Rafe

Also by Connie Mason
in Large Print:

The Outlaws: Jess
The Rogue and the Hellion
The Dragon Lord
To Love a Stranger
To Tame a Renegade
To Tempt a Rogue

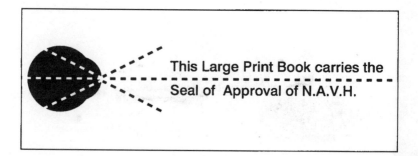

This Large Print Book carries the
Seal of Approval of N.A.V.H.

The —
OUTLAWS:

Rafe

Connie Mason

WHEELER
PUBLISHING

Published in 2003 by arrangement with Leisure Books,
a division of Dorchester Publishing Co., Inc.

Wheeler Large Print Softcover Series.

The text of this Large Print edition is unabridged.
Other aspects of the book may vary from the original edition.

Set in 16 pt. Plantin by Elena Picard.

Printed in the United States on permanent paper.

ISBN 1-58724-370-9 (lg. print : sc : alk. paper)

To my husband Jerry. My rock and anchor. This year marks our 50th year of wedded bliss. They said it wouldn't last but it gets better every year. Here's to the next fifty.

Chapter One

Ordway, Colorado, 1868

Rafe Gentry swallowed past the lump in his throat, imagining the bite of the noose as it tightened around his neck. He was going to hang. The lynch mob was storming the jail-house and the sheriff was doing little to stop it. Damn! He'd never thought he'd end up swinging from the end of a rope.

Suddenly the mesmerizing strains of music wafted through the air from the revival tent set up in the town square. The angelic voice raised in song was so profoundly inspiring that Rafe's anguish slid away for a few short moments. Only an angel could sing so sweetly. She was singing a hymn, her voice rising above the shouting outside the jail-house door. Rafe paused in the midst of his morose thoughts to listen — and to recall the events that had brought him to this sorry place.

It had been a miracle that he and his brothers, Jess and Sam, had survived the war, though their father hadn't lived through the first battle. All four of the Gentry men had joined the Confederate Army despite the twenty thousand Kansans who supported the Union. Having migrated from Tennessee to Kansas, the family's sympathies had been with the South. Jess had enlisted as a doctor, using his medical training to save lives, while Rafe and Sam had served in the Cavalry.

Rafe was the first to arrive home after the war ended. Jess and Sam showed up late in 1866. Unfortunately, it had been a sad homecoming. Quantrill's raiders had destroyed their crop and burnt most of the outbuildings back in 1863. Worn out from trying to keep the family farm solvent, poor Mama had died scant weeks after her sons returned from war. Rafe, Jess and Sam had managed to put in a crop, but for two years running, dust storms had destroyed their hopes of raising money to pay back taxes. Jess had hung up his shingle in Dodge City, intending to practice medicine, but no one came to use his services.

As a last resort they had gone to the bank in Dodge City for a loan to put the farm back on its feet. Being a staunch Union supporter, Banker Wingate had refused their request, but he did offer them a deal that would save the homestead if one of them was willing to make a small sacrifice. Rafe chuckled despite his grave situation when he recalled how he and his brothers had reacted to Wingate's shocking deal and the unforeseen outcome.

Wingate had said he would give them the loan if one of the brothers would take his pregnant daughter off his hands. The offer had been outrageous. Though all three brothers had dallied with Delia Wingate, none of them had bedded the girl, and so they had refused to marry her, never dreaming the outcome of their refusal would send them fleeing for their lives.

They were leaving the bank when Wingate burst out of his office and screamed, "Bank robbery," at the top of his voice. Rafe remembered how they had turned around, expecting to encounter a desperate criminal. Instead they saw Wingate pointing at them.

Bank robbers? The Gentry brothers? Confederate soldiers, yes, but not outlaws. But there had been no time for explanations. From the corner of his eye Rafe had seen the sheriff and his deputy running toward the bank. Fearing they would shoot first and ask questions later, the brothers had ridden hell for leather out of town. They had returned to their homestead for their belongings and divided what little cash they had on hand, taking off scant minutes ahead of the posse. They traveled a short distance together, then split up by mutual consent to confuse the posse.

Jess had ridden north, Sam south, and Rafe had headed west. Before they parted they made a solemn pact to meet one year from that day at the Antlers Hotel in Denver. If one of them failed to show up, the others would know he was dead.

Rafe hated like hell to think that one of his brothers might not survive after having gone through the war with little more than a few minor injuries, but it was something they had all accepted. Hell, he doubted he'd live through the night.

The event that had brought him to this sorry pass was a stagecoach robbery and the murder of five innocent people. He'd crossed the border into Colorado and was riding along, minding his own business, when gunshots brought him to an abrupt halt. Without thinking, he had drawn one of his matched pair of service revolvers and ridden toward the shots. He arrived in time to witness a pair of outlaws shooting off the padlock on the stagecoach's strongbox.

He'd frightened them away before they had time to make off with the money, but all three passengers inside the stage, as well as the driver and the man riding shotgun, were dead. Cowboys from a nearby ranch had found Rafe standing over the strongbox, still holding his gun.

His explanation was cut short when the dead bodies were discovered, and he was hustled off to jail in Ordway, the nearest town, to await trial.

The angelic songbird began another hymn, and Rafe walked to the narrow window of his jail cell and stared through the darkness at the revival tent, where the glow from a hundred lanterns lit up the night. Her name was Sister Angela. He had encountered her when he'd stopped to buy trail supplies at the general store in Garden City, Kansas, before crossing the border into Colorado.

Rafe had been stowing his supplies in his saddlebags when he saw a blond beauty being accosted in the street by a pair of drunken cowboys. Aware that bringing attention to himself was dangerous, Rafe still felt compelled to intervene. He had made short work of the drunken cowboys and received Sister Angela's undying gratitude. He would have liked more than her gratitude, but her religious calling made her off limits to him. She had asked his name and invited him to attend the revival that night, but of necessity he had declined.

Rafe knew it was Sister Angela's voice he heard floating to him through the barred window for he'd overheard the sheriff telling his deputy about the beautiful singer with the voice of an angel and a face to match. If he could hear but one thing before he met his Maker, he would want it to be Sister Angela's sweet voice easing his way to the hereafter.

Rafe's thoughts were violently shattered when the door to the jailhouse burst open.

Chapter Two

Wearied after the intense three-day revival, Sister Angela Abbot gathered up the sheet music and placed it in a folder. Those attending the revival that night had already drifted away, followed soon afterward by Reverend Conrad and Sister Grace, his wife. Angela intended to seek her own bed as soon as she straightened up and packed away the music that had been used during the lengthy four-hour revival. Only one more city remained on the schedule before the reverend and his wife would return to their home base in Topeka.

Being offered a place with Reverend Conrad and his wife had come at a time when Angela desperately needed to remove herself from Topeka. Her mother had just recently died of lung fever, leaving her vulnerable to her odious stepfather's whims. A few weeks later, her father's letter, forwarded by his lawyer, had reached her.

Angela's mother and father had divorced when she was very young, but Simon Abbot had kept in touch with his only daughter over the years. The gold mine her father owned along with a partner was what had separated her parents. Angela's mother had hated being stuck in a mining camp in Colorado, and her father had refused to abandon the mine, which at that time had yet to show any sign of color.

Angela was ten years old when her mother had taken her back to Topeka, obtained a divorce and married Desmond Kent, a man Angela couldn't abide. During the ensuing years, Simon Abbot had taken a partner and struck a vein of gold that made him a wealthy man. Then Angela had received that final letter from her father. According to the lawyer, Simon Abbot had died in an unfortunate accident and she had inherited his share of the mine and all his worldly assets.

Angela recalled her father's letter as if it were yesterday. For some reason her father had anticipated his own death, and he'd told his daughter to look to his partner should he die suddenly or suspiciously. Shortly afterward, a letter arrived from Brady Baxter, her father's partner. Baxter informed her that the mine had played out and he offered to buy her share at a ridiculously high price for a supposedly worthless mine.

Angela had no intention of selling her share of the mine to Brady Baxter without first inspecting her property. Flouting her stepfather's authority, Angela secretly planned to travel to Colorado as soon as arrangements could be made. She wanted to check out both Brady Baxter and the mine for herself.

Angela's stepfather had promptly produced a fiancé for his stepdaughter, and Angela knew that both Desmond Kent and Anson Chandler were more interested in her inheritance than in her future. Against her wishes, plans were afoot for a hasty wedding. Then Angela happened to hear at the church she regularly attended that a Baptist evangelist intended to carry the word of God to the Western frontier, and that Reverend Conrad and his wife, Sister Grace, were looking for a vocalist to lead the singing. As lead singer in the church choir, Angela knew that this was her opportunity to escape to Colorado.

Lying didn't come easily to Angela, but somehow she had convinced Reverend Conrad that she had her stepfather's approval to travel with the evangelists. She compounded the lie by inventing a fiancé who was to meet her in Pueblo, where they would marry before traveling on to her father's mine near Canon City.

So she had used some of the money sent to her over the years by her father to secretly outfit a wagon. And hours before her wedding she'd quietly disappeared, leaving nary a word of explanation behind for either her stepfather or her fiancé. She knew they would eventually discover what she had done, but she hoped not too soon. Only six months remained until her twenty-first birthday, placing her beyond the influence of either one. She'd be in charge of her own life and free to pursue her father's murderer, for she knew in her heart her father's death had been no accident.

Angela suddenly became aware of a commotion in the street outside the tent and sensed trouble. She rushed into the street, her gaze riveted on the crowd gathered outside the jailhouse across the road. Even as she watched, the crowd seemed to swell and undulate closer to the building. Some of the men held torches; all were armed. She started to choose an alternate path to her hotel when she saw a man with a rope around his neck being dragged from the jailhouse.

A lynch mob! She'd heard that such things happened in the uncivilized West but she'd never thought to experience that travesty of justice firsthand. She watched in horror as the hapless man was hoisted upon a horse and led to a sturdy tree at the edge of the town square, well within sight of the revival tent.

Angela's heart nearly stopped when she saw someone throw one end of the rope over a thick branch above the prisoner. They were going to hang him! What kind of barbarians would do such a terrible thing?

When the condemned man turned his head in her direction, it was like a kick to Angela's gut. She recognized him immediately. The man wearing the noose around his neck was the same man who had rescued her from the drunken cowboys in Garden City!

Forces beyond reason and past explanation made Angela react instantaneously. She had no idea what Rafe Gentry had done to warrant hanging, but she knew she couldn't allow it to happen.

"What has he done?" Angela asked the first man she encountered at the edge of the mob.

"Don't trouble yerself none over that one, Sister Angela," the man said, obviously recognizing her from the revival. "The man is an outlaw. He robbed a stage and killed five people."

Angela's blood froze. Murder? No, it wasn't possible. The condemned man might be many things, but murderer wasn't one of them. Her eyes met Rafe's. The moment stretched, held. But in that brief eternity she had learned all she needed to know about Rafe Gentry. One had but to look into his unwavering silver gaze to know he was a hard man, but not a cold-blooded murderer.

She sensed the moment he had accepted his fate, for all vestiges of emotion drained from his face and his shoulders stiffened; his

16

gaze slid away from hers. A scream gathered in Angela's throat as she pushed her way through the crowd.

"Stop! You can't hang him. He didn't do it!"

The man whose hand rested on the horse's rump froze, staring dumbly at Angela.

"Ain't you one of them traveling church people?"

"I'm Sister Angela. You can't hang this man."

"Now, Sister Angela," the man cajoled. "This ain't none of your concern."

"Saving souls is my concern," Angela persisted, "and hanging an innocent man is against the law."

A rumble of unrest rolled through the crowd.

"Has he had a proper trial?" Angela pressed.

"Don't need no trial," a man from the crowd shouted. "The stagecoach driver and the man who rode shotgun were good men; they're dead now. So are the passengers."

"He gunned down five people, Sister," the first man explained with growing impatience. "Move aside. This ain't gonna be a pretty sight."

"No, please!" She swallowed hard, took a deep breath and said, "Rafe Gentry is the man I'm going to marry. He couldn't have killed five people. He came here to meet me, not rob a stage."

Rafe's gaze returned abruptly to Sister Angela, his dark brows raised. What in the hell made her say he was her fiancé?

She appeared fragile, almost ethereal in the harsh glare of the torchlight, her golden hair a gossamer halo about her head. Her face was a perfect oval, her generous mouth sweetly curved, and there was a hint of sensuality in the slanted blue eyes that were focused on him with an intensity that startled him.

"Are you saying you and this man are gonna get hitched, Sister Angela?" the self-appointed hangman asked with disbelief. He scratched his thatch of dark hair, clearly bewildered by this unforeseen turn of events.

"That's exactly what I'm saying," Angela insisted. "He was to meet me in Pueblo, but obviously he decided to join me in Ordway instead."

"He was caught red-handed," the man argued.

Rafe was more than a little stunned when Sister Angela turned those fathomless blue eyes on him and said, "Tell these men what really happened, darling."

Before Rafe could open his mouth, Sheriff Tattersal pushed his way through the mob. "Go home, all of you. There won't be a hanging in my town." He turned to the man beside the horse. "Let the judge and jury decide his guilt, Pete."

"Let the prisoner talk," Pete said, glowering at the sheriff. "Maybe Sister Angela is telling the truth and maybe she ain't."

Outnumbered, Tattersal apparently knew when to back down. "Very well, let's hear what Mr. Gentry has to say."

"I talk much better without a rope around my neck and a nervous horse under me," Rafe said.

"Talk, mister," Pete growled. "We'll decide later if tonight will be your last on earth."

Rafe sent Sister Angela an inscrutable look, his gunmetal eyes shuttered. He cleared his throat and launched into a telling of how he had come upon the pair of outlaws after the killings and chased them away before they could make off with the money from the strongbox.

"See, I told you," Angela pronounced. "Rafe wouldn't harm a flea."

Rafe stifled a grin. Obviously Sister Angela didn't know a damn thing about him if she thought that. Suddenly the mob shifted restlessly and the horse beneath him grew agitated. Rafe squeezed his legs in an effort to subdue the skittish animal. He breathed a sigh of relief when the horse quivered, then quieted.

"Everything I told you is the truth," Rafe vowed. "I emptied my guns at the outlaws, not into the passengers or driver."

"Is Sister Angela your intended bride?"

19

Sheriff Tattersal asked.

Rafe looked down at the sweet-faced angel who for some unknown reason had lied through her teeth to save his life and wanted to grin from ear to ear. Instead, he composed his features with difficulty and said, "Sister Angela has no reason to lie. Think about it. She's an evangelist, a holy woman who spreads God's gospel. If I were guilty, would she go out of her way to lie?"

Pete glanced at Sister Angela and looked away, as if ashamed of doubting her. But he still didn't look convinced.

"What's going on here?"

The booming voice belonged to Reverend Conrad, the man responsible for bringing the revival to Ordway. Rafe felt his muscles tauten as he watched the reverend push his way through the mob. He stifled a groan, certain that the preacher's interference would seal his fate. The fire-and-brimstone preachers he had known in the past held a dim view of theft and murder, even though Rafe had committed neither.

Reverend Conrad saw Angela standing at the center of the mob and rushed to her aid. "Sister Angela, what's going on?"

"Thank God you're here," Angela cried. "You have to talk some sense into this unruly mob. They're going to hang an innocent man."

Rafe stiffened as the reverend fixed him

with a steely gaze. "What makes you think this man is innocent, Sister?"

Sister Angela looked at him squarely, neither flinching nor backing down. Rafe marveled at her temerity. She lied with such ease; had he not known better, he would have believed he actually *was* her fiancé.

"Rafe Gentry is my fiancé, Reverend Conrad. He's the man I was to meet and marry in Pueblo. We were to travel to my father's mine as man and wife. I had no idea he'd decided to meet me in Ordway instead. Rafe couldn't have held up the stage and killed innocent people. It had to have happened just like he said. He came upon the outlaws and chased them away. Regrettably, he arrived too late to save the passengers and driver."

The reverend returned his attention to Rafe. "Is that true, young man?"

"Yes, sir," Rafe said without hesitation. He could lie as easily as Sister Angela when it meant his life. "I decided to meet Angela in Ordway instead of Pueblo." His silver gaze bored into Angela. "We've been parted a long time and I grew impatient to see her again. That's the only reason I happened to be on the road when the stagecoach was attacked."

"I've known Rafe all my life," Angela added. "He couldn't kill anyone."

"That's it, then," Reverend Conrad said authoritatively. "Sister Angela has no earthly reason to lie. Obviously you have the wrong man, Sheriff."

Disappointment made the mob restive and the men surged forward. They had been primed for a hanging, and Rafe's greatest fear was that they didn't give a hoot if he was innocent as long as they were provided with entertainment.

Reverend Conrad must have come to the same conclusion, for he turned to the crowd and held up his hands for quiet.

"My good people," he intoned in a deep voice that commanded instant respect. "If Sister Angela says this man is innocent, that's good enough for me. If any of you wish to dispute her word, please step forward and speak your piece."

Rafe held his breath. No one moved, though some clearly wanted to. Who would dare look into an angel's face and call her a liar? Even Sheriff Tattersal appeared unwilling to challenge Reverend Conrad and Sister Angela.

"You heard the reverend, men. Let Gentry go," Tattersal growled as he removed the rope from Rafe's neck.

Someone untied his hands and hauled him off the horse. Rafe dragged in a shaky breath and massaged his neck where the rope had chafed his skin raw. Though no one appeared willing to debate Rafe's innocence, the crowd was still dissatisfied and restive. Rafe seriously doubted he'd make it out of town alive if he were to try to leave now.

But once again Reverend Conrad came to his rescue. He seemed to sense the ugly mood and immediately sought to diffuse it. He glanced at Angela, then at Rafe, and smiled, as if he had just arrived at a remarkable decision.

"My friends, I know you came out tonight expecting to witness a hanging, but I have something more appropriate in mind. We shall have a wedding instead. Sister Angela and her fiancé intended to marry in Pueblo. Since he has seen fit to join her in Ordway, it will be my pleasure to perform the ceremony immediately. You are all invited to the revival tent to celebrate the marriage of Sister Angela and her young man."

General pandemonium ensued. A muscle worked in Rafe's jaw. Tension kept him upright. But short of admitting he was not Angela's fiancé, there was nothing he could do but agree to the good reverend's outrageous suggestion. He cast a sidelong glance at the devious angel and was gratified to note that she appeared as stunned as he. He braced himself, waiting for her to voice some objection. But all she did was clamp her lips tightly together and glare at him. Fortunately, Reverend Conrad seemed not to notice.

"Come along, children," the reverend said,

beaming. He turned to the crowd. "Someone fetch Sister Grace. This calls for music. The piano is still in the revival tent, and she knows the wedding march by heart."

"Do something!" Rafe hissed beneath his breath. "Unless you want to be saddled with a husband. What about that fiancé waiting for you in Pueblo?"

"I want you for a husband no more than you want me for a wife," Angela shot back. "But short of admitting the truth and sending you back to the hanging tree, I don't know what to say."

"Damn!"

The crowd surged forward, sweeping Rafe and Angela with it toward the revival tent. The mood had turned abruptly from ugly to jovial. But Rafe knew it would take very little for the situation to turn again, and he was determined to do whatever it took to save his neck. But marriage?

Angela stared at Rafe Gentry. Though intuition told her he wasn't a killer, a kernel of doubt existed. How could she marry a man she knew nothing about? The dilemma she faced seemed insurmountable. Either she admitted Rafe wasn't her fiancé and let him hang, or she continued with this farce, which was becoming more bizarre by the minute. Was he completely innocent of the crime of which he'd been accused? Lord knows he looked rough enough and tough enough to be a killer. But in the end it was his eyes that convinced her to save him. Those mesmerizing silver orbs held no cruelty.

The crowd swelled, filling the tent beyond its limits. Rafe and Angela were literally pushed along with the reverend to the front of the makeshift church. Sister Grace, having been alerted, was seated at the piano, grinning from ear to ear.

"And now, children," Reverend Conrad announced, turning to face the crowd, "shall we begin?"

"We really planned to be married in Pueblo," Angela said in a last-ditch effort to escape this travesty. A husband, even a temporary one, had no place in her future.

"Nonsense," the reverend boomed in a voice brooking no argument. "I'd be remiss in my duty if I sent you two young people off without benefit of marriage. I know how impetuous youngsters can be these days." He turned to Rafe. "Do you have the ring?"

"It's . . . right here," Rafe said, shocking Angela. With shaking fingers he removed his mother's wedding ring from his vest pocket. He had taken it when he and his brothers had divided money and keepsakes before they had ridden away from the farm with the posse hard on their heels. Angela stared at the gold band he had retrieved from his pocket as if it were a snake about to bite her.

"Excellent," Reverend Conrad said. "Since

you have the ring, it's obvious you are, indeed, Angela's fiancé," he said, directing his remarks at those still-skeptical members of the lynching party.

"Get on with it, Reverend," someone in the crowded tent called out.

Rafe muttered a coarse obscenity.

Angela heard and shared his sentiment. What was she getting herself into? Abruptly she realized the sacrifice was too great and opened her mouth to stop this mockery.

Something in her demeanor must have tipped Rafe off, for he gripped her arm and hissed, "Don't. You started this, you owe it to me to see it through."

Angela stared at him and shook her head. "I can't."

His grip tightened and his silver eyes glittered. "You can and you will. I don't know what you intended when you intervened, but the die is cast. You can't back out now."

She sensed his desperation and knew that it matched her own. Never in her wildest dreams had she imagined her rash act would end like this. But Rafe Gentry was right. He had come to her defense once; she could do no less than return the favor. There were ways to end a marriage, after all. Stiffening her spine, she nodded to the reverend, giving him permission to begin.

Sister Grace played softly on the piano and the reverend opened the Good Book. His voice uttered meaningless words as Rafe's thoughts raced. He wondered how long it would take to shake the dirt of Ordway from his boots and leave Sister Angela behind in the dust. Though this farcical marriage had saved his life, he had no intention of honoring it. Sister Angela's reasons for lying to save his life were none of his business. He had his own plans, his own needs, and they didn't include a wife.

He must have responded in the right place, for the next thing he knew, the reverend was prodding him to place the ring on Angela's finger.

Focused once again, he reached for Angela's left hand and shoved the wedding band into place. It fit perfectly.

"I now pronounce you husband and wife. You may kiss the bride."

Rafe stared at Angela's lips. They were full, ripe and slightly moist, as if she had just wet them with her tongue. He could hear the crowd in the background, clamoring for the kiss. His gaze shifted upward, to her eyes, stunned to see them wide and slightly unfocused. He cupped her chin. She blinked. Then he slipped his hand to her nape, beneath the silken halo of hair. With slow, steady pressure he brought her forward to meet his lips.

He had meant the kiss to be a brief touching of lips, nothing as dramatic as what ensued. Her lips were soft, her breath sweetly scented. He slanted his mouth over hers and was lost in sensations totally foreign to Rafe Gentry, a man who loved well and loved often without engaging emotions.

The scent of her hair and skin was intoxicating. Subtle yet wildly arousing. He deepened the kiss, nudging her mouth open with his tongue. Her tentative, somewhat breathless response emboldened him and he thrust his tongue past her teeth to explore the delicate inside of her mouth. He sensed her shock, her outrage, but some perverse devil drove him to kiss her until he heard the reverend clear his throat. Only then did he become aware of the hoots and cheers reverberating through the tent.

Abruptly he broke off the kiss. Angela swayed, as if slightly unbalanced, and he steadied her with his hand upon her elbow.

"I was right to marry you two right away," Reverend Conrad said. "Especially after witnessing that rather spectacular display. I wish you much happiness and many children. If Sister Grace will bring me the church register, we'll make this legal in the eyes of God and the law."

Sister Angela murmured something Rafe didn't catch as Sister Grace produced pen and inkwell and the register that went with them wherever they traveled. Reverend Conrad presented it to the newlyweds.

With great reluctance Rafe signed first, then handed the book to Angela. She took a long time studying the page, but finally set her name to it. Meanwhile, Reverend Conrad prepared a legal document they could carry with them as proof of their marriage.

"The marriage has been duly recorded in the church register and will be entered in the church records in Topeka," Reverend Conrad explained. "This is for your own records," he added, indicating the marriage document awaiting Rafe and Angela's signature.

Angela appeared incapable of movement, so Rafe signed the document first, then handed it to his bride. She gave him a blank stare but signed it nevertheless. Then Rafe took it upon himself to thank Reverend Conrad for both of them.

"Will you leave immediately or travel with us on the morrow?" Conrad asked. "I understand we're traveling in the same direction."

"I don't know if going to Pueblo at this time is wise," Sheriff Tattersal said as he joined the group. "I've been meaning to speak with you before you left. We just got word that Comanche renegades are raising a ruckus in the area. No one knows where they're headed next. Perhaps it's best if everyone remain in Ordway until the danger is over."

"Indians?" Sister Grace said, edging closer to her husband. Her plump hand flew to her throat and her lined face crinkled in fear.

"Oh, Clarence, let's do return to Topeka. We're nearly at the end of our itinerary anyway."

"Hmmm, perhaps you're right, my dear. Thank you for your advice, Sheriff, but I think we'll return to Topeka first thing in the morning." He slid a concerned glance at Angela. "Maybe you should rethink your plans to continue west to your father's claim, Sister."

Angela gave her bright curls a vigorous shake. "Oh, no, Reverend, that's impossible. I'm sure my . . . husband and I will be perfectly safe. It's imperative that I reach Canon City and the Golden Angel."

Rafe gave Angela a sharp look, having no idea what she was talking about, though he intended to find out at the first opportunity.

"Very well, Sister," the reverend said somewhat doubtfully. "Sister Grace and I will pray for your safe journey."

"As I will pray for yours," Angela replied.

"The town has a mighty fine hotel," Tattersal offered.

"I think my . . . wife" — Rafe choked on the word — "and I will leave immediately." He didn't want to stick around Ordway any longer than necessary.

"I agree," Angela concurred.

"I hope you're not making a mistake," the reverend said. "Come along, Grace, the hour grows late."

Rafe watched everyone leave with a sense of dread. He had no idea what Angela had in mind, or her destination, for that matter. In fact, he knew nothing about her, except that she was dedicated to saving souls, the kind of woman he usually steered clear of. Those kinds of women were usually stiff as starch and holier than thou, trying to reform every soul they met. Well, he had news for Sister Angela. He was beyond redemption and had no intention of reforming.

Furthermore, he didn't intend sticking around long enough for Sister Angela to lay into him with her preaching. Once they left Ordway behind, she was on her own. By now posters were probably circulating with his picture on them, and he needed to put distance between himself and Kansas.

His thoughts turned to his brothers, Jess and Sam, and he offered a quick prayer for their safety. They were as close as brothers could get, and he hoped they weren't encountering the same problems he was.

"Are you ready to leave?" Angela asked, cutting into his reverie. "I'm serious about reaching Canon City as quickly as possible."

"I'm ready if you are, *wife*," Rafe shot back.

"You don't have to be so sarcastic about it," Angela huffed as she made her way from the tent. "I just saved your skin."

"And gained a husband in the bargain," he

31

reminded her as he followed her outside.

"My wagon is behind the tent. We have only to hitch the horses and leave." She led the way around to the back of the tent.

Rafe fumed in silent rage. Did she actually think he was going to travel with her? She might be temptingly beautiful and sexually arousing, but she wasn't his kind of woman. Besides, had he wanted a wife, he would have stayed in Dodge and married the banker's daughter.

All this he kept to himself as he hitched the team to the wagon.

"My horse is at the livery and the sheriff still has my guns," Rafe said. "You go on; I'll catch up with you."

He turned away before Angela could form a reply, only to be brought up short when the sheriff appeared in the darkness, leading his horse.

"Thought I'd save you the trouble of claiming your horse," Tattersal said. "Brought your guns, too. You might need them."

Rafe's lips thinned. "Much obliged." He shoved the twin Colts into his empty holster.

"You two climb aboard, I'll tie Gentry's horse to the tailgate," Tattersal said.

"Damn, damn, double damn," Rafe muttered beneath his breath. Nothing was going his way. Now he was forced to sit beside the tempting church woman, lusting after her while she remained untouchable.

"Did you say something?" Angela asked as she clambered onto the unsprung seat.

"Not a damn thing," Rafe said, climbing up beside her and taking up the reins.

"Good luck," Tattersal called as the horses jolted off. "Sorry about the misunderstanding, Gentry. Rest assured we'll capture those men responsible for the killings."

An uneasy silence descended as the moon rose higher in the sky and the horses picked their way along the uneven road. Angela wondered what Rafe Gentry was thinking and hoped he didn't expect marital rights just because a preacher had said words over them.

Strangers. That's what they were. Strangers with nothing in common. Whatever devil had prompted her to claim him as her fiancé had long since abandoned her. She cast a surreptitious glance at him from beneath lowered lids. A wedge of moonlight revealed tightly clenched jaw, high, unshaven cheekbones, silver eyes framed by indecently long black eyelashes, and full lips.

His expression was shuttered, but instinct warned Angela that he was angry. She couldn't blame him. She was angry, too. No, dismayed was a better word. She'd had no idea her rash action would have such dire consequences.

Married. Lord, her stepfather and Anson Chandler, the man who expected to marry her and gain a gold mine in the bargain, would be livid.

Angela's unease intensified when Rafe pulled the wagon into a stand of trees that hid them almost completely from the road.

"Why are we stopping?"

"This is as good a place as any to bed down. If I'm not mistaken, I hear the sound of water rushing over rocks somewhere nearby." He jumped from the wagon and came around to lift her down. "I'll take care of the horses while you look for the stream. Are you hungry?"

"No, I ate earlier."

"So did I. When you return from the stream, there's a lot of questions that need answering."

Angela slanted him a disgruntled look and disappeared inside the wagon for towel and soap. Then she stalked off in search of the stream. She didn't have far to look. She just followed the sound of babbling water and came upon a narrow brook several yards behind their campsite. She took her time washing, contemplating her answers to the questions Rafe was sure to ask. He deserved answers, she supposed, but how much truth should she tell him?

A twig snapped behind and she whirled, relaxing somewhat when she recognized the impressive contours of Rafe's powerful body silhouetted in the moonlight. She shivered despite the warm night. Everything about him suggested strength and virility.

He walked like a man on the prowl. Despite his calm facade, Angela sensed the tension coiled within him. He wore his twin Colts as if they were a part of his skin, and Angela was willing to bet he knew how to use them.

"What's taking you so long? Don't you know it's dangerous to linger out here alone? Pick up your towel and come to bed, Mrs. Gentry."

Angela froze. *Mrs. Gentry?* Just what did he expect from her? Hands on hips, chin tilted at a stubborn angle, she lashed out at him.

"I'll never be a real wife to you, Rafe Gentry! If you're thinking about taking advantage of me, let me set you straight."

"No, let me set *you* straight, lady," Rafe said harshly. "I never wanted a wife and have no intention of complicating my life by bedding a woman bent on saving my soul. All I want from you are answers. There has to be a reasonable explanation why you married a virtual stranger. And don't try to tell me it was to save my life."

Angela lifted her chin and stalked past him. "Ungrateful wretch!" she muttered in passing.

Chapter Three

Desire battered Rafe. The only thing he could think of was how badly he wanted to kiss Angela. He remembered the lush softness of her lips and touched his own with his fingertips, recalling the sweet innocence of her response when he'd kissed her at their wedding ceremony.

If he were the kind of man to take advantage of a woman, he wouldn't hesitate to take what he wanted. In the eyes of the law, bedding Angela was his legal right as her husband. Unfortunately, it seemed almost sacrilegious to touch so pure an angel. But Rafe had never pretended to be a saint. Far from it. He could hold out only so long against the overwhelming temptation his Angel presented. The best thing he could do for Sister Angela was to put distance between them. And that was exactly what he intended to do, as soon as he had the answers he sought.

Kneeling at the brook's edge, he removed his shirt and splashed water over his face and torso. Then he tossed his shirt over his shoulder and followed Angela back to the campsite. His limbs froze and a groan slipped past his lips when he saw Angela's slim form silhouetted against a backdrop of canvas. She was standing inside the wagon, wearing nothing but her chemise and petticoats, blissfully unaware of the spectacle she was providing Rafe.

When she stepped out of her petticoats, Rafe's loins swelled and cold sweat broke out on his forehead. Then the lantern went out and Rafe let his imagination run rampant. He envisioned Angela removing her chemise and drawers, then slipping her nightgown over long bare legs and gloriously unrestrained curves.

Madness drove him as his legs moved forward of their own accord. He wanted the angelic songbird, and the way he felt now, nothing was going to stop him. Fortunately, reason returned when he reached the tailgate and he skidded to a halt. What in the hell was he thinking? Sister Angela might be his wife but she wasn't for him. Besides, she had a fiancé waiting for her in Pueblo. It was time she told him what was going on.

He paused behind the wagon and rattled the tailgate. "Angela, come out, we need to talk."

"Can't it wait until morning?" came her muffled reply.

"I might not be here in the morning."

That brought an instant response. The lantern flared to life and a tousled blond head appeared in the back opening. "You're leaving?"

"We both knew I would eventually. I want to know why you saved my life. You didn't have to go through with the marriage, you know." His eyes narrowed suspiciously. "Maybe I'm wrong. For whatever reason, perhaps you *did* want a husband. It's difficult to believe you're simply a do-gooder looking for souls to save. If that was your motive, I'm beyond redemption."

Angela ground her teeth in frustration. "I'm sure your soul isn't worth saving, Mr. Gentry. Good night. Or should I say goodbye?" Then she removed her head from the opening and pulled the canvas together with a snap.

Frustrated beyond endurance, Rafe dropped his shirt, vaulted up over the tailgate and lunged through the canvas opening.

"We're not through talking, *Mrs. Gentry.*"

Angela grabbed for her shawl and pulled it over her flimsy nightgown. "Get out!"

"In my own good time. Sit down, Sister, and tell me what possessed you to save my life. Not that I'm ungrateful," he added; "just confused."

Angela stared at Rafe's bare chest as if she'd never seen a man in that state of undress before, as indeed she hadn't. She wanted to shut her eyes but couldn't. She'd never thought of a man's body as arousing, until she'd seen Rafe Gentry's bare torso. Tongues of flickering light lapped at his rippling muscles and sculpted chest. She tried to focus on his face but something perverse compelled her to slide her gaze down his torso, to the lean plane of his stomach.

She flushed and returned her gaze to his face. The light was bright enough to reveal wide, deep-set eyes and boldly slanted eyebrows. His hair was thick and long and black as ink against his neck and throat. His nose was straight, his jaw square and his chin blunt.

His was a handsome face, but not without character. Painful memories shadowed his silver eyes, and Angela suspected his lopsided smile hid a checkered past. Instinct told her he wasn't a killer, but common sense warned her he was no stranger to violence.

She watched the play of lamplight in his eyes and experienced a prickling rush of sensation up her spine. As unnerving as it was, Angela couldn't look away. It was the sound of his voice that finally jerked her from her bemusement.

"Do you realize we're in one helluva fix? Excuse me, Sister, if I offend your delicate ears, but I can think of no other word to describe our situation. Why did you let the preacher marry us?"

"Why did you?"

"I had a skin to save, you didn't. Hell, I would have agreed to anything to save my life. You, on the other hand, had nothing to gain."

Her chin notched upward. "I couldn't let an innocent man die."

He sent her a startled look. "What made you think I was innocent?"

She stared at his bare chest and looked away. "Would you please put on a shirt?"

Rafe gave her a lopsided grin. "Do I bother you?"

"Yes. No. I don't know. It isn't right."

"Haven't you ever seen a man's bare chest before?"

"Of course not," she said stiffly.

"We're married, or have you forgotten?"

Surely he didn't want . . . didn't expect to . . . "In name only, and that's how it's going to remain until we part company."

He was too close, filling the small space with his powerful presence and daunting body. She retreated until the backs of her legs hit the cot behind her. He took an aggressive step forward, until he was so close she felt his hot breath fan her cheek.

"What do you want? You can't . . . I won't let you . . . Why are you doing this?"

"Are you really a prissy, purse-lipped holy woman, Angel? Or is that just a facade you assume whenever it suits you? What are you *really* like beneath that angelic halo you wear so well?"

A jolt of heat surged through her veins. Angela hated to think that the sight of Rafe's naked chest bothered her, but she couldn't deny that her stomach was flooding with a strange and potent warmth.

"You're insulting," Angela said, drawing her shawl closer around her. "Say what you have to say and leave."

"All right." He grasped her shoulders and pushed her down on the cot. She wanted to jump up when he sat down beside her but she forced herself to ignore the tension arcing between them.

"Let's start off with the truth. Why did you save my skin back there in Ordway? For all you knew, I was a cold-blooded killer."

"I was simply repaying a debt. You helped me in Garden City, remember? Would a killer do that? Besides, lynching is against the law."

He sent her a guarded look. "Why didn't you stop the wedding? One word from you and the marriage would never have taken place."

"I almost spoke up, if you recall. But you convinced me that things had gone too far. I . . . couldn't let the lynch mob have you."

"No ulterior motive?" His probing gaze settled on her stomach. "You're not increasing and in need of a husband, are you?"

41

"What!" Angela sputtered indignantly. "How dare you! You're making me very sorry I saved your life."

"What about that fiancé waiting for you in Pueblo? Isn't he going to be disappointed?"

After a long pause, Angela said, "There is no fiancé. I made him up for Reverend Conrad's benefit."

"Why?"

Since she didn't expect to see Rafe again once he departed, Angela felt no obligation to tell him her life history. The less he knew about her circumstances, the better. She didn't know him. Once he learned she was part owner of a gold mine, he might turn greedy and decide to stick around. She had enough trouble with both Desmond and Anson trying to ruin her life.

"It's none of your concern. When I'm settled," she added, "I'll see to the annulment. You needn't worry yourself about it. Once you ride away, you can consider yourself a free man. I will make no demands upon you."

Suspicious by nature, Rafe found it difficult to believe Angela wanted nothing from him. No woman alive was completely selfless. There was much she wasn't telling him. He could force her to reveal everything, but on the other hand, did he really want to know? He had enough on his plate already. He was free — that was all that mattered.

"Keep your secrets, Sister. You saved my skin, that's enough for me." He stood. So did she. "I'll probably be gone when you awaken tomorrow. Can you manage the team on your own?"

"I've done it for the past six weeks. I'm close to my destination. I'll be just fine."

"Then I reckon this is good-bye."

"I suppose it is."

Rafe had no idea how she ended up in his arms. He just knew that he'd never felt anything so warm and soft in his life. He had but to bend his head and . . . He captured her mouth. Captured and possessed it, his mouth molding hers, his tongue playing along the velvety fullness of her lush lips. At first she stood frozen against his length, her breath short and explosive, her body rigid.

He drew her closer, until he felt her nipples pebble against his bare chest. He deepened the kiss, his tongue probing, exploring what he suddenly realized was virgin territory. He imagined he could feel her heart thudding in time to his own raging pulse. Then he felt her mouth move tentatively under his, and desire emboldened him to lower his palm to her breast.

She twisted and lurched back, her hand raised to strike him. He grasped her wrist before it reached his face. Her eyes were chips of blue ice and her lips were swollen, her hair disheveled. She was breathing fast. So was he. The air between them crackled. Something had just happened, but Rafe had no idea what it was.

"That will never be repeated," she said shakily. He could tell she was struggling to regain her composure.

Rafe grinned. "I was simply kissing my *wife* good-bye."

"Good-bye, Mr. Gentry. Try to stay out of trouble. I won't be around to save your neck next time you clash with the law."

Rafe decided to leave before he did something he'd regret later. "So long, Angel."

Then he was gone, leaving Angela with an empty space inside her she couldn't explain. She raised her fingers to her lips; they felt fuller and plumper than they had before Rafe kissed her. They were not afire, as they had been only a few minutes earlier when his lips were pressing against hers, but only slightly warm.

Angela wondered why she hadn't resisted more strongly. At the very least she should have placed a well-aimed knee in his groin. But she hadn't. She had rested complacently in his arms and let him kiss her, claiming her mouth as if he owned it. Her knees were still weak and her stomach roiling. For the sake of her sanity, she sincerely hoped she and Rafe Gentry never crossed paths again.

Rafe found scant rest in his bedroll that

night. He rose at the first hint of daylight, washed up at the stream, saddled his horse and rode off, gnawing on jerky he carried in his saddlebags. He rode west, toward Pueblo, deciding it was as good a place as any to buy supplies and take in the lay of the land. He was nearly out of cash, and if there were no Wanted posters out for his arrest in town, he might take a temporary job to fill his empty pockets.

For both their sakes, he hoped he didn't run into Angel Abbot again. At some point during their brief acquaintance he'd named her Angel in his head, and the name seemed to fit. It was his dearest wish to block her from his mind entirely, but he knew that was a lost hope. He would never forget his brief marriage to the woman with the voice of a songbird and the sweet face of an angel. Or the compelling attraction that made him want to learn all Angel's secrets and keep her close to him.

It was late when Rafe reached Pueblo. He stabled his horse and found a hotel room. He fell into bed totally exhausted. He arose early the next day, bought breakfast and strolled through town. Ducking into the general store, he asked about a job. The proprietor told him the Circle K foreman was hiring men for the roundup and to wait in the Whistle Stop saloon for him to show up.

Rafe headed over to the Whistle Stop,

45

pushed through the swinging doors and bellied up to the bar. He ordered a beer and carried it to a table to await the Circle K foreman.

It was still early. The saloon had few clients. A pair of Easterners sitting at the next table attracted Rafe's attention. Without knowing either of them, Rafe felt an immediate animosity toward them. He rarely judged on sight, but for some unexplained reason, these two men raised the hackles on the back of his neck. He took a swig of beer and tried to tune out their conversation, but something they said captured his attention. He could have sworn they were talking about a woman named Angela. Pretending to be engrossed with his beer, he leaned closer and listened.

"Angela hasn't shown up yet, Kent. What if she isn't coming?"

"Relax, Chandler, Angela is traveling with the Conrads and Pueblo is the evangelists' last stop on the circuit. The revival tent has already been erected in anticipation of their arrival. They'll be here. We'll give them another couple of days. If they don't show up soon, I'll wire Ordway and find out what's keeping them."

"Angela's not going to like it," Anson Chandler said. "If you recall, she left me standing at the altar. Hell, Kent, you promised we'd share in that gold mine of hers if I married her. You said we'd both be rich if that mine is producing like it has in the past."

"It's producing, all right. I had it checked out years ago, after Simon Abbot began sending money to Angela. Simon's partner thought he could pull the wool over our eyes by telling us it had played out, but I know better. Once you marry Angela, all that gold will be ours."

"It had better be," the younger man grumbled. "I'm not too keen on marriage, but beggars can't be choosers and I'm desperate for money. Since my parents squandered my inheritance, it's either marry money or find employment. When you came to me with your proposition, it seemed the answer to my prayers. I didn't know I'd have to travel halfway to nowhere to get my hands on your stepdaughter's money."

As the conversation progressed, things began to make sense to Rafe. He hadn't pressed Angel about her reasons for traveling with the preacher, but he recalled that both she and Reverend Conrad had mentioned a mine. From what he'd gathered from the Easterners' conversation, Angel did indeed have a fiancé, and his name was Chandler.

She was also part owner of a gold mine. This was getting more interesting by the minute. It appeared that his Angel had gotten herself into a potentially dangerous situation.

"Is the preacher prepared to marry us the moment Angela hits town?" Chandler asked.

"Everything is set. The old fool saw nothing but the color of our money. He'll marry you and Angela even if she's unwilling."

"I'm not taking any chance of her getting away again," Chandler returned. "You lure her away from the Conrads and together we'll drag her to the preacher's house."

Kent lifted his glass in salute and tossed his drink back. Then he wiped his mouth on the back of his sleeve and rose. "I'm going back to the hotel to pack. I want to head up to Canon City right after the wedding."

Chandler scraped back his chair. "Wait for me."

Rafe's jaw clenched as he watched them leave. He shouldn't care, but he did. He'd thought he could ride away and forget the beautiful songbird who had saved his life, but his conscience kept getting in his way. How could he leave her to her fate when he knew what awaited her?

The answer to his question wasn't surprising. He had to go back and warn Angel. She needed to be told about Kent and Chandler. From what little he'd gathered, Angel had a whole lot of baggage tagging along with her. Rafe had assumed she was one of those women who made saving souls their life's profession, but after listening to the men he assumed were her stepfather and fiancé, he realized she was in serious trouble. Though his Angel's halo was somewhat tarnished, he couldn't let her ride into Pueblo and the trap that awaited her.

Rafe swallowed the last of his beer and rose, his mind made up. Thirty minutes later he had checked out of the hotel and was riding back toward Ordway. He met Angela ten miles east of Pueblo.

Angela had awakened that morning with a sense of foreboding. Rafe was gone; he had left before daylight yesterday morning, but she hadn't expected to feel his loss so keenly. The fact that she was totally on her own was more frightening than she had anticipated. She spared a moment to wonder if she had been foolish to continue on to Canon City, especially with Indians active in the area. But she had set her course and was determined to reach the Golden Angel to discover for herself the truth about the mine and her father's death.

The afternoon sun was just setting when Angela saw a rider approaching. She watched him grow larger and larger until she recognized the limber, broad-shouldered man she had thought never to see again. Her heart beat a rapid tattoo and her breath came in short bursts of air.

Rafe!

She couldn't imagine why he was returning, but nevertheless she halted the wagon and waited. He didn't say a word as he tied his horse to the tailgate and leaped onto the seat, pushing her aside and taking the reins. She could tell by the look on his face that he wasn't in the mood to argue, so she let him have his way. But when he veered off the road that would take them to Pueblo, she sputtered a protest.

"Rafe Gentry! What's going on? This isn't the way to Pueblo."

"We're not going to Pueblo."

She tried to tug the reins from his hands without success. "You're mad!"

"No, just prudent. There are ways to reach Canon City without going through Pueblo. Canon City *is* where you're headed, isn't it?" She nodded. "We're skirting Pueblo, going directly to Canon City."

"We?"

He slanted her a look that sent goose bumps down her spine. This was crazy.

"What are you doing here? I never expected to see you again after you rode off yesterday morning."

"Who are Kent and Chandler?" he asked without preamble.

The breath froze in Angela's throat. "Kent

and Chandler? How did you . . . ? Who told you?"

"I overheard an interesting conversation between two Easterners in a saloon in Pueblo earlier today. Their names were Kent and Chandler. I assume you know them."

Angela blanched. "They're in Pueblo? Already?" Her hands flew to her mouth. "Oh, no! How did you know about them?"

"I told you, I listened to their conversation. I didn't pay much attention until your name was mentioned. They were talking about a gold mine. Then everything fell into place. I remembered your telling Reverend Conrad that you wanted to reach the Golden Angel without delay. You might as well start from the beginning and tell me everything."

After a moment's hesitation, Angela took a deep breath and said, "Desmond Kent is my stepfather and Anson Chandler is the man he intends for me to marry. Desmond paid scant attention to me until he learned my father had died and left me half interest in a gold mine near Canon City. Then one day he brought Anson Chandler around, insisting that I marry him. A wedding date was set, but I had no intention of marrying that gold digger."

"What about your mother?"

"She passed away a few weeks before I received news of my father's death. I hadn't seen Father since I was ten years old, but we kept in touch. Mama divorced him years ago and moved to Topeka. She hated Colorado and the gold camps. A few years later she married Desmond. I detested him on sight."

"So you left without telling anyone. You must have done some fancy talking to get the Conrads to take you along with them."

"They needed someone to lead the singing and I was qualified. I convinced them that I had my stepfather's blessing."

"You invented that story about a fiancé waiting for you in Pueblo, didn't you?"

"Yes. I knew it was the only way Reverend Conrad would let me remain in Pueblo at the end of the circuit. After Pueblo, the Conrads were to return to their home base in Topeka. I led them to believe my fiancé and I would marry in Pueblo and continue on to the mine together."

"Surely you weren't so naive as to think Kent and Chandler wouldn't follow you."

"I was hoping they wouldn't, but I should have known they were too greedy not to follow."

Rafe shook his head. "You know, lady, you're plumb loco. What made you think you could reach your father's mine on your own? You're so damn innocent it's disgusting. You have no idea of the dangers awaiting a woman traveling alone in this day and age. You had a taste of it in Garden City; that should have been warning enough."

"I couldn't stay in Topeka and marry Anson Chandler," Angela insisted. "I knew I had a home waiting for me out here; all I had to do was get to it. Reverend Conrad was a godsend at a time when I needed him. I figured it would be a simple matter to get to the mine from Pueblo. Father wrote that Canon City is only thirty miles from Pueblo, and the mine just three miles up Red Rock Canyon. I figured I could make it in two days."

"That's under good conditions. What if you had to contend with a broken axle, or Indians, or men bent on mayhem?"

Angela knew Rafe was right, but she hadn't let herself think about that. Besides, until Ordway and the Indian scare, the plan was for the Conrads to take the revival to Pueblo before returning home. She'd had no idea when she left Topeka that things would turn out the way they did. If not for unanticipated circumstances, she would be traveling with the Conrads to Pueblo instead of with a man who now had the right to call himself her husband.

"When I left Topeka, the plan was for the Conrads to take the revival all the way to Pueblo. It doesn't matter that things didn't work out that way. The distance between Canon City and Pueblo isn't so far that I can't travel alone."

"What did you intend to tell the reverend

when your fiancé failed to show up in Pueblo?"

Angela shrugged. "That he was late in arriving."

"And what did you intend to do when your stepfather and fiancé found you, Angel?"

"Don't call that man my fiancé," Angela retorted angrily. "And don't call me Angel."

"Why not? It fits."

In his letters, her father had always referred to her as his Angel. It had been a private endearment between them. Hearing that special nickname on another man's lips seemed almost sacrilegious.

"I prefer Angela," she said tartly.

Rafe grinned. "I prefer Angel."

She heaved an exasperated sigh, abandoning the subject for the time being. "Do you think Desmond and Anson will give up on me when I don't show up in Pueblo?"

"I doubt it. They didn't appear to be the type to give up easily. Neither man struck me as being particularly likable. Or trustworthy, and I'm a pretty good judge of character. I heard them say that if you didn't show up in a couple of days they would wire Ordway to see what was keeping you."

"I knew it was too much to hope for," Angela bit out. "Consider me warned. You can leave now, if you'd like."

Rafe sent her a disgruntled look. "I thought I'd string along with you as far as the mine."

Angela fell silent as she contemplated three, possibly four days and nights in Rafe Gentry's daunting company. Something inexplicable drew her to this man, though she willed it otherwise. And it terrified her. She had no idea who or what Rafe Gentry was.

"I'm going to start looking for a campsite," Rafe said as the sky began to darken and the forest around them thickened. "The horses are tiring. A storm is brewing over the mountains and I don't want us to be caught in it while we're still on the road."

"Are you sure it's safe to stop? What about Desmond and Anson?"

"There's plenty of cover hereabouts. I'll pull into the first likely spot I see. I don't think we'll have to worry about them for a day or two."

Truth be known, Angela was more concerned about being alone with Rafe than being found by her stepfather. Spending another night with him was a nerve-wracking proposition. She liked his kisses too well. If she wasn't careful, Rafe Gentry might become too important to her, and instinct told her he wasn't anxious to shoulder responsibility.

Rafe found a perfect campsite in a secluded spot nestled against a wooded hillside. Thick trees surrounded them; overhanging branches protected them from unwanted company.

"I intended to buy supplies in Pueblo," Angela said as Rafe lifted her down from the wagon. "There isn't much to eat besides beans and cornbread."

"Game is plentiful in these parts. Start a fire and make the cornbread. I'll take care of the horses and hunt fresh meat for our supper."

Rafe returned thirty minutes later with two plump rabbits, which he had skinned and spitted. He set them over the fire to cook.

"Coffee smells good," he said. "I found a mountain stream not far from here, if you've a mind to wash up. I notched the birches so you can find your way. I'll watch the rabbits if you want to go there before it gets too dark."

Angela gathered towel and soap and followed the trail Rafe had marked. She found the stream with little difficulty and washed quickly in the frigid water. When she returned to the campsite, she found Rafe sitting on a rock, sipping steaming coffee from a cup. She saw he had laid out plates and silverware. He poured coffee into a second cup and handed it to her. The warm liquid slid down her throat and settled comfortably in her stomach.

A rumble of thunder and a flash of lightning suddenly split the silence. Wind sloughed through the trees, showering them with sparks from the fire.

"I was afraid this was going to happen," Rafe said as he eyed the ominous sky. "Take the food inside the wagon and light the lantern. I'll put out the fire and join you. We'll have to finish our meal inside. Hurry," he urged as the first raindrops hit the ground.

Before the deluge hit, they were safely ensconced in the wagon with the remains of their feast spread around them.

"I hope you don't mind sharing your sleeping quarters tonight, Angel," Rafe said.

His voice was edged with roughness as he considered the coming night. Being in the same space, breathing the same air as his Angel wasn't going to be easy. Keeping his hands off of her was going to be the most difficult thing he'd ever done. The only way he'd touch her was if she wanted it, and he knew damn well that wasn't going to happen.

"Perhaps it will stop raining soon and you can sleep beneath the wagon," Angela said hopefully. "This is a small wagon and I don't think we'd —"

"Shall we get ready for bed, Angel?" Rafe said, cutting her off in mid-sentence.

Open-mouthed, she stared at him as if he were the devil come to earth to tempt her.

Chapter Four

Rafe knew exactly what Angel was thinking, for he was thinking the same thing, in vivid color. Sighing regretfully, he pushed his wayward thoughts aside. "Don't worry. I won't touch you unless you want me to."

The color slowly returned to her face. "I . . . wasn't worried." She dug into a chest and handed him two blankets and a pillow folded into a bedroll. "This is the best I can offer. There's just enough floor space for you to stretch out."

Rafe stared at the bedroll, then at the cot, which looked big enough for two, and frowned. "We could share the cot."

Her eyebrows rose until they nearly touched her hairline. "I think not. The bedroll will have to suffice."

Grumbling beneath his breath, Rafe spread out the bedroll and proceeded to take off his shirt.

"What are you doing?"

"I don't sleep in my clothes. It's going to be a long night; I suggest you get into

58

your sleeping gear."

His shirt hit the floor. When he worked open the buttons on his tan twill trousers, Angela blushed every way to Sunday and turned her head. With studied calm, Rafe removed his trousers but not his underwear and scooted down between the blankets.

"I'm covered," he said, eyeing Angel's rigid back. "You can look now."

Angela turned around slowly, her gaze finding him stretched out on the floor. Her sigh of relief was so exaggerated he couldn't help grinning. "Are you going to get undressed?"

"I'm fine just like I am," she said as she sat on the bunk to remove her shoes and stockings.

"I'll turn around so you can have some privacy," Rafe offered, though he was feeling far from magnanimous. When Angela looked unconvinced, he said, "Don't you trust me?"

"About as far as I can throw you. You promise not to look?"

"You have my word."

"Very well, turn around."

Rafe turned to face the opposite direction. He heard the rustle of cloth and felt himself grow thick and harden. He remembered another night, her long legs and womanly curves temptingly limned against a backdrop of canvas. He stifled a groan and willed his wayward body to subside. When he heard her slide into bed, he heaved a shaky sigh and flopped over on his stomach. He expected little sleep this night.

Rain lashed the wagon. Thunder rolled and lightning flashed. It was still pouring when the dull gray of morning chased away the murky darkness. Rafe pulled on his clothing and jammed his hat down on his head. Angel was still sleeping as he quietly left the wagon. He had stashed his saddlebags beneath the wagon the night before, and he ducked down to remove his slicker. Then he ventured out into the rain.

The ground squished beneath his feet, and Rafe spit out a curse. Getting bogged down in ankle-deep mud didn't appeal to him. He relieved himself, washed up at the stream and returned to the wagon. Angela was up when he returned, setting leftovers from last night out for breakfast.

"It's damn . . . er . . . darn nasty out," Rafe said as he shook out his hat and slicker and climbed over the tailgate.

The wagon seemed to shrink as Rafe filled it with his broad form. Angela felt intimidated by his very presence, although she had to admit that he had acted the gentleman last night. He could have forced her and she couldn't have done a thing about it, but he hadn't.

"Are you hungry? There's leftovers from last night. Help yourself," she said as she

60

drew her shawl over her head and prepared to leave the protection of the wagon. "I won't be gone long."

Seated on his bedroll, Rafe was chewing contentedly on cold rabbit and cornbread when Angela returned. The hem of her skirt was soaking wet and so were her shoes. As she removed her shawl, one wet shoe slid out from beneath her and she fell, right into Rafe's lap. His arms went around her. His skin felt hot against her cool flesh.

"You're cold."

Angela shivered, but she doubted it was from cold. Being held by Rafe was definitely disconcerting. She stared at him through lashes spiked with raindrops.

"You're soaked through. Let's get those wet clothes off of you," Rafe said.

Deftly he undid the buttons on the front of her blouse. Before she knew what he intended, he had pulled her blouse down her shoulders and out of her waistband. She made a grab for it as he pulled it off, but it was too late. Her blouse flew across the wagon.

"Now the skirt," Rafe said, tugging on her waistband. The skirt went the way of the blouse. Then he removed a blanket from his bedroll and placed it around her shoulders, cradling her against him until she stopped shaking.

"Isn't that better?"

"You had no right," she mumbled against the warmth of his chest.

Amusement colored his words. "I'm probably the *only* man who has the right."

She popped her head out of the blanket. "You can release me now."

"Not on your life, Angel. I've wanted to hold you like this for a very long time. Too bad it took a fall to land you in my arms. Relax, I told you I wouldn't do anything you didn't want."

"I don't want to be held."

"Like hell." A knowing smile touched his eyes. "You like to be kissed, too."

As if to prove his point, his mouth came down hard on hers. The kiss was thorough, fierce, devastating, an erotic rampage upon her senses. When he finally lifted his mouth, she felt all ragged inside.

Her heart jumped violently, banging against her ribs. She made a faint sound of apprehension but his mouth smothered it as he kissed her again, penetrating her with his tongue. She felt the flat of his palm move up between her legs, spreading them gently; she tried to squirm away. Her breath hitched as he stroked the silky inner skin, his hold on her tightening. His mouth moved hungrily over hers, tasting of rain and the sizzling tang of lightning.

She moaned low in her throat as her body caught fire and simmered with a sensuality she'd never known she possessed. She felt flushed and warm, her skin keenly sensitive. The flesh where his hand caressed felt deliciously chafed, and deep inside, she felt all soft and slick. She knew she had to stop this madness before her wits deserted her.

Rafe's mouth drifted from her lips to caress the rapidly beating pulse on her throat. Angela somehow found the strength to turn her face away when he would have taken her lips again. Undaunted, he pushed the blanket aside, pulled down her chemise, and pressed his warm mouth to her breast.

"Rafe! You promised."

"I want you, Angel. I want to make love to you."

"No. I . . . can't. I don't know you. When you leave I'll never see you again. It's best we both forget our . . . unusual marriage and get on with our lives. Please don't do this to me. Someday I hope to marry a man who loves me."

His gunmetal eyes were shuttered as his arms fell away. There were small lines etched at the corners of his eyes and mouth, and his skin was pulled taut over his cheekbones. A muscle worked in his jaw. Angela tensed, sensing his anger; then she relaxed when she felt the last dregs of tension draining from his body. She rose shakily from his lap, eyeing him warily, relieved when he made no move to stop her. With lethal grace, he rose

to his feet. Before he left the cramped confines of the wagon, he paused and smoothed
his rough palm along her cheek.

His voice held a note of tenderness that
startled her. "I hope you find that man,
Angel."

She heard him moving around outside,
hitching the horses to the wagon, and she
busied herself with setting the wagon to
rights. She moved slowly. Her body felt slug-
gish, as if the blood had thickened in her
veins. Her first taste of passion had left her
undeniably wanting, though she had no idea
what she wanted. But she was willing to bet
that Rafe Gentry knew precisely what she
craved, and was eager to give it to her.

They bypassed Pueblo that day and em-
barked on the last leg of the journey that
would take them to Canon City. The foothills
gave way to craggy mountains interspersed
with deep canyons. They followed a rocky
trail that had been cut through the wilderness, surrounded by thickly forested hillsides.
As the day wore on, Angela realized they
would have to camp yet another night on the
trail. And that worried her.

"What are your plans once we reach
Canon City, Rafe?" Angela asked, disrupting
the charged silence that hung between them.

Rafe shrugged. "Keep riding, I suppose.
It's a big world out there. During the war I

saw all of the South and East that I care to see. Thought I'd explore the West for a while. At least until it's time to meet my brothers in Denver next year."

"You have brothers?"

"Two. Jess and Sam."

"What about your parents?"

"Pa took a fatal bullet early in the war. Ma died three years ago. There's no one else."

"What are your brothers like? I've always regretted that I had no brothers or sisters."

"My brothers are good men. Jess is a doctor."

"Where are they now?"

Rafe wished he knew. "You ask too many questions. Shall we look for a campsite? We can pull beneath that ledge up yonder. I don't see any water nearby, but our canteens are full and the water barrel still has some water in it."

"Are you sure we can't make it to Canon City before dark?"

"I'd rather err on the safe side."

A wolf howled and Angela sidled closer to Rafe. "Was that a wolf?"

"These mountains are full of wild animals. Wolves, bears, mountain lions, to name a few."

He felt her shiver and marveled once again at her innocence. She'd had no idea what she was getting herself into when she'd left Topeka.

"Better stick close to the wagon tonight. Those wolves sound hungry. I'll keep a fire going to scare them away."

"I'm not afraid. I lived here until I was ten years old and don't ever recall not feeling safe. I love the mountains. I always dreamed of returning one day. Only I expected my father to be alive when I returned."

"With any luck we'll be in Canon City tomorrow," Rafe said. "How did your father die?"

"I was told it was an accident. But I don't believe it. His last letter hinted that something unforeseen might happen to him, and if it did, he said his partner wasn't to be trusted."

"You think your father's death wasn't an accident?"

"That's what I believe. Shortly after I received word of Father's death, a letter arrived from Brady Baxter, his partner. Baxter said the Golden Angel had played out, and he offered to buy my share at a very high price. If it was worthless, why was he willing to pay so much for it?"

Rafe shook his head. "You really are loco, Angel. What makes you think you can take on the world by yourself? You can't accuse a man of murder with no proof."

"I haven't accused anyone of murder . . . yet. I'll reserve judgment until I look into things for myself. There's a lawyer in Canon

66

City Father trusted. Perhaps he will help me."

"Don't tell me any more," Rafe said. "It's none of my business. I've got my own troubles."

They had reached the outcropping of rock Rafe had chosen for a campsite and he pulled the wagon beneath the sheltering ledge.

"Can you manage here while I hunt for our supper?" Rafe asked as he lifted Angela down from the wagon.

"I'll be fine," Angela returned. "It's growing dark; watch out for wolves."

Idly Angela wondered about the problems plaguing Rafe. She'd sensed from the beginning that he was on the run, but from what? The law? Could he actually be the killer folks in Ordway named him? She dismissed that notion immediately. But that didn't mean he wasn't wanted for some other crime. She wouldn't let herself care about a man with a shady past, and Rafe Gentry's past was as shady as they came.

Rafe returned a short time later with a pair of scrawny prairie chickens, which they cooked and ate immediately. Angela cleaned up afterward, then glanced nervously at Rafe. "I guess I'll turn in. Good night."

His silver eyes darkened to the smoky gray of desire. "Does that mean you're not inviting me to share the wagon tonight?"

"Definitely *not*," Angela huffed.

"Don't you trust me?"

She spun around to face him. "After last night I don't even trust myself. I can't think around you, Rafe Gentry. I don't know what to make of you. You're a dangerous man, in more ways than one. You're far too comfortable wearing a gun, and you appear to know how to use it. What are you, Rafe Gentry? Who are you? You spoke of the war. Did you fight for the North or the South?"

"Does it matter?"

She shrugged. "Not really."

"My family came from Tennessee. My brothers and I fought on the losing side. We were not popular in Kansas."

"Are you running from the law?"

"I didn't commit any crime," Rafe hedged. "You ask too many questions."

"I'm your wife, remember?" she said archly.

"I haven't forgotten, but I fear you have."

Angela gave an exasperated snort. "This has gone too far. We both know our marriage is a farce. It never should have taken place. Nothing is going to happen between us tonight . . . or ever. Some misguided sense of responsibility made you turn back to warn me about the danger awaiting me in Pueblo, but we both know you won't stick around long."

"You're one determined lady," Rafe contended. "Your faith must be strong indeed to afford you such confidence."

"Faith is a personal thing. Perhaps you don't have enough."

"The only things I have faith in are my gun and my wits. Both kept me alive through the war."

"I never asked: Is there a woman waiting for you back in Kansas?"

Rafe grimaced. "No specific woman, but there *have* been women. A man doesn't reach the age of twenty-eight without having women in his life."

"Don't count on adding me to your list," Angela said, turning away.

A smile lingered on Rafe's lips as he watched her march to the wagon and climb inside.

Rafe stared moodily into the fire, listening to the mournful call of a wolf and thinking about the woman who thought she could exist in a man's world on her own. She had to be the most naive woman alive, for she definitely wasn't prepared to handle all the problems piling up on her plate. Not only were her stepfather and fiancé hot on her trail, but her father's partner might be a murderer. Only a very foolish woman, or one with strong convictions, would think herself invincible.

But Angel's difficulties were none of his concern. If he wasn't careful he'd find himself mired down in her problems, and sticking around in one place was dangerous. He wouldn't be surprised if Wanted posters started appearing soon; he had to keep one step ahead of the law.

The wolf stopped howling and silence closed in on him like a suffocating curtain. Then he heard it. Her voice wafted through the darkness, sweet and dulcet, the notes startlingly pure. She sang a hymn he recognized from his youth. It took him back a good many years. She sang like an angel, and for a few minutes Rafe felt almost at peace.

Then abruptly the singing stopped. As if on cue, a wolf took up the refrain. Then another, and another. Rafe fed kindling into the fire and hunkered down to await morning. There were many places he would rather be tonight. One of them was in Angel's bed. Another was in that sweet warm place inside her body.

A weak sun broke through the clouds as the wagon lumbered into Canon City late the following afternoon.

"Do you know the way to the mine?" Rafe asked as the wagon joined the others traveling down the muddy main street.

"All I know is that it's on Red Rock Canyon Road, not too far from Canon City. I suppose we should ask someone."

"Do you have a place to live once you get there?"

"Father built a cabin. It's all mine now. Brady Baxter has his own cabin on the property. I have no idea in what condition I'll find it, but I'll manage."

"I'll park in front of the general store so you can purchase whatever you think you'll need to last until your next trip to town. Meanwhile, I'll inquire about directions. Do you have money?"

"I have enough to buy what I need. According to Mr. Goodman, Father's lawyer, there are funds in my name in the local bank."

Rafe pulled up at the general store and lifted Angela down onto the wooden sidewalk. "Have your supplies stowed inside the wagon. I won't be gone long."

He waited until Angela entered the store, then ambled off down the street. He noted Lawyer Goodman's shingle above the barber shop and reminded himself to tell Angel. Then he spotted the assayer's office and decided it was as good a place as any to ask directions to the Golden Angel.

He waited until the man ahead of him finished his business before approaching the desk.

"May I help you, sir?" the assayer asked.

"I hope so. Can you give me directions to the Golden Angel mine?"

The assayer studied Rafe through narrowed lids. "The Golden Angel, you say? Do you have business out there?"

"I'm a friend of the owner."

"Brady Baxter?"

"No, the other owner."

"If you're talking about Simon Abbot, he died some weeks back. Terrible accident."

Rafe's patience hung by a slim thread. "Just tell me how to get to the mine."

The assayer assumed an aggrieved look. "Just trying to be friendly. Head north out of town. You'll find a trail heading up the mountain. Take the first track to the right off the main trail and you'll run right into the mine. Does Baxter know you're coming?"

"Don't know and don't care," Rafe said, heading for the exit. "Oh, by the way," he said, pausing with his hand on the doorknob. "Do you happen to know the nature of Simon's accident?"

"Sure do, mister. A broken axle sent his wagon plunging off a narrow mountain trail. Tragic. Damn tragic."

"Have you heard anything about the mine being played out?"

"Played out? The Golden Angel? That's news to me, mister."

Rafe let himself out of the office, his mind awhirl. Obviously, Brady Baxter was trying to pull the wool over Angel's eyes. It had probably never occurred to him that Angel would doubt his word. Baxter was in for a big surprise.

Angela looked over the staples spread out on the counter and decided she had purchased enough food to last ten days or so. As an afterthought, she added a pistol and bullets to her pile of supplies.

"That's it, Mr. Dooley," she said. She had introduced herself and learned the proprietor's name soon after entering the store. "Add up the total. And if you'd be so kind, carry the supplies out to my wagon."

"I can't believe Simon Abbot's daughter is really here," Dooley said, smiling at Angela. "Why, I remember your ma, girl. How she hated it here. Couldn't wait to go back East. Sorry about your pa. He sure doted on you, though he hadn't seen you in years. Were he alive, he'd be one happy man right now. Are you staying long, Miss Abbot?"

"I haven't decided," Angela said, although in her heart she knew she'd never return to Topeka. There was nothing there for her.

Angela paid her tab and waited while Dooley loaded her purchases into the wagon. Then she climbed onto the seat to await Rafe.

"About time you showed up, Angela. We waited for you in Pueblo. What happened?"

That voice! Oh, no. How had they arrived here so soon?

"What's wrong? Has the cat got your tongue? You *were* expecting us, weren't you? Chandler is mighty put out at you."

Angela stared down at her stepfather and his cohort as if they were something offensive, as indeed they were. "What are you doing here?"

Chandler stepped forward. "You left me standing at the altar, Angela. I was humiliated, to say the least. But I'm here now, and there's a justice of the peace all lined up to marry us. We'll go to the mine as husband and wife, a united front against the likes of Brady Baxter."

"I'm not marrying you, Anson," Angela contended. "You came all this way for nothing. You'd be well advised to turn around and go back to Kansas."

Chandler's features no longer appeared handsome as his face screwed up into a nasty frown. "I've come too far to be denied now. You'll do as your guardian says. Tell her, Kent."

"Chandler is right, my dear. This marriage is for your own good. You need a keeper, and Chandler is just the man to tame you. He won't stand for any of your nonsense."

He reached up and yanked her to the edge of the seat. Chandler lent a hand, and together they hauled her to the ground.

"Come along quietly, Angela," Chandler

74

warned. "No need to make a public spectacle of yourself."

Angela dug in her heels. "I'm not going anywhere with you."

Kent gave her a rough shake. When she refused to budge, he hauled his arm back and slapped her. The blow sent her reeling against Chandler. Chandler caught her and lifted her into his arms. Stunned, Angela went limp as Chandler carried her off.

Rafe strode briskly toward the wagon, mulling over the information he'd gained from the assayer. If the Golden Angel was still producing, then Brady Baxter had lied to Angel. Obviously, he never expected her to show up in Colorado to claim her inheritance. He probably assumed she was like her mother, who had had a natural abhorrence for the wilderness. If Baxter thought that, the man didn't know his Angel.

Rafe's steps came to an abrupt halt, the blood freezing in his veins when he saw Angel hanging limply in Anson Chandler's arms. Desmond Kent stood beside him, abetting the abduction. Rafe broke into a run. He reached Kent first, spun him around and decked him.

The blow was a vicious one. Blood spurted from Kent's nose as he hit the ground.

"Put her down," Rafe barked as he took a threatening step in Chandler's direction.

"Who in the hell are you?" Chandler asked as he slowly lowered Angela to her feet and backed away.

"Never mind who I am," Rafe growled. "You've got a lot of explaining to do."

Holding a handkerchief to his bleeding nose, Kent rose unsteadily to his feet. "Now see here, mister, this is none of your concern. I don't know how you know my stepdaughter, but the association ends here. Mr. Chandler is her fiancé. She was so glad to see him she fainted. They are on their way to the justice of the peace to be married. If you don't back away, I'll summon the law."

Rafe thumbed his hat back and gave Kent a look that would have turned milk sour. Then he held his hand out to Angela. "Come here, Angel." Skirting Kent and Chandler, Angela slowly made her way to Rafe's side.

"I'm Angela's legal guardian," Kent sputtered. "You have no right to interfere. I've arranged a good marriage for her, and I won't see my plans thwarted by a ne'er-do-well. Anson Chandler has been more than patient with my stepdaughter. It's time she grew up and did what's expected of her."

Rafe sent Angela an inscrutable look. "Are you all right?"

Angela nodded.

He turned her face toward him, his mouth tightening when he saw the bruise forming on her cheek. "Who hit you?"

"It doesn't matter." She tugged on his arm. "Just get me away from here."

Rafe was like an immovable force. "Tell me, Angel."

She sighed. "Desmond."

Rafe whirled on Kent, his face a mask of fury. "If you ever touch Angel again, I'll personally see to your punishment. Do you understand?"

"Devil take you! I don't even know you. You have no right to threaten me."

"Let me introduce myself. I'm Angel's husband. Reverend Conrad married us in Ordway."

"You're lying!" Chandler shouted. "Who are you?"

"The name's Gentry. Rafe Gentry. If you don't believe we're married, ask Angel."

"What's this all about, Angela?" Kent asked. "I know you; you'd never marry a common cowboy."

"You must not have known me as well as you thought," Angela charged. "Rafe isn't lying. We are indeed married, and we have the paper to prove it. Show it to him, Rafe."

Rafe dug in his jacket pocket, retrieved a folded sheet of paper and handed it to Kent.

"It's not legal!" Kent shouted, tossing the document back to Rafe. "I don't believe it. Angela is promised to Anson Chandler, and by God she's going to marry him!"

"Over my dead body."

"Maybe that can be arranged," Kent said with sly innuendo.

"You aren't man enough," Rafe said with deadly calm. "Now if you'll excuse us, I'm going to see about a hotel room for the night. It's too late to start up to the mine."

"Where is Reverend Conrad?" Kent asked pugnaciously.

"On his way back to Topeka," Rafe returned.

"You won't get away with this, Gentry. If you were married in Ordway, it shouldn't be too difficult to check out your story."

"Do whatever you have to do, Kent. It won't change the fact that Angela and I are man and wife. I strongly suggest you return East and leave Angela alone."

Grasping Angela's elbow, he steered her toward the wagon.

Fuming in impotent rage, Kent watched them walk away.

"Do you believe them?" Chandler asked.

Kent spit out a curse. "I don't know what to believe, but I'm damn well going to find out. You stay here and keep an eye on them while I backtrack to Ordway. Someone there should be able to tell me what I want to know without having to run down the preacher."

"Watching that cowboy with Angela isn't going to be easy," Chandler grumbled. "He took what should have been rightfully mine.

Angela's going to pay for pulling that dirty trick on me."

"I'll get to the bottom of this, Chandler, and when it's sorted out, you'll have Angela and we'll both share her wealth. Perhaps we can even get rid of Brady Baxter so we'll have it all."

They shook hands and parted company.

"Why are we going to the hotel?" Angela asked as Rafe guided her away from the livery, where they had boarded the horses and wagon for the night.

"We don't know the trail and it's getting dark. We'll start out fresh in the morning."

"Very well, just be sure you rent two rooms."

"I don't think that's a good idea."

"Why not?"

"Don't look now, but we're being followed. Your former fiancé is tailing us. If we rent separate rooms he'll get suspicious. You'll just have to put up with my company to-night, Angel."

Alarm settled low in Angela's stomach. How much more of Rafe Gentry's company could she bear? The man was a distraction she didn't need. Granted, he'd saved her from marrying Chandler, for she knew without a doubt that had Rafe not produced a marriage license, she would have been dragged off and married against her will to a man she detested.

Worry gnawed at Angela as Rafe arranged for a room and signed the register. She didn't really panic until Rafe unlocked the door and ushered her into their room. Then she took one look at the bed and nearly bolted.

Would he expect her to sleep with him in that bed tonight?

Chapter Five

Rafe dropped his saddlebags and Angela's small carpetbag on the floor. "I noticed a barbershop and bathhouse down the street." He rubbed his chin. "I could use a shave, haircut and bath. I imagine you'd like a hot bath, too. I'll order one up for you on my way out. Bolt the door behind me and don't open it to anyone but the chambermaid or me."

"A bath sounds wonderful," Angela said, relieved that Rafe was going to let her bathe in private.

"There's a dining room in the hotel. We'll eat when I return."

"Take your time," Angela said, waving him off. "I'm going to have a long soak."

Hoisting his saddlebags over his shoulder, Rafe let himself out the door. Angela bolted it behind him. A short time later a chambermaid and pot boys arrived with a tub, hot water, soap and a bath towel. Bolting the door behind them, she undressed quickly and sank into the steaming water. It was pure bliss. The first real bath she'd had since leaving Ordway.

Soap bubbles tickled her nose as she lathered her body, then her hair. After rinsing, she lay back and rested her head against the rim. There was an almost sensual quality to the soapy water sliding over her sensitive skin, something she never would have noticed before Rafe Gentry had awakened her body to passion.

She raised her leg and rested it on the side of the tub. Then, unthinkingly, her fingers slid up the inside of her slippery thigh, mimicking the movement of Rafe's hand that day in the wagon when she'd fallen into his lap. A tension began low in her belly as her fingers explored further, brushing the wreath of hair protecting her most private place. A cry slipped past her lips; she was shamed by a sense of forbidden pleasure.

Trembling, she jerked her hand away. She couldn't believe what was happening. This was wicked. Wanton. How could she, a pious church member, even think about self-gratification, much less attempt it? Her face flamed. It was all Rafe Gentry's fault. She'd known nothing of sexual matters, nothing of desire, until Rafe entered her life.

Suddenly aware of the cooling water, Angela got out of the tub, dried herself and dressed in a clean chemise, a white, long-sleeved blouse that buttoned to her neck, and a plain brown skirt. She'd brought nothing fancy with her, for Reverend Conrad had insisted that Sister Angela dress simply and demurely.

Angela was pulling the comb through her unruly hair when a knock sounded on the door.

"Who is it?"

"Rafe. Open up."

She unbolted the door and Rafe sauntered inside, dressed in a spotless linen shirt and buckskin trousers and jacket. His face was newly shaved and his hair had been trimmed. Angela swallowed hard. He was so handsome the sight of him took her breath away.

"Are you ready for dinner?" Rafe asked.

Angela wished she had something more colorful to wear, but Rafe didn't seem to mind her somber attire as his gaze slid over her with obvious pleasure.

"Leave your hair down," he said.

"I didn't have time to put it up."

"It looks good just as it is." He offered his arm. "Let's eat. I'm starved."

The dining room was crowded but a table was found for them. Rafe ordered beefsteak and fried potatoes. Angela preferred lamb and fresh peas. Neither seemed inclined to talk as they devoured their food. Angela passed on dessert, preferring just coffee, while Rafe dug into a piece of chocolate cake as tall as Pikes Peak.

"Let's stroll," Rafe suggested as they left the dining room. "It's a warm night and the moon is full."

Glad for the reprieve, Angela readily agreed. She wasn't looking forward to sharing a room with Rafe for an entire night.

"What do you suppose Anson is doing now?" she asked, sending a cautious look over her shoulder.

Even before Rafe said, "He's following us," she saw him. "I saw him in the dining room," Rafe added. "He left when we did. Ignore him."

Angela tried. The night was so lovely, she thought as she filled her lungs with fresh mountain air. She had missed this more than she realized. If she had her way, she'd spend the rest of her life in Colorado. This was her destiny.

"What are you thinking?" Rafe asked, jarring her reverie.

"About how much I love it here," she said truthfully. "I can't wait to see the mine again. I vaguely remember it from my childhood. I was happiest here, you know."

Rafe reached for her. She gave a squeal of surprise as he pulled her into the shadow of a store awning and into his arms. Beguiled by the magic of the soft night and starlit sky, she melted into his embrace, forgetting everything but the feel of his mouth moving over hers and the hardness of his body. His tongue prodded urgently against her lips, and she opened to him. He kissed her until her body tingled and her head spun. It seemed the most natural thing in the world to kiss him back.

He was panting when he broke off the kiss. He gave her a hard look, grasped her hand and dragged her back toward the hotel.

"What are you doing?"

His voice was gruff, impatient. "Taking you back to our room. I'd rather do this in a bed."

His words finally got through the sensual fog drifting aimlessly in her brain. Panic-stricken, she pulled away. "I . . . I don't know what got into me."

"I know what's *going* to get into you," Rafe growled as he pulled her roughly behind him. "Me."

She considered digging in her heels, until she saw Chandler watching them with keen interest. Rather than raise questions in Chandler's mind about the relationship between her and Rafe, she tripped along beside Rafe. But once they were behind closed doors, she intended to tell Rafe exactly what she thought of him and his highhandedness.

Literally dragging her to their room, Rafe closed and bolted the door behind them. His face was taut, his muscles tense. Angela could almost taste his desire, and it frightened her. She felt suddenly vulnerable, too attuned to this man's lust for her own good.

Rafe said nothing as he tore off his shirt and jacket. Then he reached for her. That kiss in the street had unleashed something fierce and needy within him. He recognized desire when he felt it, and Angel had definitely wanted him. Her body had softened against his and her mouth had opened to him. That was all the invitation he needed.

"Let's get you out of those clothes," he gasped raggedly as he fumbled with the buttons holding her blouse together. "I want you naked the first time I take you."

A jolt of reality tore through the sensual fog in Angela's brain. She didn't want the same thing Rafe wanted. After he got what he wanted from her, he'd disappear and she'd never see him again. What if he gave her a baby? If she let him make love to her, she would never be able to forget him and move forward with her life. He'd always be there in the background, taunting her with memories. She couldn't bear it.

He had her blouse off and her chemise pulled down to her waist when Angela finally found the energy to protest.

"We can't do this, Rafe."

"Your body tells me different. I know when a woman is aroused. You want me as badly as I want you."

"No . . . I —"

Her words died in her throat as Rafe swept

her into his arms and deposited her on the bed. He followed her down, holding her body in place with his.

"Remember how I caressed you and kissed your breasts the other day?" he murmured against her ear. "I want to do all that and more . . . much more."

His hand delved beneath her skirts. Angela felt his rough palm slide up her leg, lifting her skirts with it. He grinned at her, then lowered his head and covered her mouth with his. He kissed her until she was breathless, until dizziness made her giddy. When he finally released her mouth, she sucked in a shaky breath and murmured his name.

"Rafe . . ."

Her voice rose on a note of panic. "I can't think when you're kissing me."

"Don't think, just feel."

Held suspended by the wealth of feelings thrumming through her, she watched in trepidation as he untied her petticoats and pulled them down her legs, stared dumbly as he swiftly removed her remaining clothing. She had no time to contemplate her nakedness as Rafe lifted a firm breast in his hand and took her nipple into his mouth. She cried out in surprise, arching against him. His lips drifted lower, leaving a trail of fire down her body. He pressed hot kisses to her stomach. She tensed and shifted restlessly beneath his tormenting mouth. She'd had no idea such intense feelings were possible between men and women.

"Angel . . . Angel, God, you're beautiful."

He shifted slightly. She heard the dull thud of his boots; then his trousers hit the floor. Her eyes squeezed shut; she refused to look at him. But she let herself touch. Naughty though it might be, she rested her palms on his chest. She heard his breath hitch. Beneath her questing hands, muscles bunched, shifted, then grew rigid. Encouraged, her hands roamed wider, over smooth expanses of chest, tight and hard and roughened by crisp hair, then over impossibly wide shoulders.

"You're driving me crazy," Rafe rasped hoarsely.

Then his hand drifted between her legs and her eyes flew open. She felt the heavy weight of his sex prodding her softness and nearly swooned when his fingers opened her and caressed her most sensitive, private place. A jolt of pure pleasure shot through her. With his hand caressing her there and his mouth suckling her nipple, she felt as if her bones were melting.

An unfamiliar pressure was building inside her as excitement intensified. Her senses focused on his wicked fingers sliding inside her, slowly moving in and out. She felt the invasion keenly, felt it clear to her soul. Then he did something with his thumb, touched a place so sensitive it sent her spinning out of control. She arched against his hand, shoving his fingers deeper, writhing against him, moaning shamelessly as pleasure rocked her.

"That's it, Angel, let it come," Rafe whispered raggedly. "Ah, love, who would have thought you'd have so much passion inside that small body?"

Angela felt herself drifting amid the stars as tiny tremors burst inside her. Her wits returned slowly, and when they did, her gaze found Rafe. He was bending over her, watching her closely, his silver eyes glittering with excitement.

"Did you like that?"

"I . . . what happened?"

"You experienced sexual fulfillment for the first time. It can get better than that, Angel, much better."

Angela's brow furrowed. She knew nothing of sexual matters. Her mother had never mentioned the things that went on in the marriage bed.

"Did you feel pleasure?" Angela asked.

"My pleasure was giving you pleasure. My satisfaction will come later, when I put myself inside you. It will be painful for you the first time, for you're still a virgin, but it will get better each time we make love."

"Make love?" She mulled that over for the space of a heartbeat, then shook her head. "But you don't love me and I don't love you."

"Men and women don't always have sex because they love one another. They do it for gratification."

Angela sat up abruptly and pulled a corner of the bed cover over her. "I'm not that kind of woman."

"You liked what I did to you. We're married, for godsake!"

"We won't be married for long. It would be improper to seek enjoyment from a marriage neither of us wanted or intends to honor. You're running from something, Rafe, and I don't think you need a wife right now."

"How did you guess?" Rafe said, pushing himself to his feet.

Angela stared at him for a suspenseful moment, then averted her eyes, dazzled by the magnificence temptingly displayed before her. There wasn't an ounce of fat on Rafe's well-honed body. He was all sculpted muscles, narrow waist and long, sturdy legs. When he turned away and pulled on his trousers, she wasn't surprised to note that his buttocks appeared as hard and unyielding as his chest. It was a sight she wouldn't forget any time soon.

"You're absolutely right," Rafe contended. "A wife is the last thing I need. I have nothing to offer a wife. Not a nickel to my name or a roof over my head. I'll see you to the Golden Angel, then move on."

Fully dressed now, he strode toward the door.

"Where are you going?"

"Obviously, neither of us will get any sleep if I stay here tonight. I don't trust myself to be alone with you. Sharing a bed without . . . I just can't do it. I'll sleep in the stable behind the hotel." He picked up his saddle-bags and threw them over his shoulder. "I'll meet you in the dining room at eight to-morrow morning."

"Rafe. I'm sorry. Fate played a dirty trick on us. We never should have met, much less married. I felt the need to save your life, that's all it amounted to. I don't want there to be any need for apologies when we part. If I let you make love to me, there are bound to be regrets on both our parts."

"Speak for yourself, Angel. I feel no regret about anything that has passed between us. But if you're so determined to remain a virgin, I wish you joy of your empty bed to-night. Sleep well."

His expression was shuttered, his eyes so bleak that Angela felt her heart constrict.

"Rafe, wait!"

He paused, his hand on the doorknob.

"I . . . nothing. Never mind. I'll see you in the morning."

The door opened and closed; then he was gone. Strangely bereft, Angela felt a lump gathering in her throat. What in the world was wrong with her? She wasn't the kind of woman to have a sexual relationship simply for the pleasure of it. She didn't know what had gotten into her. She'd allowed Rafe to kiss and caress her, to give her forbidden ecstasy. Her mother had raised her to know the difference between good and bad, but Angela had never realized that bad could feel so good.

If she had thought there was a chance for her and Rafe to have a normal marriage, she'd be tempted to let him make love to her. But unfortunately, she saw nothing to indicate she and Rafe had a future together. More important was the sure knowledge that if she let Rafe love her, her life would never be the same.

Rafe found an empty stall in the stable and bedded down. He rolled up in a saddle blanket he discovered in the stall and rested his head on his saddlebags. Despite his best effort, sleep eluded him. His body was sexually aroused, unsatisfied and still pulsing. Thinking about Angel did nothing to alleviate his painful condition. Come to think of it, being as hard as stone had become a natural state since meeting his Angel.

But she wasn't *his* Angel, was she? She might temporarily carry his name, but that didn't make her his. Damn, he was thinking with his cock instead of his head. He had nothing to offer Angel. Not even his good name. One day she would find a Wanted poster with his picture on it and learn the truth. It was best he left now, before the law caught up with him. The last thing he wanted was to make more problems for Angel.

Just when Rafe thought the night would never end, a gray dawn colored the dark sky.

They met in the dining room at eight. After devouring a hearty breakfast, Rafe went for the wagon while Angela packed her night-clothes and few belongings in her carpetbag. Rafe was waiting for Angela at the curb when she stepped out the door and onto the side-walk. The day was exceptionally fine. A light breeze blew down from the mountains and the sun shone brightly in a cloudless sky.

Rafe lifted Angela onto the seat and took up the reins.

"You really don't have to come with me, you know," Angela said. "I'm sure I can find my own way to the Golden Angel."

"The least I can do is see you safely to your destination. As you reminded me last night, you *did* save my life. Only an un-grateful wretch would abandon you now. I know you're itching to be rid of me, and you'll get your wish soon enough."

Angela gnawed on her bottom lip. She should have expected Rafe's sarcasm, but somehow it made her feel guilty.

"Rafe. About last night. I'm sorry."

"You already said that."

"Then I'll say it again. I want you to understand —"

"I do understand, Angel. More than you know. Ah, here's where we turn off to the mine. It shouldn't be far now."

Angela's eyes glowed. "Yes! It's been a long time, but I recognize the road. I traveled it often with my father."

The wagon traveled steadily upward, wobbling from side to side over a rutted trail. Thick forests rose majestically on the towering mountainsides, creating a canopy of dappled shadows and sunlight. In some places the track was narrow and steep, with one side falling away abruptly to nothing. Angela drank in the magnificent views of snow-capped mountains, dark green forests and clear blue skies, giddy with delight as memories of happy times with her father assailed her.

"There it is!" Rafe cried, pointing to a narrow track and a sign posted beside it that read The Golden Angel.

A sob caught in Angela's throat. "The sign is still there! I was with Father when he made it. He always called me his angel."

Rafe deftly turned the horses into the road. The gaping mouth of the mine sat at the end of the narrow lane. Activity was in full swing. Rafe saw four men busily engaged in various tasks, and an empty car sitting on a track leading into the bowels of the mine. From what Rafe could gather, the Golden Angel was a good-sized operation. Two sturdy cabins, built to withstand the harshest winters, stood side by side at the far end of the site, backed up against a wooded hillside. Angela stared at the larger cabin, which had once been her home.

While Rafe took in the lay of the land, a man detached himself from the group standing beside the cable car and ambled toward them.

"Are you lost, mister? This is the Golden Angel mine. We don't see many strangers up here. There's nothing beyond the mine but trees and more mountain."

"We have the right place," Rafe said as he climbed down from the wagon. "Are you Brady Baxter?"

"I'm Baxter. How can I help you?"

Rafe sized up Baxter in one glance. Big, rawboned and rangy, he wasn't old, perhaps a few years older than Rafe's own twenty-eight. His drab blond hair showed signs of graying at the temples, and his murky brown eyes held the predatory gleam of a wolf. His narrow-lipped smile suggested a mean disposition. Rafe decided Baxter wasn't to be trusted.

Not one to remain in the background, Angela stepped forward. "Mr. Baxter, I'm Angela, Simon Abbot's daughter."

95

"Abbot's daughter?" Baxter repeated stupidly. "What in the hell are you doing here? Do you want more money for your share of the mine? Is that it? You didn't have to come all the way out here. We could have conducted everything by mail, or through Simon's lawyer."

"I'm not selling, Mr. Baxter," Angela said, her tone leaving no room for argument. "I'm here to stay."

"Ridiculous," Baxter scoffed. "Simon told me your mother hated it here. I don't think you'll like it any better than she did."

"You're wrong. I love the mountains. Get used to it, Mr. Baxter, because I'm here to stay. Someone has to protect my interests."

"Didn't you get my letter? The mine is played out."

"Father never mentioned anything about the mine being played out. His last letter said it was producing just fine."

Baxter took a threatening step forward. "Are you calling me a liar?"

Rafe had let this go on long enough. Though he didn't want to interfere in Angel's business, he thought it high time he stepped in and set Baxter straight.

"I think you get the picture, Baxter," he barked. "Kindly step back. If you think you can intimidate Angel, you're wrong."

Baxter's jaw jutted pugnaciously. "Just who in the hell are you?"

"The name's Gentry. Rafe Gentry. Angela's husband. Any other questions?"

Baxter looked stunned. "Simon never mentioned a son-in-law."

"He died before I could tell him," Angela said, sending Rafe a disquieting look.

Angela didn't know whether to thank Rafe for coming to her defense or be angry at him for the same reason. She hadn't intended to tell Baxter she was married, for once Rafe rode off into the sunset, she'd have no one but herself to depend upon. Rafe wasn't doing her any favors by claiming to be her husband.

Baxter sent Rafe a measuring look. "If you married Miss Abbot thinking you married a gold mine, you made a mistake, Gentry. I told you, the mine is no longer profitable."

"Looks pretty busy around here to me," Rafe drawled.

"You look more like a cowboy than a miner, Gentry. Since you aren't qualified to make an intelligent judgment, I suggest you mind your own business and leave the mining to me."

Rafe's temper dangled by a frayed thread. Angela recognized the signs and stepped between the two men. "It's been a long trip. I'd like to settle into my father's cabin. I intend to observe the operation for a time before making any decisions."

"Just keep your husband out of my hair. I

don't want no greenhorn snooping around in my business."

"*Our* business," Angela countered. "If you'll excuse us . . ."

"Simon's cabin was larger and sturdier than mine. I moved there after . . . the accident," Baxter said. "I'll gather my things and be out of there in an hour."

"Ten minutes," Rafe bit out.

Baxter looked angry enough to spit nails as he sent Rafe a scathing glance and strode off toward the larger of the two cabins.

"You certainly know how to rile a man," Angela said, stifling a smile.

Rafe sent her an answering grin. "You weren't so bad yourself. I don't like that man. Furthermore, I don't trust him."

"Do you think he murdered my father?"

"Proving that won't be easy. If I were you, I would keep my suspicions to myself."

"You're right, of course. After you leave, I'll just bide my time until I have something substantial to report to the law."

"Whoa, lady, you're going too fast. You just got here."

"I suppose you'll be leaving soon."

"What do you think Baxter will make of it when I desert my bride so soon after the wedding?"

"I don't care what —"

"Look," Rafe said, interrupting her. "We have a visitor."

They turned in unison to watch a lone rider approach the mine.

"Anson Chandler," Angela said. "What does he want?"

"Probably just keeping tabs on us. I wonder what happened to Kent."

"Maybe he gave up and returned to Topeka."

"I wouldn't count on it," Rafe said uneasily.

He didn't like it one damn bit. He hadn't seen Kent since their confrontation in the street in Canon City. What had become of him? He didn't look like a man who gave up easily. Nor did Chandler strike Rafe as a man who would carry on alone. Warning bells went off in his head. If he were smart, he'd get on his horse and ride as far and as fast as he could.

Chandler reached them and dismounted.

"What are you doing here, Chandler?" Rafe barked.

"Just thought I'd ride out and look the mine over. Some operation. Where's your partner, Angela?"

"Around," Rafe said before Angela could reply.

Just then Baxter came out of the cabin, lugging a crate with his belongings. He saw Chandler, set the crate down and strode over to join him.

"This seems to be a busy place today. Who are you?"

"I'm Anson Chandler, Angela's fiancé," Chandler informed him.

Baxter's sandy brows rose sharply upward. "A husband *and* a fiancé. That's a new one on me. Care to explain?"

"There's nothing to explain," Rafe growled. "Obviously, Mr. Chandler hasn't reconciled himself to being a *jilted* fiancé."

"Then I suggest that he leaves. This is private property."

"I second that," Rafe said. "My *wife* and I want to get settled in. I'll let you know when we're ready for visitors. Good-bye, Chandler."

"You haven't seen the last of me, Gentry," Chandler said as he mounted up and rode away.

"You can tell your friends I don't take kindly to riffraff trespassing on my property, Gentry," Baxter warned. "I've cleared my belongings from the cabin. It's all yours."

"I'm positive my suspicions about Baxter are right," Angela muttered as Baxter strode away. "He's a nasty man. No wonder Father didn't trust him. They became partners because Father desperately needed an infusion of money, and Baxter had funds available. As it turned out, they struck gold shortly afterward."

"Just how do you propose to go about proving Baxter was responsible for your father's accident?" Rafe challenged. "I think you've bitten off more than you can chew

100

this time, Angel. I'm almost tempted to stick around and see what happens. You're a determined lady, I'll give you that. Also a very foolish one." He thumbed his hat to the back of his head. "What in the hell do you expect to accomplish by yourself?"

Angela simmered with barely suppressed anger. "Just because I'm a woman doesn't mean I'm incapable of solving my own problems. Don't worry about me, Rafe Gentry. I can take care of myself."

Rafe gave a snort of laughter. "If you say so. Shall we see what the cabin looks like?"

"I already know. I remember it as if it were yesterday. Father added on a bedroom for me when I got old enough to want one."

They entered the cabin. Angela took one look around and gasped in outrage. "It's a pigpen! I don't think Baxter did one thing to it since he moved in."

Rafe agreed with Angela. Though basically sturdy and spacious compared to some cabins he'd seen, it was badly in need of cleaning. They walked through the parlor, which contained a wooden settle and pair of rocking chairs sitting before a huge hearth that took up one wall. Peering through the kitchen door, Rafe spied a cook stove, round oak table and sufficient cupboards in which to store foodstuffs. The wooden floor was littered with dirt and debris. In contrast, the parlor floor was carpeted with a colorful rag rug. Two doors opened off the parlor, which Rafe supposed led to bedrooms.

"It's going to take elbow grease to get the place back in shape," Rafe said. "I'll lend a hand. All things considered, your father built a sturdy cabin. The logs are properly chinked, and the windows have glass panes with inside shutters to keep out the raw weather during the winter."

"Father had water pumped inside for Mama, but his efforts weren't good enough to keep her here. There's even a storm cellar beneath the cabin. Mama couldn't abide the privy outside, especially on cold winter days."

"If you want to start sweeping out some of the debris, I'll carry in the supplies," Rafe said.

"I . . . can manage," Angela said. "I know you must be anxious to be on your way."

Rafe shrugged. "I've nothing better to do. Besides" — he glanced out the dirty window at Baxter — "someone has to keep you out of trouble. I think I'll stick around awhile longer to make sure Baxter doesn't try to take advantage of you."

Angela wasn't sure whether to be pleased about that or not. Rafe Gentry could grow on her. She might become too accustomed to having Rafe around, and when he left, as he surely would, his absence would leave a void in her life. When had she come to depend on Rafe Gentry?

They spent the rest of the day cleaning the cabin and stowing away personal items and supplies. As Rafe had suspected, there were two bedrooms off the main room. The larger one contained a chest of drawers and double bed covered with a colorful patchwork quilt, and the smaller one was almost identical, except it held a single bed.

Angela threw together a haphazard meal that night that was surprisingly good. Afterward, Angela cleared her throat and said, "I've put clean sheets on both beds. You can take the large room, I'll take the smaller one."

"The double bed in the room you've assigned me is large enough to share," Rafe hinted with tongue in cheek. "We've shared a bed before."

With disastrous results, Angela thought but did not say. She shifted uncomfortably. Just thinking about Rafe's hands on her, his big body next to hers on the bed, sent chills down her spine. She feared she'd like it too well.

"We'll be more comfortable if we each have our own bed," she said, keeping her eyes downcast.

Should Rafe discover how very much she liked having him around, chances were he would increase his efforts to get her into his bed. And Lord knows she had enough problems without adding an amorous cowboy who was likely to disappear tomorrow.

Chapter Six

Rafe found scant solace in the comfortable bed. Every muscle and sinew was vibrantly aware that Angel lay a thin wall away. Unfortunately, there wasn't a damn thing he could do about it. Angel was determined to keep him out of her bed. And as much as he wanted her, he couldn't disagree with her decision. He was glad that at least one of them was strong enough to resist temptation. If it were left to him, he'd be in her bed right now, loving her every way to Sunday and to hell with tomorrow.

On the other side of the thin wall, Angela was struggling with the same emotions that plagued Rafe. She had never imagined that a man could be so distracting. Or that desire could have such a debilitating effect upon a woman. Nevertheless, in her heart she knew she was right to deny herself where Rafe was concerned.

Eventually, both Rafe and Angela found the elusive sleep they sought.

Rafe rose early and decided to have a look

around before the miners arrived for work. He fixed himself a cold breakfast, drank two cups of the strong coffee he'd brewed and left on the back of the stove for Angel, and ambled over to the mine shortly after daybreak. No one was about as he lit a lamp he found at the mine's entrance and ventured inside.

The mine seemed to burrow deep into the mountainside. Signs of digging were everywhere. New tunnels had been opened up recently, Rafe noted. Rather odd, he thought, for a mine that was supposed to be played out. He entered one of the newly opened tunnels and ran a hand along the rough walls. It came away speckled with gold dust. Further inspection revealed a narrow yellow vein that sparkled in the light and appeared to be gold, but he was no expert. He couldn't be absolutely sure until he got an expert down here to inspect the mine.

Deciding he had seen enough, Rafe made his way back toward the entrance . . . and ran into Baxter.

"What the hell were you doing in there!" Baxter barked. "Don't you know it's dangerous for an inexperienced man to go into a mine alone? I don't like snoops, Gentry. Anything you want to know, ask me."

"I don't like your answers," Rafe calmly returned.

"And I don't like your attitude. Let me

give you a piece of advice, cowboy. Steer clear of the operation. The mine is worthless; I'm thinking of closing it. I plan to dismiss the men today."

Rafe stared at Baxter, amazed at how far the man would go to make a point. He was willing to lose money in order to prove the mine was worthless. Of course, he had much to gain if Angel decided to sell to him. Rafe stifled a grin. Baxter was in for a shock. His Angel was far too stubborn to give up so easily.

"Really?" Rafe drawled. "Wouldn't that be like cutting off your nose to spite your face?"

"It might be, assuming the mine was still producing. Tell that wife of yours she'd make more money selling out to me than trying to find gold in a worthless mine."

"Something doesn't smell right," Rafe said. "If the mine is no longer producing, why would you want Angel's share?"

"Believe it or not," Baxter said, "I'm doing it for Simon Abbot's sake. We were partners and friends a long time. I thought I'd be helping his daughter by offering to pay good money for something that's worthless. Call it sentimental, if you like, but I have Miss Abbot's . . . er . . . Mrs. Gentry's best interests at heart."

"And I'm the President of the United States," Rafe muttered beneath his breath. Not a word Baxter spoke smacked of truth.

"What did you say?"

"Nothing important. If you'll excuse me, I've got things to do."

"Just don't get nosy," Baxter warned. "I can't be responsible for accidents that might occur while you're snooping around. And the same goes for your wife."

"Don't worry about me, Baxter, I can take care of myself. But the first time you threaten Angel, you'll have me to contend with."

He didn't wait for Baxter's answer as he whirled and strode away. The sudden desire to see Angel was overwhelming. He knew she was all right, but after speaking with Baxter he needed to look at her, touch her. For her own good, perhaps she should sell out and return to Topeka. He didn't relish the thought of leaving her here to cope with the likes of Brady Baxter.

Rafe found Angela on her knees in the kitchen, her pert little bottom raised high in the air as she attacked the floor with a vengeance. He thought she looked adorable. When he was able to turn his gaze away from her bottom, he saw that the kitchen stove gleamed, and that she'd taken down the filthy curtains.

"There you are," Angela said when Rafe walked through the door. "Where have you been?"

He hooked a kitchen chair with his foot

and sat down. "Looking around. Ran into Baxter. He says he's shutting down the mine. I've been thinking. It might be a good idea to sell out to him."

Angela sat back on her heels, dashed the hair from her eyes and gave him a disgruntled frown. "Why ever would you say that?"

"I don't trust Baxter. He'll try every lowdown trick he knows to gain control of the mine."

Angela's pointed little chin shot upward. "He doesn't frighten me."

"He should. He's lying through his teeth about the mine, and he's afraid we'll find out. He threatened me this morning, and in a roundabout way, threatened you. Take the money he offered and don't look back."

Angela slapped the wet rag into the bucket and rose to her feet. Her belligerent stance gave hint of her answer before she spoke.

"I'm *not* leaving. Baxter can threaten and intimidate all he likes, he's not going to scare me away. Furthermore, the mine means more to me than the money."

"I knew you'd see it that way but I felt I should warn you."

"Consider me warned. You can leave here with a free conscience, Rafe Gentry."

Rafe didn't believe *that* for a minute. He seriously doubted he'd ever be free where Angel was concerned.

"I'm sticking around to keep you out of trouble, remember?"

"I remember. But I won't hold you to it. You can leave any time you choose."

"I'm aware of that. What can I do to make myself useful?"

Rafe learned that making himself useful included carrying out the rag rug and throwing it over a line so the dust could be beaten from it. And heating kettles of water over a roaring fire to wash dirty linen, filthy curtains and their soiled clothing.

At the end of the day the cabin was as spotlessly clean as Angela recalled from her youth.

After a dinner of fried eggs and potatoes, Angela set two large kettles of water on the stove for her bath. Then she invited Rafe to leave so she could soak her sore muscles in the wooden tub she had asked Rafe to roll into the kitchen from the shed.

"I'll bathe in the creek while you have your bath," Rafe said. He paused at the door, as if waiting for some sign from Angela. When none was forthcoming, he sighed and headed out the door.

Angela knew precisely why Rafe had seemed reluctant to leave. If he was waiting for her to invite him into her bed, he would wait forever. Her body might want him, but her mind was dead set against getting involved with a stranger.

The hot water felt wonderful. After she washed, she laid her head against the rim and closed her eyes. She must have dozed, for when she opened her eyes, Rafe was standing beside the tub, his glittering silver gaze devouring her. Surprised, she lurched up, forgetting she was as naked as the day she was born. She saw his gaze lower to her bare breasts and covered them with her hands.

"I thought you went down to the creek to bathe."

"I finished. I've been gone nearly an hour. You must have fallen asleep. I knocked, but you didn't hear me." He moved behind her. "Can I wash your back?"

She swiveled around. He was already on his knees, soap and cloth in hand. "No, I —"

Her sentence died in her throat when he slowly began to spread soap over her back.

"I was going to say I've already washed," she said in a strangled voice. "Thank you, anyway."

He shoved to his feet. "Glad to oblige." But instead of leaving the room, he sank down onto a kitchen chair to watch.

"I don't need an audience, Rafe," Angela said in her sternest voice.

"I'm only looking, Angel."

"I'd prefer you didn't."

"What are you afraid of?"

You, she wanted to shout. "Turn your back so I can get out."

"We're married, Angel."

Damn him! Why must he bring that up when he knows we don't intend to remain married?

"I don't feel married."

He pushed himself out of the chair. "I could change that."

"Don't you ever stop?" Angela charged.

"I have no control where you're concerned. I've made no bones about wanting you. When I walked into the kitchen and saw you lying all pink and rosy in your bath, I wanted to carry you to bed and make love to you. But you already know that, don't you? I've never hidden my desire from you."

"Rafe, I . . ."

His expression was tense, his voice coaxing and silken as he said, "Get out of the tub, Angel, unless you're afraid of me."

"I'm not afraid of you, Rafe. I don't know who or what you are, but I don't fear you."

She rose slowly; water dripped off her breasts and ran down her torso, pooling in the thick, curling hair between her thighs. She reached for the flannel towel, but Rafe was there before her. Wrapping her in the cloth, he lifted her out of the tub and carried her to his bedroom. Then he set her on her feet and released the towel, letting it drift slowly down her body.

"This isn't my bedroom, Rafe Gentry," she

said, grabbing up the towel and pulling it around her. "This isn't going to work, you know. I'm opposed to whatever you have in mind."

He spun her around. She landed against him, breast to breast, thigh to thigh. His gaze dropped to her lips; with his thumb, he brushed their fullness.

"Do you think you can stop me?" he whispered against her lips. Her mouth opened slightly. He sucked in a breath and captured her lips for a slow, leisurely exploration of her luscious mouth.

Tentatively, she kissed him back. He groaned and deepened the kiss. He withdrew only to drag in a breath, then delved back for more.

Some small part of Angela's mind knew what was going to happen if she didn't put a stop to this. Another part didn't give a hoot. That was the part that melted against him, leaned into his embrace, opened her mouth to his probing tongue.

No man had ever sent her senses reeling like this. All the defenses she'd built over the years went out the window the moment Rafe entered her life. She'd never wanted to marry. Not after seeing the disastrous end to her parents' marriage. She'd lived too long under the domination of a man she despised to change her mind. Angela was certain her mother had regretted her marriage to Kent but had been too proud to admit it.

At some point Angela wrapped her arms around Rafe's neck, and he moved closer, the pressure of his chest teasing her sensitive breasts. She returned his kiss with giddy abandon and felt him harden against her thighs. Then he lifted one hard, buckskin-clad thigh between her legs and let her ride him. She would have pulled back from his kiss then but he wouldn't allow it. Her senses careened wantonly as he cradled her bottom, tilting her against his loins. He leaned into her; she drew him closer.

Their lips fused, eased, fused again. She tasted his need and felt his heat emanating through his clothing, wave after wave, increasing in intensity until her body turned liquid. Then she felt herself drifting downward, onto the soft surface of the bed. He followed her down.

His kisses fell like rain over her face, her neck, her shoulders, her breasts. His mouth found her nipple and he suckled her. A pounding began in her head, growing louder and louder until she could no longer ignore it.

"Rafe . . ."

"I know. Someone is pounding on the door. Dammit! I'm beginning to think fate is conspiring against us. Don't move, I'll be right back."

His weight shifted away from her, and she

shivered, suddenly chilled by his absence. "Who would come calling now?"

"Baxter. Who else could it be?"

Cursing beneath his breath, Rafe went to the door. "Who is it?" he barked through the panel. *As if he didn't know.*

"Baxter! Open up."

Rafe unlatched the door and pulled it open. "What do you want? This better be good."

Baxter shoved Anson Chandler forward. "I caught your friend snooping around the mine."

"Chandler is no friend of mine," Rafe returned shortly.

"What should I do with him?"

"Send him packing," Rafe said.

"Maybe what he needs to keep him from trespassing is a load of buckshot in his ass," Baxter contended.

"Now see here," Chandler injected. "I haven't done anything wrong. You can't blame a man for wanting to protect his fiancée."

"I'm not your fiancée, Anson Chandler," Angela charged as she sidled up beside Rafe. She was wearing a tattered robe; her feet were bare. Oddly, Rafe thought the sight of her toes peeping from beneath the robe was wildly erotic.

"Your stepfather never gave you permission to marry anyone but me," Chandler contended.

"That doesn't give you the right to spy on me," Angela shot back.

"I don't understand any of this," Baxter complained. "Get the hell out of here, Chandler. If I ever see you snooping around again, I'll fill you full of buckshot. Understand?"

Chandler shot Rafe a venomous glare before making himself scarce.

"Just tell me one thing, Gentry," Baxter said. "Are you really married to Simon's daughter?"

"I can show you the marriage paper, if you'd like. Not that it's any of your business."

"It's my business if it affects the mine," Baxter said. "If you're Angela's legal husband, then what's hers is yours."

"You've got that wrong, Baxter," Rafe charged as he sent a sidelong glance at Angela. "What's Angel's is Angel's. The decision to sell out to you or keep her interest in the mine is strictly hers to make. I won't interfere. Don't get me wrong. Try to intimidate Angel in any way and you'll answer to me. Good night."

He slammed the door in Baxter's face, then turned to Angela, who looked very small and lost in the oversized robe. "Where did you get the robe?"

Angela rubbed the worn places on the sleeves and smiled. "It belonged to my father. Mama made it for him during happier times.

I found it hanging on a hook behind the door."

He held out his hand. "Shall we continue where we left off before we were interrupted?"

Angela hung back. "I don't think so. The . . . moment is gone."

"I could bring it back."

"It wouldn't be the same. Good night, Rafe."

Another sleepless night, Rafe thought, chagrined at his unaccustomed eagerness to make Angela his in more than name only. He must be crazy, or . . . No, that notion didn't bear considering.

The next day Angela and Rafe were standing near the mine entrance when Rafe sensed danger. Glancing up, he saw a boulder hurtling toward them. Rafe had noticed the boulder balanced above the mine entrance the day before but thought nothing of it. It had appeared secure, as if it had perched in that position for generations. It happened so fast that Rafe only had time for one selfless act as he shoved Angela aside and fell on top of her. The boulder clipped his right thigh, then rolled away, coming to rest against a tree.

Waves of agony contorted his features as he eased away from Angela and rolled over on his back.

Angela took one look at his pained expression and flew to his side. "Rafe! Speak to me. Where are you hurt?"

He flexed his leg. Though the pain was excruciating, he didn't think the bone was broken. "The boulder clipped my thigh." He stretched out his limb. "It's bruised but not broken. I'll survive."

"You saved my life. Can you walk?"

Baxter came running up, accompanied by a miner named Jim Cady. Idly Rafe wondered where they had been when that boulder had become dislodged. "That was a close call, Gentry. Don't say I didn't warn you about the dangers that exist around a mining operation. Maybe now you'll believe me."

"Can't you see he's in pain!" Angela all but shouted. "Help me get him inside. Be careful, his leg may be broken."

Baxter and Cady hoisted Rafe up and carried him into the cabin. Angela directed them to his bedroom, where they carefully placed Rafe on the bed.

"I'll check back later," Baxter said as he headed out the door.

"Baxter, wait," Rafe called from the bed. "Where are the other miners?"

Avoiding Rafe's gaze, Baxter said, "I let them go. I told you the mine was played out. No sense paying men when there's no work. I kept Cady on to help shut things down."

His brow furrowed in thought, Rafe was

still staring at Baxter's departing back when Angela hurried over to him.

"I'm going to have to get your trousers off."

Rafe managed a pained grin. "I've been waiting forever to hear those words from you. Unfortunately, I'm in no condition to take advantage of the fact that you want me naked."

"You know what I mean, Rafe Gentry. I can't tend to your injury until I know what I'm treating. Can you raise your hips?"

"As high as you want, sweetheart." His lopsided grin ended in a groan. "Be gentle."

She wanted to smack him. Instead, she cautiously undid his belt and unbuttoned his fly. A lump formed in her throat when she saw that he wore no underwear. Neither drawers nor longjohns. Willing her hands not to shake, she eased his trousers down his hips and legs until the huge purple bruise on his lower thigh became visible.

"Turn on your side, away from me," she instructed, trying not to look at anything but the injury.

Rafe let out a yelp when she probed the bruise with a fingertip.

"I don't think anything is broken. There's no bone sticking out, and you seem able to move about freely. You probably should stay off your leg for a few days."

Rafe wished Jess were here. With his doctoring skills he could tell right away if there was a hidden hairline fracture. But Jess wasn't here and he would have to make do with Angel's guesswork.

"Cold compresses ought to help," Angela said. "I'll fetch water and cloths."

Before she departed, she discreetly arranged the sheet over him so that nothing showed but his bruise. Her sensibilities assuaged, she beat a hasty retreat.

The cold compresses seemed to help. The swelling subsided and the pain wasn't quite as severe as it had been. Once the pain eased, Rafe had time to think. The boulder balanced over the mine entrance couldn't have been dislodged without help. The longer he thought about it, the more convinced he became that two strong men, such as Cady and Baxter, could easily pry it from its precarious perch.

The following day Rafe tested his leg. It hurt like hell to put any weight on it, and he still wasn't sure there wasn't a hairline fracture, but lying abed wasn't an option. He'd rather limp around than lie in bed like a useless lump. Besides, that boulder was meant to kill both him and Angel. She needed his protection.

Nothing unforeseen happened during the following days. Rafe's limp eased, as did the pain, and he was finally able to sit his horse without undue discomfort. The first day he was free of pain, he suggested to Angela that they go into town and sell the wagon that had carried her across the prairie.

"The wagon is too cumbersome for these mountain roads," Rafe explained. "I noticed a buckboard behind the cabin, and some horses corralled nearby. The buckboard will do just fine to get you to town and back. I think you should buy a good riding horse with the proceeds from the wagon." He sent her an assessing look. "You can ride, can't you?"

"I can ride. Your suggestion is a good one. While I'm in town I can visit Father's lawyer. Mr. Goodman should be informed of my arrival, and I need to learn more about my inheritance. Are you healed enough to ride?"

He sent her a wicked grin. "Would you care to inspect my injury?"

"No, thank you," she sniffed. "I've already seen more of you than I care to. I'll get my bonnet and meet you outside."

Rafe watched her leave, his expression bemused. He wished things were different between them. Were he able to settle down with a woman, Angel would be his first and only choice. But circumstances beyond his control denied him the kind of life he might choose for himself. A man on the run from the law had no business messing up the life of an innocent woman like his Angel.

The trip down Red Rock Canyon Road

was every bit as harrowing as it had been going up. The prairie schooner lumbered awkwardly from side to side down the winding road, but they arrived safely in Canon City, due primarily to Rafe's expert handling of the team.

The hostler offered a fair price for the wagon, and Angela found a chestnut mare to her liking. A trade was made and they set off for the lawyer's office. Mr. Goodman greeted them with a mixture of surprise and pleasure.

"So you're Simon's daughter," Goodman greeted her.

Age and years of experience sat heavily upon his shoulders, but his forthright gaze and confident air immediately put Angela at ease. "I had no idea you intended to visit your father's property."

"My decision to travel West was rather sudden," Angela said. "This isn't just a visit, Mr. Goodman. I intend to make my home here. I'm staying up at the mine, in Father's cabin."

"And who is this young man?" Goodman asked, sizing Rafe up with a critical eye.

"I'm Rafe Gentry, sir. Angela's husband," Rafe answered.

Goodman's eyes widened. "Simon never mentioned that his daughter was married."

"He didn't know," Angela replied. "What can you tell me about Father's holdings?" she asked, adroitly changing the subject. "Your letter hinted that my inheritance was quite substantial."

"There is over fifty thousand dollars in the bank in your name. All you have to do is claim it. Baxter Brady came around after Simon's death and told me the mine was played out, and that he had already notified you in writing about it. He said he offered to buy you out. I was waiting for directions from you on how to proceed."

Clearly stunned, Angela gasped. "Father left that much?"

Rafe was impressed, but he had other things on his mind. "Do you know for a fact that the mine is played out, Mr. Goodman?"

"I'm no miner, Mr. Gentry. I had no reason to doubt Baxter. Do you know something I don't?"

Rafe and Angela exchanged speaking glances. "Nothing we can prove, sir. What can you tell us about Simon Abbot's death?"

"About as much as anyone else. His wagon went off the cliff. Baxter found him. He told the sheriff that the wagon's axle snapped, sending Simon plunging over the cliff. If it's any consolation, I made sure Simon's funeral was a grand affair. He had many friends in the area and they all came to bid him a final farewell."

"Where is he buried?" Angela asked.

"In the cemetery at the edge of town. It's a pleasant spot. I'm sure you'll approve."

"Thank you for providing Father with a proper burial. Is there anything special I need to do to withdraw funds from Father's account?"

"Just a note from me. The account is in your name as well as your father's. His will clearly stated that you were to inherit his entire estate, including cash and property. You should encounter no problems."

"Thank you again. If you'd be so good as to write the note, I'll be on my way."

"Of course." He dipped a pen in an inkwell and scribbled a brief note. "If there is anything I can do for you, don't hesitate to ask." He folded the note and handed it to her. "Please accept my congratulations on your marriage. I wish you and Mr. Gentry happiness."

Rafe offered his hand. "Please call me Rafe."

"Very well, Rafe. Are you a miner?"

"No. After returning from the war, my brothers and I tried to make a success of the family farm in Kansas. Two years of drought wiped us out. Much obliged for your help, sir. We'll certainly call on you if we have need of your services."

"Fifty thousand dollars," Angela said with a shaky sigh as they left the lawyer's office. "That's a lot of money. No wonder Anson was so determined to marry me."

"I'm not sure either Chandler or Kent

123

knows about the money," Rafe mused. "They may have guessed, but they had no way of knowing the exact amount your father left in your name."

"Thank God for that. Let's go to the bank. I want to withdraw some cash for my immediate needs."

"I realize I have no business telling you what to do, but if I were you, I'd wire the assayer's office in Denver and hire an expert to come down and check out the mine. I wouldn't take Baxter's word about the condition of the mine as gospel."

Angela beamed her approval. "That's a wonderful idea! Would you take care of it while I make myself known at the bank?"

Rafe nodded. "I'll meet you at the bank after I've sent the telegram."

The first thing Rafe saw when he walked into the telegraph office was the Wanted poster identifying the Gentry brothers as bank robbers with a five-hundred-dollar reward on each of their heads. The picture alone would hardly identify any of the three brothers, but Rafe feared that enough people in Canon City knew his name to make sticking around dangerous.

Glancing over at the clerk, Rafe saw that he had his back turned. Without a smidgen of guilt, Rafe ripped the picture from the wall and stuffed it into his pocket. Then he calmly walked to the counter and wrote out his telegram, signing it Angela Abbot of the Golden Angel mine. Without glancing at Rafe's face, the clerk sent it out. Rafe paid him and beat a hasty exit.

Meanwhile, Angela made the bank president's acquaintance. They briefly discussed her inheritance; then Angela withdrew a small amount of cash. As she was walking out the door, something caught her eye. A poster on the wall featuring three men. Drawn like a moth to a flame, Angela approached the poster with a feeling of dread.

She nearly lost the ability to breathe when she recognized a very badly drawn picture of Rafe, and who she assumed were his two brothers. Their names appeared in bold lettering above the words, "Wanted for bank robbery. Five hundred dollars reward for each man, dead or alive."

Dazed, Angela staggered out of the bank.

Who *was* Rafe Gentry? He had robbed a bank; could he have killed five people and robbed a stagecoach?

Dear God! Did she even *know* the real Rafe Gentry?

Chapter Seven

Rafe saw Angel leave the bank and strode over to meet her. Anxious to leave Canon City before someone recognized him, he grasped her arm and all but pulled her toward her horse. When he placed his hands around her waist to lift her up, she twisted free of his grasp and stared at him as if he were someone she didn't know.

"Don't touch me!"

Rafe went still. His silver gaze searched her face. She was pale and shaken, her blue eyes glazed.

"What happened inside the bank? Did someone accost you? For godsake, Angel, talk to me!"

Angela shook her head and hoisted herself onto her horse. Then she dug in her heels and took off as if the devil were nipping at her heels.

"Angel, wait!"

Rafe caught up with her on Red Rock Canyon Road. Grasping the reins from her hands, he brought both horses to a halt.

"I want to know what this is all about and I want to know now."

"As if you didn't know!" she shouted back. "This is one time my instincts failed me. You're an outlaw."

Rafe spit out an oath. That damn Wanted poster! There must have been another one posted in the bank, and Lord knows where else.

"You told me you were innocent of any crime. But there it was, staring me in the face. You and your brothers are bank robbers. For all I know, you *did* rob the stage and kill those people."

Rafe heaved a weary sigh. "I'm neither a killer nor a bank robber. It was all a mistake."

"That's what they all say. I trusted you, Rafe Gentry."

"Let me explain."

She pulled the reins from his hands. "What's there to explain? That poster said it all."

She slapped the reins against the horse's rump and the chestnut bolted, carrying her upward along the narrow trail. Rafe recognized the danger the moment Angela had taken off. Had Angel not been blinded by fear and anger, she would have seen the low-slung branch in her path. It was a branch they had avoided on the way down to town.

"Angel! Look out!"

His shout went unheeded. Blinded by tears, Angela hit the branch full tilt and was swept from her horse. She fell hard, rolling over and over, finally coming to rest precariously close to the lip of a rocky ledge.

Bringing his horse to a prancing halt, Rafe leaped to the ground and took off at a run. He grasped Angela's arms just as she started to slide downward. He was visibly shaken as he carried her across the road and through the trees to where the ground was relatively level. He found a grassy spot beneath some towering aspens and carefully placed her on a bed of leaves.

She was so still it frightened him. He placed a hand over her heart. It was beating steadily, but that didn't mean she wasn't hurt. Water, he needed water to bathe her forehead. Rafe hated to leave his Angel but he needed his canteen. Leaping to his feet, he went back to the road and fetched the horses, securing their reins to a nearby bush. Then he removed his canteen and dropped to his knees beside Angela. With shaking hands he wet his neckerchief and applied cool water to her forehead.

Angela moaned but did not awaken. "Wake up, Angel. Speak to me."

He dribbled water on her lips. She moaned again and opened her eyes. "What happened?"

"You were thrown. How do you feel?"

She tried to sit up. He placed a gentle hand on her shoulder. "Lie still a while longer. Do you hurt anywhere?"

She flexed her arms and legs. "Nothing feels broken. I have a slight headache, but I've had worse."

"You scared the hell out of me, Angel. You came mighty close to going over the edge of the cliff."

Angela shuddered. This time when she tried to sit up, Rafe didn't stop her.

"Do you remember why you were hell-bent on getting away from me?"

Her eyes widened. "I . . . oh . . . God, yes. Don't touch me!"

Ignoring her plea, he pulled her against him. "Don't be afraid of me, Angel. Forget that poster. It's all a mistake. Neither my brothers nor I robbed a bank. I can explain everything."

"With more lies?" Angela asked. "I've heard enough of those to last a lifetime. I knew you were running from something. I didn't want to let myself believe it was from the law."

"You're right. I am running from the law, and so are my brothers, but we had no choice. The law was disinclined to listen to our side of the story."

"So am I." She started to rise.

"Dammit, Angel!" He shook her gently. "I need you to believe in me."

Angela was torn. She had seen only the good side of Rafe, but that didn't mean there wasn't another side to him. A side that could rob banks and kill people. She stared into his daunting silver gaze and felt impaled by it. She forced herself to look away. She couldn't think straight. Nothing made sense.

"Angel. Look at me."

She didn't want to, but an unexplainable force compelled her to look into his face. His eyes had darkened, smoky now instead of silver. He caught her wrists and yanked her to him. He was so close she could feel his breath fanning her cheek, feel the scorching heat of his body. She blew out a ragged breath when he dipped his head and settled his lips over hers. He kissed her hard. She tasted his desperation, his longing. He kissed her as if the very force of his kiss could make her believe in him.

"Angel, oh God, Angel."

Her name on his lips loosed something deep and profound inside her as she sank into his embrace. She felt heat surround her, rise intolerably within her, lick tantalizingly at her vitals. This shouldn't be . . . couldn't be . . . yet it was.

He broke off the kiss with a bitter curse. "I can't stay now. You know that. When the law comes, pretend you know nothing about my background. They won't bother you if I'm not around. But I swear to you, Angel,

I've committed no crime."

She wanted to believe him. Ached to believe him. But a tiny kernel of doubt remained.

His mouth took hers again, shutting off her thoughts. He kissed her deeply, urgently — more intimately, using his tongue to pry open her lips so he could explore the sweet inside of her mouth. He shifted upward. She felt rather than saw him remove his shirt. His boots hitting the ground were but a soft whisper as they stirred the leaves around them.

He stared down at her. Then his hands were on the buttons of her shirtwaist, his eyes begging her not to stop him. However much she knew it was wrong, aware that she would never see him again once he rode off, Angela couldn't find it in her heart to resist. As Rafe had pointed out many times, she *was* his wife. If he was an outlaw, a killer, it was a part of him she'd never seen. Tomorrow would be time enough for regrets. For one magic moment in time, she wanted to be Rafe's wife in more than name only.

Angela closed her eyes as Rafe pulled off her shirtwaist and eased the straps of her chemise down her arms, baring her breasts. She gasped in delight when he touched her nipple with the tip of a finger, then claimed it with his mouth. Her senses were awhirl with sensations. She felt her nipple rise up, felt it harden and pucker. The sensations began anew when he gave his attention to her other nipple.

Her hands splayed over his chest. She flexed her fingers into the iron-hard muscles of his upper arms and heard him groan his appreciation. She arched her back, pushing herself into his mouth as he suckled her. How could this man be a killer? she wondered before her mind shut down and her senses took over.

She had no idea how it happened, but moments later Rafe had rendered them both naked. His mouth returned to hers, reaching deep for a response, asking for more and taking greedily when she complied. Compelled by a wanton force that surprised her, her hand moved over his body. Trailed over his hips, his lower stomach.

Fingers searching, curiosity aroused, she let her hand stray into forbidden territory. His breath hitched. She felt him quiver. Tense. Felt his muscles lock. He broke off the kiss with a soft groan, his eyes wide open, as if all his senses were focused on the one muscle in his body that ached the most.

His hand closed around hers, bringing it to his throbbing erection, pumping it slowly up and down. Angela had never felt anything like it in her life. Hard as steel. Soft as velvet. It grew larger with each stroke of her hand.

"Enough," he growled. "Sweet, sweet Angel, you can't imagine what you do to me. I've been hard since the day I met you. I still don't know if I should do this to you. You know I have to walk away from you and not look back."

Angela knew, but it didn't matter. If Rafe was a killer, she didn't want to think about it until tomorrow.

"What are you thinking?" Rafe asked.

"That I must be crazy to want this."

"No, I'm the crazy one. I'm a wanted man. An outlaw in the eyes of the law. But my need for you has stolen whatever good sense I possessed."

Angela went still. An outlaw. God, she couldn't do this. "No, I've changed my mind. I don't want this."

"It's too late, sweetheart."

He kissed her again. Voraciously, ravenously, until her wits whirled and reality became a dim memory. If he stopped now, she knew she would surely perish. She probably would hate him afterward, but now all she could think about was that part of her that throbbed with unrequited need.

His body rasped hotly along hers, causing a delicious friction. She arched wildly and nearly screamed when he pressed open-mouthed kisses over her quivering flesh, torturing the succulent tips of her beasts with his tongue and teeth. Just when she thought she had felt the ultimate thrill, he pressed hot kisses to her stomach. She tensed as the trail of fire continued downward along one thigh, then up the other.

She nearly lost the ability to think when he shifted slightly and lifted her knees, parting them. Her first inclination was to clamp her thighs tightly together, but his broad shoulders prevented her from doing so. Then he lowered his head and pressed a hot kiss to her damp curls. His kiss drove her wild. Then he licked her. And sucked her. She was dying. Mindless, she thrashed beneath him; the heavy weight of his forearm kept her from leaping up. He sent her a wicked smile as his hand slid beneath her bottom and lifted her into the hot cavern of his mouth.

She felt her blood boil; fire erupted under her skin as his lips and tongue wove their magic, until her bones turned liquid and her nerves shattered. Until she was panting and crying, her need a driving force within her. She was so hot, so needy, so ready to experience the next step of her journey into erotic pleasure. Dragging in a tight breath, she waited.

And waited.

He drew back, leaving her dangling by a thin thread. She clutched his shoulders.

"Rafe!"

"You're almost ready, sweetheart."

"Almost?" she squeaked. What more could there be?

His hands closed over her breasts, kneading them, weighing them in his hands as his gaze roamed freely over her naked body. Angela felt herself blush. She'd never known. No one had ever told her it would be like this.

Then his hand found her, opening her. She squirmed, embarrassed by his close scrutiny.

"You're so small," he said, sliding a finger inside her. "I don't want to hurt you, but it can't be helped. Open for me, Angel."

He positioned himself over her. She felt his sex prodding between her legs. She stiffened, her gaze riveted to that place where they were joined.

"Look at me. Don't look down."

Her eyes lifted to his face. His expression was tense, his teeth clamped tightly together. Then she felt his first tentative surge into her tight passage. He couldn't have been inside her very far, but the pressure of his entry left her feeling breathless and ragged inside.

"Are you all right?"

Unable to speak, she nodded; she had no intention of asking him to stop. Then a tidal wave of flame was bearing down inside her. She had to escape the devouring inferno; then it was too late. Rafe flexed his hips and broke through her maidenhead. A scream rose up from her throat. He caught it in his mouth, holding himself still until she grew accustomed to him. Then he moved.

There was still some pain, but it was quickly forgotten as his slow, confident strokes produced something far more pleasant inside her. Her body tingled. Her nerve endings sizzled. Those feelings he had produced with his mouth and tongue intensified as his hands cupped her bottom, raising her so she could take him more fully.

Angela groaned. Something tantalizing dangled just out of reach. She strained toward it, panting, writhing beneath him like a madwoman. Poignant, piercing pleasure seized her and wouldn't let go.

"That's it, sweetheart," Rafe gasped against her mouth. "You're almost there. Come to me, sweet baby, come."

Suddenly Rafe held a wildcat in his arms. She was fire and fury. Desire and need. She was wanton innocence. All that and more combined in one delectable body. He felt her stiffen, felt the tremors begin where they were joined. Her volatile explosion surprised him, but he should have known his Angel didn't do anything by halves. It was all or nothing.

Then coherent thought fled as he unleashed the full force of his passion. He convulsed and shattered as unspeakable bliss pounded through him.

Much later, after his wits returned, he

looked down and met her gaze. Her eyes were still clouded, unable to focus. He grinned at her as he pulled out and rolled to her side.

"I've been itching to sink into you since the moment the reverend pronounced us husband and wife. I've been aroused virtually since the moment I heard you singing." He sighed. "If only things were different."

"But they're not, are they, Rafe?"

"Sadly, no. We both know I must leave soon. I'll want to be gone before the law comes knocking at the door."

"I wish . . . If you're not guilty, you should stay and prove your innocence. I'll help, Rafe."

He shook his head. "Wishes don't count. Western law leaves much to be desired. Maybe if I hadn't run in the beginning, it would be easier to prove my innocence now. But I can't undo what happened. I have to leave, Angel. I don't want you involved in all this."

"If you leave now, I have no choice but to believe you truly are an outlaw."

Rafe shot to his feet. "Come on, I'll take you back to the mine. I won't make a decision until later."

They dressed in silence. More than anything, Rafe wanted to stay with Angel. Perhaps, if there was a God, He would be kind and let him do what his heart directed.

★ ★ ★

Rafe didn't leave that day. Or the next, or the next. Though he kept a sharp eye out for the law, no one came to drag him off to jail on trumped-up charges. A slim hope existed that the sheriff hadn't connected him with the Rafe Gentry in the poster.

No matter how desperately he wanted to make love to Angel again, he felt it best not to further complicate their situation. She probably hadn't become pregnant from their first encounter, and he didn't trust himself to practice control should he make love to her again. He couldn't be sure how long fate would smile on him, and he didn't want to leave Angel with a child to care for while he was running from the law.

Each time Angel looked at him, he could see doubt in her eyes, and it nearly killed him. How could she believe him an outlaw, a killer? He'd hoped that by staying he might change that look in her eyes from suspicion to trust. Truth be told, he didn't blame her for being suspicious. Perhaps one day he would prove to her that he was no outlaw.

Angela felt the pressure of Rafe's daunting presence. She knew that letting him love her had been a terrible mistake, but at the time she had wanted it desperately. If she hadn't been so darn inexperienced, she would have known how to resist his sexual allure. What she couldn't understand was his aloofness since their tryst in the forest. It was almost as if they hadn't become intimate. Did he regret it? The fact that he hadn't left her seemed to disprove that theory.

Each day Angela wondered if it would be the last she would see of Rafe. A week passed. Rafe still prowled around the mine but had turned up nothing concrete to prove or disprove Baxter's claim that it had played out. Angela eagerly awaited the arrival of the expert from Denver to clear up the matter once and for all.

Meanwhile, they went on as they had before they had made love. They were two strangers sharing a cabin. But Angela remembered. Oh, God, she remembered!

Desmond Kent returned to Canon City, eager to impart the wealth of information he'd learned from Ordway's sheriff. He found Chandler at the Nugget Saloon and took him to a table in the corner where they couldn't be overheard.

"What did you find out?" Chandler asked anxiously. "Took you long enough."

"The trip was well worth my time," Kent crowed.

"Spit it out, Kent. Is Angela legally married to Gentry or not?"

"Reverend Conrad married them, all right."

"Shit!"

"But wait until you hear this. The day she married Gentry, there was a rope around his neck and a lynch mob clamoring for his blood. He was accused of robbing a stage and killing five witnesses. Now here's the really strange part," Kent continued. "Angela claimed Gentry was her fiancé, the man she had come West to meet. Somehow she made everyone believe Gentry was innocent, and Reverend Conrad backed her up.

"Then the preacher married them on the spot. What do you make of that?"

"I think Angela must have been damn anxious to escape us if she married an outlaw." Chandler shook his head. "I can't believe she'd do something so reckless. If she's legally married, there's not much we can do about it."

"You bet your ass there's something we can do," Kent contended. "The wheels are already in motion. While I was in Ordway, the sheriff received a new batch of Wanted posters. Guess who's wanted for bank robbery in Dodge City?"

Chandler raised his glass in a silent toast. "I hope it's Rafe Gentry."

"It is. It appears that he and his two brothers robbed a bank in Dodge City a while back. I've convinced Sheriff Tattersal that Gentry tricked him, with Angela's unwitting help, of course. He now believes that Gentry really did rob the stage and kill five people. I explained that I was Angela's guardian, and that Gentry wasn't her fiancé. I had a hard time convincing Tattersal not to include Angela in the new Wanted poster he's circulating for Gentry's arrest."

"How did you do that?"

"I painted Angela as a religious fanatic willing to go to any lengths to save souls and prevent social injustice. He bought my story."

"So what do we do now? No matter who or what Gentry might be, he and Angela are still married."

"That's not all I learned in Ordway," Kent said, lowering his voice. "Reverend Conrad's wagon was attacked by renegade Comanche warriors somewhere between Ordway and Garden City. He and his wife were both killed and their wagon burned. That means the church register he carried with him no longer exists. As far as I'm concerned, no legal marriage exists."

"I agree," Chandler said with growing excitement. "What are we going to do about Gentry?"

"I picked up the Wanted poster in Ordway. I'm going to show it to the sheriff here and collect the reward for Gentry's arrest."

This time both men raised their glasses in a silent toast.

A premonition of doom plagued Rafe as he

sat down to the lunch Angel had prepared. The feeling had been with him for the past week. He knew intuitively that time was growing short for him. No matter how badly he wanted to stay with Angel, he feared the consequences.

For one thing, Chandler and Kent were a pair of loose cannons, still out there somewhere just waiting for the opportunity to take him down. Then there was Brady Baxter, who wanted nothing more than to be rid of him. Complicating matters were the Wanted posters circulating with his picture on them. Every day he expected the sheriff to come pounding on the door.

Then there was Angel to consider. He could tell by the way she looked at him that she was unconvinced of his innocence. He'd do anything to put trust back into her eyes. She was watching him now, as if she didn't know what to make of him.

"I'm not going to bite you," he said as she slid into the seat across from him.

"I know. It's just that . . . I'm so confused. Perhaps you should go into town and speak to the sheriff, explain what happened. *I* don't even know why you and your brothers were accused of bank robbery."

"Would you like to know?"

She nodded slowly.

"Very well. It happened in Dodge City. My brothers and I were trying to make a go of the family farm after the war, but drought all but ruined us. We applied for a loan at the local bank and were turned down flat. Then the banker . . ."

He paused, as someone was pounding on the door.

"Gentry, open up!"

"It's Baxter, probably with another offer to buy me out," Angela said. "I wish that mine expert would get here soon."

Rafe felt a strange tingling at the back of his neck. "Wait," he said, strapping on his guns. "I'll open the door."

Angela was hard on his heels as he strode to the door and flung it open. "What do you want, Baxter?"

"Just this," Baxter said, shoving the Wanted poster in Rafe's face. "Picked it up at the bank this morning."

Rafe heard Angela gasp and winced. Keeping his expression purposely blank, he said, "I've seen it, thank you."

Rafe glanced past Baxter, wondering why the bastard hadn't brought the law with him. "Where's the law?"

"If that stupid sheriff can't find you on his own, why should I help him?"

"For the reward," Rafe bit out.

"There is that," Baxter mused. "But I have something altogether different in mind. I scoured the town and removed all the posters I could find."

"Why would you do that?" Angela asked curiously.

Rafe's unease intensified. Men like Baxter did no favors without wanting something in return. "What do you want, Baxter?"

"That's easy enough. Sell me Simon Abbot's share of the mine and I'll keep mum about this. Change your name. You and Angela can settle someplace where no one will recognize you."

"I told you, the mine's not mine to sell. It's up to Angel, and she doesn't want to sell."

"Don't be so hasty," Baxter said. "Let's hear what the little lady has to say. If she doesn't agree, I'm going straight to the law."

Angela gazed at Rafe, noted his stony expression, and her heart fell. How could she make a choice between Rafe and the mine? What did he want her to do? His expression gave away nothing of what he felt, what he expected of her.

"Rafe, I . . . perhaps I should . . ."

"No, Angel, I won't let you do it. The mine is yours. Let Baxter go to the law. I won't be here when he returns. You're innocent in all this. You had no idea I was wanted in Dodge City when you married me. As for the other, I like to think you believed in my innocence."

"What other?" Baxter asked sharply.

"Nothing," Rafe said. "You have your answer. Angela isn't going to sell out to you."

"If that's the way you want it," Baxter growled, clearly not happy with the decision. "I'm going after the sheriff."

"Don't expect me to wait around for you."

"I could take you in myself."

Rafe's mirthless grin held an unspoken challenge. "Go ahead, try it."

"You're too damn cocky, Gentry. A stay in prison will rid you of that."

Baxter spun on his heel and made a hasty retreat. A few minutes later Angela saw him riding hell for leather down the road toward town.

Panic-stricken, Angela clutched desperately at Rafe's arm. "Why didn't you let me sell?"

"Because you love it here. Whether or not the mine is played out isn't important. Your father wanted you to have the mine. I won't let you sell out on my account."

"You're leaving." It was a statement of fact, not a question.

"I have to."

"You say you're innocent. Let me help you prove it."

He closed the door and turned to face her. "I won't let you embroil yourself in my problems, Angel."

She flung herself into his arms. "Oh, God, Rafe, why does it have to end this way?"

He pulled her against him. She felt his tension, his indecision, and responded with reckless desperation as she flung her arms around his neck and pulled his head down for her kiss.

Abruptly she broke off the kiss and gave him a little shove. Her voice held a note of panic. "Go! Don't let me stop you."

He seemed in no hurry as he lowered his head and caught her lips, kissing her until her head spun and she grew giddy. When he swung her up into his arms and carried her to the bedroom, Angela feared he had lost his mind.

"There's no time!"

"There's plenty of time," he whispered against her lips. "You don't think the sheriff will come up here alone, do you? He'll want a posse to back him up, and that takes time."

Angela opened her mouth to protest, but Rafe filled it with his tongue. A moan slipped past her throat as he deepened the kiss, tasting her more fully. Their mouths still joined, he lowered her to the bed and followed her down.

A rush of heat seared through her. Her senses stretched, reached, then stirred into pounding awareness. This was Rafe, the man who had made tender love to her, the man who had made her first time memorable. She didn't want to believe Rafe could be a killer. She didn't want to think at all. She wanted to feel.

Her fingers flew to his chest, fumbling with

the buttons on his shirt. He pushed her hands aside and tore off his shirt, scattering buttons. Lifting himself away from her, he kicked off his boots and skinned his trousers down his legs.

"I want you naked," he said in a voice made husky with desire. "I need to feast my eyes on you."

Together they rid her of her clothing, until they were both gloriously naked and panting with need. Angela stared at his erection; it was heavy and pulsing, rising upright against his stomach. He lowered himself against her. She stroked the contours of his strong back, then dug her fingers into the muscles of his hips. He was so strong, she thought, yet vulnerable to her touch. No matter where she touched, he reacted as if she had reached something deep and needy inside him.

His mouth was warm upon her skin as he spread tender kisses over her flesh, teasing her, goading her into a response. His manhood pulsed heavily against her thigh and she parted her trembling legs for him. She needed to feel him inside her. Now. If this was to be her last time with Rafe, she wanted to remember this moment forever.

"Not yet," Rafe rasped as his mouth continued to spread searing flames across her flesh. Her breasts, her nipples, nothing was left unattended as he kissed and nibbled and turned her body to quivering jelly.

She reached down and touched him. He convulsed and groaned as she brought him to her entrance. "Rafe, please!"

Heaving a sigh of acquiescence, Rafe lodged himself between her thighs and eased himself upward until his shaft was pressing against her. Then he reached down, opened her with his fingers and slowly pushed himself into her snug channel.

Rafe wanted to shout for joy. Blood flowed to that part of him buried inside her, feeding his arousal. She was wet and slippery and so damn hot he nearly lost it. His face was a dark mask of self-imposed restraint as he grasped her hips and turned with them still joined. She was astride him now, staring down at him with a surprised look on her face.

"Ride me, Angel. I'm all yours."

Chapter Eight

Her blood still pounding through her veins, her heart pumping furiously, Angela slowly regained her wits. She had lost herself completely in Rafe's arms as raw pleasure surged through her. The last thing she recalled was riding atop Rafe, feeling an incredible bliss slowly building inside her. When the explosive end came, she remembered screaming out his name. Then she must have blacked out. When she opened her eyes, Rafe was on his feet, tugging on his trousers.

He must have sensed her eyes on him, for he gave her a look that could only be described as apologetic.

"I don't have much time."

"I know. Will I ever see you again?"

His expression gave away nothing of his feelings. "I don't know. Do you really care?"

She stared at him, gnawing on her lower lip as she contemplated her answer. She didn't want to care, but her wayward heart refused to listen. "I care."

That seemed to surprise him. "You care

but you still believe me capable of committing a crime. You think I'm an outlaw."

She raised herself up on her elbows. "Rafe, I seriously don't know what to believe. In my heart I know you're not capable of committing murder. As for the bank robbery . . ." She shrugged. "I'll give you the benefit of the doubt despite your unwillingness to stay and clear your name."

He gave a brittle laugh. "You don't know the way the law works out here, do you? It's shoot first and ask questions later. Perhaps one day the truth will come out, but waiting around for a posse to string me up isn't the way to do it."

He strapped on his gun belt and stepped into his boots. His expression spoke volumes about his emotional upheaval as he paused with his hand on the doorknob.

"I can't take the Red Rock Canyon Road into town without running into the posse, so I'll try to find another way off this mountain." His voice sounded weary, so very weary. "If things had been different . . ."

"But they're not, are they?" Angela said quietly. "Don't worry about me, Rafe, I can take care of myself. I got myself out of Topeka on my own, didn't I?"

"From the frying pan into the fire," Rafe muttered beneath his breath. "You keep the marriage paper. You might find some use for it. I'll try to send word when I settle."

She looked away. She wasn't about to let Rafe Gentry know how badly she was hurting. But what else could she expect from an outlaw? "Don't bother." Then she couldn't help adding, "Keep yourself safe, Rafe."

He muttered something she didn't understand before flinging open the door and letting himself out. Angela made no move to follow. She lay there, staring at the ceiling, willing the tears not to flow. When she heard him ride away, she forced herself out of bed and slowly dressed.

It wasn't a posse who showed up a scant fifteen minutes later. The sound of pounding hooves brought Angela rushing to the window. She grimaced in distaste when she saw her stepfather and Chandler riding up to the cabin. Her steps dragged as she walked outside to greet them.

"Where's Gentry?" Kent growled. "He's wanted by the law. Chandler and I thought we'd save the posse the trouble of bringing him in and collect the reward for ourselves. You do know the sheriff is forming a posse to bring him in, don't you?"

"I don't know what you're talking about," Angela insisted. "If you're looking for Rafe, he's not here."

"Get out of my way," Kent said, shoving her aside as he and Chandler stormed into the cabin.

It didn't take them long to conduct their search. "He's not here," Kent bit out. "Check the corral for his horse, Chandler."

"I told you he wasn't here," Angela said when Chandler returned minutes later to report that Rafe's horse was missing.

"He won't get far," Kent said. "Did I tell you I paid a call on Sheriff Tattersal in Ordway? He had quite a story to tell. What in hell made you marry an outlaw, Angela? I knew you were getting too involved with your church and all that nonsense about good deeds. I should have locked you in your room until you were safely married to Chandler."

"Anson Chandler is the last person in the world I would marry," Angela contended.

"So you wed an outlaw instead," Chandler scoffed. "Tell her about the new charges against Gentry, Kent."

"Gladly," Kent crowed. "I had a heart-to-heart with Tattersal and set him straight about Rafe Gentry. Now the sheriff is convinced that Gentry *is* the man who robbed that stagecoach and murdered those poor people. There'll be another poster out for his arrest soon."

"No! Rafe's not a killer," Angela protested.

"You aren't qualified to judge that. I told Tattersal you were a fanatic about social injustice, that when you saw Gentry sitting at the end of a rope with the lynch mob clamoring for his blood, your protective instincts overrode your good sense. I had a damn hard time convincing the good sheriff that you weren't aware of Gentry's violent past."

"You're reprehensible," Angela spat. "I don't know what good it will do you. I'm still married to Rafe, no matter who or what he is."

Kent's grin was downright smug. "I'd like another look at that marriage paper, if you don't mind. I'm not all that certain it's legal."

Angela saw no harm in letting them look at the document. She and Rafe had also signed the church register Reverend Conrad carried with him. Nothing could change the fact that she and Rafe were husband and wife.

Angela fetched the marriage paper from the bedroom and handed it to Kent. He perused it, then calmly tore it into shreds, letting the pieces float away in the breeze.

"That's what I think about your so-called marriage to a vicious outlaw."

"Bastard!" Angela hissed.

"My, my, you never used that kind of language when you lived in my home. Did Gentry teach you how to cuss?"

Chandler sent her a sullen glare. "I'll bet he taught her more than that. If it wasn't for the gold, I wouldn't take a killer's leavings."

"The mine is worthless," Angela claimed.

"Surely you don't believe Baxter," Chandler scoffed. "I've been snooping around town while Desmond was in Ordway. Baxter has been making regular bank deposits since your father's death. It stands to reason that he's getting gold from the Golden Angel.

"As soon as we're married, I'm going to employ my own miners, and there's nothing Baxter can do about it."

"When will you get it through your head that I'm already married?" Angela retorted. "Reverend Conrad recorded the marriage in the church register he carries with him, and nothing could be more binding than that."

"You'd be right if that book still existed," Kent said.

Angela blanched. Did Kent know something she didn't? How could that be?

"You're bluffing. Of course that book exists. As soon as Reverend Conrad reaches Topeka, he'll enter our names in the Baptist church register. If you and Anson hoped to get rich off my holdings, you're sadly mistaken. I have no intention of obtaining a divorce."

"I fear you haven't heard the sad news, my dear," Kent said without a hint of sorrow. "Reverend Conrad's wagon was attacked by renegade Indians before he reached Topeka. Nothing but ashes remains of the wagon and its contents. That means no legal document exists to verify that a wedding took place."

"Oh, no! Poor Reverend Conrad and Sister

Grace," Angela sobbed. "How terrible."

"That all depends on how you look at it," Chandler crowed. "No marriage, no husband. That means you are now free to marry me. We'll be married tomorrow, or as soon as I can arrange for a preacher to come up here and do the honors."

"You won't get away with this," Angela spat. "You can't force me to marry you. No preacher worth his salt will perform a marriage if the bride is unwilling."

"Willing or not, you're going to marry Chandler," Kent promised with a hint of menace.

No sooner had the words left his mouth than a dozen horsemen galloped into view.

"That will be the posse," Chandler said. "And if I'm not mistaken, that's Brady Baxter with them."

In a flurry of dust, the posse reined in before the cabin.

"I'm Sheriff Dixon, Mrs. Gentry. Is your husband here?"

"You're wasting your time, Sheriff," Kent answered. "Gentry's gone. He was gone when we got here."

"I told you not to waste time with a posse," Baxter chided. "You, me and the deputy could have taken him had we left town immediately."

"Who's the sheriff here, Baxter?" Dixon blasted. "Gentry's a dangerous criminal. It's gonna take more than three men to take him in."

Baxter gave a disgruntled snort but did not contradict the sheriff.

"Do you know where your husband went, Mrs. Gentry?"

"I'm sorry, Sheriff Dixon, but I have no idea where Rafe can be found. I do know that he didn't commit the crimes of which he's accused. He's innocent."

Angela was more than a little surprised at her own words. Did she really believe in Rafe's innocence?

"They're all innocent," Dixon said with derision. "We didn't pass him on the road. He's either hiding in the forest or he's found another way down the mountain. Come on, boys, let's ride. We'll find him."

"Don't forget the reward, Sheriff," Baxter called after them. "I'm the one who led you to Gentry."

"*If* we catch him, the reward is yours," Dixon said as he kicked his mount forward.

Angela watched the cloud of dust grow smaller as the posse disappeared down the road. She wondered why Baxter had remained behind and soon found out.

"What are you two doing here?" Baxter growled when Kent and Chandler made no move to leave. "I don't believe I know your friend, Chandler."

"I'm Desmond Kent, Angela's stepfather

and guardian," Kent said, offering his hand. Baxter ignored it. "I'm here to protect my stepdaughter's interests. If there's gold in that mine, Baxter, I intend to make damn certain Angela gets her share."

Baxter didn't like the sound of that at all. It was bad enough with Gentry looking over his shoulder. Now he had a stepfather and former fiancé breathing down his neck. Of all the rotten luck.

"Get out of here, both of you. I don't care who you are, you're trespassing."

"See here, Baxter, you may have pulled the wool over my stepdaughter's eyes, but you can't fool me. Angela is going to marry Anson Chandler tomorrow, so get used to seeing us around."

Baxter's eyebrows shot up. "Are you going to commit bigamy, Mrs. Gentry?"

"I'm not marrying Mr. Chandler, no matter what my stepfather says," Angela insisted. "I'm already married to Rafe Gentry."

"Angela is a little confused, Baxter," Kent said. "You see, her marriage to Gentry isn't legal. She's free to marry whomever she chooses."

"Anson Chandler is the last man I'd choose," Angela retorted.

Baxter's eyes narrowed as he considered this latest complication in his plan to obtain sole ownership of the mine. If Angela wasn't married to Gentry, and she had no intention of marrying Chandler, then the field was free for him to step in and claim both Angela and the mine.

He wasn't such a bad-looking fellow, he thought. And he could be charming when the occasion warranted. Perhaps all wasn't lost after all. By ingratiating himself with Angela he could gain everything his heart desired. Sole ownership of the mine and a nice little bundle of femininity in his bed as a bonus.

"You heard the little lady, boys. Neither Angela nor I want you on our property. If you value your lives, get the hell out of here before I fill your carcasses with buckshot. And you'd better not be dragging the preacher up here, either."

"Very well, Baxter, we're leaving," Kent said, "but we'll be back. You don't scare us. As Angela's guardian, I have every right to see that she marries a man I approve of."

Angela breathed a sigh of relief when Chandler and Kent finally rode off. She glanced at Baxter and was surprised to see him looking at her with a strange light in his eyes.

"Is it true you were never legally married to Rafe Gentry?"

"No, that's not true," Angela contended. "Reverend Conrad married us in Ordway."

"Where is the reverend now?"

"Dead at the hands of renegade Indians."

"Do you have a marriage paper to prove

you were married?"

Angela glanced down to where tiny bits of paper littered the ground.

Baxter stooped, picked up several jagged pieces and let them fall through his fingers. "Did Kent do this?" Angela nodded. "Is this all that's left?"

Angela refused to acknowledge his question. It was none of his business. "I'm sorry, you'll have to excuse me. This has all been too much."

"By all means. I imagine learning that the man you thought you married is an outlaw has been a shock. You're all alone now, Angela. I know your father would want me to look after you. If you don't want to marry that Chandler fellow, you don't have to. You have other options," he said with sly innuendo. Then he turned and strode away.

Angela stared at his departing back, wondering what in the world he meant. Surely he didn't think . . . no, he couldn't mean that he . . . that she . . . ridiculous. Baxter and Chandler were cut from the same cloth, as far as she was concerned. Turning back into the house, she began preparations for a meal, a meal that Rafe wouldn't share with her.

Crouched behind a bush above the mine, Rafe had watched Kent tear up their marriage paper, or what he assumed was the marriage document. He was too far away to hear their words, but he knew Kent had said something to upset Angela. He'd like to strangle the bastard. Then Baxter and the posse had arrived, and Rafe briefly contemplated riding away from the whole damn mess and not looking back. But his conscience wouldn't let him. When the posse began searching the area for him, Rafe had moved himself and his horse into a cave he discovered on the mountainside above the mine.

Hours passed. Rafe walked to the entrance of the cave and peered out into the darkness. Nothing stirred. He crept out onto the ledge above the mine entrance and looked down upon the cabin where Angel slept. How could he leave her when she needed him? How could he not? His very existence was threatened. Should he be caught before he could prove his innocence, he'd surely hang. There was only one thing to do. Try to convince Angel to come with him. Together they could flee to a place where no one knew him.

One question remained: Did Angel care enough about him to abandon her father's legacy?

Determination hardened Rafe's features. Good or bad, he had come to a decision. Cautiously he made his way down the mountainside, until he reached level ground. Skirting Baxter's dwelling, he crept to Angel's cabin. A thin sliver of moon provided just enough light to guide him as he climbed the front steps and tried the knob. Locked. Remaining deep within the shadows, he made his way around to the rear and tried the back door. Locked.

Then he noticed that the bedroom window was raised slightly. It took little effort to widen the gap and slip inside. He glanced about the moon-drenched room and saw Angel stretched out on the bed, her curvy form lightly covered with a sheet. A halo of bright hair floated about her face and lay like spun gold upon the pillow. Rafe had an unaccountable urge to push it from her forehead and place a kiss there.

Instead, he crouched down beside the bed and simply stared at her, resisting the urge to touch her. He leaned closer as she stirred and murmured something in her sleep.

Angela's dreams had just taken an erotic turn. She'd been dreaming of Rafe, of course. It wasn't a particularly pleasant dream, for in it he was running from the law. He seemed to know she was watching him, for every so often he'd glance back over his shoulder and send her an anguished look, as if trying to convey something of great import to her.

Then suddenly the dream took a subtle turn. Rafe was no longer running; the posse was gone and he was in the cabin, inside her bedroom. The dream was so vivid she could feel his soft breath upon her cheek. Her skin tingled, as if he had touched her. It took but a brief moment for Angela to realize she was awake, that she hadn't imagined Rafe's presence.

She opened her eyes. His name tumbled from her lips. "Rafe . . ."

"I'm here, Angel."

"What? How?"

"I didn't go far. I'm holed up in a cave above the mine."

"What are you doing here? There's a posse looking for you."

"I know. I watched from the ledge above the mine, though I couldn't hear what was being said. What did Kent say to make you angry? Was that our marriage paper he tore into shreds? What made him do that? Reverend Conrad can easily verify the legality of our marriage."

"No, he can't," Angela revealed. "Reverend Conrad and Sister Grace are both dead, killed by renegade Indians. Their wagon and all their possessions are gone. No record of our marriage exists."

"I'm sorry about the reverend and his wife. I know how fond you were of them."

He shifted to the bed and took her into his arms. "Fate hasn't been kind to you, has it, Angel?"

"Nor to you," Angela whispered. "You shouldn't be here."

"This is where I want to be," he murmured, and then his mouth claimed hers.

Angela moaned her pleasure into his mouth. When Rafe had gone away she'd been so sure she'd never see him again. And now here he was, his body pressed against hers, his mouth writing love words against her lips. Oh, how she wished he hadn't returned. Didn't he realize the danger he was placing himself in?

Suddenly her mind grasped at something and wouldn't let go. Had Rafe returned in order to try to clear his name? Was he taking her advice about the futility of running? Then her thoughts scattered as Rafe worked her nightgown past her hips and over her head.

"I came to you tonight to ask something of you, but it will have to wait." He lowered his head and kissed her nipples. "I want you, Angel. Nothing will ever change that."

Angela swallowed past the lump in her throat. She wanted Rafe every bit as badly as he seemed to want her. Even though the tiniest doubt remained. Even though he might be an outlaw. Was he really as innocent as he claimed? Would she ever know for sure?

"Perhaps you should ask me your question first," Angela suggested.

He let out a long, slow breath. "No, I need

to make love to you first."

He placed one hand on her sex. She pulsed gently against him, her flesh already swollen with desire. He could feel the small bud straining against the pad of his thumb and he rubbed it gently. His breath came hard and labored. There was a primitive pounding in his head. His blood was boiling. His shaft swelled thick and hard, straining to be free. He fumbled with the buttons of his trousers, freeing himself into his palm. He parted her thighs with his knee, thumbed her open, then bent his head, and kissed her in a very needy, very tender place.

She sobbed his name. He smiled. His fingers replaced his mouth, easing deep inside. Her wetness scalded him; he could wait no longer. He slid into her velvety folds. Her core contracted around him as he teased a ragged moan from her throat. His senses soared when she gave a breathy little sigh and arched wantonly against him, forcing him deeper.

Wanting to give her the ultimate in pleasure, he lightly bit her nipples, then soothed them with the wet roughness of his tongue. He felt her trembling, and his own passions soared. No woman had ever affected him like his Angel.

She made a breathy little gurgle in her throat that sounded like a plea. Spurred by her need, Rafe pumped his hips, reaching deep into her core, to the very gates of her womb. She clutched his shoulders, her nails biting deep. His blood surged hot and molten. The feel of her melting heat clamping around his thickened manhood shattered what little control he had left. Gritting his teeth, he held on until he heard Angel scream out his name and go limp beneath him.

Even after her climax waned, he could feel tiny tremors squeezing him. He waited until she quieted in his arms, then finally gave himself permission to seek his own pleasure. He plunged deep, imbedding himself fully, his passion unchecked. Then everything inside him exploded. Wave after wave of incredible ecstasy washed over him, and he cried his pleasure against her mouth. He shuddered, then collapsed against her.

Several long minutes passed before Rafe lifted his weight away from Angela and settled at her side. His heart was pumping furiously and his breath came in short, tortured gasps. He glanced over at Angel to see if she was similarly affected. Her face appeared almost waxen in the sliver of moonlight shining through the window. He shifted to his elbow and stared down at her, concern worrying his brow.

"Angel, sweetheart, are you all right? Did I hurt you?"

"I'm fine." Silence stretched between them.

Then she said, "Why did you come back?"

"I couldn't leave you alone to be manipulated by Kent, Chandler and Baxter. Not one of them has your best interests at heart."

"And you do?"

"I like to think so. Have you any idea what they're planning for you?"

"My stepfather says he's returning tomorrow with a preacher. He's determined to marry me to Anson. I'm not sure what Brady Baxter intends. He's awfully congenial all of a sudden. He promised to do everything in his power to keep Desmond and Anson from forcing their will on me. I don't trust him any more than I do the other two."

"And rightly so. I have a proposition for you, Angel. I can't leave you here by yourself and I can't stick around to protect you. So . . . I want you to come with me."

Angel searched his face. Though the light was dim, she could tell he was serious, deadly serious.

"You want me to abandon my property?"

"I know it's asking a lot of you, but it's the only way I can protect you."

Angela reached for her nightgown, pulled it over her head and settled it around her hips. That simple action gave her time to let Rafe's proposal sink in. But no matter how long she thought about it, she knew she couldn't leave like a thief in the night. Tagging along with Rafe would do nothing to help his situation. She'd prove more of a hindrance than an asset. Somehow she had to change his mind.

"You'd be giving up the mine, but you'd still have the money your father left you," Rafe continued when she appeared to be wavering.

"I'd only hinder you. You said yourself you don't need a wife dragging you down. You have your own problems."

"We can go to California, start over, make a new life for ourselves."

Angela wasn't sure she'd heard right. "You want to stay married to me?"

"Is there someone else you'd prefer as a husband?"

"You know there isn't."

"I have no one else in mind for a wife, so why not stay married until either of us decides it's not right for us?"

"Desmond insists we're not legally married. There's no proof."

Rafe gave a bark of laughter. "The whole town of Ordway attended our wedding," he reminded her. "That's proof enough for me." He sent her a searching look. "Unless you're afraid to stay married to an outlaw."

"You didn't give me a chance to give you the really bad news."

His attention sharpened.

"When Desmond told Sheriff Tattersal you weren't my fiancé, he jumped to conclusions and decided you were the man who robbed the stage and killed all those people after all. You're being charged with murder in addition to the earlier charge of bank robbery."

A curse exploded from Rafe's lips. "That's another reason you should come with me, Angel. They'll want to question you about me."

"No, they won't. Desmond convinced the sheriff that I knew nothing about your background, that I'm some kind of religious fanatic who's bent on saving souls, especially those who appear to be victims of social injustice. He painted me as an innocent taken in by a slicker. I'm not wanted for any crime, nor will I be questioned."

Rafe's gaze settled disconcertingly on her. "Are you refusing to come with me? Am I correct in assuming you'd rather stay here and fight Kent, Chandler and Baxter?"

"Yes. No. I don't know. You don't understand. I can't leave here. To do so would be to admit defeat, and I'm not the kind to back down without a fight. I . . . I don't want to spend my life on the run from the law. I never expected to marry at all. Marrying an out . . ." The word died on her lips.

"Go ahead, say it. An outlaw isn't exactly husband material."

"I'm sorry, Rafe. I'm so confused. Everyone is calling you an outlaw. I don't want to believe it, but . . ."

"Why is believing me so difficult? You don't seem to have a problem making love with me."

"Can't you see I'm torn?" Angela raged. "I care about you, but I'm so afraid I'll be hurt if I allow myself to love you. I couldn't bear losing you."

Rafe went still. "I never asked for your love. You saved my life, and I'm returning the favor by offering protection. I care about you, too, but love is an emotion I'm not sure I understand. If you don't want my protection, if you have even the slightest doubt about my innocence, then it's best I disappear from your life. I reckon you care more about your mine than you do me."

He surged to his feet and set his clothing to rights. "I hope you and Anson Chandler will be very happy together. Since no record of our marriage exists, I suppose we can assume we're not married."

Angela searched his face. His stony expression and silver eyes held scant warmth, and it was all her fault. Why had fate tangled their lives together? Hurting him was like hurting herself.

"It's not that, Rafe," Angela tried to explain. "Of course I care about the mine. It's all I have left of my father. On the other hand, I never expected us to become lovers. Don't get me wrong," she added, "I don't regret it. But you have to admit it does complicate everything."

"I don't even know you," Rafe said, backing away. "Are all women as cold and calculating as you?"

"I can only answer for myself. I married a stranger. A man who might or might not be an outlaw and a killer. I saved your life. I have no further obligation where you're concerned."

Angela wanted to weep. Saying those things to Rafe nearly broke her heart. The only way she could make him ride away without looking back was to be deliberately cruel. She couldn't go with him, not because of the mine, but because she feared she would complicate his life, and he would end up hating her for it. Should the posse catch up with him, they would shoot first and ask questions later. She cared too much for Rafe to see him die because of his misguided sense of obligation to her.

"Then we'll call it quits here and now," Rafe said. "Should we chance to meet again, we will be like strangers to each other. Is that how you want it?"

Grateful for the darkness that concealed the mist of tears bathing her eyes, Angela pasted a smile on her face and said, "That's how I want it. Good luck, Rafe. Take care of yourself."

Angela held her breath. He looked as if he

wanted to kiss her, and she didn't think she could bear it.

"It's not too late to change your mind," he said softly.

"It's far too late. Go, Rafe. It will be light soon and you could be miles away from here if you leave now."

"Good-bye, Angel."

"Good-bye, Rafe."

Only then did she let the tears fall.

Chapter Nine

Cursing beneath his breath, Rafe let himself out the back door into the dark night. He was profoundly disturbed and unable to make sense out of the harsh words that had passed between him and Angel. Something wasn't right, but he couldn't put his finger on it. If he was smart he'd get on his horse and ride hell for leather away from the mine, Angel and the law. Sticking around was dangerous to his health.

Rafe skirted around Baxter's cabin and the privy. He was so engrossed in his thoughts that he didn't see the shadowy figure behind him. Nor did he sense danger as the butt of a gun came crashing down on his head. He never knew what hit him.

Brady Baxter stood over Rafe, the barrel of his gun clasped tightly in his hand. "Stupid bastard," he hissed. "The need to plow that little piece you call your wife must have made you soft in the head. You shouldn't have stuck around."

Baxter aimed a booted toe at Rafe's ribs,

satisfied when Rafe gave no indication that he felt the blow. A pressing need had brought Baxter out to the privy during the darkest part of night. When he'd finished his business, he noticed someone creeping toward Angela's cabin. At first he thought perhaps Kent or Chandler had come snooping around again, but then the shape took on a form that was too powerful to belong to either of those two city slickers.

Following at a discreet distance, Baxter saw the man crawl into the bedroom window. A smug smile stretched Baxter's lips. He knew intuitively that the night prowler was Rafe Gentry. It truly amazed Baxter that Gentry would risk capture for a little loving. His smile widened. He couldn't wait to taste the luscious Angela himself. Concealing himself in the shadows, he'd settled down to wait.

Baxter's patience had paid off when he saw Rafe leave by the rear exit nearly an hour later. He drew his gun, crept up behind the distracted outlaw, and conked him a good one on the head.

Baxter prodded Rafe again, satisfied that his prisoner wasn't going any place anytime soon. Hefting him by the shoulders, Baxter dragged the unconscious Rafe into the yawning entrance of the mine. He paused briefly to pick up a rope he found lying atop a crate and hooked it over his shoulder, then lit a lamp. Grabbing Rafe by one leg and holding the lamp with the other, Baxter dragged him into a deserted side tunnel, roundly cursing the man's size and bulk. He dragged Rafe to the end of the tunnel, leaned him against a wall, and bound his hands and feet so tight it would take a magician to work himself loose from the knots.

Then for good measure he pulled off his kerchief and stuffed it in Rafe's mouth. "That ought to keep you," Baxter said, backing away to examine his handiwork.

All of Baxter's plans seemed to be falling into place. He hadn't counted on fate delivering Rafe Gentry up to him, but he certainly recognized a good thing when he saw it. He'd been wondering how to convince Angela to marry him, and now he had the means all safely tucked away where no one would find him. Rafe Gentry was the leverage Baxter needed to bring Angela around.

Baxter laughed softly to himself as he made his way back to his bed.

Rafe awoke with an excruciating headache and various other aches, certain that he wasn't where he wanted to be. Blackness surrounded him. He knew he wasn't in the cave, for there was no circle of light where the opening should be. There was just the stygian darkness of the unknown.

His mouth felt like a desert, his limbs

ached, and there was a pain in his ribs, not to mention his sore head. As his wits slowly returned, it took less than a minute to realize he'd been bound and gagged and taken someplace where light didn't exist.

The mine.

How? Why? Who?

He figured out the how and who. It was the why that escaped him. He couldn't believe he'd been so careless as to let himself be seen leaving Angela's cabin. His distraction had allowed someone to creep up behind him and clout him a good one on the head. That someone could only be Brady Baxter. But why had Baxter imprisoned him in the mine instead of taking him to town and collecting the reward for his capture? His head hurt too badly to think.

All he could do was wait for Baxter to return and reveal his intentions. And worry about Angela.

Angela awoke late. Her body still thrummed from Rafe's loving, and her throat ached from crying herself to sleep. She'd sent Rafe away and now she'd never see him again. She'd deliberately made him angry so he wouldn't stick around out of concern for her.

Lethargic and despondent, Angela washed and dressed and went to the kitchen to fix coffee to go with the biscuits she'd made the day before. She sipped her coffee and picked at a biscuit, not really hungry. She had no idea what was going to happen next. Without Rafe to act as a buffer between her and the three men trying to cheat her out of her property, she felt lost and alone.

She was no nearer now than she had been before to proving that Baxter was responsible for her father's untimely death. Everyone in town believed Simon Abbot's death had been an accident. Would anyone believe her if she started making accusations? She doubted it. Her only hope of discovering the truth was to trick Baxter into giving himself away.

Other concerns crowded her mind. Though she seriously doubted that Desmond could find a preacher willing to marry her to Anson without her consent, it wasn't impossible. He had found one in Topeka, hadn't he?

An insistent knocking on her door jerked Angela from her morose thoughts. At first she assumed her visitors were Anson and Desmond, but she quickly discarded that notion. They wouldn't have had time to find a preacher and return so quickly. She opened the door, not too surprised to find Baxter standing on the doorstep, hat in hand, a smug grin stretching his lips across large, uneven teeth.

"Mornin', Angela. I've come courting."

Angela resisted the urge to laugh. "You what?"

The smile slipped from Baxter's face. "Marrying me is a better deal than getting hitched to the man your stepfather chose for you. Why should we have to share the mine with anyone? Marry me and it will be all ours."

"Yours, you mean," Angela charged.

He shrugged. "Whatever. No one can horn in on our profits."

Angela slowly backed away. "You're mad! Why would I marry a man I believe responsible for my father's death?"

Baxter's expression turned downright ugly. "What did you say?"

Angela could have bitten her tongue. How could she have been so careless?

"I . . . it's nothing. I didn't mean it. I'm still upset over Rafe. I have to go now. I'm going to ride to town to consult with Father's lawyer."

Baxter grasped her arm. "You're not going anywhere, little lady. And I don't want to hear another word about your suspicions 'cause you're plumb loco. You and me are gonna get hitched. Today, before Chandler and Kent show up."

"You're the one who's loco, Mr. Baxter. What ever gave you the impression I'd marry you?"

"You'll marry me because I'm holding an ace in the hole."

She tried to twist out of his grasp, but he

was too strong for her. "I don't know what you're talking about."

"Let me enlighten you. I caught your lover sneaking out of your cabin last night."

Angela's breath hitched. "You're bluffing. Rafe wasn't anywhere near my cabin last night. He's probably miles away from here by now."

"That's how much you know. He's trussed up like a Christmas goose and hidden away where no one will find him."

Panic shot through Angela. "What have you done to him? If you've hurt him I'll —"

"You'll what? He's headed for the gallows anyway."

"What do you want from me?"

He sent her a smug grin. "I knew you were a smart lady. At first I thought I'd use Gentry as leverage to force you to sell out to me, but then I thought, why not have it all? You *and* the mine. I could use a pretty little piece like you in my bed. You must be one hot package to bring Gentry back here to tumble you with a posse breathing down his neck."

"I'm not going to marry you, Brady Baxter, and I'm not going to sell out, either," Angela insisted.

"Forget about selling. I'm not interested in that anymore." He leered at her. "I want more, much more. As for giving me what I want, it's either that or watch Gentry hang. If you don't agree to my terms, I'm turning him in for the reward."

Angela searched Baxter's face. He didn't seem to be bluffing. Besides, how would he know Rafe had visited her last night if he hadn't seen him? He was so sure of himself, so smug, that he had to be telling the truth.

Angela tried hard to convince herself that she didn't care what happened to Rafe. Didn't care about him at all. To no avail. She cared *too* much. Did she care enough to marry the man who might be responsible for her father's death?

"Angela, you can think all you like, but it's not going to change things. I have Gentry and I want you."

"You never expressed desire for me before," Angela observed.

"Not so. The first time your father showed me that miniature of you, I knew you were the kind of woman I could go for. But when you showed up here claiming to be married, there was nothing I could do. Circumstances have changed. Our marriage will solidify our partnership."

"We own a worthless mine," Angela reminded him.

"Perhaps I was wrong."

"Perhaps you're wrong about Rafe. Maybe he's miles away from here."

"Maybe he isn't."

"What about my stepfather? He's determined to marry me to Chandler."

Baxter gave a brittle laugh. "I don't consider them worthy opponents."

"You don't even like me."

"You think not?"

Before Angela knew what he intended, Baxter grabbed her shoulders and pulled her against him. She struggled. She screamed. No one heard. His mouth slammed down on hers. His kiss was not gentle, nor was it pleasant. Angela endured it with stoic reserve, holding her mouth tightly shut against the violation of his tongue. When he cupped her breast and started to back her into the cabin, she took exception. Raising her knee, she jammed it into his groin.

Baxter let out a wounded scream and doubled over. "Bitch! You've done it now. Your lover is as good as dead."

He took two mincing steps and howled again. "Damn you!"

Watching him, Angela felt grim satisfaction, until she remembered what he'd said. *Rafe was as good as dead.* What had she done?

"Wait! I'm sorry. I . . . I don't know what got into me. I'll agree to anything you want, just don't turn Rafe over to the law."

"That's more like it," Baxter said, gritting his teeth against the pain. "Any more tricks like that and you can kiss your lover good-bye."

"You want the mine? Fine, it's yours. I'll

180

sign the papers over to you immediately."

Baxter's lewd gaze roamed over her with flagrant lust. "Not so fast. I'm looking forward to taming you. Normally I wouldn't be interested in an outlaw's leavings, but you intrigue me, Angela Abbot. My mind is made up. I want both you and the Golden Angel. We'll be married today."

"Only if you agree to release Rafe," Angela asserted. "I don't trust you."

"And I don't trust you to keep your word if I let Gentry go first."

The one person who stood in the way of his gaining everything he wanted was Rafe Gentry. Baxter didn't fool himself by thinking that Rafe would leave once he was set free. Oh, no, there would be hell to pay if Gentry was free to seek revenge against him for taking his woman. Gentry had to die.

"I always keep my word," Angela insisted.

"You have my promise I'll release Gentry once we're husband and wife," Baxter lied. "You don't have much choice, Angela. Delaying will only condemn your lover to an ignominious death at the end of a rope. Is that what you want for him?"

"Rafe isn't a killer. The law will soon learn that and correct the mistake."

"Do you really believe that? Come on, Angela, be realistic. You're Gentry's only hope. What is it going to be?"

Baxter knew he had her the moment her

181

shoulders slumped in defeat.

"Very well, I'll marry you, but only to save Rafe's life. Don't think for a minute I have any feelings but hatred for you. If I find out you had a hand in hastening my father's death, I'll not rest until I bring you to justice."

Baxter had the gall to laugh in her face. "Put on your prettiest bonnet, honey, we're going to a wedding. Ours. Hurry now, I want this wrapped up all nice and legal before your stepfather takes a notion to trespass again."

Her mouth settled into stubborn lines. "I want to see Rafe first."

He gave her a sullen glare. "Not now. Don't make me mad while I'm still in a mellow mood. First things first. I'll go put on my Sunday best and hitch up the buckboard while you make yourself pretty for me. You have thirty minutes, Angela. Don't dawdle."

Angela stormed into the cabin. She was angry at Baxter, at herself, at Rafe, at the whole world. Before she'd left Topeka she'd expected problems to develop, but nothing like this. Rafe had been right. She'd been a naive fool to think she could travel hundreds of miles to claim her inheritance and learn the truth about her father's death without encountering trouble. Now here she was, about to marry a man who might be a murderer, and in love with another man accused of crimes he hadn't committed.

Angela went still. Love? Was she in love with Rafe? The fact that she was willing to marry a man she despised to save Rafe's life spoke volumes about her feelings for Rafe. Unwilling to delve too deeply into fragile emotions, Angela pushed the subject to the back of her mind as she prepared for her wedding.

Fuming in impotent silence, she dawdled as long as she dared inside the cabin. When Baxter called through the door that he was coming in after her if she didn't come out, she knew she'd tried his patience to the limit. Stepping outside, she was surprised to see Baxter all spruced up in a black suit and string tie. The one discordant note was the six-shooter that rode his hip. Angela thought he looked as out of place and uncomfortable in his finery as a mule among a bevy of thoroughbreds.

Angela had done little to adorn herself for what was supposed to be her wedding day. She'd donned a simple frock and her oldest bonnet. Since she was already married, she knew in her heart this wedding was a sham, illegal in every way. She was going through the motions for Rafe's sake, but she'd never allow Baxter to touch her intimately. She wasn't helpless. She'd find some way to stop him from claiming what he would consider his marital rights.

Brady guided the buckboard down the mountain road, his smug smile giving Angela little comfort. Refusing to look at him, she gazed out over the vista of mountains, forests and valleys.

"You don't talk much, do you?" Baxter observed.

"I talk when I have something to say. You wouldn't like what I'm thinking right now."

"You're not getting cold feet, are you? You'd better say 'I do' at the right time or your lover will suffer for your stubbornness."

"I know what I have to do," Angela returned shortly.

"Good, because we're almost there. Try to smile or the preacher will think you're unwilling. This should be a happy occasion for both of us."

Looking directly into his eyes, Angela said, "I hate you, Brady Baxter."

Inside the bleak darkness of the mine, Rafe had worked his gag free but had had little luck with the ropes. His mouth was dry as dust and his stomach rumbled. He couldn't recall when he'd eaten last. He supposed it was the lunch he and Angel shared before Baxter came pounding at their door with that damn Wanted poster in his hand. After that, all hell had broken loose. He was still angry at himself for becoming careless and letting himself be taken by a bastard like Baxter.

Rafe worried more about Angel than he did himself. He feared that Baxter had some vile plan in mind for Angel and now he was in no position to help her. He wondered why Baxter hadn't turned him over to the law. The fact that he hadn't troubled him.

The waiting and wondering were driving him crazy.

Angela was a bundle of nerves by the time the buckboard pulled up in front of the parsonage that squatted beside the First Baptist Church of Canon City.

Baxter jumped down from the driver's seat and went around to hand Angela down. Spurning his help, she scampered down before he reached her.

"If I didn't know better, I'd say you were anxious for us to get hitched," Baxter said, smirking.

"But you do know better," Angela retorted. "Shall we get this over with? The sooner I carry out my part of the bargain, the sooner you can set Rafe free."

Reverend Porter wasn't too happy about performing such a hasty marriage. But the color of Baxter's gold soon persuaded him that the couple was eager to be married. Calling his wife from the kitchen to act as witness, he opened the Good Book and read the brief ceremony that joined Brady Baxter to Angela Abbot.

Angela took neither the words nor the vows seriously, for in her heart she knew this ceremony was nothing but a sham in which she was forced to participate to save Rafe's life. The real test of her mettle would come when Baxter tried to claim his marital rights.

When it came time to sign the church register, no one noticed that Angela signed it "Angela Gentry." She didn't know if it would make a difference, but it certainly made her feel better.

Baxter paid the preacher, then ushered her out the door. He literally dragged her down the front steps, then came to a screeching halt when they met Desmond Kent and Anson Chandler coming toward them.

"What in the hell are you two doing here?" Kent demanded.

Baxter gave him a cocky grin. "You just missed the wedding, boys. Congratulate us. Angela and I were just married."

"Wh . . . what!" Kent sputtered. "Are you crazy, girl? You know what this means? Baxter now owns the Golden Angel. This can't be. You're supposed to marry Chandler!"

"Too late," Baxter crowed. "You two may as well turn tail and go back where you came from. Everything is under control here."

"Under *your* control," Chandler spat.

Then he directed his venom at Angela. "Bitch!" he bit out. "Two disastrous marriages and neither of them to me. I'll teach you! I've gone through a lot for you and your inheritance."

Angela didn't expect the blow. The force of Chandler's open palm across her face sent her spinning to the ground.

To his credit, Baxter's justice was swift and deadly. Blood spurted as his heavy fist smashed into Chandler's face. Another fist to his gut sent Chandler reeling.

"I'm the only one with authority to discipline my wife," Baxter said. "It's not your place to tame her. It will be my pleasure to see that she toes the line."

Angela shuddered. If she had wondered whether Baxter would treat her with respect, she no longer had any doubts. Men like Baxter didn't respect anything but gold. Baxter would treat her no better than Chandler.

Baxter shot Chandler an ominous glare as he helped Angela to her feet and hustled her into the buckboard. Angela didn't even look back to see how badly Chandler was hurt as they careened down the street. All she cared about was getting back to the Golden Angel and setting Rafe free.

Neither Baxter nor Angela heard Chandler's words as they drove away.

"That bastard will pay for what he's done to me," Chandler pledged. "I don't know how, but I'll find a way to get even. Then the last laugh will be mine."

"Whatever you have in mind, Chandler, count me in," Kent said.

The trip up the mountain seemed to take forever. Angela chafed impatiently until she saw the mine looming ahead. Only then did she deign to speak to Baxter.

"We're here. I've kept my part of the bargain, now it's time for you to keep yours. Take me to Rafe."

Baxter frowned. "You look like hell. I should have killed Chandler for marking my wife. I may yet."

Angela shrugged aside his words. "I'll heal. About our bargain . . ."

"There's plenty of time to set your lover free. Right now I'm hankering to sample what Gentry found so irresistible." He halted the buckboard in front of the cabin and reached for her.

Nimbly she slipped from his grasp and leaped unaided to the ground. Hands on hips, she faced him squarely, her expression mutinous.

"Try it and you'll find you've bit off more than you can chew. You're stronger than I, and you might have your way, but the first time your back is turned, or you fall asleep, watch out. Do we free Rafe now or are you willing to risk your life the first time you close your eyes?"

"You drive a hard bargain, Mrs. Baxter. A little thing like you doesn't frighten me, but I can see you're going to fight me all the way unless we do it your way. Very well, I'll take you to Gentry."

Baxter had no intention of setting Rafe free. Not now, not ever. He'd thought about it long and hard and decided that Gentry was a vindictive man, the kind who would demand retribution. It occurred to Baxter that the outlaw wouldn't rest until he found a way to exact his pound of flesh. No way, Baxter decided, was he going to allow Gentry to live.

Of course, Angela wasn't going to be easy to handle, but he'd contend with her after the deed was done. Either she bent to his will or she would suffer the consequences.

"He's in the mine, bound and gagged so he can't cause trouble," Baxter said. "I'll light a lamp and take you inside."

"You've left him in there all this time?" Angela blasted. "In the dark?"

"He's a big boy."

"Bastard," she hissed. "Take me to him."

Baxter lit the lamp and entered the mine. Angela followed close on his heels. He turned down a narrow side tunnel and stopped at a blank wall.

"Where is he?" Angela asked on a note of panic.

"Right here, Angel," a raspy voice replied.

Angela's breath hitched. She followed the sound of Rafe's voice and saw him lying on the damp tunnel floor, bound so tightly she knew he must be in terrible pain. He was blinking repeatedly, as if blinded by the light.

"So you worked the gag free," Baxter growled. "For all the good it did you. I take it you're not pleased with my hospitality. You should thank me for not turning you over to the law."

Deliberately ignoring Baxter's taunts, Rafe asked Angela, "Are you all right, Angel?"

"I'm fine," Angela choked out. She couldn't stand to see Rafe this way. It reminded her of Ordway, where he'd almost lost his life at the end of a rope. She shuddered, recalling the defeated look on his face as he sat beneath the hanging tree with a rope around his neck.

"Cut him loose," Angela ordered. Baxter made no move to comply. "You promised!"

"You didn't *really* think I'd let your lover go free, did you?" Baxter crowed. "You have a thing or two to learn about human nature. Men lie to get what they want."

Baxter's words chilled Rafe's blood. What had Angel done to obtain Baxter's promise to let him go free? She should have known better than to trust a bastard like Baxter.

"What did you do, Angel?" Rafe softly asked.

Baxter forestalled her answer. Placing a

possessive arm around her waist, he pulled her hard against him. "We got hitched this morning."

Color leached from Rafe's face. His gaze bored into Angel, his brows raised in disbelief. "Is that true, Angel?"

Angela dropped her gaze, unable to meet the riveting challenge of Rafe's stare. "I had no choice. Baxter holds all the cards."

"There are always choices," Rafe bit out. "You should have told Baxter to go to hell and let him do his worst. This is my problem, not yours." His gaze shifted to Baxter. "You entered into a fraudulent marriage, Baxter. Angel already has a husband. You're looking at him."

"She won't have a husband for long," Baxter said, grinning as he set the lamp down and pulled out his gun. Steadying it with both hands, he aimed it at Rafe.

"No! What are you doing?" Angela cried, lunging at Baxter.

Baxter backhanded her, sending her flying against the tunnel wall. Momentarily stunned, Angela slumped to the ground.

"Bastard!" Rafe hissed. "I'll kill you for that."

Baxter cocked his gun. "Dead men's threats don't frighten me. I can collect the same reward whether you're dead or alive. All I have to do is drag your body down the mountain and collect my money. Before I pull the trigger, I want you to know I'll be enjoying Angela in every way a husband enjoys a wife. I'm anxious to discover for myself what you found so fascinating about her."

Rafe considered his options, which were damn few. Trussed up like he was, there was little he could do to save himself. He could lunge at Baxter and perhaps avoid the bullet, but it would only prolong the inevitable. He was utterly defenseless against a man with a six-shooter in his hand. Though he still wore his own guns, they were absolutely useless without the use of his hands.

Then he saw Angel stirring and realized Baxter was paying no attention to her. *He had to keep Baxter talking.* Angel was a resourceful woman, and the only person he could count on right now.

"As long as I'm going to die," Rafe said, "you may as well tell me the truth about the mine. It's not played out, is it?"

Baxter gave a snort of laughter. "Played out? That's a good one. I just uncovered a new vein. There's thousands of dollars buried in there, just waiting to be taken out. I got rid of Simon before he found out about it, and it all belongs to me now, every single nugget and grain of dust."

From the corner of his eye Rafe saw Angel sit up and scramble in the dirt for something, but he didn't dare look directly at her lest he alert Baxter. What was she trying to do? Then he saw what she held in her hand and stifled a groan. He guessed what she intended, and fear welled up inside him. If she failed, he knew Baxter wouldn't go easy on her. And he wouldn't be around to protect her.

"So Angel was right. You did kill her father," Rafe said with slow deliberation.

"It was easy enough to arrange," Baxter gloated. "Enough talk, Gentry. You know I'm going to kill you. Why prolong it? Killing you is the only way to get rid of you permanently. Now say your prayers."

Angela chose that moment to spring at Baxter. He spun around, but too late to stop the rock Angela held in her hand from connecting forcefully with his head. His finger jerked spasmodically on the trigger as he fell to the ground. The bullet went wild, missing a vital target but grazing Angela's upper arm as it whizzed by, leaving a bloody groove.

Baxter didn't move. Angela stared down at him, holding her arm as blood streamed through her fingers. It hurt dreadfully but she couldn't pass out, not yet. She had to cut Rafe free before Baxter came around.

"Angel, are you all right? God! Where did he shoot you?"

Angela moved forward on wooden legs. She stepped over Baxter and squatted down beside Rafe. "The bullet just grazed me." She appeared in a daze. "He killed my father, Rafe. I heard him admit it."

"I know, sweetheart. It's up to a judge and jury now to convict him. There's a knife in my boot. Get it and free my hands. I'll take it from there. You saved my life . . . again. I'm beginning to think you're my guardian angel."

Angela managed to cut the ropes binding his hands before she passed out.

Chapter Ten

His hands were free. Blood rushed into them. Excruciating pain had Rafe writhing and gasping for breath. His hands and fingers refused the simple command to cut his legs free. They felt like pieces of raw meat as he willed the pain away. He struggled to move; he had to get to Baxter before he regained his wits, and he had to help Angel, who might be seriously wounded.

Dragging in a deep, steadying breath, Rafe flexed his hands, ignoring the numbing pain as he picked up the knife Angela had dropped and sawed on the ropes binding his legs. It took longer than Rafe would have liked, but finally the ropes fell away. Then the agony began anew, spiraling upward from his feet to his knees, sharp, penetrating, debilitating. He waited a moment for the pain to subside, then dragged himself to his knees and crawled over to Angela.

"Angel, speak to me. Are you all right?"

Angela stirred, sighed and sat up. "What happened?"

"You passed out. Let me look at that wound."

"It's nothing. Take care of Baxter before he comes around. He killed Father," she said on a sob.

"Are you sure you're all right?"

"Positive." She grasped his swollen hands and stared at them. "Oh, my God, you must be in agony. What can I do to help?"

"I'll manage. We've only one lantern. I'll take you outside, then return and take care of Baxter. A few hours in the mine won't hurt him until we decide our next move."

"Let me stay."

"You're bleeding; your wound needs tending. I can manage here. But we have to hurry. Baxter won't remain out long."

"What are you going to do with him?"

"Not what he intended for me. We'll discuss it later. Come on."

Hobbling on numb legs, Rafe picked up the lantern and ushered Angela to the mine entrance. "Go on," he said, turning back into the mine. "I won't be long."

Angela heaved a reluctant sigh. "Very well. Hurry."

Angela couldn't imagine what was keeping Rafe. He'd been gone too long for comfort. She hoped Baxter hadn't come around and given him trouble. She had just about convinced herself to go back into the mine to look for him when she saw him staggering from the entrance. She raced from the cabin to help him.

"What happened?"

"My legs still aren't working like they should. If I had been left trussed up another few hours, I doubt I'd ever have been able to walk again."

"Did you have any problems with Baxter?"

"No. He came around as I was tying him up. We exchanged a few words, that's all. Forget him. Let's have a look at that arm."

"It's nothing. The bleeding has already stopped."

"Let me see, Angel."

Angela removed the cloth she had used to stem the bleeding and held out her arm. Frowning, Rafe carefully examined the wound.

"The bullet gouged a pretty deep furrow. Maybe you should have the doc stitch it up so it won't leave a scar."

"No," Angela protested. "I'm fine, really. Just help me make a proper bandage. I don't care about the scar. It doesn't even hurt that much."

Rafe followed her into the bedroom and tore up an old sheet while Angela retrieved a jar of salve from among her father's things.

"Sit down and remove your blouse," Rafe said, "so I can make a proper job of this."

Angela removed her blouse and sat down

on the edge of the bed. Rafe dropped to his knees beside her and set to work. It was all he could do to keep his hands from straying to her full breasts, but he filled his eyes with the sight of those taut mounds straining against her shift. By the time he finished bandaging the wound, his hands were shaking and sweat plastered his forehead. He yearned to carry her to the bed and make passionate love to her, but there were some important issues that needed to be cleared up.

Rafe sat back on his heels and stared at her.

"What's wrong?" Angela asked.

His words held a bitter edge. "Why did you marry Baxter?"

"How can you ask that? You know why I did it. He threatened to turn you over to the law if I didn't marry him."

"I'd rather face the hangman than see you with Baxter," he barked. "You knew he couldn't be trusted. He never intended to set me free."

"You're welcome," Angela said sweetly.

He scrambled from his knees and sat down beside her. "Angel, I'm not angry at you. I'm just . . . angry at the thought of you with Baxter. Did you think he wouldn't demand his marital rights? What *were* you thinking?"

"I didn't want you to die. Besides, you heard him. He killed Father. Oh, God, what are we going to do now?"

"I'll think of something. The bastard isn't going to walk free."

"What about you? What are your plans? You can't stay here, it's too dangerous."

He grasped her shoulders and dragged her against him. "I can't leave you behind, you know that. You can argue all you like, but I'm still not leaving you. Your marriage to Baxter isn't legal and you know it."

"I don't want him to go free. He killed my father. I've got to stay and try to convince the sheriff that Baxter deserves to be put behind bars for his crime."

"Everyone believes you're legally married to the bastard, even though you and I know different. Baxter is a smooth talker. What if the sheriff doesn't believe you? I can't take that chance. You're going with me, and that's final."

"But . . ." Her protest died on her lips as Rafe stopped her words with a kiss. His lips were hard, as unyielding as his decision. He kissed her until she was breathless, until her body tingled and dampness gathered between her thighs.

Then he lowered her onto the bed and continued his relentless assault upon her senses until Angela felt like a mindless, boneless puddle of passion. Lifting her upthrusting breasts to his mouth, he licked her jutting nipples through the thin material of her shift, then blew on them. She felt them swell and peak beneath his sensual assault, felt the aching need he created claw at her innards.

She gave a small cry of alarm when he grasped the neckline of her shift between his hands and tore the fragile material in half, baring her breasts. Then he swiftly stripped her naked. She held her breath as his heated gaze slid down her body. She burned everywhere his gaze touched her, and it touched everywhere. It felt as if he were making love to her with his eyes.

"Don't stop me, Angel." His voice was ragged with need. "Back there in the mine I thought my life was going to end and I'd never make love to you again."

Angela had no intention of stopping him. She wanted him. Whether or not she went away with him, that truth wouldn't change. She couldn't worry about tomorrow; only today mattered. That realization was like a dam breaking inside her. All her inhibitions, all her fears, were swept away on a wave of incredible longing. Passion flared hot and consuming.

Small hands swept his shirt from his shoulders. Eager fingers traced a lazy pattern in the dark pelt covering his chest . . . then slid slowly down the taut grid of his belly. One by one she released the buttons of his trousers. His manhood sprang free into her palm. A shiver slid down Angela's spine. He was scalding hot and boldly erect.

When he tried to slide between her thighs, she shook her head and pushed him onto his back. Together they removed his clothing. Then she straddled him. Head bowed, hair brushing his thighs, she placed a kiss on the tip of his turgid hardness, at the same time skimming the underside of his shaft to the root with feathery touches of her fingertips.

"Angel . . ." His breath caught. "You're killing me. Let me . . ."

"No, let *me*," she breathed against him. She heard him mutter something under his breath and felt him stiffen as she touched him with the tip of her tongue.

She plied him delicately with hot, wet strokes of her tongue, a wanton, highly erotic caress, pleasuring him as he had pleasured her on more than one occasion. Her tongue whirling, she licked and sucked and tasted, reveling in the tremors wracking his body.

Rafe's world was careening out of control. The taut muscles of his body clenched. Ecstasy consumed him as he was seduced by the captivating heat of her mouth and tongue.

His hands slid into the glorious mass of her bright curls. "Angel! For the love of God, stop!" His voice was ragged, raw with charged tension.

He caught her and dragged her upward. Then, in a swift move that produced a look of astonishment on her flushed face, he turned her about. "I want you on your hands and knees," he whispered, positioning her for his pleasure.

A tremor passed through her. He saw it and smiled. Heat tugged at his belly, blood swelled his loins, making him harder, stronger, needier. Desire pounded through him, and his manhood throbbed with impatience to be inside her. Taking his place behind her, he swept the blond curtain of her hair aside and kissed her nape.

Cupping her breasts in his hands, he heard the quick intake of her breath as he tweaked her nipples, not hard, just enough to give her a jolt of pleasure/pain. He kissed her ear and licked a trail of fire down the side of her neck and along her spine. The heat of her bottom against his loins created a blazing inferno within him and he could wait no longer.

"Part your legs, sweetheart."

He heard her make a strangled sound deep in her throat as she did what he asked. His fingers slid inside her. She was hot and slick, wet and as ready for him as he was for her. He lingered but a moment, stroking her deeply, drawing moisture from her core onto his fingers, struggling to control the surge of heat that cried for completion.

He entered her in one hard thrust, impaling her with the thick length of his shaft.

Perfect, he thought with a sigh. She fit him like a glove, clasping him tightly in her wet sheath. Easing himself out, he thrust himself more deeply, then withdrew, in and out, harder, faster, deeper with each stroke.

He heard her whimper and he stiffened. She sobbed his name, begging for release. He felt something rise up inside him. It swelled and broadened into a need he was hard put to explain. He was suddenly desperate to keep this woman from harm, to protect her for as long as God gave him breath. Then all thought ceased as Angela cried out, her body wracked by tremors. Then it happened. Everything that had been building inside him exploded. Shimmering waves of scalding pleasure washed over him, through him. Arching his neck, he shouted his ecstasy for all the world to hear.

He shuddered and collapsed against her. Her knees gave way and he fell on top of her. Aware that he was too heavy for her, he rolled away. That was the last thing he remembered before he sank into oblivion.

Rafe awoke to broad daylight. Panic swept through him, until he realized that Angela was sleeping soundly, snuggled against him, her body warm and rosy from their loving.

He hadn't meant to sleep so long. Obviously, he'd been more exhausted than he'd thought. Then he remembered Baxter and knew he had to do something about the man.

Beside him, Angel stirred, stretched and opened her eyes. She smiled up at him. "What time is it?"

"We slept through the night."

She bolted upright. "Oh, no! You have to go. I'll take Baxter to the sheriff after you're gone."

"Not on your life. We're going to leave here together. I'm not going to let you talk me out of taking you with me this time."

He rose and pulled on his clothes. "I'll wash in the kitchen. Pack your things after you've finished dressing. We'll have breakfast before I decide what's to be done with Baxter. I'll scout the kitchen and see what we can take with us. Be sure to bring any cash you happen to have on hand."

Rafe didn't give Angela time to object as he hurried to the kitchen. He was rifling through the cupboards and piling trail food on the kitchen table when he glanced out the window and spied Jim Cady rushing out of the mine, hollering at the top of his lungs and waving his hands as if he had just seen a ghost.

Rafe stifled a groan. He hadn't counted on anyone finding Baxter before he'd decided what to do with the man. He shouldn't have exhausted himself making love to Angel. Then a thought struck him. Why hadn't Cady released Baxter if he'd found him? Rafe was debating whether or not to confront Cady when Angel came rushing from the bedroom.

"What is it? What's all the commotion?" She glanced out the window. "That's Cady. What's he saying?"

"I suspect he's found Baxter."

"Where *is* Baxter?"

Rafe shrugged. "Beats me."

"Don't let him see you," Angela cautioned. "I'll go out and see what's happening."

Cady halted abruptly when Angela stepped out onto the steps. His skin was waxy and he was perspiring profusely.

"Baxter's dead. Someone murdered him. Shot him through the heart."

Angela's hand flew to her throat. "No, you must be mistaken."

"He's dead, all right." Cady started backing away, then turned and ran for his horse. "I gotta go for the sheriff," he shouted as he leaped onto his horse and raced down the road.

Stunned, Angela returned to the house on shaking legs. How could Baxter be dead? The last time she'd seen him he was very much alive. Suddenly it dawned on her that she wasn't the last person to see Baxter alive. It was . . .

Rafe.

Oh, God, why had he done it? Why had Rafe killed Baxter?

"I heard," Rafe said, eyeing her warily. "And I know what you're thinking." He reached for her.

"No! Don't touch me! Why did you kill him? No matter how despicable he was, killing him in cold blood wasn't right. Oh, God, I don't even know you."

"Angel, I did not kill Baxter," he enunciated slowly. "He was alive the last time I saw him."

She backed away, shaking so hard her knees were knocking. "Don't lie! Who else was there? Only you and I knew Baxter was in the mine. I never believed all those charges against you were true, but now . . ."

"Angel, you've got to believe me. Don't turn your back on me now. We've come too far." He grasped her shoulders and felt her stiffen. He released her immediately. Her fear was so palpable he could almost taste it.

His eyes hardened to the color of stone, cold and gray and unforgiving. "I thought I knew you, but I was mistaken. I won't stick around this time to protect you. You're sole owner of the mine now. Your marriage to Baxter makes you his beneficiary. I hope that makes you happy."

"I . . . I don't know what to say or think. You were the last person inside the mine. Baxter was alive when I left."

"You could say you don't think me capable of murder. You could say you'll come with

206

me when I leave here. You could say . . . Forget it. What's the use? I can see I'm wasting my time. I hope you have no objection if I take some trail food with me."

Rafe couldn't believe this was happening. Who in the hell had killed Baxter? He hadn't a clue. All he knew was that the bastard had been alive when he'd left the mine to join Angel. He should have known better than to think a woman like Angel would believe in him. He had nothing to commend him. No home, no money, a reputation he hadn't earned, and the law breathing down his neck. But after all he and Angel had been through together, he couldn't help feeling raw and hurting after her hasty judgment of him.

They had just spent the night making love, for godsake! Never would Rafe understand women. This was the last time he'd ever let himself trust one.

"Take what you need," Angela said dully. "I have some money —"

"No!" he all but shouted. "No," he said, more reasonably. "I don't want a damn cent of your money, lady. And I'm going to prove to you that I'm no killer. I'm not even a bank robber."

"Rafe, I'm sorry. I'm just so confused. If there had been anyone else here . . . I need time to think."

"Time has run out, Angel. You never were completely convinced that I'm not an outlaw.

There was always that tiny kernel of doubt, wasn't there? Even when we made love you had a wary look in your eyes, as if you couldn't quite decide what or who I was."

"That's not true!"

"Then prove it. Come with me now."

She took an involuntary step backward. "I can't."

Sarcasm dripped from his voice. "I didn't think you would." He brushed past her and filled his pockets with food he'd set out on the kitchen table.

"I'm taking feed for my horse with me." Angela nodded. He paused with his hand on the doorknob. "Good-bye, Angel. I've enjoyed the ride." Then he was gone.

Angela stared at the door. Her heart thumped wildly inside her chest as she blinked back the tears. She wanted to run after Rafe, to tell him she knew he wasn't a killer, but her legs refused to move.

She could have misjudged Rafe. When she looked into his eyes she didn't see a killer. She saw a man who had made a woman of her, a man who had taught her passion.

She saw a man with two faces. A dangerous outlaw and a gentle lover. Who was the real Rafe Gentry? She hadn't wanted him to touch her after she'd learned Baxter was dead, and she recalled the flash of pain her words had produced in him. But she couldn't help it. She'd always been a little confused where Rafe was concerned, and this latest incident only added to her confusion. Was she capable of loving a killer?

That question hung in the air like autumn smoke, thick, suffocating, stifling her thought processes. Would she ever know the real Rafe Gentry? Unlikely, she thought as she watched him make his way up the mountainside to the cave where he'd left his horse. She watched until she could no longer see him, then turned away. She went through the motions of fixing breakfast, though she wasn't hungry, and poured herself a cup of strong coffee.

Time passed. She was staring at an uneaten biscuit, her thoughts a million miles away, when she heard riders approaching the mine. Her mind suddenly alert, she scraped back her chair, opened the door, and stepped outside. She recognized the sheriff before he reined in at the mine entrance. His deputy and Jim Cady were with him. Cady lit a lantern, then all three disappeared inside.

Angel waited with bated breath for what seemed like an eternity before the men reappeared, this time carrying a body. They laid the body on the ground and wrapped it in a blanket the sheriff retrieved from his saddle. Cady and the deputy waited beside the body while a grim-faced Sheriff Dixon walked over to where she was waiting.

"Morning, Miz Baxter. Sorry to be the

bearer of bad news, but your husband is dead."

She raised anxious eyes to him. "I know. Cady brought the news this morning."

"When was the last time you saw your husband? You and Baxter did get hitched yesterday, didn't you?"

"We were married at the parsonage yesterday morning," Angela confirmed dryly. "The last time I saw him was early this morning. He rose before dawn. He said there was something in the mine he'd forgotten to do."

The lies rolled easily from her tongue. She was still confused and undecided about Rafe's part in Baxter's murder, but common sense told her not to mention Rafe's name. She felt morally obligated to give him the time he needed to get as far away as possible before the sheriff put two and two together and came up with Rafe Gentry.

"Were you the only two here last night and today?"

Angela couldn't meet his gaze. "To my knowledge. If someone was lurking about, I wasn't aware of it."

Dixon searched her face. "You seem mighty calm for a new widow."

"I did all my crying before you got here. Besides, Brady and I hadn't known one another very long. Our marriage was one of convenience. I preferred Brady to the man my stepfather chose for me."

Dixon nodded. Marriages of convenience took place every day. Nothing suspicious or unusual there.

"Whoever killed Baxter did it in cold blood. He never had a chance. He was trussed up and shot point-blank."

Angela shuddered and looked away. "I'm sorry. No man should die like that."

Dixon gave her a shrewd look. "Any ideas, Miz Baxter?"

"I . . . no, none at all. Brady must have made an enemy or two during his life."

"You seen Rafe Gentry lately?"

She gave him a startled look. "No. He's probably halfway to California by now."

"I thought you might have seen him recently. He was pretending to be your husband, wasn't he? Everyone thought you two were married until your stepfather set everyone straight and denounced Gentry for an outlaw. Are you sure you didn't know about Gentry's violent past?"

"I was fooled along with everyone else," Angela said. "I haven't seen Rafe since he took off. Why do you ask?"

Dixon was no dummy. "I'm thinking that Gentry could be holed up somewhere in the mountains. There's no lack of hiding places."

"Why would he do that?"

"You tell me."

"I have no idea what you're implying."

"I'm implying that Gentry had a beef with Baxter. From all reports, Gentry is a vicious outlaw who wouldn't think twice about killing a man for revenge. Baxter *did* bring the law up here. And Baxter married the woman Gentry wanted for himself. That's reason enough in my books."

Dixon made it all sound so logical, Angela thought. Though she had mulled those very same things over in her mind herself, she didn't like hearing them from another source.

"I'm sure you're wrong, Sheriff."

"Nevertheless, we have no other suspects, unless we include you, and I don't think you're strong enough to tie Baxter up, or cold-blooded enough to murder him. So that leaves only Gentry. Looks like we'll be forming a posse again, and adding another murder to the charges against Gentry. What shall we do with your husband's body, Miz Baxter?"

"Would . . . would you please take him to town and see that the undertaker prepares him for burial. I'll ride down later and make arrangements for the funeral. I'll also be looking to hire workers for the mine. You can pass the word around, if you'll be so kind. I want things back to normal as soon as possible."

"Sure thing," Dixon said. "I'll take care of everything." They parted then. Angela entered the cabin and didn't look back as the sheriff, his deputy and Cady draped Baxter's body over his horse for the trip to town.

Baxter's funeral was held the following morning. Angela had gone into town shortly after the sheriff departed and made the necessary arrangements. Baxter was buried in the town cemetery, with a few friends and business acquaintances in attendance. From the corner of her eye, Angela saw Desmond Kent and Anson Chandler standing at the rear of the small gathering, and she wondered what they were up to now. Then Reverend Porter said the words over the grave and the mourners drifted away. A few stopped to offer their condolences.

Lawyer Goodman stood beside Angela. While in town yesterday, she had paid him a visit, explaining everything that had happened. She'd told him the truth, leaving nothing out. Including why she had married Rafe, and Chandler's determination to get his hands on her inheritance. She explained about the death of Reverend Conrad and the loss of the records pertaining to her marriage. She even told Goodman why she'd gone through with the marriage to Baxter when she knew it was an illegal union.

Goodman had been stunned. His first question had been, "Did Rafe Gentry really kill Brady Baxter?" His second was, "Do you actually believe Gentry guilty of all those crimes?"

213

"Rafe swore he hadn't robbed that bank, or done those other things of which he's accused," she'd responded. "I'd begun to believe him, for he showed no signs of violence. But as far as I know, he was the last person to see Baxter alive. Despite the fact that Baxter arranged my father's death and intended to kill Rafe, his death was accomplished in such a cold-blooded way that I could never forgive Rafe if he is responsible."

She'd left the lawyer's office a short time later, giving him time to digest everything she'd told him.

Now, following the brief ceremony, he accompanied her back to his office to tie up legal matters arising from Baxter's death. Seated opposite him, Angela stared at her hands. This was all such a mess. Everyone but she thought of her as Baxter's widow.

"Well, my dear, it looks as if you're the sole beneficiary of Brady Baxter's estate."

"But our marriage wasn't legal," Angela insisted.

"I strongly suggest you keep that piece of information to yourself. Baxter had no relatives. You're the logical person to inherit. Besides, your father and Baxter signed a letter of intent before they became partners. I have it in my records. Since Baxter had no relatives, his share was to go to Simon should he not outlive your father. You're your father's heir. And if both you and Simon failed to outlive Baxter, he would have become sole owner of the Golden Angel."

"Baxter probably thought marrying me was easier than killing me," Angela mused. "When I turned up with a husband, it probably threw all his plans awry. That's why he planned to do away with Rafe. Of course, it didn't hurt that Rafe had a price on his head."

"I still can't believe Baxter was responsible for your father's death. Simon was on his way to the smelter with a load of ore when his wagon careened over a mountainside. Baxter told everyone the axle broke."

"Believe it," Angela said with a touch of sadness. "At least I have the satisfaction of knowing he was punished for his crime. I'm just sorry his death happened the way it did. I would have preferred to have the law pass final judgment."

"You're a very wealthy young lady now," Goodman said. "You can live in luxury the rest of your life, if you'd like."

"I don't want Brady's money," Angela averred.

"Nevertheless, it's yours. I'll make all the arrangements for the transfer of Baxter's assets into your personal account."

"I don't —"

"Think it over carefully before you refuse," Goodman advised. "The money might do a lot of good somewhere. Take your time, decide what you want to do, then let me know."

A slow smile spread across Angela's face. "You're right. I could found an orphanage, endow a new school or build a new church. Very well, Mr. Goodman, I'll give your suggestion serious thought." She rose to leave.

"Don't go yet, Angela. What if Rafe Gentry shows up at the mine? You shouldn't be alone out there, you know."

"He won't show up," Angela said with firm conviction. "Not if he values his freedom. As for being out there alone, I intend to hire men to work the mine before I leave town. I posted a sign at the post office this morning. With any luck, I can hire all the men I need today. The foreman can stay in Brady's cabin. He can even bring his family, if he's married. It would be nice to have another woman around."

Goodman sent her a concerned look. "Good luck, my dear. Miners are a stubborn lot. I'm not sure they'll want to work for a woman. Especially a woman who knows nothing about mining."

"I can learn," Angela said with an assurance she was far from feeling.

Angela walked the short distance to the post office. The sign she had posted asked that men interested in working at the Golden Angel meet in front of the post office at noon. She was heartened to see about ten men gathered outside the building, gossiping and smoking while they waited.

"I need mine workers," Angela began as she called the men to attention. "Experienced ones."

"Who's gonna pay our wages?" a man asked.

"I am," Angela answered. "You'll receive the going rate for mine work. Perhaps some of you worked for my father and Brady Baxter. I'd be pleased to have you return."

"You gonna be our boss?" a man challenged.

"Since I'm the owner, I'll run things," Angela stated.

"I ain't working for no woman."

"Me neither. Women got no business bossing men around."

The small band of miners started drifting away.

Panic surged through Angela.

Damn you. Damn you all, Angela wanted to shout. Instead, she bit her tongue and watched them leave her high and dry, without a crew to work the mine.

"I knew you'd have need of me one day," Chandler said as he joined her outside the post office. "They'll work for me. I can pack my things and move out there today. I'll bring workers with me, too. What do you say, Angel?"

"Bring qualified miners and I'll think about

it," Angela responded. "What about my step-father? He'd be useless up here."

"Don't worry about Kent. I persuaded him to return to Topeka."

"Good riddance," Angela muttered.

Chapter Eleven

Chandler showed up at the mine the following day with ten men and a foreman. It galled Angela to think that most of the men were the very same ones who had refused to work for her the day before. Not only that, but the foreman was Jim Cady, the man who had been Baxter's right-hand man.

"I told you I'd get the men you needed," Chandler bragged when Angela walked out to greet him.

"How did you do it?"

Chandler shrugged. "I told them we were going to be married, and that I'd be in charge of operations here."

An angry flush suffused Angela's face. She didn't like the idea of people thinking she and Chandler were romantically involved. But for the time being, it appeared to be the only way to bring workers to the mine. Men were a strange breed, she silently fumed. Women weren't supposed to have brains, and woe be to any who didn't fit the mold. Men considered women mindless creatures with little to commend them but their bodies and their housekeeping capabilities.

"Just don't get too comfortable with what you told the men," Angela warned. "I have no intention of marrying you, Anson. The only reason I'm letting you have your way is because I need men to work the mine."

Angela had done a lot of thinking since Baxter's death. If Rafe hadn't killed him, someone else had. To her way of thinking, Chandler was a logical suspect, and she hoped that having him around where she could watch him would eventually lead to the truth. The thought that Rafe had killed in cold blood was becoming increasingly difficult to believe, and she intended to do everything humanly possible to prove his innocence.

"I'm going to change your mind, Angela," Chandler promised, leaning so close Angela felt a compelling urge to slap his face. Instead, she backed away.

"You need a man to show you the error of your ways, my dear," Chandler continued smoothly. "A woman is no substitute for a man, no matter how smart or accomplished she thinks she may be. I'm determined to become your husband and take care of you."

Angela felt like laughing in his face. "I don't need a man to show me anything, much less the error of my ways. All I require of you is your cooperation. You can stay as long as you keep men up here working the mine. If I were you, I'd learn all I could about mining. You don't want the miners thinking they're taking orders from a fraud."

Chandler's smile turned downward into a scowl. "Look who's calling the pot black. You have no room to talk. You married a stranger, an outlaw, simply to save him from a hangman, *Sister Angela*. Don't worry, I'll do my job, and one day you'll realize I'm the kind of man you need. Meanwhile, I'll move my things into Baxter's cabin, unless," he added slyly, "you invite me to share your bed."

Preferring not to alienate him before she had the information she sought, Angela held her tongue, but her eyes blazed defiance. "You're welcome to Baxter's cabin, Anson, but don't push your luck."

Whirling on her heel, head held high, she left him standing with a half smile on his lips. Angela knew what he wanted to happen, and it pleased her no end to know it never would.

Several days passed. The mining operation seemed to be going well, but Angela's attempts to discover if Chandler knew anything about Baxter's death brought only frustration.

One evening Chandler stopped by Angela's cabin to report on a new tunnel just opened. He made himself at home on the battered sofa while he gave his report. As he rattled on, Angela searched her mind for ways to broach the subject of Baxter's death without raising Chandler's suspicions.

When he finished his report and appeared in no hurry to leave, Angela rushed into the conversational void. "In the short time you've been here you've done a credible job, Anson."

Chandler appeared pleased by her praise. "I'm making you wealthier than Midas, my dear."

"The foreman is experienced, and that helps," Angela said. "Brady knew what he was doing when he hired Jim Cady."

"Baxter, bah!" Chandler scoffed. "I was livid when I learned that you had married him, but his sudden death proved fortunate for both of us, eh?" He gave her a smug grin. "A stroke of luck, really. If I hadn't been here and seen . . . Well, never mind. Good riddance to both Baxter and Gentry, I say. They were in my way."

Angela pretended confusion. "I don't know what you're hinting at, Anson. I told the sheriff that Rafe wasn't at the mine the night Brady was killed."

"We both know better, don't we, Angela?"

Angela opened her mouth to offer a protest, but Chandler forestalled her. "No, don't lie. Don't say anything. Just forget this conversation ever took place. The less you know about Baxter's death, the better off you'll be."

"What do *you* know about Brady's death, Anson? You can tell me. I liked Brady no better than you did. We married for convenience's sake. I consider it a blessing that he . . . died on our wedding night. I'm just not convinced that Rafe killed him."

Chandler sent her a sharp look. "You're too curious for your own good. I suggest you turn your thoughts in another direction. It's healthier to believe that Gentry killed Baxter. What's another murder to a man like him?"

His thinly veiled threat gave her pause. She knew she was on the right track now. "It's late; you'd better leave," Angela said, rising. Chandler's remarks tonight hinted that he knew more than he was letting on about Baxter's death.

Chandler stood, surprising Angela when he grasped her arm and swung her around to face him. "I don't have to leave. We both know you're no longer a virgin; you have no need to pretend coyness with me. If you need some loving, I can give you what you're craving."

"You assume too much," Angela retorted. "I don't need a thing from you, Anson Chandler."

He stood his ground, refusing to be dislodged as she tried to free herself. His arm snaked around her waist, bringing her hard against him, making escape impossible. When she tried to turn her head aside, he grasped her chin and held it in place for his kiss. His mouth slammed down on hers. She tasted blood. When he tried to deepen the kiss, Angela's anger soared. Mustering her strength, she bit down hard on his tongue. His response was immediate and gratifying.

Howling like a banshee, he pushed Angela away, his eyes narrowed in fury. "What in the hell was that for?"

"For taking liberties," Angela responded, backing away and wiping the blood from her lips with the back of her hand.

"A kiss is the least you owe me for providing you with workers. I could leave and take them with me," he threatened. "They'd never work for a woman."

Angela couldn't allow that to happen. But kissing Anson was repugnant to her. "Perhaps when I know you better . . ." she hedged.

"You bedded Gentry without knowing a damn thing about him. I'm not hard to look at. What do you have against me?"

"You're a handsome man, Anson," Angela said, choking on the words. "Perhaps, when you decide to trust me, we can become closer."

His eyes narrowed. "I don't know what you're talking about."

Angela sent him an inscrutable look. "Don't you? I think you know more about

Baxter's death than you're letting on. Please leave now. It's late and I wish to retire."

Chandler appeared stunned by Angela's words as she pushed him out the door and locked it behind him. Once Chandler was gone, she leaned against the panel, her relief palpable as she considered everything Chandler had revealed about Baxter's death. In time, she expected to wring every last detail from him.

Moving away from the door and into the bedroom, Angela thought of Rafe and the angry words they had exchanged before he lit out. She knew now she had been wrong to accuse him of murder. At the time, the accusation seemed reasonable even though she wasn't thinking reasonably right then. Now she knew better. If what she suspected was true, she had to prove that Chandler was involved in Baxter's murder.

She owed Rafe that much for accusing him of a crime without sufficient proof. She would ride into town tomorrow and talk to Mr. Goodman about it, she decided. Even if she never saw Rafe again, she'd have the satisfaction of knowing she'd removed one charge from his roster of crimes. Only a miracle would clear Rafe of all the crimes he was supposed to have committed.

Angela undressed quickly, donned her nightgown and slid into bed. Almost reverently she touched the pillow next to her, recalling the man who had recently lain beside her. Rafe Gentry. Her husband. A man comparable to none. Would she ever see him again? Would he ever forgive her for accusing him unjustly? Probably not. Rafe wasn't a forgiving kind of man.

She sighed. Under the circumstances, how could she *not* have thought Rafe guilty? But now that another suspect had entered the picture, her belief in Rafe's innocence had been restored, and she felt like such a fool for accusing him unjustly.

Rafe wasn't as far away as Angela suspected. No matter what he'd told her, no matter how dangerous it was for him to linger in the area, Rafe couldn't make himself ride away from Angel. And he was glad he'd stuck around. He'd seen more than enough to know that Angel was doing what Angel did best . . . getting into trouble.

For the past several days, Rafe had been holed up in the cave above the mine, the same cave he'd used before. He'd easily lost the posse in the mountains, then backtracked, erasing his tracks by tying a thick branch to his saddle.

Rafe spent his idle time keeping a close watch on Angel and the activities at the mine. Concealing himself behind bushes above the mine, Rafe noted that the Golden Angel was in full production. He recognized

Jim Cady and a few others who had worked for Baxter, but what had shocked him utterly was seeing Anson Chandler strutting about as if he owned the place.

From what little he could gather, it appeared as if Angel and Chandler were on good terms, and that Chandler was taking over as boss. What was Angel thinking? he fumed. How could she flit from man to man as easily as changing her blouse? First Baxter and now Chandler. Was there a side to Angel he didn't know? He'd been right to return, Rafe thought. It didn't matter that she thought him a murderer; he couldn't let a woman as helpless as his Angel fend for herself. Seeing Chandler at the Golden Angel just proved his point.

Rafe was watching from his vantage point above the mine when he saw Chandler follow Angel inside her cabin after the workers had departed for the night. Rage roiled inside him. She was like an innocent babe when it came to men. She had married *him*, hadn't she? Which more than proved his point.

When Chandler failed to leave right away, Rafe grew wild with jealousy. Ignoring the danger, he climbed down the hillside and crept toward the cabin. Blending into the purple shadows, he crouched beneath a window. He paused a moment to catch his breath, then lifted his head to peer into the room. What he saw made him want to howl in outrage.

His Angel was in Chandler's arms, kissing him. He recalled the countless times she'd professed to hate Chandler, and he wanted to burst into the cabin and tear her out of the other man's arms. *Damn, damn, damn!* He had to save his fickle Angel from doing something she'd regret.

Having seen all he cared to see, Rafe dropped down below the sill, his mind in a turmoil. Angel was too vulnerable to be left on her own; she was an extremely wealthy woman. Chandler wanted her and wouldn't hesitate to take her against her will. Then it came to him. Rafe knew exactly what he would do.

Angela fell asleep hugging Rafe's pillow. Though she'd washed the bed linen since he'd left, she imagined she could still smell his musky scent permeating the material. She was sleeping so peacefully she didn't hear the rasping noise of a window being raised to admit a rather large man. She slept blissfully on, unaware until a blanket was thrown over her head and she felt strong arms pick her up and carry her away.

Her wits returned slowly. She was being abducted from her bed! By whom? Chandler? That didn't make sense. She opened her mouth to protest, but her voice was muffled

by the blanket. Her words were pitifully gar-
bled. Then she felt night air cooling parts of
her body not covered by the blanket, and
panic rose inside her.

Kicking and flailing didn't work. The arms
holding her were too strong, the blanket too
tightly confining. Then the slant of the land
changed, and Angela realized her abductor
was climbing steadily upward. She managed
to grunt out a few words of outrage, but they
appeared to bounce off the man. After what
seemed like hours but in reality was only
thirty minutes, she was lowered to the
ground. Immediately she tried to fight her
way out of the blanket, but her captor was
too fast for her. With a few deft strokes he
tied the blanket in place around her body
and bound her ankles so she couldn't hobble
off. She was helpless, totally at her abductor's
mercy.

Rafe glanced down at Angel, satisfied that
she wasn't going anywhere while he returned
to the cabin for her clothing and a horse.
"I'll be back," he whispered hoarsely into her
ear. Then he turned and strode out of the
cave and into the dark night.

All was quiet at the mine when Rafe returned. This time he entered the cabin by
the front door and lit a lantern inside Angel's
bedroom. He found her saddlebags and
hastily stuffed clothing into them. After a
quick look around, he added a hairbrush,

towels, soap and a washcloth. He was rummaging around in a drawer for some ribbons to bind her long, blond hair back from her face when he came across a small stack of gold coins and a wad of bills.

Since he had no money of his own, and he knew that they would need more food than he could carry away from the kitchen, he pushed the money down into one of the pockets of the saddlebags. Then he rolled two blankets into a bedroll and carried everything into the kitchen, where he emptied a gunnysack that held sticks of kindling for the stove and filled it with bacon, canned goods, beans, crackers, coffee, salt, flour and anything else he thought they might need in the way of food. Then he doused the light, carrying the lantern with him when he left the cabin.

Rafe made his way to the corral, keeping well within the shadows as he passed Chandler's cabin. He left the saddlebags, lantern, gunnysack and bedroll in the tack house while he found a saddle and carried it out to the corral. The horses whinnied a greeting when Rafe walked into the enclosure, and Rafe prayed that Chandler wasn't a light sleeper. He spotted Angel's mare immediately and used his gentlest voice to soothe her as he tossed the saddle over her back and fastened the straps.

When he finished, he retrieved the things

he'd left in the tack house, threw the saddle-bags over the mare's withers and tied the gunnysack to the saddle horn. Then he led the horse from the enclosure, past the cabins and up the hillside to the cave where Angel waited. Rafe wasn't looking forward to facing her wrath when she learned he had abducted her. Somehow he had to make her understand that it was for her own good.

Angela struggled within the suffocating folds of the blanket until exhaustion forced her to stop. How could this be happening to her? Who had abducted her and why? She couldn't imagine Anson doing such a thing, for he had nothing to gain by it. Did she have unknown enemies?

For lack of a better solution, Angela screamed. The sound, muffled by the blanket, bounced off unseen walls and echoed back to her. She shivered, letting her imagination run wild. Her keen senses told her a few things, none of them comforting. The ground beneath her was damp and the air around her cool. Her abductor was a large man who had carried her uphill with ease. Nothing else made sense to her befuddled mind.

Locked in darkness, Angela found it impossible to judge the passage of time. Minutes or hours could have passed before she heard footsteps approaching. Through the fibers of

231

the blanket she perceived light. Her captor was carrying a lantern.

"Who are you?" Angela cried. Though her words were muffled, she knew he understood her. "Why have you done this to me?"

She heard a sigh. The sound reverberated through her brain, setting off alarm bells in her head. "Release me!"

She felt his hands on her ankles, freeing them, felt the rope holding the blanket in place around her body fall away. She drew in a sustaining breath as her shroud was whisked off. She blinked and gazed up into the stoic face of her captor.

"You!"

"Hello, Angel."

"Damn you, Rafe Gentry! You scared ten years off my life." She glanced around and realized she was inside a cave. "What's this all about? What are you doing here?"

"I'm happy to hear you're glad to see me," he said with a hint of sarcasm.

"If you recall, we didn't part on the best of terms."

"If you recall, you told me you wanted nothing to do with Chandler, yet he's here, acting as if he owns both you and the mine."

Angela gaped at him. "How do you know that?"

"I know more than you think. Did you enjoy his kiss?"

Angela blanched. "You saw that?"

"Fickle bitch," Rafe muttered beneath his breath. "Don't you realize you're playing with fire? Chandler will stop at nothing to get to your money. He's already wormed his way into your good graces."

"You don't know a darn thing, Rafe Gentry. Anson kissed me, I didn't kiss him," she said defensively.

His voice held a note of derision. "There's a difference? What's Chandler doing at the mine?"

"It seems that Western men are more prejudiced against women than I thought. I couldn't find men willing to work for a woman. Anson offered to help out. He promised to bring all the workers I needed and suggested that we pretend to be engaged to be married."

Rafe gave a snort of laughter. "Pretend? You two looked pretty damn chummy to me."

"You don't understand," Angela tried to explain. "I went along with Anson's suggestion for your sake."

Rafe sent her a stunned look. "For me? You're right, I don't understand."

"Anson said something that led me to believe he knew more about Baxter's death than he should. I invited him out here to find out what he knows."

His voice held a cynical note. "Are you telling me you now believe I'm innocent?

That I didn't kill Baxter?"

"I'm telling you I'm willing to do whatever it takes to learn the truth." Her voice softened. "I'd like nothing better than to prove you innocent, Rafe."

"Forget it, Angel. Either you believe in me or you don't."

Men! Angela thought. Why did they have to be so stubborn? She tried to stand. Her legs were wobbly and she tottered forward. Rafe reached out to steady her.

"If you're finished with your games, Rafe Gentry, I'd like to return to my cabin now."

"You're not going anywhere, Angel. You're not thinking coherently. You're headed for a heap of trouble. As your husband, I'm duty bound to protect you."

Astounded, Angela asked, "You returned to protect me? After the angry words we exchanged?"

"Why else would I stick around? I know you don't trust me, that you think I'm a killer, but that doesn't lessen my responsibility regarding your safety."

Angela's chin notched upward. "I can take care of myself. Did you hear nothing I said? I'm trying to prove your innocence. You should be grateful."

"Grateful that you need proof of my innocence? My word alone should be enough."

"You forget," Angela reminded him, "I'm not the only one requiring proof. What about the sheriff? If I can prove someone else killed Baxter, your name will be cleared."

"You suspect Chandler?"

"It's a distinct possibility."

Rafe's temper exploded. "Are you mad? If Chandler is a killer, then you're in danger every minute you remain in his company. What if Chandler becomes suspicious of your questions and decides he doesn't need you? Your stepfather is your next of kin. He'd inherit the Golden Angel and everything else you own should you meet with an accident. Chandler would benefit through his deal with Kent. God, how naive can you be?"

Angela looked properly chastised. "I never thought of it that way. I'll be more careful from now on. Don't worry about me, Rafe. Just take care of yourself."

She tried to push past him.

"Where are you going?"

"Back to the mine. It can't be too far away. I want to be home before the miners show up for work."

When she tried to sidle past him, his hand came down hard on her shoulder. "You're not going anywhere, Angel."

She shrugged free of his grip. "How do you intend to stop me?"

"The same way I got you here, if need be."

Angela went still. "You'd abduct me? Where are you taking me?"

"I intend to clear my name if it's the last

thing I do. I'm going back to Dodge City to confront Mr. Wingate, the banker who falsely accused me and my brothers of bank robbery. I'm going to prove to you that I'm not an outlaw if it's the last thing I do."

"It just might be the last thing you do," Angela muttered bleakly. "I can't fault you for wanting to clear your name. What I don't understand is your reason for taking me with you. You'd be better served if I remain here and learn what I can from Anson about Baxter's death. He seems to be the only person besides you who can shed any light on the subject."

"No! I'm not leaving you behind this time. You're coming with me and that's final. If things work out, we can solve that mystery together."

"I'm *not* going with you," Angela stubbornly retorted.

"You have no choice. You're not going anywhere near the mine or Chandler unless I'm with you."

"This is totally unacceptable, Rafe. The Golden Angel is my responsibility; I can't leave it unattended."

"You're *my* responsibility, Angel. I risked a great deal to return for you and I'm not leaving without you."

Angela stared at him. He sounded like a jealous husband. "Is that all I am to you, Rafe? A responsibility? Do you take *all* your responsibilities so seriously?"

"I take my responsibility to *you* seriously, Angel. You're my wife. There are scores of people in Ordway who witnessed our marriage. We *have* been intimate. What if you're carrying my child?"

Angela's hands flew to her stomach. "That's not possible! I couldn't be . . ."

"It's very possible and you could be. Think about it while I bring your saddlebags inside the cave so you can dress."

"You packed my clothing?"

"And a few extras. Oh, I found some money in your drawer. I thought it might come in handy so I stuffed it in your saddlebags."

"You forgot one thing, Rafe."

His dark brows rose questioningly.

"I'm not going anywhere with you. It's more important for me to remain here and work on Anson. You should be grateful that I'm willing to do that for you."

"You'll come with me if I have to hogtie you to your mare."

"You brought my mare?"

"She's outside with my gelding."

"I'll hate you if you insist on kidnapping me. I'll escape."

Rafe shrugged. "You're welcome to try. As for hating me, you made your feelings for me clear when you accused me of killing Baxter."

"But I want to believe you, Rafe; that's

why I need to pump Anson for answers."

"Sorry, Angel, it's too late for retrospection. I'll go fetch your saddlebags."

She'd never seen a man as stubborn as Rafe, Angel thought, fuming in impotent rage. Or as hardheaded. Or as overbearing and possessive. Her list of his faults came to an abrupt end when Rafe returned with her saddlebags and dropped them at her feet.

"I'll ready the horses while you dress. I want to head out of here before daylight."

Staring at Rafe's departing back, Angel shivered, and not just from the damp cold permeating the cave. Rafe's rigid features revealed his determination to have his way in this. That he had resorted to abducting her didn't really surprise her. He must have known she wouldn't leave the mine of her own free will. More shocking was the knowledge that Rafe considered her his responsibility.

She knew for a fact he hadn't wanted to be married, so why this sudden concern for her welfare? Without proof of their marriage, he could have relegated it to a bad memory. His concern appeared genuine but ill-advised. He had enough problems without taking on hers. Furthermore, she was trying to help clear his name. The stubborn man had no sense. Any other man would be happy to have her working in his behalf.

Seeing no way out of the situation, Angela

shed her nightgown and donned her clothing. She was just pulling on her boots when Rafe returned.

"All ready, I see. You'll have to make do with jerky and a biscuit until it's safe to stop to eat."

"I can wait. I lost my appetite when I was dragged from my bed in the middle of the night. Are you sure you won't change your mind about taking me with you?"

"Not a chance," he said as he picked up the lantern, grasped her elbow, and guided her from the cave. Once outside, he doused the light and left the lantern just inside the entrance.

Before Angela could form a protest, Rafe tossed her atop her horse and grasped the reins.

"Give me my reins," Angela insisted.

"I'll keep them for the time being. Relax, Angel, and enjoy the ride."

Rafe knew Angel was angry but he couldn't trust her not to bolt if he gave her the reins. Talk about stubborn. He'd never encountered a more stubborn woman. Obviously, she hadn't a clue as to the kind of danger Chandler presented. Strange, he mused, he hadn't even considered Chandler as a possible suspect in Baxter's death. He'd run through a list of men who could have killed Baxter and Chandler's name hadn't even come up. But once Angel had pointed out the possibility to him, he could see how Chandler might benefit from Baxter's death.

It was obvious to him that Chandler intended to take advantage of Angel's vulnerability. With Rafe out of the picture and Baxter dead, Angel had no one to turn to. It must have occurred to Chandler that Kent stood to inherit should something unforeseen happen to Angel. It astounded him that Angel had invited Chandler up to the mine. The woman was a walking calamity. She needed a keeper. If he hadn't returned, Lord only knew what mischief she would have got herself into.

Determination to keep Angel safe stiffened his spine as he nudged his mount forward. Dodge City was but the first stop in his pilgrimage to clear his name.

Chapter Twelve

The sun was high in the sky when Rafe called a halt. He had found a secluded spot beside a bubbling creek protected by a cover of thick aspens.

"It's safe to rest now and have a bite to eat," Rafe said as he dismounted and hauled Angela down from her horse. He rummaged in a sack of supplies attached to his saddle and retrieved a battered coffeepot. "Fill the coffeepot after you've refreshed yourself. And don't forget to fill your canteen while you're at it. I'll build a fire and fry up some bacon."

Angela merely glared at him as she jerked the coffeepot out of his hands and marched away. Rafe chuckled to himself as he watched her go to the creek. He'd forgotten to bring her hat, and her cheeks were reddened from the sun. He suspected his Angel would drop from sunstroke before complaining to him. His smile broadened as he considered the enticing sway of her hips beneath her skirt.

Memory served him well as he recalled

how her supple body arched beneath his hands when he stroked and caressed her. Her breasts were especially sensitive to his lips and hands. He grew hard just thinking about the way her nipples rose up to meet his mouth when he claimed them.

Rafe swallowed convulsively when he saw Angel kneel at the edge of the brook, her bottom high in the air, and splash water over her face and down the front of her blouse. His throbbing erection pushed against the confines of his trousers; he was so close to tossing Angel on her back and making violent love to her right there on the hard ground that he had to turn away. He knew exactly how his Angel would react to his ardor. In her present frame of mind, he suspected she would reject him outright.

Stifling a groan, he watched her walk toward a clump of bushes before turning back to the task at hand. When the fire was burning well, he sought privacy behind some trees, then washed up in the stream. When he returned, he sliced bacon and fried it in a skillet. Angela returned with the coffeepot and set it to boiling while Rafe worked over the fire.

"There's stale biscuits in that gunnysack," Rafe said. "Will they do?"

"If they came from my kitchen, they're not all that stale," Angela sniffed. "I made them just yesterday."

When the coffee was done, they sat on the ground to eat the meager fare. Afterward, Angela washed the tin plates and bent silverware while Rafe repacked everything. The atmosphere was decidedly chilly when Rafe plucked off his hat and placed it on Angela's head.

"What's that for?"

"I forgot your hat. I don't want you getting sunstroke, or burning that delicate skin of yours."

"What about you?"

"My skin is already sun-darkened and a lot thicker than yours. I'll be fine. Keep the hat, I'll buy you another the first small town we come to."

He helped her mount, snatched up her reins and leaped aboard his gelding.

"I'm perfectly capable of handling my own reins," Angela protested, trying to jerk them out of his hands.

"Will you promise not to bolt back to the mine?"

Her lips thinned. "I can't promise that, Rafe Gentry, and you know it."

"Then I'll keep the reins until turning back is no longer an option," Rafe said as he kneed his horse forward. "We'll camp tonight near Pueblo and get an early start in the morning. I want to pass through town before the townspeople begin stirring."

Those were the last words spoken for the

remainder of the long day. When the sun sank below the western horizon and purple shadows crept along the ground, Rafe found a perfect camping spot beside a shallow river they had just crossed. An outcropping of rock beneath a bluff provided shelter from both the weather and predators.

"You can bathe, if you like, while I take care of the horses," Rafe said, gesturing toward the river. "Don't dally or wander too far. You'll find soap and towels in your saddlebags."

Angela merely nodded as she retrieved the necessary items from her saddlebags.

"How long are you going to continue this silent treatment?" Rafe asked, cocking an eyebrow at her. "It gets mighty lonesome out here on the prairie without the sound of a human voice."

"I'm still angry with you, Rafe Gentry. You're arrogant, manipulative and overbearing. You have no right to force me to your will."

"Force you to my will? If I really wanted to force you to my will, I'd tear off your clothes and pull you beneath me. Then I'd make love to you until we were both too exhausted to move."

Angela's mouth dropped open. She backed away. "I . . . I . . ." Words failed her as she whirled on her heel and fled to the river. She didn't slow down until she was certain Rafe wasn't following her. Gulping huge draughts of air, she dropped to her knees beside the river and waited for her breath to return.

Rafe's evocative words created an image indelibly etched upon her brain. She shook her head, but the vision refused to be dislodged. In her mind's eye she pictured Rafe, naked, muscles rippling across his chest and back, his sturdy legs braced, his sex rising long and hard between his thighs. She covered her face with her hands and groaned; the thought of him thrusting into her hot center flamed her cheeks, and she splashed them with cool water.

Desperately wanting a bath but unwilling to undress where Rafe could see her, she walked along the bank, seeking a private spot. A bend in the river provided the shelter she sought, a place where she couldn't be seen from the campsite. After a furtive glance over her shoulder, Angela stripped off all her clothing but for her shift and poked a toe into the water. It felt delightfully cool after a hot day in the saddle, and with soap in hand she waded out until water lapped at her waist.

Bending forward, she washed and rinsed her hair, twice, not satisfied until it felt free of grit and dust. After waging a silent debate in which prudence lost, she pulled off her shift and tossed it onto the bank. Then she soaped the rest of her body and sat down on the gravelly bottom to let the gentle current flow over her. She dallied so long in the refreshing water, she lost all track of time. If her stomach hadn't begun growling, she could have remained immersed for hours.

Angela was jerked from her reverie when she heard a faint sound in the distance. A twig snapping? Panic rose like a hard knot inside her. The noise could be nothing. Or it could be Indians. Or wild animals coming down to the river to quench their thirst. Either way, she could be in grave danger. She glanced longingly at her clothing lying on the riverbank. What a time to be caught naked.

Then she saw him, standing motionless on the opposite bank. The Indian's squat, muscular body was scantily garbed in breechclout and war paint. A bow hung from his brown fingers. She held her breath as his dark, unwavering gaze found her. She wanted to scream but couldn't find her voice.

Willing her legs to move, she slowly backed toward the bank. The Indian watched her, his intense scrutiny as frightening as it was nerve-wracking.

"Don't make any sudden moves."

Incredible joy surged through Angela when she saw Rafe standing on the riverbank. Never had she been so glad to see anyone in her life. Then her heart sank when she realized he wasn't wearing his gun belt.

"What shall I do?" Angela asked shakily.

"He may not be alone. He could be with a war party camped nearby."

Angela glanced back at the Indian and quavered beneath his intense scrutiny. "Maybe he's never seen a white woman before."

"Not a naked one, I'd wager," Rafe said drolly.

"This is no time for levity, Rafe Gentry."

"I'm not being funny, Angel. I'm trying to think of the best way to get us out of here with our skin intact. I'm hoping darkness will work in our favor."

Angela began to shiver. The shadows had deepened and the night air was raising goose bumps on her skin. "H . . . how long do I have to stay in here?"

Rafe glanced at the Indian. "Not much longer. I think he's alone. Or too far from his party to summon them. He's probably as surprised to see us as we are to see him. Start walking toward me," he instructed.

"I'm naked."

"That can't be helped. Now, Angel! Start moving."

Angela moved stiffly, concentrating on placing one foot before the other. Indians had killed Reverend Conrad and his wife. Were she and Rafe to be their next victims? Swallowing her fear, she waded toward Rafe, silently blessing the encroaching darkness. Nevertheless, she had to force herself to keep walking.

The water fell away from her hips, her waist, her knees. It was ankle-deep now and she had nearly reached the place where Rafe waited. Moments later she was out of the water, reaching for the towel Rafe held out to her.

"Go back to camp. Now," Rafe ordered. "I'll bring your clothing." His gaze never left the silent Indian standing on the opposite shore.

Suddenly the Indian gave a bloodcurdling yell and splashed into the river.

"He's coming!" Angela shrieked.

"Go!" Rafe shouted. "I'll handle this."

Angela turned and ran, ignoring the sharp sticks and briars bruising the tender soles of her feet. She didn't want to leave Rafe alone with the Indian, but he had given her no choice.

Once back at their campsite, she pulled clean clothing from her saddlebags and dressed quickly. Driven by fear for Rafe, she searched for his guns and spied his holster lying beside his saddlebags. Carefully she lifted out one gun. Disregarding her bloody feet, she retraced her steps back to the river. She didn't know much about guns, but she knew she could fire one to save Rafe's life.

She came to an abrupt halt when she spied Rafe locked in combat with the Indian. She raised the pistol and tried to get the Indian in her sights, but the two men were so closely entwined that she couldn't be sure she wouldn't shoot Rafe. In the meager light of the quarter moon, Angela could tell little about the fight, except that it was a fierce one. Her heart nearly stopped when she caught a glimpse of moonlight reflected off the shiny surface of a knife.

Then the men were rolling on the ground, making identification even more difficult. Angela lowered the pistol to her side, unable to shoot without hitting Rafe. She had no idea she was sobbing until she felt tears rolling down her cheeks. This was all her fault. Had she not strayed so far from their campsite, or lingered so long in the water, this never would have happened.

A strangled sound escaped her throat when she saw the blade slash downward. Uncertain who held the knife, Angela feared the worst. Both men suddenly went still, as if frozen in time; the panting and fierce sounds of battle ceased. Angela's breath hitched. She saw a movement; one man rose up from the ground. The breath she'd been holding came out in a loud whoosh.

"Rafe! Thank God!"

Rafe crouched over the dead Indian, struggling to bring enough air into his lungs to speak. He tried to frown at Angel, to show his displeasure at her for disobeying him, but he couldn't find the energy. The Indian had been incredibly strong in his determination to have Angel. He straightened finally and opened his arms to receive Angel as she rushed into them.

"Rafe! Oh, Rafe, I thought . . . I feared . . . thank God you're all right."

He hugged her close. "I told you to stay at the campsite," he said with a gruffness that belied his relief at finding her safe. He spied his gun dangling from her fingers and stifled a groan. "I hope you didn't for one second consider firing that."

She buried her face in his neck. "I only wanted to help," came her muffled reply.

"Have you ever fired a gun in the dark?"

"Well, no, but I know how to shoot."

He raised his eyes heavenward. "Then I have a lot to be grateful for. Come on, let's find your clothing and get the hell out of here. His friends may come looking for him."

"Is he dead? I was so frightened. I couldn't see who held the knife."

"He's dead," Rafe intoned dryly.

He wasn't going to tell Angel just how close the outcome had been. He could feel the blood from his wound dampening his shirt collar. The shallow cut that slashed downward from the corner of his right eye to his earlobe wasn't life-threatening but it was bleeding profusely. He was grateful Angel hadn't seen it, for he knew she would make too much of it.

Angela sat on a rock and pulled on her

boots while Rafe gathered her clothing. Then they started back to the campsite. They had gone but a short distance when Rafe noticed that Angela was limping.

"Did you hurt yourself?" She shook her head. "Why are you limping?"

"I . . . it's nothing."

Suddenly it dawned on Rafe that Angel had walked to the campsite and back again in her bare feet. She could have hurt herself badly. Without giving her a chance to protest, he swept her off her feet and into his arms.

"Wh . . . what are you doing?" Angela sputtered.

"How badly are you injured? Your poor feet must have taken a terrible beating."

"I'm fine. You're the one who battled an Indian to the death." She touched his face. Her fingers came away wet. She stared at her hand, then let out a cry of dismay. "You're hurt!"

"It's nothing. There's salve in my saddle-bags. I'll rub some on the soles of your feet before we leave. It's too dangerous to remain here now. The Indian's friends will have missed him by now and come looking for him. When they find him dead, they'll come for us."

"What about your face?"

"It's fine. The bleeding has almost stopped."

They reached the campsite; Rafe set Angela

251

on a tree stump. "Stay put while I get the salve."

He returned moments later, pulled off her boots and carefully spread the soothing mixture on the soles of her feet. When he finished, he said, "I'll put out the fire and pack up our things."

"I can help."

He sounded almost angry as he proceeded to stomp out the remaining embers of the fire. "I'll do it. When are you going to learn to obey orders?"

"When you learn to stop giving them," Angel shot back.

In deliberate defiance of his orders, she hobbled over to her saddlebags and began stuffing her soiled clothing in one of the pockets. Rafe merely gritted his teeth and said nothing as he quickly saddled the horses.

He should have known his Angel wouldn't listen to him. Returning to the riverbank when he'd told her to remain at the campsite could have been disastrous for her. Had the Indian seen her, he might have used her as a shield and dragged her away. If that had happened, Rafe couldn't have done a damn thing about it. Just thinking about the danger in which Angel had placed herself gave him the shivers.

In no time at all Rafe had finished the chores and was ready to leave. He helped

Angela to mount, then handed her the reins. "I don't suppose you're anxious to leave my company with Indians lurking nearby," he said as he leaped into his saddle. "I'll lead the way."

"Where are we going?"

"As far away from here as we can get. We'll probably have to travel all night to lose them. It will slow us up some, but it's a helluva lot healthier than staying here."

They continued in a southeasterly direction until the sun rose over the plains, bathing them in brilliant shards of light. Rafe knew Angel had to be exhausted, for he was all but done in himself. He glanced back at Angel and saw her totter sideways in the saddle. Holding his horse back until she drew up to him, he reached out and swung her before him in his saddle. He smiled when she sighed and snuggled against him. Nothing in his life had ever felt so right. Then he grasped her horse's reins and plodded onward.

A short time later Rafe spied an unusual rock formation that looked as if it might provide the protection he sought. The place appeared to be a garden of rocks, all leaning haphazardly against one another.

He guided the horses deep within the bowels of the towering stones, satisfied with his choice when he realized how secluded it was. There was a small trickle of water seeping from between two rocks, and Rafe decided it was all they needed since both their canteens were full.

Holding Angela upright in the saddle, he carefully dismounted. Then he placed her on the ground while he spread out their bedrolls. He'd thought they should eat first, but Angel was so soundly asleep he decided food could wait. Rest was more important.

He placed Angela carefully atop her bedroll, pulled off her boots and inspected her feet. His expression turned grim when he saw the torn and bruised flesh. He retrieved the salve from his saddlebags and spread another layer over the injured area. Then he covered her with a blanket and lay down beside her. His arms curled around her and he pulled her into the curve of his body.

The sun was sinking below the distant mountains when Angela awakened hours later. She sat up and glanced around, having no idea where she was or how she had gotten there. She stretched and was immediately sorry. Every bone in her body ached. She searched her brain for answers, but the last thing she remembered was following behind Rafe for what seemed like an eternity. She remembered darkness, then light, and after that she recalled little else. Her stomach gave a loud rumble and she realized she was famished.

Glancing at Rafe, she saw that he was still sleeping soundly. He was turned away from her, only the left side of his face visible. His brow was smooth, as if he hadn't a care in the world, and the dark lashes that lay against his cheek were indecently long and lush. Abruptly he turned, exposing the right side of his face. A startled cry burst from her throat when she saw the bloody streak angling downward from the corner of his eye to his earlobe.

The sound must have startled Rafe awake, for he leaped to his feet and reached for his gun. "What is it? Have the Indians discovered our hiding place?"

"Your face! What did he do to you?"

"Oh, that," Rafe said, shrugging. "It's nothing serious."

"You'll have that scar for life. Let me take care of it for you."

"Don't fuss, Angel. I can handle it. Right now there are more important things to take care of. My stomach is touching my backbone. I'll fix us something to eat."

"Where are we?"

"Hidden within a formation of rocks. It was the best I could do under the circumstances. You couldn't have ridden much farther. Sit still while I get us something to eat. It will have to be trail food; I don't think a fire is safe yet."

"Let me help," Angela said, rising. She

soon learned that attempting to stand was a big mistake. The soles of her feet were too tender to bear her weight. She gave a pained groan and fell back onto her rump.

"I told you to sit still," Rafe said, clearly exasperated. "One day you'll learn to do as I say."

"I doubt that," Angela sniffed. "Wet a cloth and bring it here so I can clean the blood from your face. I refuse to eat until I see to your injury."

Rafe glared at her a moment, then shrugged. "Very well."

He found a washcloth in his saddlebags and saturated it with water from his canteen. Then he handed it to Angela and sat down beside her. "Do your worst, woman."

Angela carefully dabbed at the cut, washing away blood and dirt. When she finished, she leaned back and studied her handiwork. Though the cut wasn't deep, it would definitely leave a scar, Angela thought. But rather than detract from his handsome features, it added a sense of mystery to his rugged appeal.

"Do you have something I can put on it to aid the healing?" she asked.

"How about some of the same salve I put on your feet?" Rafe asked. Angela nodded. "I'll get it," he said, rising.

"I should put a stitch or two in it before I apply the salve," Angela said when Rafe returned.

He reared back, feigning shock. "I don't want you anywhere near me with a needle, lady. I'll learn to live with the scar."

"It's not all that unattractive," Angela ventured.

Rafe gave a snort of laughter. "If you're trying to beguile me, it's not going to work. I'm damn angry at you for disobeying me. In the first place, you ventured too far from our campsite for your bath. You're lucky I came looking for you when I did."

"I wanted privacy," Angela said defensively. "I had no idea there were Indians in the area."

Rafe sent her a mocking grin. "Privacy? I've seen everything you have to offer, Angel."

He touched her cheek. Angel sucked in a shaky sigh as his fingers wandered downward along the side of her face. They grazed her neck; he stared into her eyes and cupped her breast. Watching her expression, he gently kneaded the firm mound, smiling to himself when her eyes closed and a soft moan tumbled from her lips. She wasn't as immune to him as she pretended.

God, he wanted her. It had been too damn long since he'd experienced the sweet thrill of loving his Angel. Bending close, he kissed her closed eyes and soft, trembling lips, drawing on them until he elicited another sigh from her.

"Let me love you, Angel."

She glanced up at him, her expression troubled. His face was tense, his silver eyes a translucent window to the hunger and longing behind them. Mesmerized by his steady gaze, she felt powerless to resist.

His breathing sounded ragged. Her own breathing was just as frazzled and she tried unsuccessfully to bring it under control. She was aware that he was leaning closer, so close she could feel the heat radiating from his body.

Though she knew she might regret it later, she had no will where Rafe was concerned. No protest was forthcoming when he lowered her to the bedroll and leaned over her. She breathed deeply, savoring his musky scent as their breaths mingled. His hands found her breasts; his mouth covered hers. With a breathy little moan she arched shamelessly into the hot, wet suction of his kiss. She eagerly accepted his tongue, relishing his taste as he boldly explored her mouth.

"I want you naked," Rafe whispered against her lips.

He undressed her quickly, tearing her shift in his haste to remove every stitch of her clothing. She squirmed impatiently as he sat back on his haunches and stared at her.

"Your body is perfection," he murmured. "There's nothing about you I don't admire. Someday I hope to hear your lovely voice raised in song as you rock our babes to sleep."

Angel went still. Did Rafe realize what he'd just said? "Are you saying you want us to stay married? To live together as husband and wife? How are you going to arrange that with the law after you?"

"I'll find a way. Help me," he whispered raggedly, fumbling with the fastenings on his shirt.

Moments later he was as naked as she. Angela's gaze slid over him with appreciation. His broad shoulders and massive chest blocked out the sun. His hips were lean, his legs long and sleekly muscled. Her eyes dropped to his sex. It was distended and rigid, the tip throbbing.

Rafe noted the direction of her gaze and smiled. "Touch me."

A tentative fingertip trailed slowly from the engorged crown clear to the root of him, then back along the ridged underside. He groaned, thrusting his hips forward, as if begging for more. Angela complied, encircling him with her fingers, holding him firmly within her palm.

He gritted his teeth against the jolt of raw pleasure that surged through him. His breath came harsh and labored. There was a primitive pounding in his head. His blood boiled in his veins. Desire churned through him. His shaft swelled, thickened, grew harder and fuller. Battered by furious need, he pumped his hips, moving faster and faster within her hand, until he was forced to exert his willpower or end this too soon.

"Enough," he growled, removing her hand from his rigid member. "I want this to last as long as possible."

Leaning forward, he took a puckered nipple into his mouth and suckled her. Moving from breast to breast, he sucked, nipped and laved, until Angela was drowning in a turbulent sea of pleasure/pain. His knuckles brushed the hollow of her belly. His fingers grazed the silken fleece between her thighs, tracing her moist cleft.

Flailing her head from side to side, Angela stifled a cry when his bold fingers explored deep inside her. She was trembling from head to toe; molten fire spread along her nerve endings. When he bent his head and touched the taut little bud at the entrance of her sex with the tip of his tongue, mind-numbing pleasure shot through her.

"Rafe! Please. Come inside me. Now."

Ignoring her, he explored her thoroughly, his tongue playing havoc with her senses. Just when Angela thought she would shatter from the pressure building inside her, he parted her wide with his knees and nudged her entrance with the velvet tip of his shaft. His hands slid beneath her buttocks, lifting her high. Then he thrust deep. She felt the scalding length of him clear to the gates of her womb.

A cry ripped from her throat and she clutched at his shoulders, her nails biting deep into his skin. She rose up eagerly to meet the wild pounding of his hips. Sweat dripped from his forehead onto hers, but she didn't notice. Nothing mattered but the desperate need to reach that distant pinnacle. Then abruptly she was there, drenched in profound bliss as she exploded around him.

Rafe heard Angel's cry, felt her contract around him, and his blood surged thick and molten. The feel of her sheath tightening around his engorged shaft destroyed what little control he had left. Bowing to the frenzied demands of his body, he plunged inside her silken heat, imbedding himself deep, his passion soaring, inciting him toward a rapturous release. He felt her pulsating around him as he gave up his seed.

Rafe waited until his heartbeat settled to a steady roar before he pulled out and rolled to his side. His eyes closed and he drifted off.

Eons later, or it could have been only moments, Rafe felt something brush against his face. Startled awake, he opened his eyes, smiling when he saw Angel leaning over him, her fingers gently tracing his scar. A jolt of tenderness passed through him when she placed a gentle kiss where her fingers had been.

"It's my fault you were wounded, Rafe. You were right. I shouldn't have strayed so far from camp."

"Forget it, love. At least I no longer have to worry that you'll bolt. I doubt you'll try to return to the Golden Angel, now that you realize the danger involved."

"I suppose you're right," Angela agreed sweetly. Too sweetly for Rafe's peace of mind.

Rafe searched her face. "I don't like that look, Angel. What are you planning?"

"I know better than to return on my own, but you can't stop me from trying to convince you to take me back. We're not so far away that turning back is no longer an option. Anson could steal me blind during my absence. He might even construe my disappearance as license to take over the mine in my stepfather's name."

A predatory gleam lit the centers of Rafe's silver eyes. "Hmmm, you've got me curious. I'm sure I'll enjoy your brand of persuasion if it requires more of what we just shared." He pulled her down on top of him. "Go ahead, sweetheart, do your worst. I can hardly wait."

Chapter Thirteen

Rafe and Angela approached Pueblo the following morning just as the stores were opening for the day. Angela felt wonderfully alive after a night of nearly nonstop lovemaking. She and Rafe had made love, then napped briefly, only to awaken and turn to one another again in the night, until darkness gave way to a glorious dawn.

"I thought you wanted to avoid towns," Angela said when Rafe turned down the main thoroughfare.

He reined in, waited for her to come abreast of him, then plucked his hat from her head and settled it on his own. "You need a hat. I'll wait outside the general store while you go inside and purchase something to your liking. Buy a sack of coffee — we're almost out — and anything else you think we might need. I'd like this to be the last town we visit until Dodge City."

Angela glanced furtively down the street. Vendors and early shoppers were just beginning to stir. "What if you're recognized?"

He pulled the hat down low over his forehead. "I'll be careful." He started forward and Angela plodded after him. They reined in at the general store.

"There's money in your saddlebags," Rafe said as Angela dismounted.

Angela found the money, peeled off a few bills and put the rest back. "I won't be long."

She tied her horse to the hitching post and started toward the store. She hadn't gone five steps when she stopped abruptly, her eyes focused on one of the Wanted posters placed prominently on a post outside the store. Blood rushed to her head, and her heart pounded erratically. She glanced over her shoulder to see if Rafe had seen the poster bearing the pictures of the Gentry brothers.

"I see it," Rafe said quietly. "Pretend the poster doesn't mean anything to you and go about your business."

Angela nodded jerkily and walked into the store without a backward glance.

Rafe's eyes narrowed as he studied the poster bearing a rather bad likeness of him and his brothers. Rafe wondered why there wasn't another poster beside it, charging Rafe Gentry with the murder of five people.

Pulling the brim of his hat down lower, he turned his head away from passersby. He thought it highly unlikely that he would be recognized, but he wasn't taking any chances.

He breathed a sigh of relief when Angela came out of the store wearing a tan hat atop her blond hair and carrying a cloth sack filled with supplies. Rafe dismounted, took the sack from her and fastened it to his saddle horn. He didn't relax until the town was behind them.

Each night after that, Rafe selected secluded spots for them to camp. Though he kept a sharp eye out for Indians, Rafe saw nothing to indicate their presence in the area through which they traveled. Whenever they were fortunate enough to camp beside water, they soaked away trail dust and grime. On most nights they shared a bedroll. If they were too tired to make love, Rafe just held Angela close, wondering how long fate would give them before snatching away his happiness.

Rafe couldn't begin to describe the kind of contentment he'd found with Angel. Nothing about their meeting had been conventional. She had saved his skin and ended up married to him, something neither of them had really wanted. But now felt bound to her by an emotional bond that cut deep into his soul.

One night they camped on the banks of the Arkansas River, giving Ordway a wide birth. Rafe said they might rest the next day, so Angela took advantage of the leisure time to wash their dirty clothes and string them over bushes to dry. Then she stripped, washed the clothing she was wearing and immersed herself in the cool water.

Rafe joined her a short time later, having caught and spitted a pair of rabbits for their supper. He shed his clothes and waded in, splashing water over his wide shoulders as he made his way unerringly to Angel's side.

"There will be more than beans and bacon tonight for supper," Rafe said, smiling. "I set two rabbits beside the fire to cook."

"My mouth is watering already," Angela returned.

Her mouth *was* watering but it was due more to watching Rafe strip than from want of food. Never would she tire of looking at him. She'd seen a statue once in a museum in Topeka that didn't hold a candle to Rafe's magnificent form. There wasn't an ounce of fat anywhere on his body. The best part was that no fig leaf concealed that male part of him which was more powerfully arousing than a cold marble statue could ever be.

"What are you thinking?" Rafe asked. "You're so quiet. Not still conjuring up ways to convince me to return you to the Golden Angel, are you?"

"I suppose we've passed the point of no return now," Angela said. "I've resigned myself to seeing this through, whatever it is you're trying to prove. I just hope you don't regret it."

Rafe frowned. "Regret what? Taking you

with me or trying to prove my innocence?"

"Both," Angela said. "I'm afraid you've set yourself an impossible task. You should have disappeared while you had the chance. Gone west to California, maybe, or north to Montana. Anywhere the law couldn't touch you."

He shook his head. "I need to prove something to you."

"But at what cost? Honestly, Rafe, sometimes you can be so stubborn it boggles my mind."

She dipped her head beneath the water and began working soap into her long tresses.

"Let me do that," Rafe said, shoving her hands aside.

A moan slipped past Angela's lips when Rafe, having finished washing and rinsing her hair, turned his attention to her body. He soaped her upper torso first, then dipped down below the water to run the soap over her limbs and private parts. When she felt his hands sliding up the inside of her leg, she moved restlessly.

"Rafe! Behave yourself."

He gave her a wicked grin, not in the least apologetic. "How can I behave with an alluring temptress seducing me?"

"You're insatiable. For your information, I'm not trying to seduce you. Turn around so I can wash your back."

Rafe handed her the soap and dutifully

turned around. After she scrubbed his back, she moved around to his front and soaped his chest. Her hands wanted to stray downward, but she knew where that would lead, so she handed him the soap and told him to finish bathing himself. He looked so disappointed she wanted to laugh.

"Don't leave yet," Rafe said when she started to wade back to shore.

"Shouldn't the rabbits be turned? They might burn."

His voice was rough with need, his silver eyes glazed. "The hell with the rabbit. I'm the one burning."

She gave him an exasperated look. "Rafe, this isn't the right time to —"

"I disagree, Angel. This is exactly the right time. It hasn't been easy just holding you while you slept, but I knew you were exhausted. I realize this constant riding hasn't been easy on you. That's why I decided we should rest a day before going on. After I make love to you tonight, you can sleep the entire day through tomorrow."

She threw him a saucy glance over her shoulder and continued toward shore. He shook himself, sending great droplets of water in all directions, then took off after her. Soon it became a lighthearted romp, something badly needed by both of them to relieve the tension they'd been under since leaving the Golden Angel. He caught her by

268

the ankle before she could scramble up the riverbank and pulled her back into the water. She went under, and came up sputtering when he lifted her from the water by the shoulders.

"Rafe Gentry, are you trying to drown me?"

"Drowning you isn't what I have in mind, sweetheart."

As if to prove where his mind dwelt, he scooped her into his arms and carried her to their bedroll. Then he knelt beside her, lowered his head and licked the droplets of water that had gathered between her breasts. When the rough pad of his tongue lapped at her erect nipples, she moaned and clasped his head between her palms, holding it in place against her swollen breasts.

"Rafe! This is madness," she gasped, arching into his mouth. "Every time we make love it increases our chances of making a baby."

He lifted his head and stared at her. "Would that be so bad? You're my wife."

"This isn't a good time. Children need a full-time father."

Rafe's eyes narrowed as he leaned back on his haunches. "You could already be carrying my child."

"Don't say that!"

It wasn't the thought of having Rafe's baby that upset Angela; it was the uncertainly of

Rafe's future, of their future.

"I'm sorry the thought of having my child disturbs you," Rafe bit out.

"That's not what I meant and you know it," Angela protested. "Neither of us knows what tomorrow will bring."

"That's why we should live for today."

"And if there is a child?"

"I hope to be around to help raise it." His silver eyes grew opaque. "But if I'm not, I know you'll be the best mother a child can have. The mine will give you all the security you need."

Angela scooted onto her knees, her eyes fiercely challenging. "Damn you, Rafe Gentry! Do you think I care about security? Those aren't the words I want to hear from you."

Rafe's jaw jutted out pugnaciously. "What do you want me to say? That I need you? Very well. I need you. Are you satisfied?"

"Tell me more," Angela whispered.

"You're my guardian angel. When we met, marriage was the last thing I wanted from you. I should have listened to my conscience before you snared me in your tender web. I should have walked away and never looked back. I'm not good enough for you, Angel."

Angela felt tears gathering at the corners of her eyes and dashed them away with the back of her hand. Rafe needed her; he didn't love her. That wasn't what she wanted to hear. His words had sounded almost desperate, as if love were something that would complicate his life.

"Did you abduct me from my bed simply because you needed me? Is that all you've got to say?"

His hands clenched into fists at his sides. "I . . . I can't explain it. I couldn't stand the thought of Chandler having you. You belong to me, Angel, whether or not I deserve you. Leaving you unprotected wasn't an option after I saw you kissing Chandler. That scheming bastard doesn't want you; he's after your money."

Angela lurched to her feet. "Don't you think I know that?" She glared at him. "Do you want to know how I feel about you?"

Rafe's expression grew glum. "I already know. You married me because you're an angel, a woman who hadn't the heart to let a man hang. You never meant for our marriage to be permanent. I'm the one who stuck around when I should have left you. You deserve a better life. One without me."

Angela gave an exasperated snort. "How typical of a man. If you believe that, you're dumber than I thought. I wanted to prove Chandler had something to do with Baxter's murder. He could be the killer, but you saw fit to remove me from my home, thus curtailing my investigation. How do you expect to clear your name without my help? Surely you know by now that I'm . . . fond of you."

His eyes glinted pure silver in the waning light. His stance broadened, his arms wound around her, crushing her to him, bringing her into the vee of his widespread thighs. He wanted to absorb her, to feel her melt beneath him, to feel her softness accommodate his hardness. He needed to hear her say she loved him even though he didn't have the right yet to unburden his heart. He was an outlaw, wanted for multiple crimes.

"Just fond? If I were an optimist, I'd read more into those words."

His head lowered and his mouth covered hers. His tongue swept between her lips, caressing hers in a deep, carnal stroke. He kissed her until she was breathless, until her knees buckled and she was his to do with as he pleased. He seemed to recognize the moment of her capitulation, for he lowered her to the bedroll and followed her down.

"Just how fond of me are you, Angel?" he growled against her lips. "I know you enjoy making love with me. Dare I hope for more?"

"The truth, Rafe Gentry, is that you're an insufferable, overbearing despot who doesn't deserve an answer. You should know without being told how I feel about you. I wouldn't allow these intimacies with a man if I felt anything less than love. Right from the first I felt an affinity to you. I looked into your eyes and knew you weren't capable of murder."

"Yet you thought I'd killed Baxter," he charged.

She bit her lip. "That was my first reaction. After I had time to think about it, I knew I'd wronged you. That's why I was so eager to prove you innocent of Baxter's murder. I love you, Rafe. I don't know if we'll ever find happiness together, but you deserve to know."

Incredible joy surged through Rafe. Until he realized how utterly futile it all was. "Oh, God, Angel, I'm so sorry our lives are in such a mess. You'd be better off if we had never met. I already had two strikes against me that day you saved my life. Being accused of Baxter's death only muddied the waters further. I want to clear my name. Returning to Dodge City is the first step in proving to you I'm not an outlaw."

She took his face between her hands and brought his mouth to hers. Her kiss was gentle, forgiving, soothing.

"You don't have to prove anything to me, Rafe Gentry. I believe you. One day you'll prove to the world that you're a decent man."

They sank to the bedroll in mutual accord. He covered her lips; her mouth opened to his hungry tongue. She sighed, her head fell back, her throat arched. With a hoarse groan he kissed the slender column, licked the salty sheen from the tender spot at its base. She moved against him, as if to ease the tingling of her flesh as his fingers sought the wet heat between her thighs. He probed the slick petals of her sex, spreading her, easing his erection inside, nearly mad with the need to possess her fully.

Angel. His Angel. She loved him. God help her. God help them both.

He entered her slowly. She smiled at him, a knowing, womanly smile, opening herself wide to receive him. She rocked against him, holding him tightly in the cradle of her slender arms and legs, squeezing him snugly inside her. But it was not enough for Rafe.

Reversing their positions, he brought her on top of him, letting her set the pace as he feasted on her breasts.

Moving together in fierce possession, they strove for fulfillment, breaths mingling, voices raised in exultation. The hunger they felt for one another was nurtured and sustained by their searching mouths, and when the ultimate pleasure surged over them, Rafe buried himself deep within her, spilling himself inside her as her fingers dug into his shoulders. Tremors rippled through him into her, and she came with a loud cry, her body stretched taut, her head thrown back, neck arched, eyes tightly closed.

Overpowering emotions burned behind Rafe's eyes and deep within his heart as he held his Angel tightly within the circle of his arms. He knew intuitively that he would do whatever it took, go to any lengths, to clear his name and give Angel the kind of life she deserved.

They rested the following day, stirring themselves only to eat, make love, bathe and make love again. After their evening meal, Angel folded up their clean clothing and packed their saddlebags. They left their private Eden early on the second morning.

Unwilling to risk being identified in Ordway, they gave the city a wide berth and continued into Kansas. When they rode through a small settlement, Rafe was pleased to note that no Wanted posters bearing his likeness were prominently displayed. In fact, the town lacked a sheriff or lawmen of any kind. What it did have was a rather crude hotel.

"What do you say?" Rafe asked, giving the hotel a once-over. "Shall we spend the night in a real bed and eat a decent meal in a restaurant?"

"All I see is a Mexican cantina," Angela noted.

"Some pretty good food can be had in cantinas," Rafe said. "I'm willing to give it a try if you are."

"A bed does sound good. A bath in warm water sounds even better. Are you sure it's safe?"

"I seriously doubt that anyone in this town has ever seen a Wanted poster," Rafe assured her. "It may be our last chance for a bed until we reach Dodge City."

Rafe checked them into the Siesta Hotel and they were given the key to a room on the ground floor. Apparently they were the only guests, for the sleepy-eyed clerk seemed rather startled when Rafe asked if he had a vacant room.

"They're all vacant, mister," he said. "Take your pick."

"You don't have many visitors passing through, do you?" Rafe observed.

"Not many. Sometimes a few drovers on their way back from a trail drive will stop in, but this is the wrong time of year."

"We'd like a tub and hot water," Rafe said.

"That costs extra, mister, in advance. So does the stable out back for your horses."

"I'll take the horses around back and bring in the saddlebags," Rafe told Angela as he dug in his pocket for money to pay their tab. Before they'd entered the hotel, he'd taken some of the cash from Angel's saddlebags and stuffed it into his vest pocket. "Wait here for me."

Rafe returned a few minutes later with their saddlebags and guided Angel down the dim hallway to their room. Though the room was sparsely furnished, the sheets and counterpane appeared clean, as did the curtains flapping in the breeze at the open window. Rafe gazed longingly at the bed, dropped the saddlebags and flopped down on the quilted counterpane with an exaggerated sigh. He grinned and held his hand out to Angela.

Further persuasion wasn't necessary. Angela joined him, but when he turned and reached for her, she pushed him away.

"No, not yet. Baths first, then dinner."

"You drive a hard bargain, Mrs. Gentry," Rafe growled. "Very well, we'll do it your way, but I intend to put this bed to good use tonight."

The meal they purchased at the cantina after they each had bathed in a huge wooden tub was surprisingly good. The only discordant note to the evening came when a rough-looking character dressed in buckskins kept staring at Rafe. He wore a week's growth of beard, and his hair looked as if it hadn't seen a comb in days. Angela must have noticed too, for she insisted they leave before Rafe finished his coffee.

"I don't like the way that man looked at you," Angela said once they were back inside their room.

"He was looking at *you*," Rafe teased, trying to put her mind at ease. He'd noticed the man himself and hoped he wasn't a bounty hunter. That was all they needed now.

Rafe sauntered over and locked the door.

"I'm ready to make use of that bed now."

Rafe loved Angel with a fierceness that surprised even himself. The uncertainty of their future produced an urgency in him that drove everything from his mind but the woman clinging to him in sweet surrender. His worries melted away when he heard Angel cry out and felt her body convulse around him. Giving his own passion free rein, he spilled himself inside her. Blissful moments passed as the last dregs of passion flowed from him into her.

Hugging Angel close against him, Rafe finally succumbed to the concern that had plagued him since spotting the stranger in the cantina. He sensed danger. Even now he felt it closing in on him. He must have been loco to think he could single-handedly clear himself and his brothers of bank robbery charges. He was beginning to think that bringing Angel with him was a mistake, too, that he was endangering her life instead of protecting it.

The longer Rafe thought about the stranger in the cantina, the more certain he became that the man had recognized him. He glanced at Angel. She was sleeping soundly. Carefully he extracted himself from her arms, rose and dressed. He was the kind of man who faced danger head on once he identified it.

The hotel lobby was deserted when Rafe

walked past the desk and out the door. He headed for the cantina, expecting to find the stranger sitting at a table with a bottle of tequila before him. But he wasn't there now. Rafe was a realist; he knew the man wouldn't leave town if he had recognized Rafe.

He turned away from the cantina and retraced his steps to the hotel. Maybe he'd been wrong all along. Maybe the man *had* been staring at Angel. And maybe pigs fly, Rafe thought, disgruntled. He recognized a bounty hunter when he saw one.

"Rafe Gentry?"

Rafe went for his weapon, but the gun barrel pressing against his back was a powerful deterrent.

"That would be a mistake, mister," the disembodied voice behind him growled. "Keep your hands where I can see them."

Rafe cursed the full moon that made him a clear target. "Who are you?"

"Name's Clyde Dudley."

Rafe stifled a groan. He knew Dudley, not personally but by reputation. He was a bounty hunter, and a damned good one. He'd heard that Dudley brought in more men than all the other bounty hunters combined.

"What do you want?" Rafe asked, though he already knew the answer.

"I've been waiting for you. I knew you recognized me back there in the cantina, just

279

as I recognized you."

Cautiously Dudley moved around until he was facing Rafe, his gun in one hand and a crumpled sheet of paper in the other. He handed the paper to Rafe. Rafe smoothed it out and saw his face and those of his brothers staring back at him.

"I'm not guilty," Rafe said. "Neither are my brothers. We were falsely accused."

"Sure you were," Dudley said with a smirk. "I've been looking for you and your brothers for a long time. It would be quite a coup to bring in all three Gentrys."

Rafe blanched. "You haven't . . . My brothers . . ."

"They're still at large. Haven't been able to track them down. Heard you were wanted over in Colorado for another crime, so thought I'd head this way. I can't believe I found you in a dump like this. Who's the whore with you?"

Rafe stiffened at the insult. "Leave her out of this," he bit out.

"Her name," Dudley persisted. "Is she wanted?"

"Angela is my wife. She's as innocent as the day is long."

Dudley gave a snort of laughter. "Not if she married you, she isn't. Where's your horse?"

"Stabled behind the hotel. Why?"

"The closest sheriff is in Garden City. I'll

turn you in there and collect a tidy little reward for your capture."

Carefully Dudley removed Rafe's guns from his holster and stuck them in his own belt. "Don't try anything funny. The reward says dead or alive."

Angela awoke with a start, aware that Rafe was no longer sleeping beside her. Panic surged through her. Call it intuition, call it the special bond linking her to Rafe, Angela knew Rafe was in trouble. She rose quickly and dressed. She was halfway out the door before deciding she might need a weapon. She spied Rafe's rifle propped beside his saddlebags and went back for it.

No one was stirring in the lobby as she slipped out the door. She heard voices and flattened herself against the building. Hidden from view by deep shadows, she held her breath as two men walked past her. One of them was Rafe.

The man walking behind Rafe was holding a gun on him!

Angela froze, stifling the scream gathering in the back of her throat. Why had Rafe left their bed? Who was the stranger holding a gun on Rafe? Where were they going?

"I need my saddlebags," she heard Rafe saying.

"Where you're going you won't need a damn thing," the man answered. "I'm good at what I do, Gentry; you'll not escape me."

"I need to tell my wife what happened," Rafe insisted.

"She'll figure it out."

Angela had indeed figured it out. The man with Rafe was the same man they'd seen in the cantina. She'd heard about men like him. They were bounty hunters, men who dealt in human flesh. A shudder raced through her. She glanced at the rifle in her hands and visibly paled. She knew how to aim and fire but wasn't certain she could shoot a man. But there were other things she could do with the weapon, she decided as she hefted it in her hands to test its weight.

She watched, hardly daring to breathe as Rafe and his captor turned the corner, heading for the stables behind the hotel. She followed close behind, hugging the shadows. When both men disappeared into the dark building, she scampered across the open space and crouched behind a bale of hay inside the stables.

A lamp flared. "Saddle up," she heard the bounty hunter order.

She held her breath and watched as Rafe turned around. She prayed he wouldn't do anything foolish until she'd found a way to help him.

"I'm not going anywhere until I speak with my wife," Rafe insisted, crossing his arms over his chest.

Dudley shrugged. "I'd just as soon take you dead as alive. Less trouble. Don't have to feed a dead man. Now, for the last time, you ain't gonna talk to anyone."

He grabbed a rope from his saddle horn and said, "If you're gonna be obstinate about it, I can fix that. Put your hands behind you. You can ride to Garden City on your belly."

Angela heard Rafe mutter something beneath his breath as the bounty hunter shoved him around and pulled Rafe's hands behind his back. Both men were facing away from her; it was time to act. Taking a deep, steadying breath, she moved from behind the bale and took a step forward, then another, the sound muffled by the straw beneath her feet. She was within striking distance now. She stopped, muttered a brief prayer, and raised the rifle by its barrel. Closing her eyes, she swung it with all her might at the bounty hunter's head.

Rafe saw her shadow outlined against the wall, and the breath caught in his throat. He spun around, his expression frozen in a grimace of shock as he stared over Dudley's shoulder. Dudley must have realized something was amiss, for he cast a nervous glance behind him. But it was too late. The rifle smashed against his head with deadly accuracy.

Rafe heard a satisfying thud seconds before Dudley hit the ground. Then, somehow,

Angel was in his arms, clinging to him, her body quaking. He held her tight, kissing her forehead, her cheeks, the top of her head as his heartbeat slowed.

"Are you all right?" he asked, holding her at arm's length so he could look at her.

"A little shaken. What about you?"

"I'm fine." He pulled her against him again, loath to let her go.

"Who is that man?" Angela asked, glancing down at the prone form lying at her feet.

"His name is Clyde Dudley. He's a bounty hunter. One of the best. He identified me from a poster he had in his possession and intended to turn me over to the sheriff in Garden City for the reward. How did you know where to find me?"

"I awakened and found you gone. Something told me you were in trouble, so I grabbed your rifle and set out to look for you. I had just left the hotel when I heard voices and saw you with the bounty hunter." She dragged in a shuddering breath. "I waited until you turned the corner and followed. After that it was just being patient until the right moment to strike arrived."

"I owe you again for saving my skin." He sent her a lopsided grin. "You've got guts, Mrs. Gentry, I'll give you that."

She returned his smile. "What are we going to do with him? He isn't dead, is he?"

"He's still breathing," Rafe said, noting the

steady rise and fall of his chest. "Hand me that rope hanging on the wall and I'll tie him up. Then we're going to get the hell out of here. I want to be far away from here before he comes around. Dodge City is the last place he'd think to look for us, so I don't think we'll be bothered by him again."

"Do you still want to go to Dodge City?" Angela whispered.

Rafe's face hardened to match his resolve. "I've never been more sure of anything."

Chapter Fourteen

They reached Dodge City without mishap.
Rafe reined in at the outskirts of town. Not
for the first time he questioned his own
sanity. Returning to Dodge City, where he
would be recognized on sight, had to be one
of the worst ideas he'd ever concocted.

He'd thought he had it all figured out. He
would simply confront Mr. Wingate and
wrest the truth about the robbery from him.
Recanting his original story wouldn't be easy
for the pompous banker, but determination
drove Rafe. He had too much at stake to fail.

Rafe saw Angel staring at him with a puz-
zled look on her face, and he mustered a
heartening smile. "Maybe you should wait
here for me."

Angela gave a vigorous shake of her head.
"No. You might need me."

"You know what I'm up against, sweetheart. I'm apt to be tossed in jail the minute
I'm recognized."

"Will you speak to the banker first?"

"That's my intention. I hope I can persuade him to recant his story about the bank robbery before I'm recognized."

"Aren't there any townspeople willing to attest to your character?"

Rafe gave a derisive snort. "Hardly. My brothers and I fought on the losing side during the war. When we returned, we were outcasts among the good citizens of Dodge City. Kansas supported the Union, Angel. Our entire family fought for the South. Jess hung up his shingle to practice medicine, but no patients showed up."

"The war was over a long time ago, Rafe," Angela reminded him.

"For some people it never ends. I wouldn't be surprised to find it's still an issue a hundred years from now."

"Let's turn around before it's too late," Angel urged with growing panic.

"I've come too far to back down."

"Then I'm going with you."

In the daylight the notorious cow town displayed little of the wild reputation it had earned. The rutted streets were no different from those in any other frontier city Rafe had passed through. The stores and houses basking in the noonday sun seemed peaceful enough, but Rafe knew what Dodge City was like once the sun went down and the saloons and streets teemed with cowboys and buffalo hunters vying for space with every kind of criminal known to mankind. Sometimes the violence spilled into the daytime hours, but today everything appeared peaceful.

Rafe rode down the main street and reined in before the town's only bank. "Wait for me," he told Angela. "If you see anything unusual happening, hightail it out of town."

"Unusual like what?" Angela asked.

"You'll know when you see it," Rafe said grimly. He dismounted and handed his reins to Angela. "Wish me luck."

"Good luck, and be careful," Angela called after him.

Luck definitely was *not* with Rafe. He opened the door of the bank and ran headlong into Sheriff Diller. Rafe tucked his chin down and tried to sidle past him, but it was not to be.

"Well, I'll be damned," Diller blustered, clearly stunned. "Look who's come back to the scene of his crime."

He drew his gun and casually pointed it at Rafe. "Looking for more easy pickings, Gentry? It's not gonna work this time. You're gonna be cooling your heels in jail until the circuit judge comes through again."

"You got me wrong, Sheriff," Rafe tried to explain. "I came back to Dodge to clear my name. If I could just speak to Mr. Wingate, I'm sure he will clear up this misunderstanding."

Diller removed Rafe's gun belt and slung it over his shoulder. "You'll have your day in court, Gentry. Did you bring your brothers with you?"

"I came alone," Rafe said, deliberately failing to mention Angela.

"Move along," Diller said, prodding him into the street.

Angela didn't want to believe what had just taken place at the bank's entrance. What rotten luck! She had to do something, but what? She caught the warning in Rafe's eyes as he passed by and debated for all of five seconds whether she should heed it. Caution fled as she quickly dismounted and rushed after Rafe and the sheriff.

"Sheriff, stop! Rafe isn't an outlaw. He returned to Dodge to prove his innocence."

She heard Rafe groan.

"And who might you be, little lady?" Diller asked.

"I'm Angela, Rafe's wife. Rafe never robbed the bank. It was all a misunderstanding."

"That's not what Mr. Wingate says. Don't know how Gentry hoodwinked a pretty little thing like you into marrying him, him being an outlaw and all. He may have lied to you about his violent past, but he can't fool the law. Move aside, Mrs. Gentry, I'm taking your husband to jail."

"Am I allowed to visit him?"

"Dammit, Angel, there's nothing you can do," Rafe chided. "I should have left you back at the Golden Angel."

"Don't see why you can't visit the prisoner," Diller said. "Come to the jailhouse later, Mrs. Gentry."

"Is there a hotel in town?" Angela asked.

He sent her an assessing look. "The Dodge House is the best, if you can afford it."

Angela gave him a curt nod. "Thank you."

"I'm sorry," Rafe mouthed to Angela as the sheriff led him off.

Angela was sorry, too. Sorry she hadn't been able to turn Rafe away from this folly. Only an innocent man would think he could clear his name by confronting his accuser and shaming him into telling the truth.

Rafe might be helpless, but she wasn't. Squaring her slender shoulders, Angela knew exactly what she had to do. It wasn't going to be easy, but she had justice on her side. And love. She loved Rafe too much to see him end his life behind bars.

Angela engaged a room at the Dodge House, had a bath and changed into clean clothing. Then she ordered a meal and ate it in her room. Fortified by the food and fresh clothing, she left the hotel and headed over to the jailhouse.

She spied Rafe the moment she walked through the door. He occupied a cell at the far end of the room. His head was resting in his hands, as if he were too weary to lift it.

"I've come to see my husband," Angela

said, prepared to do battle if her request was denied. From the corner of her eye she saw Rafe's head lift at the sound of her voice.

Fortunately, Sheriff Diller did not deny her request. "Fifteen minutes, Mrs. Gentry; that's all I can allow."

"Very well. Can we have a few moments of privacy?"

"I'll step outside if you swear you don't have any weapons on you. But don't get any foolish ideas. I'm taking the keys with me, and the guns are locked in a cabinet."

"I carry no weapons, Sheriff," Angela said stiffly.

Jenkins shot her a warning glance, then stepped outside the door.

Angela hurried over to Rafe. His knuckles were white from gripping the bars, and his silver eyes mirrored the bleakness of his soul.

"You were right and I was wrong," he admitted gravely. "If I wasn't hell-bent on proving my innocence, I wouldn't be in this predicament now. I should have taken off for healthier climes when I had the chance."

"I understand, Rafe. No man wants his reputation ruined by false charges," Angela said. "What can I do to help you?"

"Buy a ticket on the next stage to Canon City while you still have money," Rafe advised. "Forget me. I thought I could protect you, but I can't. You should have let them hang me in Ordway."

Blue flames shot from Angela's eyes. Hands on hips, she shook her head in vigorous denial. "It's not like you to give up without a fight, Rafe Gentry."

"I don't have anything left to fight with. What an arrogant fool I was to think people would listen to me. I must have been mad to force you to accompany me. No," he corrected himself, "I was jealous. I couldn't bear the thought of Chandler having you. You're mine."

He gave her a look filled with such anguish, it nearly broke Angela's heart.

"Go home, love," he reiterated. "There's nothing left for you here, and everything waiting for you in Colorado."

"I'm not going anywhere without you, Rafe Gentry," Angela persisted.

His thoughts seemed to turn inward. "You know what puzzles me?" Angela shook her head. "The sheriff hasn't mentioned those charges stemming from the Colorado stagecoach robbery and murders. Perhaps word hasn't reached Kansas yet."

"Thank God for that," Angela said with heartfelt relief. She clasped his hand through the bars. "Don't give up, Rafe. I'll find some way to help you."

A long, weary sigh slid past Rafe's lips. "The best thing you can do for both of us is to leave. Forget about our marriage. Nothing exists to show we were ever husband and wife. Find a man who can offer you more than I."

The door opened and Sheriff Diller re-entered the room. "Time is up, Mrs. Gentry."

"I'll be back," Angela whispered. Aloud, she said, "Thank you, Sheriff. I'll return to-morrow, if I may."

Rafe watched Angel disappear through the door, wishing he knew what she had in her devious little mind. He saw no way Angel could help him, no matter how eager she was to come to his aid. This time he was on his own; all his options had suddenly dried up. Fate had dealt him a losing hand. The only good thing that had happened to him was meeting Angel.

After a restless night's sleep, Angela dressed with care for her confrontation with Rufus Wingate, the man who held Rafe's life in his hands. Now, poised in front of the bank, she straightened her newly purchased bonnet atop her head, smoothed down her skirts, and pushed through the bank's en-trance. She bypassed two clerks waiting on customers and marched directly to the door marked private and knocked.

"What is it, Stanley?" a voice called from the other side.

Angela took that as a sign to enter and pushed the door open. She stepped inside, closed the door softly behind her and waited to be acknowledged.

"What do you want, Stanley? Can't you see I'm busy?" Rufus Wingate said without looking up.

"I need to talk to you, Mr. Wingate."

Wingate's head shot up. "How did you get in here? I thought you were Stanley. Do I know you, young lady?"

"No, you don't know me. I'm sorry to barge in like this without an appointment, but my business is urgent."

"My bank doesn't lend money to women. Send your husband around and I'll see what I can do for him." Having clarified bank policy, Wingate gave Angela a nod of dismissal and went back to the ledger he'd been perusing.

"I'm not here for a loan," Angela said, refusing to be ignored. "I'd venture to say I can buy your bank and have plenty of money left over."

That bald statement caught Wingate's attention. "What did you say your name was, young lady?"

"I didn't say," Angela replied dryly. "It's Mrs. Rafe Gentry."

"Well, Mrs. Gentry, why don't you sit down and state your . . ." His words fell off. He stared at her as if she were an apparition from hell. "You did say Mrs. Rafe Gentry, didn't you?"

Angela took her time seating herself and

arranging her skirts to her satisfaction. "You heard me correctly. My business concerns my husband, Mr. Wingate."

Wingate avoided Angela's gaze. "Sheriff Diller informed me that Gentry returned to Dodge yesterday. He's in jail now, exactly where he belongs."

"Rafe told me everything that happened here that fateful day. One word from you will clear his name, Mr. Wingate. Rafe and his brothers never robbed your bank, did they?"

"The Gentry brothers are outlaws," Wingate claimed. "I'm not going to lie to the law. I have a reputation to uphold."

"What about Rafe and his brothers? Your false charges ruined their reputations, their lives. You lied to the law about them."

Wingate leaped to his feet, knocking his chair over in the process. "Now see here, Mrs. Gentry. I don't know what your husband told you, if Gentry really is your husband, but none of it is true. He and his brothers did indeed rob my bank. Leave now, before you find yourself occupying a cell with your husband."

Undaunted, Angela rose slowly and with great dignity. "I'll go, but you haven't heard the last from me."

Only after Angela left the bank did she let her dejection show. She didn't wear defeat easily. She allowed her shoulders to slump and her chin to sink before shaking herself and turning her mind to other ways to persuade Mr. Wingate to tell the truth.

Rafe paced his cell like a caged animal. Knowing Angel as he did, he feared she would get herself into trouble. Trouble seemed to follow her despite her good intentions. He was more than a little relieved when Angel visited him later that day. She nodded to the sheriff and hurried over to his cell, clutching his hands through the bars.

"Did you buy a ticket to Canon City?" Rafe asked. "When does the stage leave?"

"I'm not leaving, Rafe." She searched his face, then let her gaze drift down his body. "Are they feeding you?"

"I'm being fed," Rafe assured her. "The food is tolerable. The sheriff said the judge will be coming through town in three weeks or thereabouts."

"You'll be gone long before then," Angela said with a conviction she was far from feeling. "I've been working on a plan."

"Angel —"

"Don't fuss, Rafe. I'm sure things will turn out the way we want them. Is there anything I can do for you?"

"Yes, don't do anything at all. Your schemes have a way of going awry."

"Sorry, Rafe, you should have thought about that before you dragged me out here. I'll see you tomorrow."

"Angel, wait." Their hands were still clasped; he drew her forward until she was pressed against the bars. Then he angled his face and kissed her.

She kissed him back. The sweetness of her response brought a suspicious moisture to his eyes. Then abruptly he released her, gave her a gentle push and backed away from the bars.

"Go back to the Golden Angel, love. Knowing you're safe will do more for me than anything you can do for me here."

"Sorry, Rafe, you're in no position to tell me what to do. I'm going to prove your innocence if it's the last thing I do."

Back stiff, she walked away, nodding goodbye to the sheriff as she headed out the door.

Angela's heart was heavy as she walked back to the hotel. She had no idea what she was going to do next. Wingate hadn't been the least bit intimidated by her. His pride demanded that he stick to his story no matter how false or hurtful it was to others.

Back in her room, she pulled a chair over to the window and stared out into the street, ideas flitting through her brain in rapid succession, only to be just as quickly discarded. Rufus Wingate was the only person besides Rafe who knew the truth about the alleged robbery. She couldn't give up now, not with things going against Rafe the way they were. Determination stiffened her spine. She wouldn't give up. She'd badger Wingate until he admitted the truth.

Angela ate dinner in her room and retired early. First thing in the morning she intended to wire her lawyer for money. She might need more than she had on hand if her stay at the Dodge House was to be a lengthy one. Then she would visit Wingate at his office and try one more time to talk some sense into him. She fell asleep pondering the words she'd use to sway Wingate into admitting he'd lied.

A clap of thunder awakened Angela from a fitful sleep. She heard the sound of rain falling down from the heavens in unrelenting sheets. A flash of lightning jolted her upright. It didn't appear as if the downpour was going to stop any time soon. She washed, dressed and ate breakfast in the dining room. Then she sat in the hotel lobby, tapping her foot in time to the steady beat of the rain as she waited for it to stop.

Eventually the rain did stop. A weak sun broke through the clouds shortly before noon, rewarding Angela's patience. She had business to be about and could waste no more precious time twiddling her thumbs. She stepped out onto the wooden sidewalk and groaned in dismay when she saw the quagmire the rain had made of the roads. Unfortunately, she had to cross the street to reach the bank and telegraph office.

Angela lifted her skirts high and stepped off the sidewalk into the muddy street. She had trudged halfway across when she noted a woman encountering difficulty crossing the thoroughfare. The woman was heavily pregnant, her footing unsure as she dragged a foot out of the sucking mud and attempted to set it down in front of her.

Intuition told Angela the woman wasn't going to make it across without taking a nasty spill. She looked around to see if anyone else was out and about, but the street was deserted.

"Stay there!" she called out to the woman. "I'm coming to help you."

Despite the treacherous footing, Angela reached the woman's side, placed an arm around her ample waist and held her steady as they crossed the street together.

"Thank you," the woman said gratefully. "I shouldn't have attempted to cross the street but I wanted to see my father before my husband and I returned to our ranch. I'm Delia Poppins. You're new in town, aren't you?"

"I'm Angela. My husband and I arrived yesterday," Angela said. "Can you manage on your own now?"

"Yes, thank you. I'm sure I would have fallen if you hadn't helped me. I'm pretty awkward these days. Besides, I'm only going as far as the bank."

"I'm going to the bank, too. I'll walk along with you."

"Ted and I stayed in town with my parents last night because of the storm," Delia offered. "Papa left for the office early this morning, before I got to say good-bye. I don't get to town often. Ted is at the feed store, that's why he's not with me now."

Bells went off in Angela's head. "Your father works at the bank?"

"He owns the bank," Delia revealed. "You may have heard of him. Rufus Wingate. I was Delia Wingate before I married my Ted."

The color leached from Angela's face. This was the woman Wingate had tried to force on one of the Gentry brothers. She wondered how much Delia knew about her father's nefarious scheme to wed her to whomever would have her. Apparently, Wingate's machinations had been premature, for Delia seemed very happily married to her Ted. Was Ted the father of Delia's child?

"What a coincidence," Angela said. "I am going to see your father, too."

"Then we'll go together," Delia said, winding her arm in Angela's. "I won't interfere with your business. I'll just say good-bye and leave."

Angela had no intention of letting Delia leave her father's office until every detail of the bank robbery was laid before the woman.

If Delia was an honest person as Angela suspected, she would be appalled at her father's plot to marry her off.

They entered the bank together. One of the clerks saw Angela with Delia and did a double take. He hurried from his cage to waylay her.

"Miz Poppins, if you're planning on visiting your father, you can't go in there with —"

Delia waved him aside. "It's all right, Mr. Stanley. My father will see me. And Angela has business with him."

"But you can't . . . That woman . . . I've orders . . ."

Delia paid little heed to the clerk as she sailed past him with Angela in tow. She opened the door with a flourish and ushered Angela inside.

"Hello, Papa. I just stopped in to say good-bye. Ted and I are leaving as soon as he finishes his shopping."

Wingate looked up, his welcoming smile faltering when he saw Angela standing beside his daughter. "What's that woman doing here? I gave orders to keep her out."

"I don't understand," Delia said, clearly confused. "Angela said she had business with you."

"I've already spoken with Mrs. Gentry. There's nothing I can do for her."

Angela stepped forward, her chin raised pugnaciously. "There's a great deal you can do for me, Mr. Wingate. Telling the truth, for starters."

"Gentry? Your name is Angela Gentry?" Delia asked, staring curiously at Angela. "Which brother did you marry?"

"Rafe," Angela said. "He's sitting in jail right now for a crime he didn't commit. He returned to Dodge hoping your father would tell the truth about the alleged bank robbery and clear the Gentry brothers of a crime they didn't commit."

Delia, a pretty woman with piquant features and big brown eyes, gave her father a startled glance.

"What is Angela talking about, Papa? I'm acquainted with the Gentry brothers. None of them exhibited outlaw tendencies. That's why I was so shocked when you accused them of bank robbery."

"Don't listen to the woman, Delia. Obviously, she's a liar and a troublemaker. Sit down; you're not supposed to get excited in your condition."

"I'm not excited," Delia said calmly. "If you won't tell me, I'm sure Angela will." She turned to Angela, her eyebrows raised in question. "What makes you think Papa is lying about the bank robbery? What did he have to gain?"

Angela cleared her throat. This was a delicate subject, one she felt sure Delia wouldn't like, but it had to be broached. "The Gentry brothers came to your father for a loan to pay the taxes on their farm. They'd had a run of bad luck and couldn't come up with the money. Your father refused them."

Delia sent her father a wary look. "Papa bought the Gentry place for back taxes and gave it to me and Ted for a wedding present."

"It was up for grabs, honey," Wingate was quick to explain. "I bought it fair and square."

"The farm *was* up for sale," Delia said, as if challenging Angela's claim.

"Did your father tell you about the deal he tried to cut with Rafe and his brothers before the alleged bank robbery?" Angela asked.

Wingate shot up from his chair. "Don't listen to her! She's trying to poison your mind against me. Everything I did was for your sake."

"What did you do?" Delia asked. A tense silence followed. "Since Papa isn't talking, why don't *you* explain, Mrs. Gentry?"

"Very well. The Gentry brothers asked your father for a loan. Your father refused, but he did offer them a way out of debt. He said he'd loan them the money if one of them married you and gave your child a name."

"What? Papa! How could you? I didn't need you to buy me a husband. I loved Ted. I knew he'd return once he had time to think about his obligation to me. I was willing to wait. Why couldn't you?"

"I . . . well, I . . ." Wingate stammered. "We have a name to uphold in this town. I couldn't have my daughter bearing a child out of wedlock. I became overwrought when the Gentrys refused my offer and I acted . . . er . . . thoughtlessly."

"So you charged them with bank robbery," Delia accused. "How could you, Papa? Your lies ruined the lives of three innocent men. Even if one of the brothers had agreed, I still wouldn't have married anyone but Ted. I'm not proud of everything I've done in my lifetime, but I was sure of one thing. I loved Ted. Mama is sure to be livid when I tell her what you did."

Angela was amazed when Wingate, a big, bluff man, literally cowered at the thought of being held accountable by his wife.

"Now, honey, there's no need for that. What's done is done."

"What's done can be undone," Angela persisted, facing Wingate squarely. "It's never too late to right a wrong."

"You have to do it, Papa," Delia charged. "Whatever it takes, the Gentry brothers must be cleared of those false charges."

"Daughter, think of the shame, the embarrassment of recanting now."

"If you don't come to the sheriff's office with me now, I'll go alone," Delia said. "Rafe and his brothers have prices on their heads. They're on the run from the law because of you. I love you dearly, but I can't condone what you've done. I'm sure Mama will agree with me once she's told."

Wingate sent Angela a sour look. "It's all your fault, young lady. Very well, I'll go to the sheriff and try to make amends."

A measure of relief swept through Angela. She thanked God for her chance meeting with Delia Poppins. Without her, she never would have been able to convince the arrogant Wingate to tell the truth.

Fortunately, they weren't required to cross the muddy thoroughfare to reach the sheriff's office. They had but to walk down the sidewalk a short distance. Wingate hung back with marked reluctance, but Delia would have none of it. Grasping her father's arm, she pulled him along with her.

Sheriff Diller looked up from his desk as they entered. "Well, well, what have we here? What can I do for you, Mr. Wingate, Mrs. Poppins? I know what Mrs. Gentry wants. Her husband has been pacing all morning, waiting for her visit."

Delia prodded her father in the ribs. Wingate cleared his throat. "There's a rather . . . delicate matter I wish to discuss with you, Sheriff."

"Very well, have a seat. Does this concern you, also, Mrs. Poppins?"

"Indeed it does," Delia said, accepting the chair her father held out for her. "And Mrs. Gentry, too."

Diller's eyebrows shot upward as he stared at Angela. Then he dragged another chair over for her and seated himself, looking expectantly for someone to begin.

"Perhaps Rafe should join us," Angela suggested. "This concerns him as much as it does us."

Now Diller really did look baffled. "Perhaps someone should tell me what this is all about."

Wingate and Delia exchanged meaningful glances, but it was Angela who jumped into the void. "Mr. Wingate has come to tell you that he lied about the bank robbery. Rafe and his brothers are innocent. There was no bank robbery."

"Well, now, those are some mighty strong accusations, Mrs. Gentry. Perhaps we should let Mr. Wingate speak for himself."

Wingate looked properly abashed, refusing to look at the sheriff. "I . . . that is —"

"Papa, tell the sheriff the truth," Delia prodded.

Misery marched across Wingate's face as he raised his eyes to the sheriff. "I lied, Sheriff Diller. There was no bank robbery. I . . . I was angry with the brothers and unjustly accused them."

"And you waited all this time to tell me?"

Diller sputtered angrily. "Good God, man, whatever possessed you to do something like that?"

Wingate glanced at his daughter, then at Angela. "I'd prefer we spoke in private, Sheriff. Perhaps you'll understand when you hear my reasons."

Angela glanced at Rafe. He was plastered against the bars, his brow furrowed, his body tense. "I'll tell Rafe what's going on while you two talk," she said, rising.

"I'll go with you," Delia chimed in. "Perhaps he'll accept my apology."

Rafe couldn't hear what was being said across the room, but whatever it was must have shocked the sheriff, for he seemed highly agitated. When Angel and Delia walked toward him, his heart jumped into his mouth. He prepared himself to receive bad news. Nothing good had come of his return to Dodge City thus far. Why should he expect anything different now?

He grasped Angel's hands the moment she reached him. "What is it, Angel? What's happened?"

"Hello, Rafe," Delia said.

"Delia," Rafe acknowledged.

What in the hell was Delia Wingate doing here? he wondered. She looked ready to pop out her babe. Was Wingate still trying to find her a husband? Delia wasn't a bad girl; he hoped she'd find the right man one day. She probably hadn't even known about her father's plans to buy her a husband.

"I'm Delia Poppins now," Delia said. "You remember Ted Poppins, don't you? He courted me a while back. He left town for a time but returned. We were married soon afterward."

There was a bitter edge to Rafe's voice. "Congratulations." He couldn't help being caustic. He wouldn't be a wanted man today if Delia hadn't gotten herself in the family way. Obviously, Ted Poppins was the father of her child. It was good that he'd found his conscience and returned to marry the mother of his child.

"What's Wingate doing here?" Rafe asked, turning his attention back to Angela.

"He's come to recant his story about the bank robbery, Rafe," Angela said.

Rafe stared at her, his face a mask of utter amazement. "I don't know how you keep doing that, love."

"Doing what?"

"Saving my life."

Chapter Fifteen

"How did you get Wingate to tell the truth?" Rafe asked, shifting his gaze from Angela to Delia.

"It was Delia," Angela explained. "I met her by chance. I was headed to the bank to beg Mr. Wingate to admit the robbery was a hoax when we ran into one another. We got to talking. She was with me when I confronted her father in his office. When she learned what her father had done, she urged him to make amends."

"I never asked Papa to find me a husband," Delia explained. "He took it upon himself to deal with you and your brothers in that fashion." She blushed and looked away. "I know you and your brothers must think ill of me, but once I met Ted and fell in love, I wanted no other man.

"Ted was somewhat . . . reluctant to marry me when he learned about the baby," she continued. "He left town in a hurry, but I knew he'd come back when he realized he had a responsibility to me and our child. But

Papa couldn't wait. His pride got in the way. I'm sorry, Rafe. I feel as though this is all my fault."

"You couldn't have known what your father intended," Rafe grudgingly allowed. "All I want now is vindication for me and my brothers."

"And you're gonna have it," Sheriff Diller said as he walked over to join them. He unlocked the cell and swung the door open. "You're free to go, Gentry."

Rafe stepped through the opening and breathed deeply. Then he pulled Angela into his arms and kissed her soundly. "Don't you ever follow orders?" he asked after he'd kissed her breathless.

"Not when it concerns your life," she responded saucily.

Rafe lifted his face from Angela's and saw Delia dragging her father forward.

"Papa wants to apologize," Delia said.

"Er . . . yes, indeed. I was concerned about my daughter's reputation and acted unwisely. You and your brothers angered me; I never expected to be turned down. Once I made the accusation, pride prevented me from backing down."

"You ruined the lives of three men, Wingate," Rafe said with bitter emphasis. "What happened to our family farm?"

"Well . . . er . . . I . . ." Wingate blustered.

"He bought it for back taxes and gave it to me and Ted for a wedding present," Delia revealed. "I'm sorry, Rafe."

"There's nothing you can do to get the farm back," Wingate insisted. "You would have lost it in any event."

"I've grown quite fond of the place, Rafe," Delia said. "I don't think I can give it up, and Ted is trying hard to make it as productive as it was before the war. I hope you'll settle for knowing the land is being taken care of by people who love it."

"I've already accepted that we've lost the farm," Rafe allowed. "Jess is a doctor, not a farmer, and Sam would rather chase after rainbows than be tied to the land. As for myself" — he sent Angela a tender look — "I have other interests right now."

"Here are your guns, Gentry," Diller said, handing Rafe his gun belt. Rafe promptly buckled it around his hips.

"Before I leave," Rafe asserted, "I want something official to take with me, words to the effect that the Gentry brothers are no longer wanted for bank robbery."

Jenkins nodded. "It will take a few minutes to write out the paperwork. I'll make sure the Wanted posters are removed from circulation, so you needn't worry about that. However, word might not reach every city in which a poster is placed, so don't lose the document I'm preparing for you."

"Don't worry, Sheriff, I won't let it out of my sight."

Wingate and Delia had already taken their leave when Rafe tucked the document affirming his innocence inside his vest pocket, took Angela's arm and walked out of the jailhouse.

"I've taken a room at the Dodge House," Angela said, eyeing the sea of mud standing between her and her destination.

A grin split Rafe's features as he swung her into his arms and stepped into the street with the chivalry of a knight. "I've been looking for an excuse to hold you in my arms ever since I left the jailhouse," he bantered.

Rafe skirted around a stagecoach that had just pulled into town to discharge passengers and carried Angela across the street to the hotel. He didn't give a damn what people thought. He'd gone through hell for the right to hold Angel in his arms. Unfortunately, he still had a long way to go before he could claim Angel without fear of being hanged for murder.

Pressing her face against his chest, Angela whispered her room number and Rafe headed down the long corridor. She produced the key from her reticule and unlocked the door. Rafe carried her inside and kicked the door shut with a booted heel. Then he lowered her to her feet and kissed her with all the love and longing in the depths of his soul.

Her fingers plucked at the buttons on his shirt. Rafe moaned against her mouth. Her touch scorched him. His loins turned to stone. He wanted to topple her on the bed, throw up her skirts and thrust himself inside her. It nearly took more control than he possessed to break off the kiss and hold her hands away from him.

"I'm filthy and I need a shave," he choked out.

"I don't care," Angela whispered as she dragged him toward the bed. "Love me, Rafe; love me now."

They sprawled across the bed. Rafe moaned as need pounded through him. Loving Angel was his destiny. He kissed the corner of her mouth, her jaw, the sensitive spot just below her ear. His fingers made short work of the buttons on her dress as he pushed it off her shoulders and lowered his mouth over a nipple, sucking it through the thin material of her shift. Everything he wanted to say to her went out of his head as she arched against him, crying out her need.

Rafe raised himself enough to shed his gun belt, push his trousers down around his ankles and rid her of her dress and petticoats.

"Hurry, Rafe," Angela panted.

There was no time for finesse, no time to love her properly; they were both too needy, too hungry for one another. His hand slid down between their bodies, into her moist heat, and came away wet. Her slender thighs came around him as he covered her with his body. He kissed her deeply and slowly. When she returned his kiss, Rafe felt as if she'd reached inside him and ripped out his heart. With a groan of surrender, he opened her with his fingers and pushed himself inside her tight passage.

He heard her breath hitch, felt her tighten around him, drawing him deep inside her, until she had all of him. His hips lifted and fell as he surged forward, creating a glorious rhythm that brought them both to a gasping, explosive climax.

"I'm sorry," Rafe said when his breathing returned to some semblance of normalcy. "You deserve better than that." He gave her a quick kiss and rose from bed. "I'll do better when I return."

"Where are you going?"

"To the bathhouse down the street. I won't be long." He pulled up his trousers and buckled his gun belt in place. "Wait for me."

Rafe sank down into the tub of hot water with a grateful sigh. He washed quickly, then rested his head against the rim and relaxed. He must have dozed, for he was jerked awake by the unmistakable sound of a pistol hammer being drawn back. Instinctively he reached for the gun belt he'd placed on the floor beside the tub, but it wasn't there. He glanced upward, into the eyes of the last man he expected to see in Dodge City.

"Desmond Kent! What in the hell are you doing here?"

"Chandler wired me that Angela had disappeared. I deemed it my duty as her next of kin to return to the Golden Angel and see to the running of the mine. I boarded a stage in Topeka for the return trip to Canon City.

"I happened to see you carrying my stepdaughter across the street when the stage stopped in Dodge to discharge passengers. I feared you might have spotted me, but you had eyes only for Angela."

"Remove that gun from my face," Rafe said tersely.

"Oh, no, you're not getting out of this one, Gentry. News travels fast in a town this size. While I was pondering how to proceed, I heard that the banker had lied about the bank robbery, and that the Gentry brothers are no longer wanted for that crime."

"That's right," Rafe said warily.

"How do you suppose the sheriff will react when he learns Rafe Gentry is wanted in Colorado for murder?"

Rafe bit out a curse. "Damn you, Kent! What do you want from me? Why are you so determined to hurt your stepdaughter?"

"Angela was always a haughty little bitch. I stayed with her mother because I knew that one day Angela would come into a lot of money from her father. I handpicked Chandler to marry her after he promised to share the wealth with me. Then the little bitch had to strike out on her own for Colorado. She couldn't wait for me or Chandler to accompany her after the wedding.

"But that's not the half of it. You entered the picture and screwed up everything. When I saw you and Angela on the street today, I knew my luck had changed. Step out of that tub and get dressed."

Rafe didn't argue. Being caught with his pants down, so to speak, was embarrassing. He dried quickly and dressed. He made a quick move toward his guns, and felt the business end of Kent's pistol pressing into his back.

"It seems like you hold all the cards," Rafe drawled.

"Indeed I do."

"What do you want from me?"

"You're going to return to the hotel, ask for paper and pen and write a note to Angela."

"And what exactly is this note supposed to say?" Rafe asked warily.

"It's to say that you've thought it over and decided to go it alone from here. You're to tell Angela that you'll never be free of those murder charges, and that returning to Colorado isn't healthy for you. Tell her she'd be

316

in your way. Then wish her a happy life."

"You're mad if you think Angel will believe that."

"You'd better make her believe it," Kent warned. "Do you want to drag Angela down with you when I inform the sheriff you're wanted in Colorado for murder? I have the Wanted posters with me. It would take little effort to present them to the sheriff.

"I gather Angela fancies herself in love with you," Kent continued. "She'd be devastated to see you swinging at the end of a rope. Is that what you want for her? She'd be better off if you quietly disappeared from her life. Your violent past will catch up with you one day; then what will become of Angela?"

"All you want from Angel is her money," Rafe charged. "You care nothing about her or her future."

"Not true. I'll make sure she weds well and that the mine prospers under my direction. What can you do for her but make her life miserable?"

"I can protect her from you," Rafe said.

Kent gave him a flinty stare. "You know," he said thoughtfully, "I can shoot you now and take you in dead. The reward says dead or alive. Make your choice, Gentry. Write Angela that note or die."

"How do I know you won't kill me after I write the note?" Rafe charged.

"I'm not a violent man. I won't kill you

317

unless you force me. As for collecting the reward, I suspect Angela would think harshly of me if I turned you over to the law. On the other hand, if she believes you've left of your own free will, she'll be hurt but will eventually get over it."

"You're a devious bastard, Kent."

"I don't have time to bandy words with you," Kent said. "Someone might barge in here, and then I *will* be forced to shoot you. Name your poison, Gentry."

"You don't leave me much choice, Kent. I'll write the letter."

"I knew you'd see things my way." Kent smirked. "Walk beside me and don't try anything foolish. There's a cocked pistol in my pocket." He picked up Rafe's gun belt and prodded him out the door.

They left the bathhouse and crossed the street to the hotel. Rafe asked for pen and paper at the desk and moved down to the end of the counter to write his note. Kent dictated as Rafe wrote. When Rafe finished, Kent snatched the note from Rafe's hand, read it and handed it back to him.

"Tell the clerk to deliver it to your room," Kent ordered.

Rafe folded it in half and carried it back to the clerk, instructing him to deliver it personally to Mrs. Rafe Gentry. Kent added a five-dollar gold piece to assure prompt delivery.

"Now what?" Rafe bit out.

"Now I'm going to watch you ride off into the sunset with a great deal of pleasure. Where's your horse?"

"I assume he's stabled at the livery."

"Very well, we'll walk to the livery together."

Rafe waited for the right moment to escape but it never arrived. He could feel the barrel of Kent's gun poking him in the side and knew Kent wouldn't hesitate to shoot. Murder was a serious charge; no one would condemn Kent for shooting an accused murderer for the reward. Besides, maybe Kent was right. Proving himself innocent of two separate murder charges seemed an impossible feat. He was probably doing Angel a favor by walking out of her life.

Pain lanced through him. He'd already tried leaving Angel, twice, in fact, without success. Something stronger than the life force beating inside him kept drawing him back to his Angel. It wasn't Kent's cocked gun that kept Rafe walking toward the livery. It was the hopelessness of his situation. Kent was right about his dismal future. Pure luck and his guardian Angel had helped to clear him of bank robbery charges. But he'd be a fool to think he'd be that fortunate again. He'd probably find himself swinging at the end of a rope should he return to Ordway and boldly proclaim his innocence.

The livery loomed ahead. Rafe found his

horse and waited patiently while the hostler buckled on the saddle. When Rafe attempted to lead his gelding from the building, the hostler said, "That will be two dollars, Mr. Gentry. A dollar a day."

Rafe turned out his pockets and shrugged. "You're the one who wants me to leave, Kent. Pay the man."

Muttering beneath his breath, Kent dug two crumpled dollar bills from his pocket and handed them to the hostler.

"My guns," Rafe said, holding out his hand. "You wouldn't leave a man defenseless on the prairie, would you?"

Kent mulled over the request before handing Rafe his gun belt. "I don't suppose you'll risk your freedom by shooting me. It would serve no purpose."

Rafe buckled his gun belt around his slim hips, his expression fierce. "Then again," Rafe added, "what's another murder to a man already charged with so many?"

Kent blanched and backed away. Rafe laughed in his face. "Coward. If I made a practice of shooting men in cold blood, you'd be the first to feel the bite of my lead."

"Bastard," Kent hissed as Rafe mounted and kneed his horse into a hard trot. "Don't worry about Angela," Kent called after him. "I'll see that she's taken care of."

Rafe exerted every ounce of his willpower to keep from turning around and beating

Kent to a pulp. He imagined Angel's expressive face when she read his note. He suspected she would be disbelieving at first, then hurt, then finally, angry. He prayed her anger would be enough to sustain her, for this time there was no turning back for him. He loved her too much to drag her from town to town, one step ahead of the law.

Angela paced the confines of the small room, waiting for Rafe to return from the bathhouse. What was keeping him? she wondered not for the first time. He'd been gone so long she was debating whether or not to venture forth and find out for herself what was keeping him. Relief shot through her when she heard a knock on the door. Nearly tripping over her feet, she rushed to open the door.

"Rafe! You've been gone so long I . . . oh, you're not Rafe."

The desk clerk handed Angela a folded sheet of paper. "Your husband asked me to deliver this to you, Mrs. Gentry."

Angela's hands shook as she stared at the missive. "Th . . . thank you," she stammered, turning away from the door and closing it behind her.

Angela stared at the paper, waves of fear going through her. She knew intuitively that the missive contained ill tidings. She carried the note to the window, where the light was better, but still she couldn't bring herself to read what Rafe had written. Why had he written her in the first place? Why couldn't he just tell her what he wanted to say?

Oh, God, she couldn't read it. The note fell from her hand and floated to the floor. She stared down at it as if it were a snake about to bite her. With trembling fingers she bent and retrieved it. Very carefully, she unfolded the single sheet of paper. The words seemed to leap out at her.

She read the note in its entirety, then wadded it into a tight ball. Without knowledge of what she was doing, she pressed her head to the window, letting the tears spill unchecked from her eyes. Unwilling to believe what Rafe had written, Angela carefully smoothed out the paper and reread Rafe's hurtful words.

He was leaving her. He wanted to go it alone. He knew he couldn't prove himself innocent of murder charges and she was a hindrance he didn't need. He intended to leave the territory to escape the law and bounty hunters. He encouraged her to forget him and return to the Golden Angel.

No! her heart screamed. Rafe couldn't have written those cold words. Rafe cared for her; he'd never hurt her like that. They had made love on the rumpled bed less than two hours ago. When he returned they were going to make love again. The agony his words evoked caused her to double up in pain. Hurt and disbelief slowly dissipated as shadows deepened outside the window. Then, like a raging storm, anger filled the empty chambers of her heart, squeezing out the love that had so recently occupied it.

How could Rafe be so heartless? How could he abandon her without a word of good-bye? Contemptible wretch. Despicable miscreant. How dare he! She couldn't count the times she'd saved his skin, and *this* was how he repaid her? By leaving her stranded? Dear God, how could she have ever thought him the kind of man she needed? She had given him her heart. Together they could have worked miracles. Instead, he'd decided she was a hindrance and had left her behind to fend for herself.

Well, she wasn't helpless. She didn't need Rafe to take care of her. Her course was clear. She'd take the next stage to Canon City and take charge of her inheritance. She had the Golden Angel; nothing else was necessary for her well-being. Not even Rafe Gentry.

Who do you think you're kidding? a small voice inside her chided. Her inner self whispered that no man would ever make love to her like Rafe Gentry; no man would ever take his place in her heart.

"I will do just fine without him," Angela firmly declared. Her words echoed hollowly in her ears, but her fierce determination to survive without Rafe overrode the pain of rejection.

Angela went through the motions of ordering a supper she didn't eat and preparing for bed. She couldn't concentrate and was unwilling to delve too deeply into her pain. Wiping her mind clean of all thought, she dropped into a restless sleep.

Angela awakened to a dull gray sky, which suited her mood perfectly. Yesterday's events, which she'd been trying to forget, suddenly came crashing down upon her. The anguish was nearly unbearable. Dragging in a sustaining breath, she concentrated on washing and dressing, her thoughts skirting around the hard-hearted bastard who had abandoned her.

The first thing Angela decided was to sell her horse and buy passage to Canon City with the proceeds. In all the excitement yesterday, she'd forgotten to wire Lawyer Goodman for funds, and she didn't intend to stick around Dodge City any longer than necessary.

That thought had barely been born when a knock sounded on the door. Even though she told herself it couldn't possibly be Rafe, a surge of joy rushed through her. Two steps took her to the portal. She flung it open.

The smile died on her lips. "You! What are you doing here?"

"Hello, Angela. Your greeting leaves much to be desired."

"What do you expect after trying to marry me off to a man I despise? You know I hold no love for you, Desmond. What are you doing here?" she repeated.

"Chandler wired me that you had disappeared. I suspected Gentry was somehow involved and booked passage on a stagecoach to Canon City. I intended to take a hand in running the Golden Angel in your absence. You can't imagine my surprise when I saw you yesterday as I stepped off the stage to stretch my legs. It made a brief stop in Dodge to discharge passengers. Where is Gentry?"

"Not here, as you can plainly see. Why are you still here?"

"I decided to take a later stage. I understand the bank robbery charges against Gentry and his brothers were dropped. I wonder why the sheriff didn't seem to know about the murder charges in Colorado."

"If that's all you've come to say," Angela said coolly, "you can leave."

Kent ignored her. "What are your plans, my dear?"

"I'm returning to the Golden Angel to run my mine, not that it's any of your business."

"Without Gentry?" he goaded.

"Do you see him anywhere around?"

"Actually, I saw him ride out of town yesterday. That's another reason I stuck around. I took the liberty of purchasing a ticket for you on the afternoon stage."

"I can buy my own ticket," Angela retorted.

"Of course, my dear, I've just saved you the trouble. With Gentry gone, I assumed you'd be anxious to leave town. The ungrateful wretch owes you his life. He never should have skipped town and left you stranded."

"You don't know anything," Angela bit out. She lowered her head, unwilling to allow Kent a glimpse of her heartbreak.

"Perhaps you're right, Angela. Let's call a truce. If Chandler still wants to marry you, he's on his own. I won't interfere. I truly want to be of help to you."

Angela didn't believe him for a minute. But perhaps, she thought sagely, she could use him to glean the truth from Chandler about his involvement in Brady Baxter's murder. As greedy as she knew Kent to be, she suspected he'd agree to anything to stay in her good graces.

"Very well, a truce," Angela offered. "But with one condition."

"And that condition?" Kent asked warily.

"I want no interference from you in any of my dealings, whether they concern the mine or Anson Chandler."

Though Rafe had left her, she still intended to seek the truth regarding Brady Baxter's murder. Proving Rafe's innocence would restore her faith in her own judgment, if nothing else.

Kent's eyebrows shot up. "Are you saying you're seriously considering Chandler's suit?"

"I'm admitting nothing except that Anson and I are currently on friendly terms. Or we were until Rafe abducted me."

"Gentry abducted you?" Kent asked.

Angela could have bitten her tongue. That was not what she'd meant to say at all. "I misspoke," she amended. "There was no force involved. I left with Rafe of my own free will."

"I hope you've learned your lesson," Kent said. "Very well, I agree to your terms. The stage leaves at two this afternoon. I'll wait for you at the Wells Fargo office."

Angela left the hotel well in advance of the time she was to board the stage. It took the better part of an hour to purchase a bag in which to pack her clothing, sell her horse and saddle and check out of the hotel. The coach was already loading when she arrived at the station.

"I feared you'd changed your mind," Kent said, apparently relieved to see her.

"No reason for me to stick around Dodge City," Angela replied as Kent gave her bag to the driver and handed her into the stage-coach.

Then they were off. Squeezed between her stepfather and a traveling salesmen who kept eyeing her with undisguised appreciation, Angela didn't look forward to the long trip back to Canon City. As the horses jolted forward, she glanced out the back window. She'd always remember Dodge City as a place where she'd experienced the full gamut of emotions: happiness, sadness, anger.

Angela tried to envision a future without Rafe, but all she saw was darkness. The sunshine suddenly lost its sparkle and the clouds scudding across the sky turned gray and forbidding.

Chapter Sixteen

Rafe approached the city of Ordway with every intention of giving it a wide berth. Unfortunately, things didn't turn out the way he'd planned. He had camped for the night some distance from the town and was feasting on a rabbit he'd shot for his supper when he was surprised by unexpected visitors.

He heard them tramping in the woods and kept his hand poised on his gun as they approached. He watched warily as two men rode to the edge of his camp and dismounted.

"Howdy, mister. Mind if we share your fire?" one of the men asked. "We have our own food."

"Damn!" Rafe cursed beneath his breath. Sheriff Tattersal and one of his deputies. Of all the rotten luck. He pulled his hat down over his eyes and turned his face into the shadows.

"Howdy. Help yourself to the fire. I'm kind of short on supplies right now, so if you want coffee you'll have to make your own."

"I'm Sheriff Tattersal and this is Deputy Wilton. We've plenty of supplies. We're tracking an outlaw who robbed a stage and killed a man. Meet anyone on the road today?"

"Not a soul, Sheriff," Rafe replied.

"Are you traveling east or west?"

"West. Left Dodge City a couple days ago."

"Damn! Looks like we're following a cold trail, Wilton. I suppose we should return to Ordway and wait for another lead to come along."

"I can continue on if you like," Wilton offered.

"No, sooner or later we'll get him. We've been gone too long as it is," Tattersal said.

The two lawmen unpacked their food, poured water from their canteens into a coffeepot, then sat down to wait for the coffee to perk.

Rafe didn't like the way the sheriff kept staring at him. If he was recognized, his goose was cooked. In the thick silence, Rafe feared his thoughts were loud enough to be heard. His suspicions were confirmed when Tattersal said, "Say, I know you. You're Rafe Gentry."

Rafe's breath escaped in a loud whoosh. His hand was halfway to his gun when Tattersal said, "I've been hoping you'd return one day so I could apologize for charging you with robbing the stage and murder. I shouldn't have taken the word of a man I didn't know. I should have realized Sister Angela wouldn't have lied. But when Desmond Kent came to town and told that wild story about you, I jumped to the wrong conclusion."

"Apologize?" Rafe repeated, dumbfounded.

"We caught one of the outlaws responsible for those murders five days ago. He and his partner robbed another stage and killed the driver. One of the outlaws was mortally wounded by the guard riding shotgun and was brought to town. Before he died, he confessed to helping his partner kill those five people in that earlier robbery. I reckon he wanted to clear his conscience before meeting his maker."

"You mean I've been exonerated?" Rafe asked, disbelief turning to joy. He wanted to jump up and shout but restrained himself.

"Completely," Tattersal said. "I've already notified the proper authorities and recalled the Wanted posters naming you a killer. Of course," he added sternly, "there is still that bank robbery charge against you."

"Not anymore." Rafe grinned. "I've been vindicated and have the pardon to prove it."

Rafe reached into his pocket and handed Tattersal the pardon. Tattersal read it and handed it back.

"Congratulations. I hope you'll accept my

apology. I fear those false charges complicated your life."

Rafe gave a derisive snort. Complicated his life? They damn near ruined it. He'd lost Angel because of those charges and the ones stemming from Brady Baxter's death. But suddenly things were beginning to look up.

"How is that pretty little Sister Angela?" Wilton asked. "Did you leave her in Canon City?"

"No, she's . . . er . . . in Dodge City. She's returning to Canon City on the stage."

The sheriff and his deputy fell silent as they ate their food and drank their coffee. Rafe helped himself to the coffee and sipped thoughtfully.

"You *did* say you were returning to Ordway tomorrow, didn't you?" Rafe asked.

"Sure did," Tattersal allowed.

"Might I accompany you? Angela's stepfather claims we were never married. Both Reverend Conrad's records and our marriage paper were destroyed. No written proof of our marriage exists. Since our wedding was witnessed by many of your townspeople, I thought you might help me round up signatures of those willing to swear that a marriage took place."

"My name will top the list," Tattersal said.

"And mine will be next," Wilton averred.

"I was going to ask you to ride with us, anyway," Tattersal revealed. "You'll want

332

something to prove you're no longer wanted for murder."

"I would welcome written proof that I've been cleared of murder charges," Rafe said, grateful to have yet another crime erased from his record.

Two down and one to go, Rafe thought. For the first time in a very long time he had reason to be optimistic. But he feared it was too late. He'd been forced to hurt Angel badly. Would she ever forgive him?

Rafe rode to Ordway with Tattersal and Wilton the next day. Tattersal wrote up a pardon and Rafe spent most of the day obtaining signatures of people who had witnessed his marriage to Angel. He didn't know why he bothered, for she probably hated him, but for some reason it seemed important to prove that he and Angel had a legal marriage. Should Angel be carrying his child, no one could question its legitimacy if a legal marriage was substantiated.

The following day Rafe left Ordway with a full pardon for the stagecoach robbery and subsequent murders in his possession. He also carried a document bearing the signatures of dozens of people who had witnessed his marriage to Angel. Before he'd met up with Sheriff Tattersal, Rafe had intended to head north in hopes of running into Jess. Rafe knew Jess would be overjoyed to learn he was a free man. As for Sam, Rafe had no idea where to find his youngest brother. The hell-raiser could be anywhere.

So many things had changed now. Rafe no longer felt the hangman breathing down his neck. With two charges against him dismissed, he had but to prove himself innocent of killing Baxter and he'd be totally free to win back Angel's love. With that in mind, Rafe set his sights on Canon City. He had a lot of miles to traverse and plenty of time to ponder all the ways in which he could clear his name and gain back his life.

Rafe knew he hadn't set an easy task for himself. Baxter's death was a complete mystery. Angela believed Chandler was somehow involved, but proving it wasn't going to be easy. Rafe could ride into town and display his pardons before the sheriff, but that didn't mean he would be automatically cleared of Baxter's murder. No, his pardons weren't going to help him one damn bit in this instance. The only way to ferret out the truth, he decided, was by lying low and waiting for the real killer to make a mistake and reveal himself. He supposed a good place to start was with Anson Chandler.

Weary beyond words and carrying a world of hurt buried deep inside her aching heart, Angela stepped off the stage in Ordway to stretch her legs and have a bite to eat.

Angela wasn't all that hungry but knew she

had to eat to keep up her strength for the rest of the grueling trip. Lost in her thoughts, she started violently when she felt someone grip her arm. She relaxed somewhat but remained vigilant when Kent said, "There's a restaurant across the street. We have an hour before the stage leaves."

Angela nodded curtly and shook free of Kent's grasp. She couldn't stand his touch; he made her skin crawl. They had crossed the street and turned into the restaurant when she heard someone calling her name.

"Sister Angela, do you have a moment?"

Angela turned toward the voice and saw Sheriff Tattersal hurrying toward her. A shiver of apprehension slid down her spine. What could the sheriff want with her? Did it involve Rafe?

"Sheriff Tattersal, how nice to see you again."

"Likewise, Sister Angela."

"You remember my stepfather, don't you?"

Tattersal aimed a frown in Kent's direction. "Indeed I do. I'd like a word with him, too." He turned back to Angela with a smile. "I saw your husband a day or two ago."

Angela blanched. "My husband?"

"Yes, Rafe Gentry. He said you'd be coming through on the stage. He didn't mention that you'd be accompanied by your stepfather. I hardly thought you'd welcome Mr.

Kent's company after what he did to you and Mr. Gentry."

"Now see here, Sheriff," Kent blustered.

"No, *you* see here, Mr. Kent," Tattersal said, poking him in the chest with his forefinger. "You led me to believe Mr. Gentry was an outlaw, when in truth he was exactly what Sister Angela claimed him to be. Her fiancé. You even named another man as her intended."

"But Gentry *is* an outlaw," Kent argued. "What about the stagecoach robbery? And those innocent people he killed?"

"We caught one of the men responsible," Tattersal elaborated. "He gave a deathbed confession. I'm confident we'll have the other man in custody very soon. And by the way, Gentry has a full pardon in his possession for the bank robbery in Dodge City. Another case of mistaken identity, no doubt."

"No doubt," Kent repeated dryly. "But there's still that murder . . ."

Angela poked Kent in the ribs, her look warning him to keep silent if he expected to remain in her goodwill. "My stepfather was referring to Rafe's pardon. You did say the murder charges were dropped against Rafe, didn't you?"

"I did indeed, Sister Angela. But if I were you, I'd be careful who I trust in the future. Your stepfather doesn't seem to have your best interests at heart."

"I'm fully aware of my stepfather's failings, Sheriff," Angela asserted, "but thank you for the warning."

"Well, ma'am, I'd best get on with my business. Have a good trip." He tipped his hat and walked away.

"Gentry must have the devil's own luck," Kent muttered darkly.

"I'm happy for him despite the fact I no longer have deep feelings for the man," Angela claimed. "Nothing he does matters to me anymore."

"You're wise, my dear. Gentry is unworthy of you," Kent said. "Only a heel would abandon you in a strange city. What if I hadn't been available to escort you back to the Golden Angel?"

"I imagine I'd survive," Angela said with a hint of sarcasm.

Her retort seemed to infuriate Kent but he kept his thoughts to himself as they entered the restaurant and ordered their meal. Angela picked at her food until it was time to board the stage for the next leg of the journey.

The rattle of traces and pounding of hooves kept Angela from dozing in the hot coach as the other passengers were doing. She rested her head against the cushion and stared out the window, recalling the cold words Rafe had written in his note. With a few short sentences he had shattered her life.

If he were to turn up tomorrow and beg for forgiveness, she'd deny him. Never would she give him the satisfaction of knowing how badly he had hurt her, how completely he had destroyed her happiness.

She'd been a fool to think Rafe needed her. She'd known from the beginning he wasn't a marrying man. She'd forced him into marriage, for godsake! How could she not expect him to bow out when he'd had his fill of her?

Even feeling as she did, she was still pleased to learn he'd been given pardons for crimes he hadn't committed. No man deserved to be falsely accused. No Christian would allow that travesty to continue. Christian duty was her only reason for wanting to find Baxter's killer, she told herself. Even if she never saw Rafe again, she'd have the satisfaction of knowing her ingenuity and persistence had won his freedom.

Anson Chandler was on hand to meet the stagecoach when it arrived in Canon City. Kent had wired Chandler from Pueblo, informing him what time to meet the stage.

"I never expected to see you and Angela traveling together on the same stage," Chandler said by way of greeting. "Where did you disappear to, Angela?"

"That's a long story, Anson, one I'll recount later," Kent said. "Did you bring the buckboard?"

"Of course," Chandler said. "So glad you decided to return, Angela." His voice held a note of derision.

"How are things at the mine?" Angela asked, ignoring his sarcasm.

"Couldn't be better. I think I have a flair for this kind of thing."

"Too bad you don't have a flair for courting," Kent muttered derisively.

Angela bit her lip to keep from laughing out loud. Obviously, Anson and her step-father still harbored hopes of sharing her money. They could believe what they wanted, but it simply wasn't going to happen. The only reason Chandler was still around was because she had a murder to solve and Chandler was the prime suspect.

Chandler loaded the bags in the buckboard and climbed onto the driver's seat. Kent handed Angela up and crowded in beside her.

"I'd like to stop off at Lawyer Goodman's office before going up to the mine," Angela said as Chandler drove through town.

"Why?" Chandler asked sharply.

"Does Mr. Goodman know I left town?"

"I informed both him and the sheriff that you were missing. You really gave us a fright, Angela," he scolded. "The sheriff formed a search party but gave up after a couple of days. The obvious conclusion was that you took off with Rafe Gentry. I knew you'd return, though. The Golden Angel means too much to you. You'd never abandon it. We were right about Gentry, weren't we? You did run off with him, didn't you?"

Angela's answer did nothing to appease his anger. "I don't have to explain my actions to you, Anson."

"I won't have my future wife playing whore for an outlaw!" he exploded.

"Uh, Anson," Kent cautioned, "you'd be better served to hold your tongue. I suggest you apologize."

Chandler must have heeded the warning in Kent's voice, for he turned to Angela and said, "Forgive me, Angela, but surely you understand my concern when I discovered you had suddenly disappeared in the middle of the night."

"I don't care what you think of me, Anson," Angela snapped. "The only reason I suffer your presence at the mine is because the miners refuse to work for a woman."

"I'm determined to change your mind," Anson said. "I want you for my wife, and you need a man to look after you."

"Oh, there's Mr. Goodman's office," Angela said with obvious relief. "He'll be glad to know I've returned safely."

Chandler's confident manner set Angela's teeth on edge. He could believe what he wanted, she thought defiantly. The truth of the matter was she didn't need a man. As soon as she solved the mystery of Baxter's murder, she'd have no further use for either Anson or her stepfather.

Angela had given the miners and their reluctance to work for a woman a great deal of thought during the long trip from Dodge City and had hit upon a solution. She intended to offer twice the normal wages for a day's work. Money talked. She suspected miners would flock to take advantage of her generous offer. But for now, she'd bide her time.

Lawyer Goodman was delighted to see Angela safe and sound when she entered his office. He leaped from his chair and hugged her exuberantly.

"My dear Angela, you can't imagine how worried I've been since Mr. Chandler advised me of your disappearance. He claimed you had run off with Mr. Gentry. I didn't know what to think. I just wanted you to be safe and happy. Was Chandler right? Did you go off with Rafe?"

"I did, though not willingly."

Goodman searched her face. "He didn't hurt you, did he?"

Only my heart. "No, I'm fine."

"You appear troubled. How may I help you?"

Mr. Goodman's concern deeply touched Angela. It gave her courage to speak frankly.

"What I tell you is to be held in strict confidence, Mr. Goodman," Angela confided.

"Of course, my dear, your secrets are safe with me."

"The truth is that Rafe forced me to accompany him, then stranded me in Dodge City. He no longer holds my . . . regard. I desperately need legal advice concerning our marriage.

"As you know, Rafe and I were married in Ordway by Reverend Conrad," she continued. "Unfortunately, no written record of that marriage exists. But the marriage was witnessed by dozens of people. I want to know how to proceed. Is a divorce necessary under those circumstances?"

"Are you sure severing ties with Mr. Gentry is what you want, my dear?"

"Yes," Angela said after a moment's hesitation. "I don't intend to stay married, if indeed I am married, to a man who doesn't want me. How shall I proceed? What about my marriage to Brady Baxter?"

"A divorce would be necessary to legally dissolve your marriage to Gentry," Goodman counseled. "You said the exchanging of vows was a public affair, with many witnesses present. Those witnesses can be as valuable as a license in proving that a legal union took place. Furthermore, your marriage to Baxter was fraudulent. But since he's no longer alive, it's a moot point."

"Will you handle the details for me?"

"If that is your wish, I will draw up the papers. I can understand your reluctance to remain married to an outlaw, although it's difficult to imagine Rafe robbing a bank or killing people in cold blood. Come in next week to sign the legal documents and I'll take care of the rest."

"Thank you, but there is something you should know. Rafe received full pardons for those crimes. All charges have been dropped. The bank robbery was a sham, perpetrated by the banker, who has since admitted he lied, and the real killers confessed to the stage robbery and murders in Ordway. There is only one charge remaining against Rafe; that of killing Brady Baxter, and I know Rafe's not guilty."

"You have a lot of faith in a man who walked out on you," Goodman observed.

"As a concerned Christian, I would feel the same about any man unjustly charged," Angela claimed. "That's why I hope to prove Rafe didn't murder Brady Baxter."

"Do you intend to marry that Chandler fellow after you obtain your divorce?"

"Good Lord, no! I've reason to believe Anson Chandler killed Brady, and I intend to prove it. I thought someone I trusted should be aware of my plans."

"You could be playing with fire, my dear. Why not let the sheriff take care of it?"

"No, I'll do this on my own."

"Be careful, Angela. I've grown mighty fond of you." He sighed wistfully. "My own daughter would be about your age now had she not died of fever. Her death hastened that of my beloved wife."

Angela's heart went out to him. How lonely he must be. "I'm sorry."

"No need, my dear. It happened a long time ago. I've learned to live with my grief. It's you I'm worried about. You will take care, won't you?"

"I'll be careful. If Anson Chandler committed murder, he should be brought to trial."

"Something tells me you care more about Rafe Gentry than you're admitting."

Angela's chin notched defiantly upward. "I loved Rafe, but he killed whatever feelings I held for him. What I want now is to see justice served. I'll return next week to sign those papers. Good-bye, sir."

"Better yet," Goodman said, "I'll bring them out as soon as they're drawn up. I feel responsible for your welfare."

Impulsively, Angela kissed his cheek. "Very well. I'll see you soon."

"It's about time," Kent complained when Angela returned to the buckboard. "There's a storm brewing. I'd hate for us to be caught in it."

They reached the Golden Angel minutes

ahead of the storm. Winter arrived early in the mountains. Angela felt its bite in the chill wind that buffeted her and in the crisp mountain air that filled her lungs. The aspens had already begun to shed their brilliant golden leaves, and a rim of white appeared on the peaks of the mountains.

Kent jumped from the buckboard and lifted Angela down. "There's going to be a change of weather," he said with a shiver. "The mine will close down for the winter very soon. I think you should move to town during those cold months, my dear."

"Father lived up here quite comfortably the year around, and so shall I," Angela proclaimed. "The next time I go into town, I'll lay in a supply of food to last several months. You and Anson can move to town any time you'd like."

"Someone has to remain here to protect you," Chandler interjected. "You're far too headstrong and impetuous for your own good. You wouldn't recognize danger if it stared you in the face. You see only good in people."

"You're wrong there, Anson," Angela argued. "I see people for exactly what they are." *You're a greedy man and quite possibly a murderer,* she wanted to add.

Chandler lifted her bag from the buckboard. "I'll come inside with you and lay a fire in the hearth."

"Very well, if you insist. I hope you don't mind sharing your cabin with Desmond. I doubt it will be for long. He's unaccustomed to living without creature comforts. You did send for him, didn't you?"

Chandler aimed a warning glance at Kent. "I merely informed your stepfather that you were missing. He is your next of kin and had a right to know. His coming out here was his own idea. Lucky for you he did or he wouldn't have been available to escort you back to the Golden Angel after Gentry abandoned you."

Angela entered her cabin with Chandler hard on her heels. "I suppose Desmond told you everything while I was in Mr. Goodman's office."

"He told me enough," Chandler said. "I already guessed at most of it. I hope you've had your fill of Rafe Gentry."

"Don't worry, Anson, I believe we've both seen the last of Rafe Gentry."

"Good riddance," Chandler muttered. "Gentry may have been cleared of those charges in Dodge City and Ordway, but he's still wanted for the murder of Brady Baxter."

"I haven't forgotten," Angela said. "Brady's killer won't go free, I promise you."

Chandler sent her a curious look but said nothing as he stacked dry wood and kindling in the fireplace. Once he finished, he appeared in no hurry to leave.

"Thank you," Angela said, "I'll see you tomorrow. The trip has exhausted me."

"I can stay longer if you need me," Chandler offered, obviously not taking her hint.

"Thank you, but no. I'd like to be alone."

"Very well," Chandler said, clearly disgruntled. "But I'd like to leave you with one thought. I'm determined to marry you, Angela. I know you consider yourself still married to Gentry, but as far as I'm concerned, that marriage doesn't exist."

"What about all those witnesses in Ordway?" Angela maintained. "I'm sure it wouldn't be difficult to find people willing to testify that a legal wedding took place."

Chandler grasped her shoulders and gave her a rough shake. "Admit it, you're glad Baxter is dead. His death solved a lot of problems. I know you married Baxter to save Gentry's skin."

Angela broke his hold and pushed him away. "You couldn't have known that unless . . ."

Chandler went still. "I know what you're thinking, but you're wrong. And I strongly suggest you keep your suppositions to yourself."

"Are you threatening me, Anson?"

"What a silly goose you are," Chandler laughed. "I have no reason to threaten you. Good night, my dear."

"Good night, Anson. Tomorrow we'll discuss everything that transpired at the mine during my absence. I'll expect a full accounting."

Chandler gave her a menacing look, then turned on his heel and strode out the door, slamming it behind him. Angela shot home the bolt and leaned against the door, shaking with repressed anger and a small measure of fear.

Never had she felt so alone. She was surrounded by people who cared nothing for her, people who wanted to use her. Even Rafe had used her . . . and she had let him.

Sighing regretfully at what might have been had Rafe not deserted her, she fixed herself something to eat and went to bed.

The next two days were busy ones for Angela. Close inspection of the accounts revealed discrepancies in Chandler's records concerning the amount of gold mined and monies deposited in the bank in her account, and she suspected Chandler was lining his pockets at her expense. She let it pass for the time being but intended to have Mr. Goodman confirm her findings.

Meanwhile, plans were put into effect to close down the mine for the coming winter.

One day Angela happened to walk behind Chandler's cabin while gathering kindling and heard voices through the open window. She stopped in her tracks when she heard her name spoken.

"You're getting nowhere with Angela," Kent chided.

"She's stubborn, Kent," came Chandler's disgruntled reply. "You're doing nothing to help."

"Angela and I agreed on a truce. I promised to stay out of her affairs in return for the pleasure of living in this rustic cabin in this godforsaken country," he said sarcastically. "If it wasn't for her money, I wouldn't be living like a hermit on the outskirts of civilization. For godsake, marry the little bitch so we can share her bank account. It galls me to be nice to her."

"I've done more than you give me credit for," Chandler said.

Had Angela been able to see him, she felt certain he'd be smirking. She sidled closer to the window, for Chandler had lowered his voice.

"What in the hell are you talking about?" Kent asked.

"Brady Baxter's murder was rather fortunate for us, don't you agree?" Chandler continued. "I was out here the night he was killed."

"You saw Gentry kill Baxter?" came Kent's incredulous reply.

"Not so loud," Chandler hissed.

Angela jerked back against the wall as the

window banged shut. Damn! Just when it was getting interesting. A few moments more and she would have had a full confession from Chandler with Kent as a witness. Kent might balk at testifying against Chandler, but Angela felt certain money would loosen his tongue once he realized he could no longer use Chandler to cash in on her wealth.

It wasn't the money Angela cared about. She'd gladly share her wealth or give it up entirely for a man who really loved her. But Chandler wasn't that man, and Kent wasn't the kind of stepfather who deserved her consideration. Not after the way they'd plotted against her.

She had to admire the fact that Rafe hadn't married her for her wealth. He'd seemed genuinely fond of her. What a fool she'd been. She had trusted unwisely and loved recklessly. But she had learned her lesson well, and it was one she was not likely to forget.

Angela made her way back to her cabin and dropped her load of kindling in the woodbox. Dimly she wondered when Mr. Goodman would arrive with the divorce papers for her to sign and considered going into town herself to see the deed done. Perhaps the official end of her marriage was what she needed to put Rafe behind her and get on with her life.

Angela went to bed that night with a heavy

heart. She tried not to think about Rafe, but her body kept reminding her how much it missed his touch. Her nipples rose up in shameless anticipation as she recalled the mindless passion he aroused in her. A bitter smile touched her lips. The emptiness inside her was something she would have to live with for the remainder of her life. If she had to rely on anger in order to forget Rafe, then so be it.

Sleep, when it came, was fraught with dreams. She felt Rafe's hands on her body, his kisses against her mouth. Smelled his masculine scent, tasted his essence on her tongue. She awoke abruptly in a cold sweat. She wasn't alone! The jangle of a spur. A shadow outlined against the wall. The slow, steady beat of a heart not her own. Whether real or imagined, she felt his life force pounding within her own breast. Her body tingled in sudden awareness.

"Who's there?"

"Hello, Angel."

"No! Go away!"

Chapter Seventeen

Rafe stepped into a puddle of moonlight. Angela could see his face now. The play of shadow and light brought definition to his features, sculpting the bold jut of his jaw, revealing the glitter of his gaze, the earthy sensuality that was so much a part of him. She tried to blink him away, but when she opened her eyes he was still there, his powerful form filling the room. "This can't be happening, not again."

"I'm not an apparition, Angel; stop looking at me like that."

"Just when I think I'll never see you again, you turn up. What do you want from me, Rafe Gentry?"

He moved closer. Alarm swept through her.

"Things have changed," he said. "I'm no longer wanted for those murders in Ordway. One of the real killers confessed."

"I know. The stage made a stop in Ordway and Sheriff Tattersal told me all about it. I can't see how that changes anything. Your farewell note explained your feelings for me quite adequately. What are you doing here? Why do you continue to torment me?"

He sat on the edge of the bed; she scooted to the opposite edge.

"Because you never stopped tormenting *me*. Not a day or night goes by without me driving myself crazy wondering what you are doing, who you are with, whether you are safe."

"You brought it on yourself, Rafe. I thought things were fine between us. Then you abandoned me. I'm tired of saving your skin. The day you deserted me in Dodge City was the day I stopped caring about you."

Rafe reached over to strike a match and light the lamp. The glow illuminated her face, highlighting the misty brilliance of her eyes, shadowing the delicate texture of her skin. He raised his hand to cup her cheek. She flinched away, and Rafe fervently wished he could undo the damage he'd done with that blasted note.

He closed his eyes and breathed in his wife's sweet scent: soap and sunshine and her own special fragrance. His groin ached, and he grew instantly hard; he felt ragged and needy inside. His hands reacted independently of his mind as he grasped her shoulders and pulled her against him. He hadn't meant to touch her; he'd only intended to explain his actions that day in Dodge City.

He hoped she'd forgive him but feared it was asking too much from her.

Rafe felt her resistance, sensed her reluctance, her fear, and knew he deserved her scorn. God, he wanted to kiss her!

"You're not going to hoodwink me again, Rafe Gentry," Angela charged. "How dare you think you can pop in and out of my life like a jack-in-the-box! Do you think I'm a toy, existing for your convenience?"

"Dammit, Angel, I don't think that at all! Will you hear me out?"

"Why? I won't believe you," Angela hissed. "I've been a fool where you're concerned, Rafe. Just when I've convinced myself I'll never see you again, you turn up like a bad penny. I don't want to hear your explanation. Nothing you can tell me will change my mind about you."

"Have you and your stepfather reconciled?"

Angela's eyes narrowed. "How do you know Desmond is here? Have you been spying on me again?"

"It doesn't matter how I know." Rafe realized Angel was in no mood to listen to him now.

"Before you leave, there's something you should know," Angela said. "I'm filing for divorce. Mr. Goodman is drawing up the papers for my signature."

Rafe reared back and stared at her. Her words were like a blow to the gut. "Had I known you were filing for divorce, I wouldn't have bothered gathering the signatures of people who witnessed our marriage."

She looked confused. "You did that? Why?"

"Isn't it obvious?"

"Nothing is obvious where you're concerned, Rafe. You're the most thoroughly confusing man I've ever met. At least I know where I stand with Desmond and Anson."

"And where is that, Angel?" Rafe asked with disapproval. "Are you planning to marry Chandler?"

"Not that it's any of your business, but I wouldn't marry Anson if he were the last man on earth."

"Then why is he still here?" Rafe challenged.

"Because I intend to prove he killed Brady Baxter!" Angela all but shouted.

Stunned, Rafe stared at her. "I thought you didn't care what happened to me."

Her chin rose defiantly. "I don't."

He gave her a lopsided grin. "Then why are you so anxious to prove my innocence?"

"You should know the answer to that. I can't stand to see an innocent man falsely accused of a crime. I learned from Reverend Conrad that each person is responsible not only for himself but for his fellow man. I know you're not a killer, Rafe."

"Your purity and goodness humble me, Angel. I don't deserve you."

"My thoughts exactly," Angela returned. "My heart can stand only so much pain."

This time she stiffened only slightly when he pulled her into his arms. She knew she'd regret it, but resisting this thoroughly exasperating man was impossible. Common sense told her he'd break her heart again . . . and again, that she should turn away from him and not look back. Common sense flew out the window when Rafe's mouth sought the shell of her ear, whispering her name on a ragged breath. He kissed her eyes, her cheeks. He slipped the nightgown from her shoulders and tasted her skin at her shoulder and at the hollow of her throat.

Her nightgown drifted down to her waist. His tongue followed it down, leaving a vertical path of fire between her breasts. Her breasts felt hot and tingly, and she arched closer, pushing herself into the torrid heat of his caress.

She groaned a protest when he shifted away. Abruptly she realized she was making this too easy for him and somehow found the strength to shove him away. Taken by surprise, Rafe fell backward off the bed and onto his rump.

"What in the hell was that for?" Rafe demanded as he picked himself up off the floor.

Angela's breathing calmed. "For thinking I have no willpower where you're concerned."

He grinned. His gun belt hit the floor.

"Have you? Any willpower, I mean." He tore off his kerchief and ripped his shirt apart. Buttons flew in every direction.

"I like to think so."

He stripped his belt off and unbuttoned his trousers. Air spilled from Angela's lungs as the rest of his clothing melted away. He was fully erect, his shaft thick and pulsing against the rigid muscles of his stomach. Her hands slowly curved in the fabric of the sheets. She willed herself to look away, but she was so weak, so utterly, impossibly enthralled with this man.

Struggling to quell her mounting passion, she scooted over to make room for him when he lowered himself to the bed. His hands slowly curved around her waist, bringing her closer. For a desperate moment they shared a single breath as his mouth sealed hers with a heated kiss.

The delicious pressure of his hands on her breasts made her blood thicken and her heart pump faster. Her lips parted; his tongue eased inside. Too soon, he broke the kiss, his breathing ragged as he searched her face. "You want me as much as I want you, Angel, admit it."

"You know I'm weak where you're concerned. But I despise the fact that you're using my weakness against me," Angela said, sighing despairingly.

"The only thing I want to use against you

is this," he said, bringing her hand to his groin and clamping her fingers around his erection.

Angela stared into his face and saw a flash of raw hunger in the depths of his silver eyes. And something else. An emotion that came from within the deepest part of his soul. He was overpowering her with his desperate need, with his words, and with those incredible, expressive eyes.

Holding her captive with his gaze, he placed a hand on her belly, pressing it as he stroked, wringing a gasp from her. The raging tumult of blood in her veins, the mad rush of sensation, cleared her mind of everything but Rafe, the man she loved . . . no, hated. She was so confused.

Thought skidded to a halt as his hand flattened between her thighs. She closed her eyes and parted her legs for him, anticipation mounting. Her body cried out for his, and it irked her that he knew it. His mouth took hers again, their bodies melded together, breast to breast, hip to hip. She felt his muscles growing rigid as his need escalated.

His fingers parted her, dipping inside, gently soothing the burning ache. Her body screamed for completion, her hand working him in a sliding motion that drew a guttural moan from him. She tried to draw him inside her. He removed his hand and settled between her legs.

He kissed her eyelids, the tip of her nose, her mouth, as he guided himself into the torrid heat of her body. Her muscles clenched around him. Her body was flayed by fire as the storm of his passion ravaged her. Tossing her high. Tumbling her down. He drove harder, deeper into her core, pushing her toward the summit as cresting waves of sensation buffeted her.

She gripped the corded muscles of his upper arms, staring into his eyes as he held himself above her. Despite her tumultuous state of arousal, Rafe seemed in no hurry for his own climax as he forged relentlessly on. The end came suddenly, explosively, as she yielded herself to the firestorm sweeping her to sweet oblivion.

Rafe watched her face closely, not slacking his pace as she found rapture. Then he began to move again, seeking his own pleasure. He gave her a startled look when her body stirred around him and she clutched his shoulders.

"Can you come again, sweetheart?"

Angela seemed beyond coherent speech as she rose up to meet his strokes; she seemed as genuinely surprised at her renewed passion as he was. Rafe moved faster, the smell of sex and sweat a powerful aphrodisiac. His stomach clenched, his muscles jumped. If she didn't . . . soon . . . . Then he heard her cry out, felt the tiny contractions flutter around him, and with a ragged cry of pleasure he spilled himself inside her. His last cogent thought was that he was exactly where he belonged.

"Are you happy now?" Angela asked after the firestorm abated.

For long minutes nothing stirred the air but their harsh breathing. "I want us both to be happy," Rafe finally answered.

Angela turned away. "I want that, too, but it's not going to happen."

"Leaving you in Dodge City wasn't my idea."

It took a moment for her to absorb his words. When they finally registered, she gave a bitter laugh. "I suppose you're going to tell me someone held a gun on you while you wrote that disgusting note."

He gave her a strange look. "That's exactly what happened."

"Really, Rafe, I'm not stupid."

"Far from it, but I'm not lying. Kent got the drop on me in the bathhouse that day. He was the last person I expected to see in Dodge City. He forced me at gunpoint to write that note. If I didn't do as he directed, he would have killed me and claimed the reward. There were still those Colorado warrants for murder that Sheriff Diller seemed to know nothing about.

"I'd just been cleared of bank robbery charges and you were waiting for me back at the hotel. Leaving you was the furthest thing from my mind. Kent changed my plans quickly enough. My situation seemed hopeless. I wanted only the best for you, even if it meant leaving you. I decided you'd be better off without an outlaw dragging you from town to town, one step ahead of the law."

"What changed your mind?"

"Learning that I was no longer wanted for those murders in Ordway gave me renewed hope. After those charges were dropped, I felt confident I could find Baxter's killer and emerge a free man, one without a tainted name.

"But those weren't the only reasons. I couldn't stay away from you, Angel. We're meant to be together, whether you choose to believe it or not. I could no more leave you than I could cut off my right arm."

Her gaze wavered, then fell away. "I want to believe you, Rafe, truly I do."

"But —"

"I'm afraid of being hurt again. I'd be forever holding my breath, wondering when you're going to disappear again."

"Never," Rafe vowed. "I'm never going to leave you again." Rafe hadn't planned on falling in love when Angel claimed him as her fiancé, but she had sneaked up like a thief in the night and stolen his heart. Unfortunately, he still wasn't free to declare his love, so he held his tongue.

"Why, Rafe? Why should I believe you?"

Rafe frowned and looked away. "I know I've given you ample reason in the past to distrust me. I never felt I was right for you because I don't have anything to offer a woman who has everything."

"All I ever wanted was you. I would have given up everything to hear you say . . ." She paused, gulping back her words.

Rafe wanted to reach out to her as she struggled for composure and had to forcibly restrain himself from telling her he loved her. She probably wouldn't believe him in her present state of mind, anyway.

"Oh, what's the use," she sighed. The note of despondency in her voice nearly broke Rafe's heart.

"Angel, listen to me, love. I know what you want to hear, but I can't say the words until I'm a free man. You'll just have to be patient and trust me until that happens."

"Like I trusted you in the past?"

"I know I'm asking a lot of you, but I'm still a wanted man. I can't even offer you my good name."

"I already have your name," Angela reminded him. "But I expect to change that soon."

The violent sound he made was born of pain. "Dammit, Angel, I don't want you to divorce me."

"Exactly what *do* you want, Rafe?"

"I thought I'd made myself clear. I want *you*. I'm determined to find Baxter's killer, and when I do, I'll be free to tell you what's in my heart."

She gave him a disgusted look. "Until then I'm supposed to guess how you feel?"

He sent her a tortured look. "I'm asking you to trust me, Angel. I have to leave soon. No one must know I'm here."

"Have you a plan?"

"Not yet, but I haven't given up."

"Let me help."

Rafe reared up on his elbow. "Absolutely not! We're dealing with two greedy, vicious men. You could be hurt."

Her blue eyes glittered defiantly. "You have no choice. Even if you hadn't returned, I would have pursued this on my own. I over-heard Anson all but admit to Desmond that he killed Baxter. I have an idea how to prove his guilt, but it needs more thought."

"Think all you want, sweetheart, I simply won't allow you to become involved. It's too dangerous."

Angela decided to change the subject. Arguing with Rafe was getting her nowhere. "Are you hungry?"

His stomach growled at the mere mention of food. "Starved. I've existed on the sparse leavings in my saddlebags and whatever game I was lucky enough to bag."

Angela rose from the bed and pulled on a

dressing gown. "I'll fix you something to eat. Then I'll pack up whatever I have on hand for you to take with you. What about blankets? You're staying in the cave, aren't you?" He nodded. "That can't be too comfortable."

"I'll manage."

Angela hurried to the kitchen and lit a lamp. By the time Rafe had dressed and joined her, she had built up the fire in the cookstove, sliced bacon and set the coffeepot on the burner to boil.

"It will be light soon," Rafe said, glancing out the window.

"This won't take long."

"Angel, I meant it when I said you're to keep out of trouble," Rafe said as Angela cracked eggs in the frying pan and cut thick slices of bread from the new loaf she had baked the previous morning.

"You asked me to trust you, Rafe. Now it's your turn to trust me."

She set the plate before him and he dug in with gusto. Angela couldn't help smiling at his healthy appetite. While he ate, she placed a loaf of bread, some canned goods, the rest of the slab of bacon, potatoes and whatever else she thought he could use into a pile on the table. She left the room and returned with two thick blankets, which she placed beside the food.

"Does this mean you forgive me?" Rafe asked between mouthfuls.

"It means I'm thinking about it," Angela said, not giving an inch. She'd been hurt once too often by this powerfully seductive man.

"I have to go," Rafe said, pushing away his empty plate. He glanced at the supplies Angela had readied, then back at her. "How am I supposed to carry all this?"

"In this," Angela said, shaking out the linen pillowcase she had brought with her from the bedroom.

When the pillowcase was filled, Rafe placed it on the table and pulled Angela against him. "I'll be back, Angel." His eyes had darkened with desperate yearning but his humor was still intact as he said, "It would help if you didn't lock the back door. I'm getting too old to climb through windows."

"You *say* you'll return, Rafe, but I don't know what to believe anymore."

"Believe this," Rafe said as his lips settled possessively over hers. His mouth was warm; he tasted of coffee and Rafe. She leaned into him, savoring his unique scent, painfully aware of how easily Rafe had seduced her into trusting him.

He broke off the kiss. "If I don't leave now, I'll never leave," he groaned against her lips. "I have a killer to smoke out into the open, and taking you back to bed isn't the way to do it. Promise you'll stay out of trouble while I find a solution to our problem."

Angela gave him an innocent stare. "Rafe Gentry, I never get into trouble. Getting people, especially you, *out* of trouble is what I do best."

"I know, sweetheart, you're my guardian angel," he said with such tenderness it brought tears to Angela's eyes. "But this time you're out of your league with Kent and Chandler. Let me do this my way."

"Of course," Angela said, crossing her fingers behind her. She pushed him toward the door. "The sun is coming up over the mountains. Hurry, before someone sees you."

"One more thing," Rafe said. "Forget that divorce. I'm not letting you go, Angel."

Wanting desperately to believe him, Angela blinked back tears as Rafe grabbed the sack of supplies, gave her the last kiss and slipped out the door. She watched from the window as purple shadows swallowed him and he became one with the wooded hillside.

Turning away, Angela poured herself a cup of coffee and sat down at the table to ponder the ramifications of Rafe's unexpected return. Could she trust him this time? she wondered. Had Desmond truly forced him to leave Dodge City without her?

It all made sense when she thought about it. Neither Rafe nor Desmond had known that he was no longer wanted for murder in Ordway. Had Desmond shown Sheriff Diller the Wanted poster, Rafe would have found himself behind bars again. Given the choice of fleeing or possibly swinging from the end of a rope, Angela would have chosen the same route Rafe had taken. And Rafe *had* returned to explain, hadn't he?

Not only had Rafe returned, but he'd made love to her as if he truly loved her. He'd done everything but say the words to show her how much he cared. Deep inside, Angela believed those words would come when there was no longer a price on his head. The Rafe she knew wasn't a killer, nor was he an outlaw. He was a man unjustly accused of crimes he hadn't committed.

Whether she liked it or not, helping Rafe seemed to be her purpose in life, the reason God had placed her on earth and put Rafe in her path.

Rafe Gentry was exasperating, hardheaded, possessive and stubborn, but Angela wouldn't have him any other way. Even when she thought she hated him, she loved him.

No matter what Rafe Gentry said, she *was* going to help him find Baxter's killer. She was in a far better position to help him than he was to help himself. Besides, she already had a plan in mind and intended to see it through.

That morning Angela went about her daily chores as usual. No snow had fallen yet, so the miners were still at work. Angela found little opportunity to speak to Kent alone and bided her time. Meanwhile she kept her eyes and ears open.

That evening she left a plate of food in the warming oven, unlatched the back door and waited up for Rafe. He came just after midnight. She took him into the kitchen, poured him a cup of coffee and watched him wolf down the food she had prepared. When he finished, he grasped her hand and led her into the bedroom.

What followed next was a repeat of the night before, only their coupling wasn't as urgent. This time Rafe made a leisurely assault upon her senses, arousing her like a lover who had all the time in the world. First he undressed her, exploring her body with a thoroughness that brought tears to her eyes. Her breasts, her nipples, the tender insides of her thighs, the moist cleft and sensitive nubbin at the entrance of her sex. Then he pushed his tongue inside her, bringing her to gasping completion.

When he would have entered her, Angela turned the aggressor, pushing him back against the mattress and plundering him with her mouth and hands. She felt his broad chest quiver as she licked his flat, brown nipples, felt his stomach clench as she nipped and kissed a path to that thick, hardened part of him that gave her so much pleasure.

He nearly shot out of bed when her mouth closed around the head and drew on him.

His hands tangled in her hair, holding her against him as her eager tongue licked down the ridged underside and back again.

"No more! You're driving me mad."

With a thick, guttural growl he grasped her shoulders, hauled her up on top of him, spread her legs and thrust himself into her core. Shaking and whimpering his name, she came almost immediately; he found his own rapture scant seconds later.

Afterward they slept. They awoke before daybreak and made love a second time before Rafe left her sleeping and crept back to his lair.

Angela awoke more determined than ever to bring Chandler to justice for Baxter's murder. It wasn't right that Rafe should fear to show his face in the light of day. If she ever expected to share a future with Rafe, something had to be done, and fast. Angela knew that Anson would never admit the truth about Baxter's murder to her. But she was almost certain he had told Desmond. Desmond was a greedy man. Therefore, it stood to reason that Desmond could be bribed to betray Chandler's confidence for enough money.

As if her thoughts of Chandler had conjured him up, he showed up at her cabin a short time later.

"It's time to close down the mine for the winter, Angela," Chandler said as he walked into the cabin and made himself at home. "It's October. The miners fear they'll get caught in an unexpected snowstorm and be unable to return to their families."

"They're probably right," Angela agreed. "They know this country better than either you or I. Inform the men that today will be their last day until spring thaw. I'll prepare their paychecks."

Chandler had no sooner left to inform the men about the mine closing than Lawyer Goodman arrived with the divorce papers for Angela to sign.

"You should move to town," Goodman said after greeting Angela warmly. "Colorado winters are harsh, especially up here in the mountains."

"I know," Angela agreed. "I remember a little about them from my youth. That's one of the reasons Mama divorced Papa. She hated the isolation. But I'm not Mama. I'll manage. Come into the kitchen and share my lunch. I just made some fresh coffee."

"Coffee and lunch would be welcome," Goodman said. "How are things going, Angela? Is your stepfather or Chandler causing trouble for you?"

"Anson is still determined to marry me, but Desmond is behaving for now. They both depend upon my goodwill for their livelihood."

Goodman waited until after they had finished lunch before producing the petition for divorce he had drawn up for Angela's signature.

"You'll find everything in order," Goodman said, spreading the document before Angela. "Sign here." He pointed to a place at the end of the document. "I hope you're aware that I can't promise a quick dissolution of your marriage. These things take time, you know."

Angela stared at the paper for a breathless moment, then tore it into small pieces. "I've changed my mind."

Goodman didn't seem at all surprised. "May I ask why?"

"I've seen Rafe. He explained his reason for deserting me in Dodge City to my satisfaction." She launched into a shortened version of the story Rafe had told her.

"And you believed him?"

"Not at first. It took a long time for him to convince me. Rafe may be a lot of things, but he's not a liar. I'm determined to prove he didn't kill Brady Baxter."

"Where is Mr. Gentry now?"

"Nearby," Angela said, fearing to reveal Rafe's hiding place to anyone, even a man she trusted.

"How may I help?"

"By not repeating what I have just told you."

"You have no worry on that score, my

dear. Are you still convinced of Chandler's guilt?"

"More than ever. In fact, I'm convinced he admitted his guilt to Desmond. I think I've figured out how to get Desmond to tell what he knows to the sheriff. I know Desmond. He'd betray his own mother for money."

"Does Rafe know what you're planning?"

Angela studied her hands. "Not exactly."

"Just as I thought. I want to be with you when you confront your stepfather."

"I have to do this my way. I have to wait for the right moment."

"I don't like it, Angela. What if Chandler gets wind of it?"

"He won't. I'll be careful, I promise. Once Desmond agrees to my terms, we'll head right down to the sheriff's office. The only way Rafe and I can have a future together is to bring the man who killed Baxter to justice."

"Very well, my dear, I'll stay out of it for the time being. When do you intend to close down the mine for the winter?"

"Today is the last full workday. The miners are storing tools and putting things in order for their return next spring."

"Tell you what. If I don't see you and Kent in town within . . . say the next three days, I'm coming up here to take you to town myself. You can afford to stay at the best hotel the town has to offer."

"That's too soon. Make it five days and you have a deal."

If she couldn't convince Desmond to betray Chandler in five days, then nothing was going to change his mind. Should she fail, she and Rafe could flee, live someplace where no one knew them. She had enough money for both of them to live on for the rest of their lives. They could buy a ranch in Montana, or a farm in California. Rafe was more important to her than the mine. It had taken a while to realize that, but now she knew without a doubt that she would choose Rafe over the mine any day.

With marked reluctance Goodman left. Angela gathered up the bank drafts for the men, put on a warm wrap, and went out to find Chandler. She found him near the mine entrance.

"I've brought the miners' paychecks," Angela said, handing the drafts to Chandler for distribution. "I've included a small bonus for each man. Tell them we'll be needing workers next spring and we hope they'll return. Your check is in there, too, Anson. You should see about accommodations in town."

"Absolutely not," Chandler retorted. "Now that the mine is closed down, I'll have more time to devote to you. How does a Christmas wedding sound?"

"You should ask the woman you intend to marry that question. Have you seen my stepfather? I need to speak with him."

Chandler's lips flattened. "Dammit, Angela, you know our marriage is inevitable. You need me."

"You're wrong, Anson, I don't need you." Whirling on her heel, she walked away.

Three days passed before she found the opportunity to speak to Kent in private. She encountered him leaving the privy and asked him to join her in her cabin for a private word.

"What is this about, Angela? I know your lawyer was here the other day. Shouldn't I have been called to represent you?"

"I'm quite capable of representing myself, thank you. My business with Mr. Goodman is a private matter."

"Humph," Kent spat. "You always were a conniving little . . . witch. All that aside, I've been thinking about moving to town for the winter, but I'm short of funds. It's not right that you should hold the purse strings."

"If you're lacking money, Desmond, I think I have a solution to your problem."

Kent's face lifted. "You've agreed to marry Chandler!"

"Hardly. Come to my cabin where we can talk without Anson interrupting us."

"If this is some trick, daughter, I'll have none of it. I'm still your guardian."

"My husband is my guardian and I'm not your daughter," Angela contended.

"You have no husband."

"The entire city of Ordway would argue that point with you. Are you coming or not?"

"Only if you agree to part with some of your money."

"I promise you won't be disappointed with my generosity, Desmond, if you agree to my terms."

Chapter Eighteen

"Sit down, Desmond," Angela invited as they entered the cabin.

Neither she nor Kent noticed that a curious Anson had seen them conversing and followed behind at a discreet distance. Nor did they see him make his way around the back of the cabin and slip through the back door. Flattening himself against the kitchen wall, he listened intently to their conversation.

"Just say what you wanted to say and give me the money so I can leave," Desmond said, warming his hands before the fire. "If you and Chandler were wise, you'd follow my example and find lodgings in town for the winter."

"Perhaps I will," Angela hedged. "The reason I asked for a private word with you is to tell you that I know Anson is lining his pockets with my gold."

Divide and conquer, Angela thought sagely. It was an old ploy that just might work.

"How do you know?" Kent challenged.

"The figures in the books don't add up. Anson is wrong if he thinks I'm stupid. I'm very good at adding and subtracting."

"The bastard has been holding out on me," Kent muttered darkly. "Some friend he turned out to be. He'd better share with me after you two are married."

"For the last time, Desmond, I'm *not* going to marry Anson."

Kent's eyes narrowed. "Accidents happen, you know. The same thing that happened to your father could happen to you. As your next of kin, I stand to inherit."

"Your threats don't worry me. You inquired about Lawyer Goodman's recent visit, did you not?" Angela said. "He drew up a will for me to sign."

Kent blanched. "A will? Why would you need a will?"

"For the same reason anyone needs a will. This will has a special provision. Should anything unforeseen happen to me and I die without issue, the mine is to be sold and the proceeds given to charity. The money in my bank account is to be used to open an orphanage and build a church. Not a cent will go to either you or Anson."

Actually, inventing a nonexistent will had just occurred to Angela. And it coincided nicely with Mr. Goodman's recent visit. If either Anson or Desmond had thoughts of harming her, the will would provide a powerful deterrent. In fact, having a will drawn up might be a good idea in any event. She wanted Rafe to have everything that had been hers.

"You little bitch!" Kent shouted. "I should have known you'd find a way to thwart my plans." He jumped to his feet and began to pace.

"Sit down, Desmond," Angela said. "I told you I was going to help you and I will."

Eyeing her warily, Kent perched on the edge of a chair. "What's in that devious little mind of yours, Angela?"

Angela leaned close, her voice lowered to a whisper. "I'll give you ten thousand dollars if you'll tell the sheriff what you know about Brady Baxter's death."

"What!" he blustered. "Everyone knows Rafe Gentry killed Baxter. I wasn't even here when it happened."

"But we both know Rafe didn't kill Baxter."

"I know no such thing."

"I overheard you and Anson discussing Baxter's death one day when I happened to pass behind your cabin while collecting kindling for the stove. I always suspected that Anson had killed Brady but couldn't prove it. Now I have a witness to his confession. You."

"What? How dare you eavesdrop! Besides," he said more reasonably, "you're mistaken. I can't recall that conversation."

"Listen carefully, Desmond," Angela said. "I've fixed it so you'll never touch a cent of my inheritance. You've no funds of your own. You're completely dependent on my good-will."

"It wasn't always that way," Kent said. "I ran a profitable family business. I can't help it if I made a few unwise investments. At least I was smart enough to sell out and come away with a tidy profit. Unfortunately, your mother's illness exhausted all my re-sources."

"Don't blame my mother's illness for your impoverished circumstances," Angela blasted. "You liked gambling too well and you had no head for investments. The family business was only profitable until your father died and left you on your own. You're no businessman, Desmond. That's why you hatched that un-holy plan to marry me to Anson and share my inheritance. That didn't work, so now you have nothing. Agree to my terms and you'll have money again, enough to live the way you wish."

"On a measly ten thousand?" Kent laughed. "Surely the price of my betrayal is worth more than that to you."

Aware of Desmond's mercenary nature, Angela had already considered sweetening the pot. She could well afford it. "Very well, Anson, this is my final offer. Twenty-five thousand in gold. You tell the sheriff what you know, collect your gold and leave town. I don't ever want to see you or hear from you again."

"What if I refuse your 'generous' offer?" Desmond growled.

"You can't afford to. Anson has done nothing to earn your loyalty. There is no way, legal or otherwise, that you and Anson can get your hands on any part of my inheritance."

"I should have beaten you when you were a child," Kent muttered. "Maybe you'd be more manageable now if I'd done so."

Angela's patience was swiftly eroding. "What will it be, Desmond? The choice is yours. Live comfortably on my largesse or find work to support yourself."

"You drive a hard bargain, daughter."

Angela gritted her teeth against the frustration riding her. "I'm protecting my interests. Mine and Rafe's."

"Gentry? He's gone."

"Is he?"

"Bastard! I should have known he'd be involved in this."

"This is strictly my idea, Desmond. If Rafe had his way, you wouldn't receive a cent of my money. Do we have a deal?"

Desmond looked as if he wanted to kill someone. His eyes spewed hatred at her. "You've backed me into a corner; I have no recourse but to agree to your terms. When do you plan to make the trip into town?"

Excitement thrummed through Angela. At long last Rafe would be a free man. Free to love her and free to plan a future.

"Tomorrow morning."

"When will I get my gold?"

"Right after we talk to the sheriff."

"I want to be as far away from Canon City as I can get when Chandler learns I betrayed his confidence."

"Don't worry, he'll be behind bars where he can't hurt you. Meet me at ten tomorrow morning with the buckboard. If Anson asks, tell him you're taking me to town for supplies."

Kent nodded curtly. "If you're finished, I'll leave now. I've got plans to make and clothes to pack."

He headed for the door. Angela didn't stop him. Elation was a heady emotion. Success was another. *Soon,* she promised herself; *soon Rafe will be free to love me.*

A raw wind ruffled Kent's hair as he slowly made his way back to the cabin he shared with Chandler. Soon, he thought, soon he'd have the money he desperately needed. So what if he had to betray Chandler? It wasn't as if Chandler had done anything for him. Chandler had failed at the simple task of persuading Angela to marry him. Furthermore, Chandler had killed a man in cold blood.

A shiver passed through Kent. Had he not heard Chandler's confession with his own ears, he wouldn't have believed his friend capable of killing a man who'd been bound and gagged and unable to defend himself. He knew little of the details except that Chandler had told him he'd been in the right place at the right time and had turned the situation to his advantage.

The cabin was empty when Kent arrived. The fire in the hearth flickered lifelessly, and Kent fed it until the flames leaped high. Winter wasn't even here and already he was feeling the cold. He couldn't wait to leave the mountains for civilization. He pulled out a carpetbag and began tossing his belongings inside.

Moments later the door opened and Chandler blew inside on a chill wind.

"What did you and Angela talk about?" Chandler asked, moving close to the fire to warm himself. "I saw you both entering her cabin." His gaze settled on the carpetbag. "Going somewhere?"

"Thought I'd move into town for the winter," Kent said, unable to look Chandler in the eye. "Angela and I just talked about my leaving."

"I could use your help before you leave. I'd like you to accompany me inside the mine to collect any tools the miners might have left behind. Four hands are better than two."

"Can't you do it alone? I'll fix something for us to eat while you're gone."

"I really do need you, Kent. It won't take long if we work together."

"Very well, but you know I don't like going into the mine."

Ignoring his complaints, Chandler hustled Kent out of the cabin. Chandler struck a match to a lantern he found at the mine's entrance and all but pushed Kent inside.

Thirty minutes later only one man emerged from the mine. He returned to the cabin and left again a few moments later carrying a carpetbag. He reentered the mine and walked out not long afterward . . . empty-handed.

Angela couldn't wait for Rafe to appear that night. She knew he'd be thrilled with what she'd accomplished despite his warning not to meddle. Telling him he'd be a free man tomorrow was bound to soothe his ruffled feathers.

Rafe arrived shortly after dark, several hours earlier than usual. He seemed excited when he greeted her with a hug and a kiss.

"I've decided on a course of action," Rafe revealed.

"Rafe, that's not necessary," Angela began, "I've already —"

"Don't interrupt, sweetheart. I'm determined to end this infernal waiting once and for all."

"But Rafe, let me explain —"

"You, Chandler and Kent are alone up here now that the mine is closed," Rafe continued, ignoring Angela's attempts to explain. "Tomorrow, ask Kent to drive you to town for supplies, then leave Chandler to me."

"But, Rafe —"

"Your job will be to bring the sheriff back up here with you. I don't care how you do it, just do it. Leave the rest to me. By the time I finish with Chandler, he'll be eager to confess to Brady's murder."

"But, Rafe —"

"No, I know what you're going to say. You're afraid I can't make Chandler talk. Well, you're wrong. You'll see."

"But —"

"Don't try to talk me out of this, Angel. I'm tired of running, sick of hiding. I want to show my face in public without fear. I want to walk the streets a free man."

"I know," Angela said sympathetically. "It's going to happen, Rafe. That's what I've been trying to tell you. I convinced Desmond to testify against Anson. We're going to town to see the sheriff in the morning."

"You what? What did I tell you about courting danger? My God, Angel, this whole thing could have blown up in your face. Kent could have told Chandler." A shudder passed through him. "They both could have turned against you."

"It worked, Rafe. Desmond is desperate for money. He knows I'll never marry Anson, and rather than lose everything, he's agreed to tell the sheriff that Anson told him he killed Baxter."

Rafe's lips flattened. "How much did it cost you?"

"I can afford it. Aren't you pleased? Tomorrow you'll be a free man."

"It just seems too damn easy. Listen, Angel, I wouldn't count on Desmond coming through for you."

Angela refused to let herself believe that. All her hopes and dreams rode on Desmond's compliance. "You'll see, it will all work out. Desmond can be trusted when it involves money. Are you hungry?"

"Hungry for you," Rafe said, hugging her fiercely. "Let's go to bed. I want to sleep with you in my arms all night long. When dawn arrives, I hope it will be the last time I'll have to leave you. I want a home, a family." He searched her face. "How do you feel about children?"

"I'd love your children."

He touched her stomach. "You're not . . ."

Placing her hand over his, Angela gave him a mysterious smile. "I don't know yet, but it's definitely a possibility."

His arms tightened around her. "If Kent doesn't come through for you, I'll find a way to clear my name so we can move on with our lives. Our children won't have an outlaw for a father if I can help it."

Angela touched his brow, smoothing away the worry lines. "You're no outlaw, Rafe. Soon the whole world will know it."

If ever a time existed for Rafe to tell his Angel that he loved her, this was it. But he resisted the urge to bare his soul. He wasn't free yet to give his heart. When he told Angel he loved her, he wanted nothing to spoil that special moment. No worries about the law, just a bright future stretching before them.

Sweeping her from her feet, he carried her to the bedroom. Their clothing flew in every direction as they undressed each other. With one goal in mind they fell into bed, both aroused to the point that no further foreplay was needed. Rafe entered her quickly. She climaxed immediately, then climaxed again when Rafe sought his own pleasure.

They slept, made love a second time, then slept again. Shortly before dawn, Rafe shook Angela awake. "It's time for me to leave, sweetheart."

"So soon?" Angela answered sleepily. "You just got here."

"I've been here for hours." He kissed the tip of her nose and tenderly pushed a silky strand of tangled blond hair away from her face. "Go back to sleep, Angel. You don't have to meet Kent for hours yet. You won't be alone. I'll be trailing behind you to make sure nothing goes wrong."

"I'm so happy," Angela murmured drowsily. "Everything is finally going our way."

Angela had already fallen back to sleep when Rafe tiptoed out the back door and into the cold, gray dawn. He wished he were as confident as Angel about today's outcome. What if the sheriff didn't believe Kent? What if Kent reneged on the deal and refused to talk? Rafe shook his head, trying to think positively and not dwell on the disastrous things that could happen. He hoped for the best but would prepare for the worst.

Angela awoke late to a bright day filled with hope and promise. Excitement thrummed through her. After today Rafe would be a free man. She sang her favorite song as she rose and kindled the banked fire in the hearth. She always sang when she was happy, and today she had so much to be thankful for.

Angela dressed carefully, choosing a blue serge skirt with a wide waistband that emphasized her small waist and a white blouse with lace collar and cuffs. Too excited to eat a hearty breakfast, she drank two cups of strong coffee and nibbled on a stale biscuit. At the stroke of ten she stepped outside to meet Kent. Warning bells went off in her head when she saw Anson Chandler waiting beside the buckboard.

"Where's Desmond?" Angela asked in a strangled voice.

Chandler's deceptive smile was far from comforting. "I drove him to town at dawn. He left on the early stage." He pulled out his watch. "He's long gone by now. He asked me to drive you to town today. He said you needed supplies."

Angela's hand flew to her throat. No, this couldn't be happening. "Desmond didn't mention anything to me about leaving when we spoke yesterday. You're lying."

"What reason would I have to lie?"

Desperation rode Angela. "Desmond had no money."

The sun suddenly slid behind a cloud, turning the promising day dark and dismal. But it couldn't compare with the bleakness within Angela's heart. Why would God do this to her?

"I had some money set aside," Chandler said. "Desmond seemed so eager to return home that I gave it to him."

Anson's smug smile hinted that he knew something about the deal she had struck with Desmond. Had Desmond betrayed her? What was she going to do now?

"Are you ready to go to town? I've got some business there myself."

Angela backed away. "I . . . I've changed

my mind. I'll go tomorrow. But you go on. Find yourself lodgings while you're there. I have no further need of you, now or in the future."

Chandler took two menacing steps forward. "You can't dismiss me that easily, Angela. I've devoted too much time to you and the mine to leave now."

"Is that so?" Angela challenged. "We'll see what the sheriff has to say about that. As of this moment you're trespassing on my property. Move away from the buckboard. I can drive myself to town."

"You're not going anywhere," Chandler threatened. "Let me remind you that we are virtually isolated out here. Soon we'll be snowed in for the winter. You and I . . . alone."

"Never!" Angela vowed.

Her protest made little impact upon Chandler. "Do you know what's going to happen, Angela?"

Angela remained silent. She didn't have the foggiest notion what Chandler had in his devious mind. But she didn't have long to wait to learn the answer.

"I'm going to move into your cabin and share your bed. When your belly swells with my child, you'll have to marry me."

"You're mad! There's no way I'll share your bed. I have . . . friends. You won't get away with this."

"Friends?" he guffawed. "You mean that over-the-hill lawyer? A fat lot of good he'll do you."

Angela remembered Mr. Goodman's promise to come up to the mine and move her to town if he didn't hear from her in five days. She had just two more days to wait for him to arrive. But even more heartening was the sure knowledge that Rafe was nearby. She knew he was watching, and when he didn't see her and Desmond leave together in the buckboard, he'd come to investigate.

What truly disappointed Angela was the fact that there was virtually no hope now of proving Rafe's innocence. Anson might confess to her, but it wouldn't mean a thing without witnesses.

"Have I rendered you speechless, my dear?" Chandler taunted. He moved closer. "Can I hope that you're looking forward to my attentions? It's been a long time since you and that outlaw have been together. You're probably hurting for it right now." He touched her breast. "I'll not disappoint you."

A gasp of outrage exploded from Angela's lips as she swatted Chandler's hand away. "How dare you! You have no right to touch me. Your touch makes me want to retch."

"Bitch!" Chandler snarled. "I'm going to enjoy taming you. You're going to lie with me every night until you swell with my child." He swung his arm to encompass the mine. "I've come too far to lose all this because of one obstinate woman."

Angela let her gaze drift beyond Chandler to the hillside above the mine. "I wouldn't be too confident if I were you."

"Go inside and fix me something to eat," Chandler growled. "I'm thoroughly sick of my own cooking. And Kent's clumsy attempts were even worse than mine."

"Cook for yourself," Angela shot back. "I'm going to town for the law. If you're smart, you'll clear out of here before I return."

She tried to move around Chandler but he blocked her path.

"You're not going anywhere. Look up at the sky. Those are snowflakes, if I'm not mistaken."

"Then I'd best get going if I want to reach town before the roads become impassable." She pushed past him. "Get out of my way."

He grasped her arm, bringing her up short. "You're not going anywhere, Angela, except inside that cabin to await my pleasure. I'm partial to roast beef. We can while away the afternoon in bed while the beef cooks. There are no duties, no one around, nothing to keep us from enjoying one another."

"Cook your own roast beef!" Angela spat, jerking her arm from his grasp. "I'm moving to town."

She flew past him toward the buckboard.

She didn't get far. This time when he grasped her arm he bent it behind her. Pain exploded through her. "Don't, you're hurting me!"

"That was my intention. I'm tired of acting like a suitor. It's time you learned to take me seriously. I'm not someone you can push around."

"Since when have you ever acted like a suitor?" Angela hissed.

He twisted her arm higher. Angela rose to her toes, the pressure so great she feared her arm would break.

"I can't cook your dinner with a broken arm."

"That's more like it," Chandler said as he eased the pressure on her arm. Angela wanted to sob with relief but wouldn't give him the satisfaction. "Go inside and wait for me while I unhitch the horses from the buckboard and pack up my belongings for the move over here. I like mashed potatoes with my roast beef," he called over his shoulder.

"I'd like to give you poison with your roast beef," Angela muttered beneath her breath.

This is absurd, Angela thought as she returned to her cabin. Roast beef indeed. If Anson wanted to eat, he'd have to cook the food himself.

The first thing Angela did was retrieve the pistol she'd bought in town from the dresser in her bedroom. She loaded it and shoved it inside her skirt pocket. Chandler was crazy if he thought she'd let him get her with child. A slow smile curved her lips. Besides, she was almost certain she was already carrying Rafe's child.

Angela left the bedroom, the gun a comfortable weight against her hip.

She glanced out the parlor window, letting her gaze drift upward, to the hillside above the mine. She wondered if Rafe was nearby as she pondered her dilemma.

Angela had no idea what had sent Kent fleeing at the crack of dawn. He was a coward, that much was certain. He must have feared Chandler more than he wanted money.

Where was Rafe? she wondered anxiously. Was he waiting on the trail for her and Kent to pass by? Too many puzzles, too few solutions. She had just turned away from the window when Chandler burst into the cabin.

"It's that lawyer fellow. He's coming up the road. What in the hell does he want?"

A great shudder of relief passed through Angela. But it was short-lived when Chandler said, "Get rid of him if you value his life. It wouldn't be difficult to arrange an accident. These mountains are full of hazards. And he *is* an old man."

Angela blanched. "You wouldn't!"

"Wouldn't I?"

The question hung in the air between them

as a knock sounded on the door. Angela moved to answer it. Chandler held her back. "Don't say anything to arouse his suspicion."

"Angela, are you there?"

"He's becoming impatient," Angela hissed. "Let me go." He released her arm and she hurried off to answer the door.

"Mr. Goodman, what brings you up here on such a raw day?" Angela asked brightly. "Come inside and warm yourself by the fire."

He followed her to the parlor and lowered himself into a chair beside the fire. "I told you I'd return, my dear. The promise of snow brought me a day or two early. Are you ready to . . ." His gaze found Chandler. "Am I interrupting?"

"Actually, you came at a good time," Chandler said, placing an arm around Angela's waist and pulling her against him. "You see, Angela has just agreed to marry me."

Goodman's startled gaze swung around to Angela, his shaggy brows raised nearly to his hairline. "Are congratulations in order, Angela?"

Angela fidgeted nervously. If she told the truth, Chandler's threat against the lawyer could become reality. But to admit to being engaged to Anson was unthinkable.

"I haven't agreed to anything," Angela finally said. "I fear Anson is overeager. My divorce isn't final yet and may not be for a long time."

The word *divorce* sent Chandler's eyebrow shooting upward. "Divorce? What divorce?"

Goodman sent Angela a look that indicated his understanding of the situation.

"I advised Angela to obtain a divorce from Mr. Gentry," Goodman said. "She couldn't claim their marriage never took place when dozens of people witnessed the ceremony. Divorce is a long, sometimes exhausting process."

Angela could see the wheels turning in Chandler's head.

"I'll wait for as long as it takes," Chandler said. "We are both eager to cement our relationship with a child. It's quite possible," he announced with sly innuendo, "that we may not wait for the nuptials to start a family. It's going to be a long winter."

"I see," Goodman said, stroking his chin thoughtfully. He knew darn good and well that Angela had torn up the divorce document. Something was definitely amiss.

"I told Angela when I saw her a few days ago that I'd help her find lodgings in town for the winter. You haven't changed your mind, have you, my dear?"

"That's out of the question," Chandler retorted. "Angela and I are remaining here for the winter. Don't worry, I'll take good care of her. After all, she's almost my wife."

"If you have no other instructions for me, my dear," Goodman said, rising, "I'll take my leave. The weather is worsening."

Angela jumped to her feet. "Yes, you mustn't linger. I'll see you to the door."

Goodman wasn't surprised by Angela's haste to push him through the door; he knew she was maneuvering him for a private moment alone. He glanced over her shoulder and saw Chandler following them.

"What's wrong?" he asked softly. "Can you tell me?"

"Find Rafe," she hissed. "He's living in a cave above the mine. Kent has disappeared. Anson is . . ."

"What are you two talking about?" Chandler asked harshly.

"Mr. Goodman just asked about Desmond," Angela lied. "I told him my stepfather returned to Topeka on the morning stage."

"Is that all?" Chandler asked sharply.

Angela faced him squarely. "Of course. What else is there?"

"I'll bid you both good-bye," Goodman said. He hated to leave Angela alone with a killer, but it was imperative that he find Rafe. In fact, it was past time he alerted the sheriff to Angela's suspicions and let him handle Chandler.

Sleet and driving snow prevented Goodman from locating either Rafe or the cave. After an hour of wandering around in the blinding storm, Goodman headed down the mountain.

Covered with snow and numb with cold, the old man stumbled into the sheriff's office and spewed out a story that sounded more like fiction than fact.

"That sounds pretty far-fetched to me, Mr. Goodman," the sheriff said, scratching his head. "Are you sure you've got your facts straight?"

"Every charge against Rafe Gentry except the one stemming from Brady Baxter's murder has been dropped," Goodman said through chattering teeth. "Rafe Gentry is not a killer. Someone else killed Brady Baxter, and Mrs. Gentry has sufficient evidence to prove that Anson Chandler is the killer. She's alone with Chandler at the Golden Angel. You have to go up there now, Sheriff. I fear for her life."

"Then we'd better pray for her, Mr. Goodman. Even the bravest soul wouldn't venture into those mountains tonight."

Chapter Nineteen

"You were wise to send the old man away," Chandler said after Goodman left. "Have you put on the roast beef yet?"

"There's nothing left in the larder but beans and potatoes," Angela informed him. "Why do you think I was going to town for supplies?" She didn't mention that she'd been feeding both herself and Rafe as well as sending food back with him to the cave.

Chandler's nose wrinkled in disgust. "I don't need you to fix food for me."

"That was my next suggestion. You're perfectly capable of cooking for yourself. I'm going to my room."

"Don't you mean *our* room?" He leered at her. "I'll join you."

"On the other hand," Angela hastily added, "I'm hungry."

"So am I. Fix whatever you have on hand. The lawyer interrupted my packing. I'm going to return to my cabin and bring the rest of my things over here before the snow piles up any higher."

A fine dusting of snow blew inside as Chandler opened the door and stepped outside. Angela stared at the door a moment, then went into the kitchen to fix something to eat. The warm weight of the gun inside her pocket gave her a small degree of comfort as she opened a can of beans and threw together the makings for biscuits. She had just taken the biscuits out of the oven when Chandler returned.

"What miserable weather," he complained, shaking the snow off his hat and dropping his bag beside the door.

"Get used to it, there's plenty more like it ahead," Angela warned.

"Let the snow fall. We'll be warm and snug in our bed," Chandler said meaningfully.

Angela placed the biscuits on the table, set out a jar of jam and dished out a plate of beans. Then she sat down to eat her meal.

"What about me?" Chandler asked.

"You can have what's left."

Chandler gave her a surly look but helped himself to beans and biscuits.

Angela scraped the last of the food from her plate into her mouth. With outward calm, she placed the empty plate on the sink and left the room.

"Where are you going?"

"To my room."

Chandler leaped up and headed her off.

"Fine, I'll go with you. It's about time I learned what that cowboy found so irresistible about you. You must be damn good in bed to keep him coming back."

He grasped her shoulders and pushed her through the bedroom door. He followed her inside and slammed the door behind him.

"Take off your clothes."

"No." *Rafe,* she silently implored, *where are you?* Didn't he wonder why she and Desmond had never left the mine?

"Dammit, Angela, I'll tie you up to accomplish this if I have to. It would be easier on both of us if you cooperated."

She turned her back on him and realized too late it was a mistake. One never turned one's back on a snake. He was on her in seconds, pinning her arms to her sides, twisting her around and wrestling her to the bed. She bit his neck, hard. He released her right arm and slapped her. She saw stars. He insinuated his knee between her legs and hiked her skirt up to her thighs.

It took Angela a moment to realize her right arm was unfettered and another to remember the gun in her pocket. When Chandler lifted his hips to remove his gun belt and unfasten his trousers, Angela reached for the gun and worked it free. When Chandler pressed his naked loins against hers, she jammed cold metal into his gut and cocked the hammer.

He reared up. "What the hell!"

"Move off of me," Angela hissed.

"Where did you get that gun?"

"I bought it in town. Did you think I'd come up here without protection?"

He glanced longingly at his discarded gun belt. "Don't even think about it," Angela warned. "Now get out of here."

He hiked his trousers up and backed away from the bed.

"All the way out."

She rose slowly from the bed, holding the gun steady on him as she kicked his holster under the bed and prodded him through the door, all the way to the front of the house.

"Go back to your own cabin. No, better yet, leave the Golden Angel. You don't belong here."

"You may have the upper hand now, but I'm stronger and smarter than you," Chandler blasted. "How long can you hold out against me?"

"As long as I have to," Angela promised. "Move!"

An icy blast buffeted Chandler as he opened the door. "I don't have a coat."

"You should have thought of that before you assaulted me." She aimed the gun at his privates. Chandler took one look at her steady hand and stepped out into the cold. Angela slammed the door and shot home the bolt.

Her heart was still pounding as she lowered the gun and leaned against the door. Dragging in a shaky breath, Angela realized she wouldn't be safe until every window and door was latched. Fear gave her feet wings as she latched the shutters at each window and bolted the back door. The cabin was plunged into darkness but for the light from the hearth. She lit a lantern and took stock of everything she had on hand.

She had enough firewood to last several days, thanks to her foraging trips into the forest. She could make do with the food she had on hand, too. The snowstorm raging outside had arrived too early in the season to last more than a day or two, and she knew she could depend upon Mr. Goodman to bring help. Had he found Rafe? she wondered. Obviously not, for Rafe would be here if he'd known she needed him. She sat down to wait for help. Somehow she would survive until Goodman returned or Rafe arrived.

Dragging himself a few inches at a time, Rafe slithered down the hillside through the driving snowstorm. Pain so intense it stole his breath slowed his progress. The numbing cold that ate through his clothing and into his bones was the least of his worries. The cold was a blessing in disguise, for it dulled the pain caused by his broken leg.

What a helluva mess, he reflected as he

rested against an ice-covered stump to catch his breath. A broken leg was the last thing he'd expected when he'd started down the hill toward the mine. He'd known something was terribly wrong when Angel and Kent failed to leave the mine. Crouched above the mine's entrance, he had waited hours for the buckboard to appear, until blowing snow obscured his view. Fear for Angel brought him from his concealment and he'd started down the hillside on foot, slipping and sliding through snow and sleet.

His feet had found an icy patch, sending him tumbling head over heels. He'd landed hard, with his right leg twisted beneath him at a strange angle, and then everything had gone black. He'd awakened in excruciating pain, certain that his leg was broken.

Crawling on his elbows, Rafe had found a sturdy tree branch and dragged it along with him until he located a spot where two young tree trunks grew close together. It had taken him long, painful minutes to maneuver the foot of his broken leg between the two trunks and wedge it firmly. Lying flat on the ground, he had reached behind him and grasped another sturdy tree trunk. Then he pulled with all his strength, until he heard the bone snap into place. He remembered screaming before passing out.

When he had awakened he'd removed his belt and strapped his leg to the branch he'd dragged with him for that purpose. It wasn't as professional as Jess would have done, but it would have to do.

Rafe crawled inch by painful inch through the snow, making slow but steady progress down the hill. Instinct told him that Angel needed him. She was alone with two vicious men who would do anything to get what they wanted. Why hadn't she and Kent gone to town as they were supposed to? The question hung ominously in the air, reminding him of Angel's vulnerability.

Dulled by pain, Rafe's mind began to drift. He remembered those days after the war when he'd learned that both his brothers had survived. He recalled the sadness of their father's death and the loss of their mother shortly after they had returned home for a joyous reunion.

Wind howled overheard. Blasts of icy air slowly penetrated through the pain. He couldn't go on. He was going to freeze to death before he reached his love. Come spring they'd find his bones in the hills. Then he heard it. The lilting melody of a hymn. Angel's sweet voice floated to him through the fog of his mind. Whether real or imagined, it gave him the will to go on. Renewed strength flowed through him as he continued his struggle toward the angelic voice calling to him.

Dragging his crudely splinted leg behind

him, Rafe slithered down the hillside, aware of nothing but his need to reach Angel. His elbows were scraped raw through his jacket as he used them to propel himself. Gripped in the throes of pain, Rafe focused on his goal with unswerving intensity.

Angel.

He was scarcely aware of the passage of time; it could have been hours or days later when he finally reached the bottom of the hill. He stopped and rested, groaning in frustration when he realized he hadn't the energy to go on. Then, once again Angel's voice floated to him on the frigid wind. She was singing something he recalled from his childhood. The mesmerizing sweetness of her voice gave him the impetus to drag himself to her back door. Slumping in total exhaustion, Rafe stared at the insurmountable obstacle the closed door presented and feared he'd freeze to death before he could muster the strength to make himself heard.

His last thought before he passed out was that he shouldn't have dragged himself to Angel's door. He didn't want her to be the one to find his stiff, frozen body.

Angela wouldn't allow herself to sleep. She sat up in a chair by the fire with the gun in her lap. Occasionally she went to the window and peered through a crack in the shutters to check on the weather. The snow seemed to be diminishing, though the wind was still howling down the chimney. She prayed for the sun to appear tomorrow and melt the snow, opening the road to the mine.

Angela knew Mr. Goodman had understood her message and hoped he'd arrive soon with help. Meanwhile, she felt confident she could handle Anson; she had outsmarted him so far, hadn't she?

Angela rested her head against the high-backed chair and began to sing softly. Singing during times of stress always soothed her. She kept on singing to stay awake. She sang several hymns first, then a lullaby she recalled from her childhood. It reminded her of happier times, when her mother sang to her at bedtime, and somehow it eased her loneliness.

Angela sang until her throat became too dry to continue. She recalled the bucket of spring water she'd carried into the house earlier, before all the trouble had started, and went into the kitchen for a drink. The water was sweet and cool and it soothed her throat. She was about to return to the parlor and the beckoning fire when she stopped abruptly and stared at the back door. A frown darkened her brow.

The door was still latched, but something . . . something she couldn't name drew her closer. Her first thought was that Anson was outside, waiting to pounce once she opened the door, but she quickly discounted that notion. She doubted Anson would stand long in the cold without his heavy jacket. No, it was something else. Then she heard it. A scratching sound, like fingernails scraping against wood.

She placed her ear against the door, but all she heard was the wind whistling around a corner. *Foolish girl,* she chided herself. *It would be folly to open that door. Not only would she let in the cold but perhaps Anson as well.* She turned away but was drawn back by a silent plea she heard only in her head, a sound that had nothing to do with the wind. She listened again but heard nothing further. *You're being fanciful,* she told herself as she returned to the parlor.

Angela's head began to nod; then suddenly she jerked upright. Her gaze returned to the kitchen. Something propelled her to the back door. Her shaking hands moved unerringly toward the door; aware of the risk she was taking, she unlatched the door. Dragging in a sustaining breath, she cracked the door open. A cry of dismay ripped from her throat when the door was jerked from her hand and an inert body fell into the room.

The body was covered with snow, from the top of his hat to the soles of his boots. Ice rimmed his eyebrows and lashes, and his mouth was twisted into a grimace of pain.

Rafe! Oh, God, was he dead?

He was lying unconscious, half in and half out of the door. She grasped his shoulders and tried to pull him inside so she could shut and latch the door. Her first tug brought an unholy scream from his bloodless lips.

"Rafe, what's wrong?"

His head rolled from side to side. Then she spied the crude splint on his right leg, and tears sprang to her eyes. The agony he must have suffered getting here was beyond comprehension.

"Rafe, I can't leave you like this. I'm sorry, my love, but I have to get you inside."

Grasping his shoulders again, she slowly and, as carefully as she knew how, maneuvered him until his entire body was inside. She quickly shut and latched the door, then returned to Rafe. He was shivering uncontrollably. Since she couldn't move him by herself, she did the next best thing. She hurried into the bedroom and returned with pillows and all the blankets she had on hand. Once she'd made him comfortable, she sat back on her heels and brushed the snow from his face.

She was heartened when he opened his eyes and tried to smile.

"Am I in heaven?"

"You're too stubborn to die," Angela said, smiling through her tears.

"I see an angel, I must be in heaven," he

said, his teeth chattering. "I didn't realize it would be so cold in heaven."

"You must have been out in the cold a very long time," Angela said, pulling the blanket up to his neck.

He tried to move and grimaced. "I hurt. What happened?"

"You tell me. I found you at my back door."

Rafe's brow furrowed in concentration. Suddenly it cleared. "Are you all right? Why didn't you and Kent go into town as you were supposed to? I feared something terrible had happened to you. I waited as long as I could, then started down the hill to make sure you were all right. I reckon haste made me careless, for I lost my footing and fell. The bone in my lower leg snapped but didn't break through the skin."

"Who set your leg?"

"I did."

Amazement colored her word. "*You* did? You need a doctor. As soon as the roads become passable, I'll put you in the buckboard and take you to town."

"Forget about that for now. Why didn't you and Kent go to the sheriff as planned?"

"Desmond left. Anson said he took Kent to town early this morning to catch the stage to Topeka. I don't know why he'd do a thing like that. It just isn't like him to turn down a large sum of money."

"I told you not to count on Kent," Rafe reminded her.

"But I was so sure. I don't like this, Rafe. I was so sure. Something is desperately wrong."

She decided not to tell him about her problem with Anson, for Rafe had enough on his plate right now.

Rafe frowned. "Why am I on the floor?"

"I couldn't carry you, and dragging you caused you too much pain. Your leg needs attention. A better splint might ease your pain some."

"I agree. Help me up. I can hobble on one leg to the bed while you find something more suitable for a splint than this tree branch."

Angela braced herself as Rafe used her shoulders to pull himself up. His face was ashen and she feared he would pass out, but he hung on tenaciously until he was balanced on one foot. Then she placed an arm around his waist and took his weight while he hobbled the short distance to the bedroom. When she eased him down and lifted his legs onto the mattress, he sighed and drifted into unconsciousness.

Taking advantage of Rafe's senseless state, Angela lit a lamp so she could properly inspect his injury. The first thing she had to do was replace the crude splint with something sturdier. She rummaged in the wood box and found several two-foot lengths of aspen sapling she had chopped for the fireplace. She stripped the bark off of two of them and carried them into the bedroom. Rafe was still out as she unwound the belt and carefully removed the tree branch from his leg.

Using the knife she found in a sheath at his waist, she slit his trouser leg to his thigh and cut his boot away from his foot. Then she carefully ran her hands over the break. Rafe had been right. The skin wasn't broken, and the bone had been snapped back into place. With tender care she placed the splints she had prepared into position and began tearing strips from the top sheet. Rafe awoke while she was tying the last strip of cloth into place.

"I'm sorry," Rafe apologized.

"Why?"

"For passing out. I hate weakness."

"Weak? You call a man who sets his own broken leg weak? The fact that you made it down here at all proves you're made of strong stuff. Are you feeling any warmer now?"

"Not much." He patted the bed. "Lie with me, Angel. Keep me warm."

"How about some hot coffee first?"

"Body heat," Rafe said, shivering. "I need your body heat."

Angela couldn't refuse his plea, nor did she want to. "Let's get you out of your wet clothes." She tugged off his soggy jacket, then his vest and shirt.

"I'm going to have to finish cutting your trousers away." She removed his gun belt, then picked up the knife and carefully sliced away the remnants of his trousers.

"You've cut off my boot," Rafe said when he noticed his bare right foot.

"I had no choice." She pulled off his other boot and dropped it beside the first. "I'm going to the kitchen for blankets," she said, hurrying off.

Rafe was still shivering after Angela had tucked several blankets around him.

"B-b-body heat, Angel," Rafe repeated. "It's the o-o-only way."

Without hesitation Angela quickly shed her clothing and climbed beneath the blankets with Rafe, careful not to disturb his injured leg. His arms came around her and she snuggled against him, feeling safe for the first time in a very long time.

Rafe felt the heat from Angel's body seeping through his pores and warming his bones. If it weren't for the throbbing pain in his leg, he would be a contented man. Though he was in no condition to make love, just holding Angel in his arms was better than any medicine a doctor could prescribe. He sighed, feeling himself being sucked down into a dreamless void. But something important kept tugging him back, some significant piece of information that was missing.

Forcing his mind to concentrate, he finally recalled what he'd wanted to ask Angel. "Are you asleep, Angel?"

"No. It's almost dawn."

"You haven't told me everything, have you?"

A long silence ensued.

"Angel, something is troubling you. Is it Chandler?"

"I didn't want to tell you yet. You're in no condition to do anything about Anson."

Rafe stiffened. "You may as well tell me what he's done."

"You're right about Anson. After Kent left, he told me he intended to share my . . . bed. He said I would *have* to marry him once my belly swelled with his child. He's desperate, Rafe. He said he's spent too much time and energy on me and the mine and he wasn't going to lose it because of a stubborn woman."

"Where's my gun? If he touched you, I'll kill him."

"He didn't get a chance. I had the gun I bought in town. I forced him to leave and locked him out. Mr. Goodman came up to the mine yesterday before it started to snow, and I managed to get a message through to him. I expect him to bring help as soon as the roads are passable."

"What brought Goodman up here?"

413

"I had no one else to confide in, so I told him about my plan to clear your name. Though he thought the plan dangerous, he allowed me five days to get Kent to agree to testify against Anson. If my plan didn't work, I promised him I'd move to town for the winter.

"Mr. Goodman didn't wait five days, thank God. He turned up ahead of time. He feared the weather would take a turn for the worse and worried that I'd be snowed in. He intended to take me back to town with him. Anson was here when Mr. Goodman arrived, and he had the gall to tell the lawyer we were going to be married."

"The bastard," Rafe hissed.

"Not only that," Angela continued, "Anson told Mr. Goodman we weren't going to wait for the wedding to start a child. I managed a moment alone with Mr. Goodman before he left. He already suspected things weren't right here. I told him where to find you, but obviously the snow hindered his search. I expect him to arrive tomorrow, weather permitting, with the sheriff."

"At times you're more a tiger than an angel," Rafe said, summoning a grin. "You'd probably find a way to conquer the devil himself if he challenged you. You look and sing like an angel but have a warrior's strength and courage. Did you know your singing gave me the strength to go on when I would have given up?"

Angela gave him a startled look. "You couldn't have heard me singing."

"You *were* singing, weren't you?"

She stared at him. "I . . . yes, I was singing, but no one outside this cabin could have heard me."

Rafe knew differently. Had he been halfway to hell, he would have heard her calling him back.

"You saved my life, Angel. How many times is that now? I lost count long ago. Now it's my turn to help you. I won't let anything happen to you, love. A broken leg won't hamper my aim. I'll kill Chandler before I'll let him hurt you. Go to sleep. There are still a few hours left before dawn."

"Are you in pain? I believe I saw a bottle of laudanum in Father's medicine kit."

"I can stand the pain," Rafe said. "I don't want to take anything that will spoil my aim."

"No shooting, Rafe. You don't need another murder charge hanging over your head."

"Let me worry about that. Go to sleep."

Rafe waited until Angela fell asleep before scooting to the edge of the bed and reaching for his guns. Sliding them out of his gunbelt, he placed them under his pillow. Only then did he allow himself to relax. Finally, he slept.

Rafe awakened first. Sunshine streamed through the shutters. It appeared as if the early storm had blown itself out, leaving clear blue skies and sunshine, which wasn't an unusual occurrence in Colorado. He shook Angela awake.

"Wake up, sweetheart. It's daylight."

Angela stretched, felt the warmth of Rafe's body beside her and smiled.

"I hope that smile is for me."

She opened her eyes. "I thought I'd dreamed you."

"Like a bad penny, I keep turning up. Open the shutters."

Angela threw back the blanket and gasped as cold air hit her warm skin. "Oh, it's freezing." She drew on a warm robe and stepped into a pair of slippers. Then she went to the window and opened the shutters.

"Oh, look! The sun is shining and the snow is beginning to melt."

Rafe balanced himself on an elbow and gazed out the window. "Last night's storm was a freak occurrence. I wager we'll have a few days of Indian summer before winter arrives for good."

"Do you think the road up to the mine will be open?"

"Muddy, perhaps, but negotiable. Are you sure Goodman will arrive with the sheriff?"

"I'm as certain as I can be. They won't know you're here, though. No one does.

416

You're safe as long as you remain in the bed-room."

"What are you going to tell the sheriff?"

"The truth as I know it about Brady's murder. He has to believe me. If only Desmond hadn't left. He seemed so anxious to get his hands on the money I offered him."

"Perhaps he didn't leave willingly," Rafe suggested.

"You don't think he —"

A commotion at the front door halted her in mid-sentence.

"It's Anson," Angela hissed.

Anson's voice, accompanied by loud pounding, reverberated through the cabin.

"I came to apologize, Angela," Anson shouted through the door. "I wasn't myself yesterday. Open up. Give me another chance to prove I can be the kind of man you need."

"I'm not dressed, Anson," Angela called back.

"I'll wait, Angela. I want to apologize to your face."

"What shall I do?" Angela whispered to Rafe.

"Stall him. Tell him anything."

"Angela, please. I promise to be on my best behavior," Chandler whined.

Angela moved to the door. "Come back later, Anson, after I've made myself present-able."

"You're stalling."

"I swear I'm not. Besides, how do I know you'll behave if I let you in?"

"You have my word. Give me a chance to persuade you that marrying me is best for both you and the Golden Angel. I'll court you until your divorce is granted and I'll not force you, if that's what's worrying you. I never realized you could be so fierce. I was foolish to underestimate your determination."

"Tell him you'll hear him out when he returns, but he should give you enough time to dress and eat breakfast," Rafe whispered.

Angela relayed the message.

"If you insist," came Anson's petulant reply.

"Don't forget," Angela added, "I still have my gun and know how to use it."

"I won't forget," Anson mumbled.

"He's gone," Angela said, moving away from the door. "I'll build up the fire and fix us something to eat. We can decide what to do while we're eating."

Angela ate in the kitchen, then prepared a tray for Rafe. While he ate, she fetched a shirt and pair of trousers that had belonged to her father. She cut off the right leg to accommodate the splint and helped him to dress.

"I know what I have to do," Rafe said after he drained the last drop of coffee from his cup.

Angela liked neither his grim tone nor the way his mouth tautened. "What is that?"

"When you let Chandler inside, I'm going to meet him with both guns drawn and order him off the property."

"What if he refuses?"

"That's his problem," Rafe said tersely. "I'll do what I have to do to make sure he doesn't bother you again. I can shoot straight even if I can't walk."

"No! If you kill Anson, we'll have no way to prove your innocence. There's got to be another way."

"There's no other way, Angel."

"I won't let you be carted off to jail again."

Rafe smiled wearily. "I'm tired of running, Angel. Mr. Goodman is a capable lawyer; I'll ask him to defend me. It's a chance I have to take in order to protect you from Chandler."

Angela's mouth turned downward. There was no way she was going to allow Rafe to act unwisely. She'd think of something; she had to.

Chapter Twenty

Angela was ready for him when Chandler knocked on the door a short time later. When she'd returned to the kitchen to fetch Rafe another cup of coffee, she'd added a liberal dose of laudanum. He'd fallen asleep in the middle of a sentence. She knew he'd be livid when he awakened, but it was the only way she knew to keep him from killing someone or getting killed himself.

"Are you going to let me in, Angela?" Chandler called through the closed door.

"Only if you behave," Angela returned.

"I said I would."

Angela cast an anxious glance at the closed bedroom door and prayed that she'd given Rafe enough laudanum to keep him from interfering.

"Very well."

She patted her pocket to reassure herself that her gun was still there and opened the door to admit Chandler. She had no idea what she intended to do, but anything was better than allowing a confrontation between Anson and Rafe.

"It's about time," Chandler complained as he strode through the open door.

"What is it you wanted to talk about?" Angela asked.

"Don't pretend with me, my dear. You need a man to protect you, someone who can control the miners when they return in the spring. You know from experience how reluctant they are to work for a woman. There's enough wealth here to share. Our marriage will be a positive step for both of us."

"I'm still married to Rafe."

He grasped her shoulders, giving her an ungentle shake. "I can wait for the ceremony. As I said before, getting you with child is more important."

Angela wrested herself free and took an involuntary step backward. "Touch me and you're a dead man."

Chandler retreated a step. "Do you still have that blasted gun?"

"I wouldn't have let you inside if I wasn't armed. Sit down. Let's discuss this like civilized people."

"I don't feel civilized," Chandler grumbled as he dropped down into the nearest chair. "You can't begin to know the things I've done to get what I want."

Angela's heart nearly stopped. "Tell me what you've done, Anson," Angela said sweetly. "Maybe I'd appreciate you more if I knew what you'd done to achieve your goal. Strong men intrigue me."

Chandler gave her a suspicious glance, but Angela knew she'd struck a nerve when he preened for her benefit.

"You think I'm a strong man? Funny you never mentioned it before."

"Indeed I do. You've never given up on me. That's more than I can say about Rafe Gentry. Tell me, Anson," she whispered seductively; "tell me how much you want me. What have you done or are willing to do to get me?"

Chandler smiled obsequiously. "If you only knew."

"Knew what?" Angela taunted. Even if no one else heard Anson's confession, her word should count for something.

Anson stared at her, as if trying to decide whether or not to trust her sudden interest in him. "Why should I trust you?"

"Why not? We're alone. No one can hear what you say. Besides, it could change my mind about marrying you."

While Angela and Chandler verbally sparred with one another, two riders approached the mine. They reined in a short distance down the road to assess the situation before forging on.

"You'd better know what you're talking

about," Sheriff Dixon said to his companion. "Are you certain Mrs. Gentry is in danger?"

"As sure as I am of sitting here on this horse," Lawyer Goodman declared. "Angela's message yesterday was unmistakable. Thank God the storm abated and the roads weren't in as bad shape as we thought."

"Hmmm," Dixon said, stroking his chin. "If you're right, I don't want to go busting in there and endanger the woman's life. We'll leave our horses here and walk to the mine on foot. That way we can nose around without calling attention to ourselves."

"Good idea," Goodman agreed, dismounting. "There's plenty of cover around the cabins."

"You did say Mrs. Gentry was alone out here with Anson Chandler, didn't you?"

"I did," Goodman said. "I told you what he said about not waiting for a marriage ceremony to get a baby on Angela. And you are aware, of course, that Angela believes Chandler killed Brady Baxter. I sincerely believe Chandler presents a grave danger to Angela."

"Then we'd best find out what's going on," Dixon said. "Let's go."

Frustration gnawed at Angela. Anson was leaning close, preparing to confide in her, and as luck would have it, no one was around to hear his confession. If only . . . She glanced out the window to contemplate her dilemma and swallowed a gasp when she glimpsed two faces pressed against the pane. Sheriff Dixon and Mr. Goodman! Fearing Anson would see them, she jumped to her feet and walked toward the kitchen, turning Chandler's attention away from the window.

"Where are you going?" Chandler asked, turning to follow her. "I thought you wanted to hear what I had to say."

"I just made fresh coffee," Angela improvised. "I thought you might like some before we have our talk."

"Why, thank you, Angela, coffee sounds wonderful. My own tastes like mud." His brow furrowed. "You're not thinking of leaving through the back door, are you?"

"No, I have no intention of walking away from you. I'm more than anxious to hear what you have to say." She glanced toward the window, relieved to note the faces had disappeared. "I'll be right back."

Chandler appeared lost in thought as Angela ducked into the kitchen. She made a beeline for the back door and prayed it wouldn't squeak as she cracked it open. Her prayers were answered when the sheriff and Goodman slipped inside. She motioned for silence and nodded her head toward the parlor.

"Angela, are you still there?"

Chandler's voice sounded petulant, and Angela was quick to answer. "I'm still here,

Anson." She carefully poured out two cups of coffee. "Do you like sugar in your coffee?"

"Two spoons. Whatever is keeping you?"

"I'll be there directly."

"Are you in danger?" the sheriff asked in a hushed voice.

"Stand by the door and listen," Angela whispered as she picked up the coffee cups and headed out the door.

"Ah, there you are," Chandler said. "I was just about to come after you." He accepted the cup from her hand and took a cautious sip of the hot liquid. "Now, where were we?"

"You were just about to tell me some of the things you've done on my behalf. I need to know how strong and smart you really are, Anson."

"Smarter than Brady Baxter," Chandler snorted. "I know why you married him, you know. I followed you and Baxter home after that farce of a wedding ceremony. I suspected funny business was afoot the moment I heard you had married that man. I followed you and Baxter into the mine and heard everything."

"You know Brady had overpowered Rafe, tied him up and dragged him into the mine?" Angela asked. "You know that he threatened to kill Rafe if I didn't marry him?"

"All that and more," Chandler said smugly. "I saw you knock Baxter unconscious, and I saw you and Gentry tie him up and leave the mine together."

"You killed Brady!" Angela blasted. Though she'd expected it all along, it still came as a shock to hear him calmly admit killing a man.

"Yes, but you already knew that, didn't you? I thought it was rather smart of me. I knew Gentry would be blamed, and that he'd have no choice but to flee and leave you to me."

"I suspected you killed Brady, but had no proof," Angela said.

"You have proof now. I'm a strong man, Angela. Strong enough to get rid of the competition."

"I suppose one could consider murdering a helpless man a show of strength," Angela said with scathing sarcasm. Chandler seemed oblivious to her derision.

"Yes, well, you have to admit I rid you of a nuisance. Two, if you count Gentry. Three, if you include Kent."

Angela was quick to pick up on Chandler's remark. "Kent? What about him? How did you get him to leave?"

Chandler gave a snort of laughter. "I eavesdropped on your conversation with Kent. I knew you suspected me of Baxter's murder the moment I heard you offer Kent a ridiculous amount of money to tell the sheriff what he knew. I couldn't allow that to happen so I took measures to ensure Kent's silence."

"You offered him more money?" Angela asked, not sure where this was leading. Kent's disappearance hadn't been fully explained and she hadn't really given it much thought. But Chandler had raised a subject that begged for clarification.

"As if I had enough money to outbid you for his loyalty," Chandler scoffed.

Suddenly it all became clear to Angela. "My God, you killed Desmond!"

"He was a fool. I'm not Kent's bootlicker like you thought I was. Now that you know everything, I want your word that you'll marry me when you're free. And don't think to use my 'confession' against me, for I'll deny it."

Abruptly the bedroom door crashed open and Rafe burst through, balancing himself on one leg. That he had found the strength to drag himself out of bed in his drugged state stunned Angela, but she could tell by his white face and pained expression that he was suffering untold agony. He leaned against the doorjamb, a gun held firmly in one hand while he balanced himself with the other.

"I heard, Chandler. Every damn word."

Angela started to go to Rafe, but Chandler grabbed her around the neck and produced a gun from somewhere on his person. "Well, well, if it isn't Rafe Gentry," Chandler sneered. "What ill wind blew you to the Golden Angel?"

"Release Angel and move away from her," Rafe demanded.

"Not on your life," Chandler responded, pressing his gun more firmly against Angela's unprotected throat.

"You won't get away with this," Rafe threatened. "You killed two people in cold blood."

Chandler gave a mirthless laugh. "You're a fool if you think the law will believe you. I'm not the outlaw, Gentry, you are."

Suddenly Lawyer Goodman stepped from the kitchen into the parlor. Angela waited for Sheriff Dixon to appear, and when he didn't, she wondered what had happened to him.

"I also heard everything, Chandler," Goodman said. "You may as well give up and turn yourself over to the law."

"What in the hell are you doing here, old man?" Chandler growled. "I thought I saw the last of you yesterday."

"Surely you didn't think I believed that cock and bull story about you and Angela getting married, did you? Your days of freedom are over."

"Like hell!" Chandler shouted. "I'm leaving and I'm taking Angela with me. If either of you try to follow, Angela will die. I'm desperate. I've lost everything. One more murder won't matter at this point."

Rafe felt himself starting to slide, felt his senses dull. He couldn't imagine what had made him so damn groggy and suspected Angel of drugging him. She hadn't wanted him to challenge Chandler and had taken steps to prevent a confrontation. Probably she had slipped laudanum into his coffee. Dammit! Why couldn't she have trusted him?

He watched as if from a great distance as Chandler began dragging Angel toward the front door. He felt so damn helpless, as if his body was paralyzed, his mind numb. Even if he could raise his arm, he doubted he had the strength to pull the trigger with any accuracy should he have a clear shot at Chandler. He could only watch . . . and fight to remain conscious.

Then he saw his Angel stomp on Chandler's foot. Rafe uttered an anguished cry when Chandler struck her a glancing blow on the head with the butt of his gun. She went limp in Chandler's arms, and Rafe felt such rage that he forgot his broken leg and lunged forward. His roar of outrage turned into one of pained dismay as he tumbled to the floor. He heard Chandler's laughter and watched through a red haze of pain as Chandler dragged Angel's limp form toward the front door.

"You won't get far," Goodman said as he went to Rafe and helped him to sit up.

"Are you going to stop me, old man?"

"No, but I will. Drop your gun, Chandler."

When Sheriff Dixon had divined Chandler's intention of using Angela as a shield, he had instructed Goodman to distract Chandler while he sneaked out the back door to cut off Chandler's escape.

Chandler glanced over his shoulder and spit out an oath. "Where did you come from?"

"I've been here long enough to hear your confession. Drop the gun, Chandler. I'm taking you in for the murders of Baxter Brady and Desmond Kent."

"Like hell!" Chandler bit out. "I've got the upper hand." He pressed his gun deeper into the soft flesh of Angela's throat. "Come one step further and I'll kill her."

"You won't get far," Dixon warned.

"We'll see about that. Move away from the door."

Angela suddenly came alive, catching Chandler by surprise. Bringing her elbows forward, then back, she rammed her captor in the ribs. The blow was hard enough to stun him. Caught off guard, Chandler inadvertently lowered the gun, allowing Angela to spin away from him. Sheriff Dixon took over from there. Grasping Chandler's arm, he wrested the gun from him and pinned his arms behind him.

"Someone get a rope," he called out as he wrestled with Chandler.

"There's a rope hanging outside the kitchen door," Angela said.

"I'll get it," Goodman said as he strode past her. He returned seconds later and helped Dixon tie up the struggling Chandler.

While they were occupied with Chandler, Angela turned her attention to Rafe. He was sitting on the floor, his back against the wall, his face ashen. She dropped down beside him.

"Are you all right?"

"I'll live," he said through gritted teeth. He lifted a hand to caress her face. "What about you? I wanted to kill Chandler for striking you. Unfortunately, my body refused to react as I wanted it to."

Angela rested a hand on his chest, warmed by the steady beat of his heart. "It's over," she choked out. "It's really over. You're free, Rafe. You can go wherever you please, do whatever you want without looking over your shoulder, wondering when the law will catch up with you."

"Thanks to you," Rafe said hoarsely. "My guardian Angel."

Angela gazed up at him, taken aback when she saw moisture gathering in the corners of his eyes. Her own eyes were ready to overflow.

"Are you two all right?" Sheriff Dixon asked. He and Goodman had subdued Chandler and left him lying on the floor.

"I'm fine except for a rather large bump on my head," Angela said, "but Rafe needs a doctor to see to his leg."

"I'll send one up as soon as we reach town," Dixon promised. He gestured toward Chandler. "I'll be carting this one to jail. Wouldn't be surprised to see him hang for his crimes, but we'll leave that to the judge and jury to decide. Can I help you back to bed, Mr. Gentry?"

Rafe allowed Dixon to help him up, and with the sheriff's help, he hobbled into the bedroom. Angela fussed over him as he settled into bed.

"I'm sorry for all the problems you've encountered with the law," Dixon continued. "It's a damn shame when an innocent man is accused of crimes he didn't commit. You're a free man, Gentry. You'll no longer be troubled by the law, if I have anything to say about it. If you and the missus ever need my help, you have but to ask."

"Much obliged, Sheriff," Rafe said. "You don't know how good it feels to finally be free of all those false charges. I just wish I knew how to contact my brothers and let them know they're no longer wanted men."

"Well, if there's anything I can do, let me know. I'd better get this scum to jail and send the doctor up to see to your leg."

"I'll be off, too," Goodman said from the bedroom doorway.

"I can't thank you enough, Mr. Goodman," Angela said. "I don't know what I would have done if you hadn't interpreted my message correctly when you were up here yesterday. I shudder to think what would have happened had you and the sheriff not arrived when you did."

"It's all over, my dear," Goodman said. "You and your husband have a lifetime together. Don't waste a moment of it."

Angela kissed Mr. Goodman on the cheek. "Come back and see us often."

Goodman touched his cheek and beamed. "You couldn't keep me away."

Angela watched dispassionately from the doorway as Chandler was hefted onto his horse and led away by the sheriff. Though she knew she had nothing more to fear from Chandler, she flinched when he shot her a hate-filled look. Suppressing a shiver, she hurried back to Rafe.

Rafe held out his arms to his Angel. She went into them gladly, snuggling against him. His leg hurt like the very devil but he needed to feel her against him. He loved her so much, and at long last he could tell her exactly what was in his heart. He was a free man. Free to live where he pleased. Free to love his Angel. Free to raise a family with her.

"What are you thinking?" Angela asked. "Are you in pain? Can I give you some laudanum?"

Rafe scowled. "I've had enough laudanum, thank you. Why did you drug me?"

"I was afraid you'd kill Anson, or he would kill you, and I couldn't let that happen. Are you angry?"

He picked up her hand and placed a kiss in the center of her palm. "I can never stay angry with you for very long, Angel. What does upset me is the fact that you placed your life in danger. You always assume you can handle yourself in any situation, and that frightens me. It's going to take a lifetime of constant surveillance to keep you safe."

"A lifetime?" Angela asked breathlessly. "Does that mean . . ."

"Surely you don't think I'd ride away from you now, do you?" Rafe asked, smiling. "I love you, Angel. I've always loved you."

"You do? Why haven't you told me before now?"

"I wasn't free to tell you. I was a wanted man; I had no right to claim your love."

"You claimed my love long ago, Rafe. I've been helplessly and hopelessly yours for a very long time."

"I wish . . ."

"What do you wish?"

"I can't help thinking about my brothers. Jess is a good doctor. As long as he thinks he's wanted by the law, he's not free to practice his profession. And then there's Sam. Sam is a hothead and there's no telling the kind of trouble he'll get himself into. If only there was some way to tell them they're free men."

"Do you know where to find them?"

"I wish I did. We agreed to meet in Denver a year from the day we left Dodge. Jess rode north and Sam headed south. They could be anywhere. All I can do is hope and pray they get the word that they're no longer wanted for bank robbery."

"What about us, Rafe? What are your plans for the future?"

"You love me and I love you; for now that's enough."

"And the mine?" Angela wondered. "I know becoming a miner doesn't exactly thrill you."

"The mine is yours, sweetheart. You decide what you want to do and I'll abide by your decision. We have the entire winter ahead of us to make plans. Come spring . . . well, we'll cross that bridge when we come to it."

Angela sent him a cheeky grin. "Things are definitely going to change come spring."

"How so?" Rafe asked curiously.

She grasped his hand and placed it on her flat stomach. "You can't feel it yet, but I'm pretty positive your child is growing inside me. I hope you're as happy as I am about it."

Rafe's hand tightened around hers. "What! How long have you known?"

"Long enough."

"Whatever possessed you to place your life in danger when you knew you were increasing? Dammit, Angel, I ought to toss you over my knee and spank you." He shuddered. "God, I could have lost you. My life wouldn't have been worth living without you."

"Rafe, you're hurting my hand. I thought you'd be happy."

Rafe released her instantly. "I'm sorry, love. I *am* happy. Words can't express how I feel about starting a family with you. I've dreamed about it but never allowed myself to believe it would happen." His eyes grew misty. "A baby. I hope it's a girl. I want her to look just like you; our own little songbird."

Angela sighed happily.

"We're going to move into town for the winter," Rafe said decisively. "I'm not taking unnecessary chances with your health. Should you need a doctor, I want to be where one can reach us."

"I suppose you're right," Angela allowed. "I'm a rich woman. We can rent the best house in town."

Rafe stiffened. "I'm not the kind of man willing to live off his wife's bounty, Angel. Once this leg heals, I'll be looking for something to do. I've always wanted to be a rancher, to raise horses. I'd like to buy a ranch somewhere in Colorado if I can negotiate a loan. How does that strike you? Colorado is beautiful country. I'd like to stay, if that's acceptable to you."

"Hmmm, a ranch sounds like a wonderful place to raise our children. I love it here, too, and I've known for a long time that I'm not an enthusiastic miner. This place holds memories for me, some good ones from my youth and some bad ones from the present. I think Father would understand if I sold the mine and became a rancher's wife."

"God, I love you," Rafe said, hugging her against him. "Do you know how badly I want to be inside you right now?"

"Almost as badly as I want you to be," Angela replied huskily. "Forget it, Rafe. You're in no condition to make love right now."

Rafe's silver eyes gleamed wickedly. "You want to bet?"

His hands settled on the neckline of her dress. "Take it off."

"But, Rafe . . ."

"Do as I say, love."

"Your leg . . ."

"I don't make love with my leg."

Rafe brushed aside her protests as he unbuttoned her bodice to the waist and untied the strings holding her chemise together. When he lowered his head and sucked a pert nipple into his mouth, Angela's willpower melted. Grasping his head between her hands, she held it in place and arched upward into his heated caress as he stroked the tender peaks with the rough pad of his tongue.

"Your . . . clothes," Rafe groaned as he tore at the offending cloth denying him full access to her heated flesh.

Utterly lost to passion, Angela tore off her clothing, tossing it carelessly aside, anxious to consummate their love. Rafe's clothing was not so easily disposed of. It took skill on both their parts to strip him without jostling his broken leg.

"Are you sure you can manage this?" Angela asked, eyeing him with misgiving. "I don't mind waiting, Rafe."

Rafe's eyes gleamed. "*I* mind. I need you, Angel. Lean over me so I can reach your breasts with my mouth."

Angela eagerly obliged, and it wasn't long before she discovered just how capable Rafe was despite his broken leg and obvious pain.

Their loving was slow and delicious as they aroused one another with hands and mouths until their bodies were slick with sweat and their passions heightened to a feverish pitch.

When Rafe could take no more, he lifted his Angel atop him, spread her legs and drove himself home. He heard her gasp, felt her tighten around him, and he pushed his engorged sex as far as it could go.

"Rafe!"

Rafe let out a ragged sigh. Nothing had ever felt so right, so damn good. "You've got all of me, sweetheart. You're in control; do your worst."

Angela moved slowly at first, as if fearing she would hurt him, but Rafe seemed impervious to pain as he arched his hips upward into each of Angela's downward strokes. Gripping the bedcovers in his fists, he gritted his teeth to keep this loving torture from coming to a quick end. But when Angel's movements became almost frenzied, he unleashed his barely restrained passion.

Grasping her buttocks in both his hands, he guided her movements, driven by the furious need to spend himself inside her. When he raised his head to suckle her nipples, Angela cried out his name and exploded around him. Rafe was not far behind her. Two more strokes and he was there . . . his hoarse shout echoing loudly in the waiting silence.

"Did I hurt you?" Angela asked anxiously.

"The only way you can hurt me, Angel, is by leaving me."

"I'll never leave you, Rafe. Fate brought us together and love will keep us together."

"Forever," Rafe vowed.

"Forever," Angela echoed.

Epilogue

Angela gazed out the window, admiring the herd of fine horses grazing on the hillsides. The land as far as she could see belonged to her and Rafe. She couldn't recall when she'd been this happy. In a few short weeks she and Rafe would have a child to share their love. She couldn't wait to hold her son or daughter in her arms. Moving to the piano Rafe had shipped out from Denver, she sat on the bench, ran her fingers over the keys and began to play.

She tested her voice on a hymn, then went directly into a lullaby she hoped to sing to her babe. Her voice rose and swelled sweetly as the haunting melody trilled from her throat. The last note still hung in the air when Rafe entered the parlor and placed his hands on her shoulders.

"Did you know I fell in love with your voice?" Rafe said. "It gave me great comfort as I sat in that jail cell, awaiting death."

A shudder slid down her spine. "I couldn't let you hang, even though I didn't know you well enough to judge your guilt or innocence. I looked into your eyes and saw a man incapable of committing murder."

He helped her from the bench and brought her into the circle of his arms. "Shouldn't you be resting?"

She grimaced. "I'm fine, truly. How soon are you leaving?"

Rafe sighed. "I don't want to leave at all. Not now, when you're so close to your time."

"Not all that close," Angela scoffed. "I've weeks yet to go."

He eyed her burgeoning belly with misgivings. "Not from the looks of you."

She clipped him playfully on the shoulder. "How ungallant of you to mention my girth."

His eyes darkened. "You've never looked more beautiful to me than you do now. Seriously, though, I don't have to go."

"Of course you do. You promised your brothers you'd meet them in Denver a year from the day you left Dodge. They'll be expecting you. I know you've been worried about them. I'll be fine. We're not far from town; I can easily reach a doctor should I need one. And Bessie is a godsend. We were lucky to get her. She's both housekeeper and companion. She knows what to do in a crisis, though I seriously doubt there will be one."

"I don't know," Rafe hedged. "I'd hate like hell to miss the birth of our first daughter."

"Trust me, you won't. Besides, how do you know the baby will be a girl?"

"Wishful thinking, I suppose."

He tilted her head and kissed her lightly on the lips. "If you're so anxious to be rid of me, I reckon I'll leave in the morning. I'll be back in plenty of time for the birthing."

"I hope your brothers have fared well this past year," Angela said wistfully. "As well as we have. We made a fortune selling the Golden Angel to that Eastern mining company. They even built a new smelter near the mine so they wouldn't have to transport the ore down the mountain to town."

"By the way," Rafe said, "I made the last payment on the money you loaned me to buy the ranch. I deposited it in your account yesterday."

Angela sent him an exasperated look. "The money has always been yours, Rafe. You were just too stubborn to realize you could have had it any time you wanted it."

"I don't work that way, love. Living off my wife's money isn't my way. Now that the ranch is becoming a profitable enterprise, I don't feel so guilty about using your money."

"*Our* money," Angela reminded him.

"Our money," Rafe concurred. "How about another song? I want to carry the sound of your sweet voice with me to Denver."

Angela returned to the piano. She paused

with her hands on the keys, looked up at Rafe and said, "I hope you find both your brothers well."

"No more than I do, love."

He placed his hands on her shoulders, staring out the window, his thoughts returning to that fateful day when he and his brothers had ridden off in different directions. Would his brothers find their way to Denver as promised? Were they still alive?

"Don't worry," Angela said, patting his hand. "If your brothers are anything like you, they'll find their way to Denver. Who knows, they may have launched themselves into great adventures. Perhaps they've even found someone to love."

"If they have, I count them almost as lucky as I have been." He kissed the top of her head. "There's only one Angel in this world, and she's mine. I'm going to miss you."

"Not as much as I'll miss you. Now go on up and pack. I know how anxious you are to see your brothers."

Rafe walked slowly up the stairs of their rambling two-story ranch house, Angel's sweet voice echoing through the halls. He would miss her dreadfully, and this was a very bad time to leave, but he had to know how his brothers had fared . . . if they had survived. Denver was but a short, two-day journey. He'd be back before Angel even knew he was gone.

Both Jess and Sam had been on his mind a lot lately. Soon, very soon, he'd learn what Fate had dealt his brothers.

The employees of Thorndike Press hope you have enjoyed this Large Print book. All our Thorndike and Wheeler Large Print titles are designed for easy reading, and all our books are made to last. Other Thorndike Press Large Print books are available at your library, through selected bookstores, or directly from us.

For information about titles, please call:

(800) 223-1244

or visit our Web site at:

www.gale.com/thorndike
www.gale.com/wheeler

To share your comments, please write:

Publisher
Thorndike Press
295 Kennedy Memorial Drive
Waterville, ME   04901

W